Battlefield Missouri

by Arnold P. Montgomery

Three Ravens Publishing
Chickamauga, GA USA

Battlefield Missouri By Arnold P. Montgomery
Published by Three Ravens Publishing
threeravenspublishing@gmail.com
P O Box 851, Chickamauga, Ga 30707
https://www.threeravenspublishing.com
Copyright © 2023 by Arnold P. Montgomery

Credits:
Battlefield Missouri was written by Arnold P. Montgomery
Cover art by Christine Montgomery
Battlefield Missouri by: Arnold P. Montgomery /Three Ravens Publishing – 1st edition, 2023

Ebook ISBN: 978-1-962791-13-7
Trade Paperback ISBN: 978-1-962791-14-4
Hardback ISBN: 978-1-962791-15-1
Audiobook ISBN: 978-1-962791-16-8

Table of Contents

Dedication

To my loving wife. Thank you for your unconditional support as I struggled to publish this novel. I could not have done it without you.

To my father. Thank you for introducing me to books at a young age. My love for reading made me an author.

Chapter 1

October 3, 2014, North of Pyongyang, North Korea

General Lee Hyun Do and his deputy, Lieutenant General Song Ho Sung, sat at a ten-meter-long conference table. The table's mahogany, harvested in Thailand, gleamed from hundreds of hours of hand polishing. The table sat within the executive conference room located in the center of the military command post that served the Supreme Leader, often called the 'Dear Leader', of North Korea; Kim Ha Jun. The room's walls consisted of floor to ceiling glass and provided an unobstructed view of the command post around it.

A dozen South Korean-produced seventy-inch flat screens sat high on each glass wall. They displayed status reports from key North Korean military units and live video of air bases and missile launch facilities. One even displayed a real-time radar picture of all aircraft flying over the Korean peninsula. Outside the room's walls, dozens of men and women manned desks and computers. None paid any attention to the two senior officers seated within the conference room. An executive elevator and a set of stairs sat next to the conference room. Both rose through six stories of solid granite to one of the Dear Leader's seventeen luxury palaces. Experts stated the granite would protect the command post from even a direct hit by a nuclear weapon.

Lee, a veteran of the original Korean War and decades of bloody skirmishes between the divided Koreas, served as North Korea's Defense Minister. This year he celebrated his seventy-ninth birthday by sharing common mess hall fare with a dozen low ranking conscripts.

Song had not experienced combat. Powerful political connections, and at least one undiscovered assassination, allowed him to attain his rank and position. This year, for his fifty-third birthday, he dined with influential party members at a restaurant visited by only the most powerful citizens in North Korea.

At the end of World War II, world leaders decided to partition Korea along the 38th parallel. A communist dictatorship, backed by the Soviet Union, came to power in North Korea. South Korea became a democratic republic supported by the United States and other free nations.

Five years later the north launched an all-out war to bring all of Korea under its control. They failed, and each year since saw continued hostilities between the two nations.

Lee turned to his much younger deputy. "Song, are you sure you want to do this? I do not know what your proposal entails, but I suspect any promises you make carry much risk. The Dear Leader does not tolerate failure in any form. For your sake, I feel I must review your plan for any flaws before you present it."

Song sat ramrod straight. Dozens of medals, many of them unearned, decorated his tailored uniform. In comparison, Lee displayed just a few medals on his standard issue uniform.

Song did not look at Lee. He looked at one of the flat screens and spoke. "Lee Hyun Do. Thank you for your offer. I'm certain your experience and wisdom would benefit my plan." He turned to face Lee. "However, I know what I am doing. I will give a splendid briefing and I will await the guidance of the Dear Leader. He will approve my plan and order its immediate implementation. There is little risk of anything else."

Lee's eyes narrowed. A fool occupied the seat next to him. Deluded by his ambition, Song thought his proposal, once presented to the Dear Leader, would push Lee into retirement and earn Song his fourth star. Lee knew of many generals that rotted in unmarked graves because they showed similar desires. Desires that brought them to the attention of the Dear Leader.

Before he could dress down the impertinent general, the door opened, and Kim Ha Jun swept into the room. An entourage of military and civilian aides followed close behind. Both generals leaped to their feet and bowed. The young, but overweight, leader positioned himself at the head of the table in a large, black executive chair.

The grandson of Kim Il Sung, the founder and first supreme leader of North Korea, Kim came into power in 2011 when a heart attack killed his father, Kim.

Educated in expensive Swiss boarding schools, some party officials wondered if the young ruler's ascension meant a positive future for North Korea.

However, thirty days into his rule, Kim's five brothers and sisters all died under mysterious circumstances. Within two years, provocative acts against South Korea increased, the population of North Korean concentration camps swelled, hard wrought international agreements waned, and the nation's nuclear and ballistic missile programs accelerated.

All while sixty percent of his people lived below the poverty line and often struggled to feed themselves.

Kim looked at the two generals and a smile crossed his face. "Gentlemen, it is good to see you both."

The top three buttons of Kim's Mao-style jacket were undone, his hair needed combing, and he reeked of cigarettes. Lee recognized the odor of raw, pipe-smoked opium that wafted off the Dear Leader. He suppressed a look of contempt that tried to cross his face. He never liked this fat asshole.

"I have exactly twenty minutes for this meeting. Please be brief, General Song."

Lee assumed the young leader desired a quick return to the dozens of concubines that waited above.

Kim's smile grew. "However, before we begin, I have some business to conduct."

He nodded to a staff officer seated outside. Every flat screen within the room blanked and then displayed a color picture of a sprawling, outdoor weapons range. Both generals stiffened. Lee recognized anti-aircraft target range #57; one of the most modern in North Korea.

The camera panned back and showed four ZSU-23-4 anti-aircraft guns parked at the range's firing points. Their sixteen cannons pointed down range. Crews manned each weapon, and stacks of ammunition sat behind the vehicles. A red flag waved behind the vehicles indicating they were ready to shoot.

The camera moved away from the vehicles and zoomed in on a small object at the far end of the range. Lee recognized the North Korean Minister of Culture lashed to a wooden post. A powerful man; his ministry supervised their nation's Olympic athletes. However, his pampered athletes failed to win even one medal at the last Olympic Games.

The minister, Kim's great uncle, wore an expensive suit, and his frail body shook in the freezing rain. The old man sagged against the post, but the ropes kept him in an upright position. His unheard pleas escaped his mouth in small wisps of vapor. The minister seemed to recognize that the camera framed him. He looked at it and yelled his unheard pleas. He showed no stoic dignity as he faced death.

The old man looked to his left. He shook his head and struggled against the ropes. Lee read the old man's lips. "No! No! No!"

Two uniformed soldiers appeared in the frame. They dragged the minister's wife towards her husband. The frail woman wore a traditional "hanbok" dress, now splashed with mud. The rain pelted her, and her mascara ran down her face in dark smears.

The two soldiers threw the old woman to her husband's feet and ran to safety. The camera panned back and centered the terrified victims in the frame.

Kim raised his right arm. A staff officer in the outer room, a telephone held to his ear, watched the Dear Leader. The arm dropped, the officer barked into the phone, and the anti-aircraft guns on screen fired.

Both generals showed no emotion and kept their eyes on the screen. If they looked away, it could lead to their own executions. In less than a second, hundreds of high velocity rounds impacted upon and around the couple. A red mist filled the air as the couple disintegrated. Thick, black smoke from the explosions obscured the picture. Soon the screen blanked.

Kim looked away from the screen and stared off into space. "I'm going to miss my aunt and uncle," he said. "She made the most wonderful soybean soup with oysters." He turned to his two generals. "Adopting anti-aircraft target range #57 for state executions was an excellent idea, don't you agree gentlemen?"

Neither general responded. Kim blew cigarette smoke into the air. "I'm ready for your briefing, General Song."

Song stared at the Dear Leader but said nothing. Kim returned his stare. The silence lengthened. Lee kicked his deputy under the table. Song yelped and jumped from his seat.

A PowerPoint briefing appeared on the flat screens. The title page read 'Operation Ferguson' in Korean.

"What is the significance of the word Ferguson?" Kim said. "What does it mean?" He pronounced the English name with difficulty. He enunciated it as 'fur-goo-san.'

Song grabbed a laser pointer. "Ferguson is a small village located in the United States. Its significance becomes clear later in my briefing. May I continue, Dear Leader?"

Kim stared at Song and turned to Lee. The old general shrugged his shoulders.

"Continue, General," Kim said.

Song's first charts displayed routine information; the disposition of North Korean military forces and South Korean and American forces arrayed in defense of South Korea.

After five minutes Kim spoke. "General Song. I have many beautiful and skilled women waiting for me in my residence above. These women can do things to me that you cannot imagine. I interrupted my morning session with them at your request." Kim paused and stared at Song. "So, why do you brief me on information I receive every morning?"

Song again stared in silence at the Dear Leader and sweat appeared on his brow.

A look of disgust crossed Lee's face, but he rescued his idiotic deputy. "General Song, please show us your summary chart. Explain to the Dear Leader the most important aspect of your proposal, and the significance of this Ferguson village."

"Yes, of course, General Lee." He spoke up at microphones in the ceiling. "Display slide number twenty-one." Song faced the dictator. "Dear Leader, during the war of reunification our forces fought the South Koreans and their capitalist American allies to a standstill. Today, however, the Americans have an advantage that allows them to win any ground war against our forces. Wouldn't you agree, General Lee?"

Lee frowned at his deputy but spoke. "General Song is correct Dear Leader. Our forces match our enemies in terms of personnel, equipment, and tactical skills. But any attack by our forces into South Korea bogs down against their strong defense. While we fight to a stalemate, American military strength increases due to a massive military and logistics response from the United States."

Song used his laser pointer to highlight a map of the Korean peninsula. "My point exactly. Consider a full-scale attack against South Korea. Sixty days after we crossed the demilitarized zone, we would occupy no more than one-third of South Korea's territory. Our forces have exhausted their fuel and ammunition, and our resupply proceeds in a slow and limited fashion. This stalls our advance."

He moved the pointer to tables displayed alongside the map. "The Americans, however, can call on six mechanized and armored divisions, one marine division, eight fighter and bomber wings, and stockpiles of fuel and ammunition in or on the way to South Korea. They will defeat our spent forces, restore the original border, and advance into our territory to achieve reunification on their terms. Their Iraq invasion in 2003 shows the Americans will conduct military operations until they have regime change."

Kim's face flushed, and he gripped the table's edge. "So, General Song, your expert opinion is we will lose a war with the South and the Americans."

"Yes, Dear Leader."

Kim's voice pitched low, and he spoke slowly. "So, my family's dream of reunifying the Korean people will never happen? That my military, which receives our best technology and over eighty percent of our national budget, will fail in a war for reunification? And better still, if I attack the South to take what is mine by birth, enemy forces attacking into my own nation will arrive here at my favorite palace and force me from power?"

"That is correct, Dear Leader."

Kim pointed at the flat screen that displayed the recent Hwasong-6 ballistic missile launch, a missile that flew over Japan and landed three thousand miles away in the Pacific Ocean and rattled off his response. "Then I shall destroy these attacking forces with our nuclear weapons. If the Americans respond with their own atomic weapons, they risk our nuclear bombardment of Hawaii or their precious West Coast." Kim laughed and his underlings laughed in support. "If we invade the South, their fear of escalation prevents them from 'going nuclear' as they like to say."

Song glanced at the flat screen. "It is true you could destroy any attack from the South with our nuclear weapons, but the Americans know we have no missile capable of reaching their territory. If we use our nuclear weapons, they will target their own weapons of mass destruction against this facility and many others in our sacred homeland."

Kim's face flushed and a blood vessel appeared at his temple. Members of his entourage exchanged looks. One took out his cell phone and gestured to the security detail standing outside the room.

Song continued. "In a typical war with the south, our enemies prevail. However, what if we could change the status quo and defeat America's logistics capability? Their military logistics is their greatest strength and secured them many strategic victories including their own civil war one hundred and fifty years ago. But it is also their greatest weakness. My plan exploits that weakness."

Kim's body shook and he slammed his fist down on the table. "How is that possible? You just stated our own poor logistics limit our capabilities. How can our forces fight South Korean and American divisions and defeat their logistics at the same time?"

Song highlighted a map of the United States. "By stopping America's logistics capability at its origin. Our special operations forces, teamed with our new Islamic State of Iraq and Syria allies, slip into the United States and conduct an attack on our enemy's own territory. Destroying a few key logistics-focused military installations delays their response to our invasion by at least ninety days. This delay allows us to consolidate our military gains within South Korea and hold off any American response. No matter how large."

Kim ceased shaking and stared at Song.

"Impossible!" Lee said. He sat up straight and pointed at Song. "American military forces within the United States will crush our special forces and any ISIS rabble we send to their country."

Song puffed his chest out. "Again, we use another American weakness against them. We disguise our actions as internal disturbances based on America's increasing racial, immigration, and political unrest. One of their most important laws, the Posse Comitatus Act, forbids their military from responding to our fabricated civil issue."

Kim's forehead furrowed. "You joke with me General Song; no nation, least of all the United States, would tie the hands of its military in such a way. There is no such a law."

Song nodded. "This law is real, and their military obeys it to the letter, Dear Leader. We will convince the American leaders that our attacks are mere civil disturbances. When that happens, their military is powerless to intervene."

"What about American law enforcement?" Lee said. "No laws prevent them from responding to your attacks. What will you do when American policemen arrive at these facilities to investigate your civil disturbance?"

"This leads to the significance of Ferguson." Song displayed a chart with several recent headlines from US newspapers. "It is true the American police could oppose us. However, the recent deaths of American minorities at the hands of law enforcement, in villages such as Ferguson, deprived their police of much authority. American citizens, armed with cameras, often confront their police officers and make even veteran police reluctant to act. American citizens have even ambushed and killed police using firearms they own."

The Dear Leader's mouth dropped open. "General, that is unbelievable. No government could maintain control of its citizens when its law enforcement has no teeth."

Song nodded again. "It is true, Dear Leader. We have the American news reports that show this."

Kim looked at General Lee. "This is amazing."

"Also, most American policemen carry a simple sidearm. If they do have an automatic weapon, they must lock it inside their patrol vehicle. In any type of emergency, they must seek approval from higher authority for its use."

Kim again slammed his fist down on the table. "General Song, if you continue to ply me with untruths, I will end this briefing. When I lived in Europe, their police always carried assault rifles and submachine guns. Are you stating the American police are not equal to their European counterparts?"

"General Song is correct," Lee said. "Throughout America, police autonomy and morale plummeted following well-publicized incidents in Ferguson and other villages. I believe our special forces could handle any American police forces that opposed them."

A look of disbelief crossed Kim's face. He turned to Song. "What logistics facilities do you need to attack in America?"

A map of the United States, with two red circles in the center of the nation, appeared on the screens. Song highlighted the circles with a laser pointer. "Dear Leader, our models show that destroying two key facilities, one in the American state of Kentucky and the other in Missouri, eliminates America's ability to make war."

Lee recognized the facilities. He sat up and pointed at the screen. "General Song, these munition facilities you describe are hundreds of square kilometers in size. You would need thousands of men to seize and destroy such a sizable base."

"Yes, General Lee, they are large," Song said. "But both have singular vulnerabilities." A satellite photograph of one of the facilities appeared on the screen. Song swung his pointer. "Here we see bridges, rail switching yards, loading facilities, road networks, vehicle staging areas, and communication networks. Our forces need to destroy just a few of these key nodes to eliminate a facility's ability to deploy its ammunition. Even if the Americans do deploy ground or air forces to our conflict, they carry only a few days of munitions. Without ammunition resupply, their forces cannot counterattack. We will retain our captured territory and force surrender talks. Talks that put you into the South Korean president's office, Dear Leader."

It took all of Lee's self-control to keep a straight face at Song's fawning. But he had to admit the little shit's plan could work.

Kim nodded and members of his entourage smiled and nodded. "When can you implement this plan?" Kim said.

"Dear Leader, I propose we attack the American facilities on September 13th; two days prior to our Chuseok holiday.

"Why Chuseok?"

"As you know Dear Leader both our nations consider this our most important holiday. The South all but ceases functioning during their holiday festivities. This includes their armed forces. Their celebrations result in a significant drop to their military readiness."

Another map appeared on the screen. "Movements of our units to invasion start points requires several weeks. Enemy intelligence is bound to spot these movements and warn of possible invasion. To counter this, we direct our sympathizers in South Korea to plant the seeds of doubt by protesting that our movements are peaceful in nature. Just another routine training exercise designed to protect us from American aggression. Once our forces arrive at their starting points, they begin immediate radio silence. After that we inform our enemies that we completed an unannounced exercise. We state our forces will return to their previous locations after our shared Chuseok holiday."

Song used the remote to blank the screens. "Our citizens, with over a million disguised as soldiers, flood into our cities and villages for several days of highly visible, holiday festivities. The Americans and the South detect our 'soldiers' celebrating and stand down their forces and any movements to the Korean peninsula. At noon on September 15, at the height of the South's celebration, you, Dear Leader, will give the order to begin the invasion. We achieve complete surprise and advance into South Korean territory."

Kim showed the smallest hint of a smile. He leaned back in his executive chair and stared at the ceiling. He took out a cigarette, and an aide appeared and lit it. He took several puffs and continued to stare at the ceiling. Kim brought his gaze down to the two generals.

"Your plan is approved, General Song. Make all preparations for an attack on the American logistics facilities. You will also update the operational plans for the invasion of South Korea and the glorious reunification of the Korean people."

Song smiled. "You will have it, Dear Leader."

"Excellent." Kim pointed at the two generals. "Our long-delayed reunification is within reach. I require victory, gentlemen. Do not fail me." Kim stood and strode out of the room followed by his aides.

Lee and Song leaped to their feet and bowed. When the door closed, both men sagged and let out loud sighs.

Chapter 2

October 8, 2014, Kandahar Province, Afghanistan.

Lieutenant Colonel Jack Black Eagle stared at the fresh bullet hole between his feet. The morning's growing light showed through the hole in the helicopter's aluminum deck. His eyes followed the bullet's path to another hole above his head. A small drop of hydraulic fluid formed at the edge of the hole and fell onto his sleeve. Fortunately, the vital engines above him maintained their reassuring roar. Jack's closest call in his twenty-two years of service banished his usual morning fatigue.

The sleek Sikorsky UH-60M Blackhawk helicopter utilized many redundant systems, and two long wars in Iraq and Afghanistan proved it could take a lot of punishment. As the US Army's main utility helicopter, they designed it to carry eleven fully equipped soldiers. However, this morning Jack was the helicopter's sole cargo as he returned from his inspection of a remote division outpost.

Jack raised his eyebrows at the helicopter's crew chief, Specialist Roberts, and shifted his position on the bench seat away from the hole. The young crew chief shrugged and resumed his scan of the ground below. Jack keyed the intercom. "Chief, we're taking fire. Is something going on?" Jack's upper body swayed as the helicopter made several quick zig zags and climbed to a safer altitude.

Chief Warrant Officer Two Thomas came on the intercom. "Sorry about that Sir, we didn't see them in time, and we took a couple of rounds. We're OK now." She paused for several moments. "It looks like something's happening behind us. COP Armstrong is up on the net, and they say they're taking heavy fire."

Jack knew most Americans have never heard of a combat outpost or COP. They are small US Army-manned bases positioned throughout the Afghanistan countryside to guard against Taliban intrusions and attacks. He often told uninformed people to imagine an Army cavalry fort positioned deep in hostile Indian Territory in the 1870s; it's a lot like that.

Jack's brow furrowed. "Now? We just left there. Why didn't we see anything?"

"I don't know Sir. You know the hadjis hide themselves good. I'm just glad they didn't shoot at us. I'm sure we were sitting ducks."

Normally Jack approached each morning with a positive attitude. But upon hearing the Taliban threatened COP Armstrong, great apprehension overwhelmed him. He ticked off the lethal shortcomings of the small, under manned outpost located far into Taliban territory.

"How bad is it?"

"Sir, I'm no expert but it doesn't sound good. I'm gonna connect you to the radio so you can hear for yourself."

Jack listened as someone, it sounded like a junior sergeant, spoke to the battalion tactical operations center. Static, the sounds of explosions and heavy small arms fire almost drowned out the excited voice as it reported the situation. "We can't find the lieutenant anywhere, and they took out the mortar position! There's smoke pouring from the DFAC! Oh God…I don't know if anyone got out of there! And the God damned Afghanistan army soldiers ran and left the perimeter unguarded!" The voice rose in desperation until the man screamed over the radio. A loud explosion cut him off.

A new speaker, maybe the platoon sergeant, broke in. "Tango three three this is Romeo two one. Our situation is bad. We're under heavy attack and the enemy will not disengage. We need the QRF here now."

Jack knew the quick reaction force, or QRF, for this brigade consisted of thirty soldiers carried by helicopters. An attack helicopter would accompany them. If they could get to COP Armstrong, they could hold off any Taliban attack.

After a long pause, the battalion three stated bad weather prevented the QRF from responding.

Jack leaned out the door. The slipstream rushed around him, and he looked behind the helicopter. He spotted several columns of black smoke rising from the vicinity of the small camp.

He pulled his head back inside. Jack sighed and keyed the intercom. "Chief, turn around and head back to COP Armstrong."

"What was that Sir?"

"You heard me. Turn the aircraft around and get me back to that landing zone. Make it fast. Everything's going to hell down there, and the weather grounded the QRF. So, I'll be the QRF."

The young African American pilot turned and looked back at Jack. "Are you sure it's that bad?"

Jack nodded. "I spent the longest night of my life in that outpost. With no QRF, it's that bad. Let's go."

Thomas shook her head and turned back to her controls. "Yes, Sir. Heading back now. Be there in a few minutes."

The helicopter banked into a tight turn. The barren landscape flowed under the fast-moving helicopter. Jack tried to recall all the tactical training he received in his younger days. He checked his M4 carbine, a compact version of the reliable M16 rifle, and waited.

They approached the LZ that sat outside the COP's razor wire perimeter. Jack's throat tightened as he observed the COP from the air. Explosions blossomed across the outpost, and the plywood mess hall, where he ate a quick meal last night, belched flame and smoke. Heavy enemy fire, identified by bright green tracers, hit the tactical operations center; known as the TOC, the mortar pit, and the platoon's vehicles located at each corner of the compound. Friendly and enemy machine gun fire tore up the ground in front of the COP. Furtive figures moved across the mountain that loomed above the barricaded outpost.

Jack frowned at the sight. Whoever chose this spot for a manned outpost had no common sense. Once he returned to headquarters, he would meet with the division's operations officer. Jack's report would convince him to relocate the outpost to a better location.

The Blackhawk flared above the LZ. Jack stared open-mouthed as lines of tracers reached for their helicopter. He found the tracers beautiful in a weird sort of way. He hoped he lived so he could tell someone about it.

Thomas came on the intercom. "Roberts, get off your ass and get that two forty moving!"

"What's my target?" the crew chief said.

"Anything!" Jack and Thomas yelled at the same time.

Roberts' machine gun thundered, and gouts of earth, rock, and withered plants flew off the mountain. An intense pain racked Jack's ears followed by a ringing noise. He hoped his hearing was not permanently damaged from the tremendous racket.

The helicopter descended and Jack tightened his helmet strap and stood. He used his boot to sweep piles of links and brass from under his feet and out the door. He felt a flurry of thumps hitting the helicopter, and a line of jagged holes appeared on the floor in front of him. Red lights flashed on the helicopter's dash, and it yawed to the right. Jack's arms wind milled, and he fell and slid backwards towards the door. His heart raced, and he scrambled for a handhold. He grabbed a dangling seat belt and pulled it to his chest. For one sickening moment, he looked over his left shoulder straight down to the ground. An orange object shot underneath the helicopter and exploded on the far side of the LZ. He recognized the Soviet-designed rocket propelled grenade, or RPG; just one could knock down his struggling helicopter. The Blackhawk leveled off and gained altitude. Jack jumped back in his seat and buckled in.

Thomas came on the intercom. "The aircraft's ok, the aircraft's ok, but that LZ's too hot. I can't get you in."

They flew in a circle above the outpost. The heavy enemy fire continued. "Our gunner can provide some support to the COP, but the weather is closing in. We won't be able to see, and we won't be able to fly. We need to return to base."

Jack took several deep breaths to slow his thumping heart. He scanned the terrain below. A small Afghan village, nicknamed 'Waco' by the outpost's soldiers, sat a kilometer to the north.

He keyed the intercom. "Drop me on the other side of that village."

"Say again, Sir. I didn't get that last."

"Drop me on the other side of Waco. Put me on the road about a kilometer out. I'll run through the village and get to COP Armstrong in no time."

Thomas turned and looked at Jack with wide eyes. "Sir, that's crazy! There's at least a company of Taliban down there."

Jack held her stare. "Radio the TOC and inform them I'm on my way. Tell them to support me with fire when I make my run."

She shook her head. "I can't do that, Sir. They'll court-martial me if I let you out of this helicopter."

"I'm giving you a direct order, Chief. Get me on that road. I don't have time to argue."

Thomas stared at Jack for several seconds. Her shoulders slumped. "Okay, Sir. If you say so."

The aircraft turned and headed towards the village. Jack grabbed two red smoke grenades and a squad radio from a box under his seat. He attached them to his load carrying equipment and placed the microphone up near his face.

"Chief, when I go you head out before the weather gets too bad?"

"Roger, Sir. Get ready; we're getting close." The helicopter descended. Jack locked and loaded a round into his carbine. He noticed his hand shook, so he clenched his fist until it stopped. He crouched in the door and watched the aircraft's shadow rush across the ground to join them.

They touched down and Roberts yelled. "Go! Go! Go!"

Jack jumped to the ground and folded his six-foot two-inch frame down to one knee. He closed his eyes tight while the rotor blades churned the dust into an impenetrable cloud. He said a silent prayer asking the Great Spirit to protect him and to guide him well. In less than a second, the aircraft lifted off. Soon the dust cleared, and an odd silence fell over him. Jack sucked water from his camelback and rinsed the dust from his tongue and teeth. He spit a brown gob onto the ground.

Jack assumed a steady running pace with his carbine at port arms. He scanned the area ahead of him but, as he predicted, he saw no one. When he reached the village, he crouched behind the stoop on the first dingy, mud-brick house he came to. He scanned for movement. The ancient village smelled of dust, goat droppings, and primitive sewage systems. No one walked the grimy paths, no animals stood in their pens, and he heard none of the sounds expected in a populated Afghan village. Jack frowned. Yesterday the village teemed with life. Now its residents had vanished; at least until the Taliban departed.

Faint voices yelled from within the village. He also heard a machine gun and several AK-47 rifles firing from rooftops somewhere ahead of him. Jack knew no one spotted him leaving the helicopter; if they had he'd be lying dead back on the road. He needed a distraction to get through the village unseen. He ran back outside the village to the house farthest from the COP. He popped a red smoke and threw it into the home's rear courtyard. In a few moments a large cloud billowed up around the home.

Jack ran back to the stoop. Soon five men, dressed in traditional Pashtun clothing and carrying AK-47s, darted across the village's main path and headed towards the smoke. Their dress identified them as local tribesmen that had gone over to the Taliban. Once he lost sight of them, he sprinted into the village. When he reached its center, he turned right and darted down an alley. Jack soon discovered the villagers used this particular corridor to butcher their livestock. He gagged and almost vomited but continued running. When he reached the last home, he threw his last smoke grenade behind it.

He took a different alley and ran back to the village center and turned right towards the COP.

Again, he spotted no one.

At the edge of the village, he crouched in the shadows and aimed his rifle back the way he'd come. Despite the Taliban gunfire, the village remained quiet. Soon a skinny cat appeared and rubbed up against his boots. Keeping his eyes on the village center, Jack scratched it behind its ears. With the cat luxuriating in his touch, Jack whispered to it. "Looks like you got left behind kitty. Should I take you home to Janet? Would you like that?"

Five new Taliban stepped into the village center. Jack froze and watched the men. They wore traditional kufi hats, pieces of cast-off Russian uniforms, and cheap Pakistani-made tennis shoes. All held their AK-47s at the ready. The men argued and gestured towards the second cloud of smoke. Jack guessed they wanted no part of the putrid-smelling alley. After a few moments, they darted between structure into another.

Jack opened the door to the nearest house and placed the cat inside. He turned and sprinted towards the police station located on the edge of the village. He reached the station and kicked open the building's door. He entered with his carbine at his shoulder.

An older man sat at a desk in the center of the building and observed the battle through a large window. The man held a small radio in his right hand and a cell phone in his left. An electronic tablet and a pistol lay on the desk. The startled man reached for the pistol, and Jack shot him once in the head. He flew from the chair and landed face down on the floor.

Jack ignored the dead man and swept the large, one-room building. He found no one else and approached the final hiding place; the closed restroom door. As he prepared to kick it in, the door opened, and a small boy, no more than ten years old, emerged holding a metal tea kettle. The boy's mouth formed a small O upon seeing the huge American soldier.

The faces of Jack's children flashed before his eyes. He reversed his carbine and tapped the boy's head with the weapon's butt. The kettle clanged to the floor, and the boy dropped unconscious into the puddle of spilled water. Jack wondered if the dead man brought his grandson to the battle.

Jack moved back to the dead man. He looked out the window and saw a defender's nightmare and an attacker's wet dream. Heavy fire poured into the COP from the village and from the mountain behind it. Every few minutes a mortar round or RPG exploded inside the COP perimeter. He spotted dozens of Taliban fighters firing from depressions and tree stumps in the open ground in front of the COP. Return fire came from the infantry platoon manning the compound, but he saw it was not enough.

The COP's entrance sat six hundred meters distant, but it looked miles away.

Jack grabbed the tablet and the cell phone. He checked the man's pockets and found several handwritten notes and a small notebook. The notebook held a photo of the boy lying behind him. In it the boy posed nude while wearing a cheap, blond wig. Jack scowled. He cleared his throat and spit the result onto the floor next to the dead man.

He again looked out the window. It appeared none of the enemy fighters heard his shot or knew he watched them from his position. All focused on the distant COP. To his left, three men manned a heavy machine gun in the remains of a collapsed mud hut. They fired the big gun over their comrade's heads hitting positions within the COP.

Jack took a sip of water and prepared for his final run. Movement outside caught his eye. A team of Taliban fighters streaked for the COP's perimeter. Taliban fire increased in support of the enemy's rush. A few friendly weapons fired and kicked up dust on that portion of the perimeter. Unfortunately, the dust helped to conceal the Taliban as they moved forward. One fighter fell, but the rest jumped the triple strand razor wire and entered the compound's interior.

Jack keyed his radio. "COP Armstrong, you have enemy inside your wire. I say again Armstrong you have enemy inside your wire."

He got no response and knew he had to move. He found a back door and peered outside. Seeing no one, he went through the door, hugged the wall and shuffled around to the front of the building. Once there he faced the backs of many Taliban focused on COP Armstrong.

Jack risked a glance at the heavy machine gun crew. They continued to fire at the outpost. He assumed a stable firing position and took up a good sight picture on the back of a nearby Taliban.

It felt like hunting antelope in South Dakota.

Jack fired and a fighter fell.

He shifted his target and fired again. Another fighter slumped to the ground. He shifted his target again and fired. This fighter collapsed behind the scrawny tree that sheltered him.

Jack fired at another fighter but missed. The errant round threw dirt on the fighter. The man looked to his left and right but saw no one. Jack fired again and the man dropped. He shifted his target and fired. A fighter jerked and his rifle flew several feet into the air.

Three rounds hit the corner of the building inches above his head. Shards of brick hit his face and helmet. Jack ducked.

Shit! That was close!

A fighter stood and waved at the heavy machine gun crew. The man pointed in his direction and yelled. Jack fired and the fighter dropped behind a large rock. The machine gun crew swung their weapon in his direction.

Jack stood and fired the remainder of his magazine into the heavy gun's position. The three Taliban ducked out of sight.

Slapping a fresh magazine into his carbine, Jack sprinted towards the COP. To his front, many Taliban fired at the American outpost. All failed to spot the running American in their midst.

He zigged and zagged and headed for terrain with the smallest concentration of fighters. When a Taliban got in his way, he slowed to aim and fire. When he spotted a fighter to his right or left, he maintained his pace, aimed from the waist, and fired several rounds to keep their heads down.

He received no return fire; the Taliban fighters thought his shots were their own. Jack made it halfway to the outpost before the heavy machine gun behind him resumed fire. Its rounds impacted around his feet, and dirt and rocks flew into the air.

A Taliban fighter stood up right in front of him and turned toward the heavy machine gun. Before the man could react, Jack lowered his shoulder and drove it into the man's chest. The stunned man flew backward and landed in a heap in front of the large rock he'd sheltered behind. Jack dropped and scrambled behind the rock, placing it between him and the enemy machine gun.

Heavy rounds slammed into the rock and the ground around Jack. The injured Taliban grasped his chest and groaned until rounds from his buddies' gun silenced him. Jack squirmed behind the rock doing his best to keep out of sight. Dirt and stone chips rained onto his helmet, face, and uniform.

A Blackhawk helicopter tore out of the overcast sky and raked the Taliban machine gun position with accurate fire. Jack looked around the now smaller rock and saw a cloud of dust covering the enemy gun. His radio squawked.

"Get moving Sir!" Thomas said. "We've got you covered!"

Jack leaped up and resumed his run. The Taliban around him pointed at the Blackhawk. A few even fired at the noisy helicopter.

The outpost's front gate stood one hundred meters away with no other Taliban in front of him. Jack flipped his rifle onto his back and sprinted. He kept his head down and worked to avoid any holes and large stones.

His legs and arms pumped as he ran for his life. Soon his muscles screamed for oxygen, and his body begged him to stop.

With the Blackhawk still shooting above him he raced through the open vehicle gate. Rounds cracked the air around him, and he hurdled over the charred corpse of an Afghan security guard. Looking like something from a movie, the boots of a US soldier protruded from under the collapsed guard shack. Pieces of a third body, torn apart by an explosion, lay between the two men.

He raced across the gravel parking lot. Three meters from the closest fighting position, Jack gathered his remaining strength, and without breaking stride, leaped over the row of large, earth-filled baskets. He landed hard on the position's dirt floor.

Behind him, a long burst of enemy fire thumped into the barricade. Jack stayed on his back, his eyes closed, and gasped for air. A full minute later he heard a loud groan. He opened his eyes and found himself lying on top of an Afghanistan Army soldier. He stood and pulled the smaller man to his feet. He continued panting and brushed dirt off the shocked Afghan.

He doubted the stunned ally had ever had an American jump on him before. He smiled at the man. Jack noticed a US soldier in full battle gear lying motionless behind the Afghan. The US soldier had an obvious bullet wound in the back of his head just under his helmet. A wallet, MP3 player with earbuds, and class ring lay near the dead soldier's boots.

Jack examined the shorter man's face. The man avoided his eyes. Without warning, the man pushed Jack away and lunged for his AK-47 leaning against the wall.

Frustration burst from Jack's throat. "You bastard! You murdered him!"

He pushed the soldier backward into a pool of the dead trooper's blood. The soldier pulled his bayonet but struggled to regain his footing. His movements flung drops of sticky blood on himself and the surrounding sandbags. Jack drew his sidearm and shot him in the eye. The soldier collapsed with his bayonet still in his hand.

Specialist Paul Craig, the unit's radio operator, burst into the fighting position. "Sir, you came back!"

Jack holstered his weapon and turned to the young man. "What happened at the gate?"

"A raghead suicide bomber came in wearing an Aghan Army uniform. When he got close to our local security guard, he blew his vest. After that everything went to hell."

Jack nodded. "The guard's dead. What about the soldier in the shack?"

"I saw it go down. Kirby's dead." Craig spotted the two bodies behind Jack. A look of resignation crossed his face. "Damn. They got Sergeant Hopkins. That sucks big time. Battalion tagged him for morale leave next week."

Jack looked at the dead soldier. "The Afghan soldier murdered him a few minutes before I got here."

"For real, Sir?"

Jack nodded. "Yes, it's real. We need to get to the TOC and warn everyone. Also, you have a squad of Taliban inside the perimeter near your maintenance shed."

Craig's mouth dropped open, and he took a step back. "I ran by the maintenance barn on my way here." He looked at the sandbagged path to his rear. "We'll have to take a different way back." Without waiting for Jack, he took off and disappeared around a corner.

Jack looked at his watch. It read 07:33 A.M. Thirty-one minutes ago he departed from the now cut off helipad. He took a deep breath and followed Specialist Craig.

Sergeant First Class Robinson looked out of the sand bagged position and observed the maintenance barn sitting fifty meters to his right. Their maintenance facility didn't look like a barn to him. In fact, it was a Quonset-hut-shaped aluminum frame covered by a form fitting, tan colored tarp. Large concrete barricades served as the frame's base and a large opening with no door allowed vehicles to pull inside for routine maintenance. The barn could hold two MRAPs along with spare tires, fuel, lubricants, and a few toolboxes. However, once the platoon's lieutenant called it a barn the name stuck. Before this morning's attack the barn sat empty as all the platoon's vehicles sat on the perimeter.

Incoming rounds ricocheted off the nearest mine resistant ambush protected vehicle, or MRAP. Sergeant Robinson scanned the inside of his compound. To his left the fire that consumed the mess hall showed signs of dying as it ran out of combustibles. He did not know how many of his soldiers remained inside. When the Taliban dropped their first mortar round through the mess hall's plywood roof, he knew his enemy was very good or very lucky. He guessed it was good. He also suspected the attackers had a detailed sketch of his compound. Detailed enough to sight in their mortars. He wrinkled his nose as he caught the odor of burning flesh.

He still could not believe the Taliban got inside without his unit seeing them. It was a good thing Lieutenant Colonel Black Eagle spotted them and made his crazy run from Waco. His jaw clenched as he recalled his surprise when Craig led the senior officer into the TOC. It was a miracle one of his guys had not shot him by mistake. When he heard the officer's report about the Taliban in the barn his mouth went dry. He needed a big gulp of water before he could speak again.

His gaze returned to the barn. He saw no one but he had no doubt they were there. According to Lieutenant Colonel Black Eagle, the small group jumped the wire ten minutes ago. Why they didn't break out from the barn and run amok inside his compound was unknown to him.

He turned and looked at the three soldiers crouched behind him. All three looked frightened but determined. They knew what happened at the mess hall and volunteered to take out the barn.

He spoke to them. "When we go, keep it down and stay below the barricades. If you don't, my grenades will take your head off." All three took big swallows. "We rehearsed close combat drills a couple of months ago. Entering that barn is no different than that."

He looked at the soldier next to him. "Ski, give me those grenades as soon as you see my hand."

The young soldier looked at the barn. "How did they get in, sergeant?" Ski said.

Sergeant Robinson's lips formed a thin line. "How do you think they got in? The damn Afghan Army squad is hiding in the latrine. That's how."

The young man looked in the direction of the latrine. Sergeant Robinson grabbed Ski's load carrying equipment and shook him. "Focus!" he said. "We're hitting that barn. We'll figure out how they got in after they're dead."

He shifted an iron gaze to each man. Finished, he focused back on Ski. "Grenades, Ski. When you see my hand and not before."

The young soldier nodded.

Sergeant Robinson gave the compound one more glance. "Let's go."

He led off in a crouched walk with his M4 at his shoulder and aimed at the barn. Outgoing fire from the platoon vehicles increased as the men moved. He wanted any Taliban observers focused on his vehicles' fire and not his team. He moved carefully and did his best not to make any noise.

In a few moments they covered the fifty meters to the back of the barn. He paused and his team put their backs to the concrete barricade. All kept their weapons pointed at potential hiding spots. Sergeant Robinson heard muffled conversation coming from inside the barn. He had no understanding of Dari or Pashto, but he thought the speaker sounded upset or maybe even frustrated. He heard a radio squawk along with more heated language. The voices confirmed there were no friendlies inside the barn...at least none alive.

He moved along the barricades towards the barn's entrance. with his team close behind. He came to the final corner and stopped. Sergeant Robinson peeked around it and saw no one. He moved around the corner with his team following and stopped two feet from the barn's entrance. The third man in line moved up next to Ski and covered the entrance with his M4. The fourth man covered their rear.

He lowered his carbine and reached behind him. Ski placed a grenade into his right hand. Sergeant Robinson pulled the pin and released the spoon. It made a metallic ping sound as it fell to the ground. He waited two seconds and stepped forward and threw the grenade into the back of the barn then returned to his crouch.

Excited shouts came from the barn's interior, and he heard people scrambling about. He reached for his second grenade.

The grenade inside the barn detonated with a chest crushing thump and an earsplitting blast. The barn's tarp bulged out like a jellyfish and black smoke burst from the entrance. The men inside screamed. He threw the second grenade inside, spoon and all, and followed with a third. Both exploded and the screaming ceased.

"Execute!" he said.

With their M4s pointing forward, the team launched towards the door. Sergeant Robinson entered the barn, went to the right corner, and faced the rear. Ski went to the left corner and the third soldier in line took the center. The fourth soldier secured the door so no one could come in behind them.

When all three faced the rear of the barn they advanced on line. Sergeant Robinson spotted five Taliban sprawled at the back of the barn. Three men still holding their rifles tried to regain their feet. Sergeant Robinson, Ski, and the other soldier each fired two rounds into the moving Taliban. They fell back to the ground and moved no more.

Ski approached the dead men to see if they missed anything. He finished checking them and yelled. "Clear!"

Sergeant Robinson lowered his weapon. "Search 'em." Ski and the other soldier lowered their weapons and stepped among the still forms.

Jack looked through one of the TOC's firing ports and tried to spot the Taliban hiding within Waco. He exposed himself as little as possible in case the enemy had a skilled sniper out there. Soldiers at each wall stood on ammo crates as they monitored their assigned areas through the firing ports. A bank of radios that sat in the center of the TOC squawked as the platoon's squads communicated with each other. A long burst of outgoing machine gun fire came from a fighting position to his right. Jack looked but saw no hits by the gunner.

Since his arrival, the enemy fire had slacked off and no more mortars or RPGs dropped into the compound. Jack wondered if the Taliban ran low on ammunition for their heavy weapons. The possible lack of heavy ammunition and the lull in enemy fire gave the outpost time to rally. He should be relieved, but he sensed the Taliban planned a final push into the COP.

Jack stepped away from the firing port and looked at his surroundings. Despite being made of plywood and two by fours, the TOC was a very large room. It held maps, radios, surveillance equipment, chairs, desks, bulletin boards, and computers. On a far wall cardboard boxes containing meals, ready-to-eat and bottled water sat under a table that held a spotless Keurig and a filthy microwave. Empty water bottles and torn MRE containers spilled from a large trash can.

Jack examined the multiple rows of sandbags that made up the TOC's walls and roof. Openings that served as firing ports, sat high up on each wall. The TOC sat upon a large earth mound pushed up years ago by a bulldozer. The additional height gave Jack a view that stretched all the way to Waco.

Sergeant Robinson entered the TOC and moved towards Jack. "Sir, take a look at this." The stocky African American platoon sergeant held a US Army-issued M-183 demolition charge. A crude canvas bag with attached carrying strap held the charge. Jack spotted a 2013 production date stenciled on the bag indicating someone removed it from US Army control not long ago.

"Jesus!" Specialist Craig said. "Those are satchel charges. What did they plan to do with those?"

Sergeant Robinson ignored the outburst. "Each Taliban in the maintenance barn had two of these. I think they planned to take out our vehicles, the TOC, and our key fighting positions. Once those charges went off, their buddies in Waco could waltz right in here and finish the job." He dropped the charge on a table.

"Anything else?" Jack said.

Sergeant Robinson shook his head. "They had their rifles and one hand-held radio." He rubbed his chin and focused on something Jack could not see. "There was one strange thing. Before we assaulted the barn, I heard one of them using the radio. I think he was asking for a go ahead to take us out, but I don't think he got any response." He paused for a moment. "Or maybe his radio was junk. I'm not sure. But whatever was going on, that Taliban fighter sounded pissed off."

Jack reached down and placed his hand over his cargo pocket. He felt the radio he took from the dead Taliban leader.

"Good work sergeant," Jack said. "Those satchel charges would've knocked us on our ass." He gestured at the radios. "Especially if they got one in here. Without you to coordinate the platoon's defense they could get a large force inside here in no time." He paused as another burst of machine gun fire interrupted him.

"Do you think it's over?" Sergeant Robinson said.

Jack started to pace and continued to tap the captured radio. "No. I'd bet a month's pay the Taliban in Waco were waiting for a signal from your pissed off fighter." Jack went to the firing port and stared at the enemy held village. "The Taliban brought a large force here and the bad weather works in their favor. They're not going to quit and go home just because they lost contact with their inside guys." He looked at Sergeant Robinson. "We're still vulnerable. If they rush us and get a platoon close to our wire they'll get inside."

"I agree Sir," Sergeant Robinson said. "But I don't have enough men to drive them off."

"Can we evacuate?"

Sergeant Robinson thought for a moment. "We can fit everyone to include our wounded into our vehicles. It'll be tight but we could do it." He looked at Jack. "But the bad guys have RPGs." He turned to the soldiers within the TOC. "Specialist Craig, you've observed the Taliban today. Do you think we could get out of here using the platoon's vehicles?"

The young man turned away from his perch at the firing port. "No sergeant. From the rounds we have taken so far, I think they have at least six shooters armed with RPGs. Maybe more. We might get the first couple of vehicles out, but our trail vehicles will soak up the rounds."

Sergeant Robinson nodded and turned back to Jack. "If the Taliban hit even one of our vehicles, we'll be out in the open trying to extract soldiers and wounded." He crossed his arms over his chest. "I think ground evac is our absolute last course of action."

Jack looked outside at the low, heavy overcast that drove off his helicopter. "Do you have any air support?"

"Battalion got us two F-15 fighters carrying Mark-82 JDAMs." Sergeant Robinson looked at his watch. "They were due at our initial point five minutes ago."

"What are JDAMs?" Craig said.

"God dammit, Craig," Sergeant Robinson said. "Quit interrupting Colonel Black Eagle."

Jack looked at the platoon sergeant. "It's Ok sergeant. They're just nervous." He faced into the room. "JDAMs are bombs that use GPS for guidance. They're perfect for bad weather like this."

Sergeant Robinson shook his head. "Colonel, even if the Air Force is up there, they can't help us."

"Why is that?"

"My attack controller was eating breakfast when the mortar's started." Everyone in the room looked at the ground for several moments. Sergeant Robinson pointed in the direction of the local village. "Besides, most of the Taliban are hiding inside Waco. Those pilots won't drop on a village no matter how much we scream."

"Where's the JTAC's radio?"

Sergeant Robinson pointed. "It's right behind you."

Jack looked at the modern air force radio. A bulletin board behind it held an aeronautical chart showing Waco and COP Armstrong. He walked up to the chart and studied it. The now deceased attack controller, or JTAC, used blue ink to mark the aircraft initial point, designated YANKEE, four miles east of the COP.

"Do you have a translator?"

"Sure. George Muhammad from Sacramento. He's good people. Been with us since we rotated into this hell hole. He's sitting with first squad right now."

Jack picked up the satchel charge. He opened the bag and counted sixteen blocks of explosives inside. He faced the big platoon sergeant. "Get your translator and your squad leaders up here. I've got an idea."

Specialist Janofsky, known as Ski by his platoon, ran from the maintenance barn. He carried a shovel, a spare tire, and an ammunition can full of gasoline. One of the captured satchel charges hung off his right shoulder. He sprinted for his squad's MRAP, located at the northwest corner of the compound. The spare tire was heavier than he expected and soon he sucked in huge gasps of air. He spotted three other soldiers, all with the same load, running to their vehicles.

When he reached the vehicle, he threw the heavy tire against its side. It bounced off with a thump and fell to the ground. He placed the gasoline behind the vehicle's large front tire to shield it from the explosion and grabbed his shovel. He moved six feet from the vehicle and attacked the soil. A helmeted head popped out of the top of the vehicle.

"Quit throwing stuff against my vehicle, Ski," the soldier said.

Ski continued working. "Fuck you, Patrick. I'm doing what Robinson told me to do."

"If you scratched my ride, I'm going to fuck you up when this is over."

Ski blew a raspberry. "You and what army?" He threw a shovel of soil at the MRAP. "Quit bothering me. I'm working."

Ski removed five more shovels of soil and finished his hole. He reached into the satchel charge and removed four sticks of C4 explosive taped together with an electric blasting cap. He placed the charge within the hole and threw two shovels of loose soil over the explosives.

He looked at the soldier still watching him. "Hey Patrick. Stay right there while I detonate this explosive. The sand will make a nice exfoliant for your ugly face."

The soldier smirked at Ski but dropped down within the vehicle. The top hatch closed.

Ski laughed and backed away from the hole. He headed for a fighting position fifty meters away. As he did, he uncoiled the electrical wires attached to the explosives. Halfway to the position he placed another four sticks of C4 on the ground and unwound its electrical wires.

He reached the fighting position and sat down behind a solid wall of sandbags. He connected the wires for the buried charge to an electrical firing device then keyed his squad radio. "Second squad ready." A few moments later he heard the soldiers from the other three squads check in.

Ten seconds later Sergeant First Class Robinson came on the radio. "All squads fire."

Ski squeezed the small firing device and detonated the buried charge. A loud thump hit his position and black smoke and pulverized soil flew into the air. He heard the other explosions come from near the other vehicles. As instructed, he waited a full minute and detonated his second charge.

When the other explosions came, he sprinted back to his MRAP. He looked at the big vehicle and saw it suffered no damage. However, the soldiers inside did not fire at Waco and the vehicle's mounted machine gun pointed down at the ground. He pushed the tire into the now much larger hole and drenched it in gasoline. He lit the tire on fire and a cloud of black smoke surged into the sky. A lot of the smoke covered the still functional MRAP.

Ski turned and ran to his fighting position.

Jack watched the explosions burst across the compound. He knew the Taliban in Waco heard and saw the blasts. He stepped away from the firing port and faced George. He handed the dead Taliban leader's radio to the translator.

"Tell them they destroyed the vehicles and killed many of the soldiers inside," Jack said. "They can attack the compound and there is no one to stop them." Jack pointed out the firing port facing Waco. "Tell them to come through that wide open gate."

George smiled as he took the radio. "With pleasure, colonel."

The translator, a small man who emigrated to California from Northwest Pakistan when he was twelve, connected with the Taliban and screamed into the radio. Jack didn't speak Pashto, but he was pretty sure he heard half a dozen 'Allah Akbar' or 'God is great' comments along with many other exclamations to the listening Taliban. They asked a few questions, and George jumped around the TOC with excitement as he spoke. After a minute he shut off the radio. He turned to Jack. "They're coming."

Jack and Sergeant Robinson moved to the firing port facing Waco. Both used binoculars and scanned the occupied village. Soon two men carrying snare drums at their waists, stepped from behind a fence and banged out a loud, marching beat. Jack wondered where the two Taliban learned to play the drums. He turned and noticed several soldiers inside the TOC nodded their heads to the pounding rhythm.

A line of Taliban fighters trotted out from between two houses and headed for COP Armstrong. The fighters all carried AK-47s or light machine guns. A few men ran with rocket launchers on their shoulders. Others wore long belts of linked ammunition draped around their necks. The men remained in single file and kept about a meter apart. As they ran the fighters all brought their knees up towards their chests, and each man's right foot struck the ground in time with the accompanying drums.

Another line of fighters appeared from within Waco. They also moved in a single file and high stepped towards the compound.

"Did not expect to see that," Sergeant Robinson said. "It looks like the University of Michigan marching band coming onto the field at half time."

"Their commander must be a big ten fan," Jack said. Sergeant Robinson laughed but kept his binoculars on the approaching enemy.

The two columns of fighters, keeping about fifty meters apart, followed the same path Jack had taken earlier. Jack's knees went weak as he counted at least fifty fighters in each line. He spotted the smiles on their faces as they marched towards an easy victory. He wondered how he ever made it through the village.

When the two groups reached the halfway point Sergeant Robinson gave a command over his radio. Every rifle and machine gun in the compound fired on both columns. The first runners went down in bloody heaps and the rest threw themselves to the ground. The drummers disappeared back into Waco. Two fighters in the rear sprinted for the village but gunfire cut them down.

Sergeant Robinson again used his radio and soon red smoke and infrared grenades from the platoon's M-203 grenade launchers burst among the sprawled fighters.

Jack keyed the JTAC's radio. "Falcon one one this is Romeo two six. Standby for hasty nine line. I am not a JTAC."

He received an immediate response. "Romeo two six we don't do hasty nine-line missions. Too dangerous. Put your JTAC on."

"Falcon one one our JTAC is dead, and this is a danger close mission."

After a short pause the pilot responded. "Are you sure you don't have a JTAC?

"Positive. The Taliban killed our JTAC, and we may lose this outpost if you can't make a bomb run."

The pilot paused longer this time. "Romeo two six. Acknowledged. Ready to copy your hasty nine line."

Jack read off the data needed by the pilots. "Initial Point is Yankee. Heading is two seven zero magnetic. Distance from IP is four miles. Target elevation is four five niner seven feet above sea level. Target is enemy infantry in the open. Use JDAM. Target location is grid echo foxtrot two one zero zero four six two one. Located between the village and the combat outpost. Target marked by red and IR smoke. I say again target marked by red and IR smoke. Friendly forces are three hundred meters south marked by black smoke. Friendly forces are black smoke. Egress is two seven zero. No read back and no BDA. Both aircraft are cleared in hot."

"Acknowledged Romeo two six. Both aircraft cleared in hot. Be there in thirty seconds. Get your heads down."

Jack moved next to Sergeant Robinson at the firing port. He watched as a Talban fighter rallied his team and got them moving forward. Another fighter stood and urged his soldiers forward. Heavy machine gun fire from within Waco resumed and the prone fighters poured heavy fire into COP Armstrong.

A burst of machine gun fire hit the side of the TOC and Jack and Sergeant Robinson ducked below the firing port. When he lifted his head back up, he saw a white Toyota pickup with a large machine gun in its bed as it sped around the left side of Waco. The gun truck, called a 'technical' by the US military, headed straight for them as a Taliban soldier stood in the truck's bed and fired long bursts into the compound.

Sergeant Robinson spoke into his radio and the closest platoon MRAP fired at the truck. The truck took a few hits but did not stop. The technical's gunner focused on the MRAP and soon his rounds hit the ground and sandbags around the vehicle. A few tracers bounced off its armor and shot into the sky. The MRAP's remote weapon station ceased firing. The enemy hits wrecked the MRAP's weapon.

Specialist Craig pointed and yelled. "Another vehicle on the right!"

A second vehicle, a small four door sedan, sped around the right side of the village. The sedan threw up a large rooster tail of dust as the driver gunned it through a sharp turn and headed for the COP. The sedan sat low and even bottomed out as it sped over ruts in the ground. Jack put his binoculars on the vehicle. He saw the driver and cardboard boxes stacked in the back seat.

Jack's pulse pounded and he raised his voice. "It's a suicide vehicle! Stop it before it reaches the perimeter!"

Sergeant Robinson spoke into his radio and the outgoing tracers moved away from the sprawled Taliban and the technical and towards the sedan. Soon rounds peppered the speeding vehicle. A moment later steam gushed from the punctured radiator. Jack heard the sedan's small engine racing as it struggled through the terrain.

More rounds found the sedan and it slowed. A long burst of machine gun fire shattered its windshield. It turned to the left and rolled to a stop two hundred meters from Waco. Jack could no longer see the driver.

Five seconds later a huge explosion obliterated the sedan. The blast and shockwave rocked the TOC and hurt their ears. The sandbagged ceiling bowed in, and loose sand rained down on the soldiers. Large pieces of crushed and twisted steel, along with a few burning boxes, rained down around a large cloud of smoke. None came close to COP Armstrong. The smoke drifted away and revealed a large crater surrounded by blackened car parts. Small fires burned among the debris.

The technical stopped and its driver and gunner took in the spectacle of the destroyed suicide bomber. The outgoing gunfire moved back to the technical and the Taliban fighters. The technical resumed its fire but did not approach the compound.

Jack heard the scream of a jet engine as it approached from his right. He could not see the aircraft, but he knew the pilots released their bombs at five thousand feet. The lack of visibility did not concern him. If the pilots entered the correct grid coordinates into their fire control computers, their bombs would fall on the Taliban and not the COP.

Three large explosions burst among the Taliban fighters. Pieces of weapons, clothing, and body parts flew. The blast knocked down the group of fighters running towards him. A wall of dark smoke enveloped the two columns of prone fighters. Less than a second later, a fourth bomb exploded on the technical's front bumper. The vehicle flipped into the air and disintegrated into hundreds of pieces. The blasts pummeled Jack's eardrums and the concussions slapped his face. Loose sand filled the air as the TOC's walls and ceiling shook.

The smoke cleared and the closest fighters lay motionless or writhed in pain. A dozen men near the rear of the columns ran for the village. Platoon machine gun and rifle fire chased them and at least one man fell to the ground.

Four more explosions shook the ground and more dark smoke blanketed the area. Jack ducked as the TOC again shook. Three intact bodies flew from the smoke and flew in a wide arc, fifty meters to each side of the columns. Before the smoke cleared another dozen Taliban sprinted for the village. Jack had no idea how they could move, let alone run, after they suffered the concussion of so many bombs. Weapons fire chased the runners, but all reached the safety of the village.

Jack looked at the battlefield. At least fifty Taliban fighters lay in various poses across the ground. A few moved but most did not. Small fires and black smoke marked the remains of the two vehicles. Enemy fire from Waco ceased. Sergeant Robinson spoke into his radio and all outgoing fire stopped.

A minute later the radio squawked. "Romeo two six this is Falcon one one. You owe me a beer for getting that technical."

Jack smiled. "No problem, Falcon one one. We've got some cold ones down here. When can we expect you?"

After a long pause the pilot responded. "Romeo two six. On second thought we'll pass on that beer." Everyone in the TOC laughed at the pilot's response.

The radio squawked again. "Romeo two six, getting back to business, our infrared targeting pods show many personnel leaving the village and heading away from you. Your Taliban infantry are bugging out."

Jack swung his binoculars onto Waco. He saw no movement in the village. "Roger Falcon one one. Can you hit them when they get away from the village?"

It took a moment for the pilot to respond. "Negative Romeo two six. We see no weapons with the males and the groups have women and children with them. That's a no go with our rules of engagement. We'll hang around until we're bingo fuel in case they come back."

"Thank you, Falcon one one. We appreciate your assistance. Romeo two six out."

Jack placed the handset on the radio. He found a chair and sat down. His shoulders slumped and, despite a terrible headache caused by the close explosions, the tension left him. He knew the Taliban would not come back...at least not tonight.

Chapter 3

July 1, 2015, Western Arkansas

He Who Watches lounged atop an isolated hill deep in the Ozark National Forest. He watched two humans as they followed four dogs running through the valley below. He stood eight feet tall and weighed over seven hundred pounds. He feared no man or dog, but he would keep close watch on these humans.

A handful of his kind lived quietly in his territory covering five Midwestern states. He endured twenty-four winters here; fifteen with his mother, and the rest on his own. Fortunately, the winters were mild, and he always found or caught enough food to sustain and even develop his massive body.

His coal black fur and his keen perceptions allowed him to move unseen, day or night. In fact, most forest animals, even with their highly tuned senses, have never seen him. Several times in his life humans glimpsed him from afar, but the color of his fur, along with doubts planted in their minds, convinced them they saw a bear. Only once has a human ever seen him for what he is.

Unlike others of his kind, humans had always fascinated He Who Watches. Whenever he discovered a human in his forest, he followed it. Sometimes, he spent hours or even days watching an unsuspecting human. Their activities were curious and confusing, and this captivated him.

Their amazing, but terrifying, machines also intrigued him. He remembered when many years ago, on a moonless night, he approached a silent, green machine sitting in a field. Darting from tree to tree, He Who Watches studied the machine and wondered if it slept. Soon he threw small rocks at it, but it continued to slumber. When that got no response, he crept up to it, poked it with a stick, and fled to safety. Hours later he approached the great machine and ran his hands over its curves and hard edges. He soon grasped that the machine was a made thing; a tool used by the curious humans. Their big yellow machines, and their cars and trucks, were also made things. He ran his discovery through his brain. He still wondered if the machines came alive when the humans merged with them.

Despite his attraction to humans, He Who Watches knew they were dangerous. Especially when they carried their thunder sticks. Once during his eighteenth winter, he spotted a human male sitting in a tree deep within his forest. Curious, he approached the male from behind and studied him. Later a large buck, unaware of the human and He Who Watches, approached a pile of apples located in front of the human's tree. The buck lowered its head, and the male pointed a black stick at it. A tremendous bang blasted from one end.

The sound was louder than the thunder that accompanied the strong storms in the spring. He Who Watches bellowed with fright and ran. The male in the tree turned and saw him. The male leaped from the tree and landed on the ground in a heap. He thought the male had hurt himself, but he jumped up and ran away. Days later He Who Watches crept up to the same tree. The thunder stick, made of wood and metal, lay in the leaves where the male dropped it. The large buck, a jagged hole in his middle, lay close by. After that he moved with great caution near any human that carried a thunder stick.

Below him the dogs caught the scent of a large wild hog hiding in the forest. *Good! I hope the humans kill them all!*

He hated the voracious hogs released generations ago into the forest by the foolish humans. The ground birds in his forests were almost gone and deer, rabbits and squirrels sometimes starved when the thousands of greedy hogs ate all the forest's food.

The dogs howled as they searched, but the hog was smart and fooled the dogs when he moved to new hiding places. Soon the dogs grew frustrated and fought among themselves. The humans separated the dogs and dragged them to one of their noisy machines. They drove away in a cloud of dust and left the unseen hog behind.

He Who Watches observed the road from his hiding place for several hours in case the humans returned. Satisfied they were gone; he descended to the valley and silently called the undiscovered hog. When the confused animal came close, He Who Watches swung a large tree branch and crushed its skull. He tore the back legs off the hog and returned to his secluded spot at the top of the hill.

That night he gorged on the meat. Later, he built himself a soft bed under the branches of a cedar tree. Insects avoided the fragrant tree and that meant not swatting mosquitoes all night. He soon fell asleep and snored softly.

However, his sleep was fitful. He dreamed of savage hogs with long tusks and vast herds of deer. The hogs and deer threatened a small human cub; a female with a misshapen face. A hideous round human, all in white, danced among the animals and mocked the small cub. A great eagle did its best to protect the cub as the animals closed in.

His nightmare jarred him awake. Grass ripped from the ground filled his huge hands, and his powerful legs had torn great gouges in the forest floor. Upset, he threw the grass to the ground. He scanned the area and found two coyotes sleeping near the dead hog. Nothing else stirred.

He Who Watches had never experienced such a terrifying dream before. His mind reeled at the things he saw. He sensed the dream warned him of something terrible.

Since the sun would rise soon, he rose, stretched and walked further west into his territory. Soon he reached the top of a small hill. He stopped and faced north. Something tickled his brain; almost as if a ground squirrel scratched for a nut buried within his skull. This scratch told him to go north and to go quickly. Confused, He Who Watches walked in a small circle and made soft hooting noises. These unknown feelings or instructions disturbed him. Curious, he walked west again. He traveled several hundred paces but found he could walk no more. He again faced north. Soon he swayed back and forth. He did this for many hours as he stared into the distance.

After some time, he took one final look west and walked north. He took great strides and moved quickly towards his unknown destination. As the forest fell behind him, he remembered his dream, and his large body trembled with fear.

Chapter 4

July 7, 2015, Cedar City, Missouri

Jack drove south on the two-lane US highway that wound through western Missouri. His new SUV purred as it ate up the miles to their new assignment. The vehicle had less than three thousand miles on the speedometer; with most of that from his trip from Fort Bragg to South Dakota, and now the trip from South Dakota to Missouri. He patted the vehicle's dash as he drove. He enjoyed his new car and expected to keep it for a long time.

Jack adjusted his sunglasses and gazed out at the landscape before him. For the last hour he saw nothing but thick forests and the occasional farm or cattle ranch. Even small towns were rare in this area of the state. Jack suspected the area looked today as it had at the founding of the republic over two hundred years before. He hoped his new assignment would provide him some time to explore and hunt in this still wild land.

For the umpteenth time, he considered how he ended up in rural Missouri. While in Afghanistan, the notification for his promotion to full Colonel put him over the moon. For days afterward he waited for the next announcement that would give him command of a support brigade in one of the Army's ten active divisions. His entire military career led to this point, and he hardly slept from the excitement.

The day the message came, his boss, Major General McNally, brought Jack into his office. He informed him he would take command of Show Me Army Depot when the division rotated home from Afghanistan. Jack was so surprised he could not speak for several long moments. Throughout his career Jack felt second tier officers, those who couldn't hack it in the divisional Army, received depot assignments. He argued politely with the general for a different position, and even admitted the truth; he knew nothing about army depots and wanted nothing to do with them.

His argument got him nowhere. "It doesn't matter Jack," McNally said. "I spoke to General Chisum, and he wants someone with zero depot experience to take command. Show Me Army Depot is our largest, most critical ammunition depot and it has some real problems. Something about union and safety issues. He's concerned the depot cannot perform its wartime mission." McNally paused and took a sip of coffee. "He's looking for a hard charger to break paradigms and turn things around. I told him you're the man to do it." Now he frowned at his subordinate. "So shut your mouth, Jack. It's time for you to salute and move out and take the command you're offered."

Jack smiled at the memory. He glanced in his rearview mirror at his girls in the back seat. All three, and the families' dogs and cats in their carriers, dozed or stared out the windows.

To this day his unique daughters still amazed him. Mary, his eleven-year-old, composed and sang her own music. It seemed every day she came up with a new grouping of chords or a stanza that stunned Jack with its creativity. He often wondered where her musical genes came from. Neither he nor his wife ever displayed any musical talent. Despite being a growing 'tween', Mary loved her role as big sister.

Their middle child, Carol, loved to dance. Starting as a toddler, she spent hours in front of the TV emulating the latest dance steps from movies and talent shows. Jack even found copies of the 80's dance program, Solid Gold, on YouTube and played them for her. When he returned from Afghanistan, she showed him videos of Swan Lake and the Nutcracker. He wondered if the small city near Show Me Army Depot had any ballet studios. He also wondered if he could afford the cost of a university education in ballet. A typical middle child, Carol often quarreled with her older sister despite loving her unconditionally.

Janet, their youngest, arrived six years ago. Born with Downs Syndrome, she functioned close to the level of a normal child. When she became a toddler, Jack and his wife, Soo Jong, observed many odd interactions between Janet and her pets. Finally, after much denial, they confirmed their youngest had an astonishing sixth sense that allowed her to communicate with animals of all types. At first, they did not know what to do or how to react. After several years of worrying, they simply accepted it as a gift from the great Sioux spirit Wakan Tanka. So, when a bird landed in Janet's open hand, or a herd of cows followed her around her great grandfather's ranch, the family took it for granted. Jack felt it made his little girl even more special.

Jack glanced to his right at the empty passenger seat and sighed. He met Soo Jong when he visited her parents' restaurant during his first tour to Korea. Despite their different cultures, and him towering over her, they became sweethearts and married within a year of meeting. Everyone noticed her beauty and her sparkling personality. His bosses throughout his career always informed Jack that he had married up. He always agreed. More than one of his evaluations improved due to his superiors' approval for his Korean-born wife. He could not imagine life without her.

Two years ago, in their eighteenth year of marriage, Soo Jong passed away from an aggressive cancer. Her death devastated Jack, and for many months he felt he could not endure. He struggled for a long time, but each new day brought a comment or hug or crying fit from one of his girls. Each event brought him back to reality and eventually gave him the closure he needed.

Then, four months after her funeral, it started. It seemed every friend, colleague, relative, and superior tried to fix Jack up with a replacement for Soo Jong. Jack had his hands more than full with his young children and his career so he politely declined all offers. He even had no interest in a casual, no-strings-attached blind date. Jack knew his friends tried to help but he was not sure he could ever date again.

With the help of numerous live-in nannies, and his understanding bosses, Jack stayed in the service. During his tour to Afghanistan, he moved the girls to South Dakota where they lived with Jack's grandparents. As expected, the yearlong separation proved difficult. Phone calls once a week from Afghanistan could never fill the void of his girls' absence. However, the girls adapted and came through the year with no serious issues.

The best thing about his new assignment: it required no overseas deployments and little official travel. Once he found a reliable nannie, he would spend all his free time reconnecting with his girls.

The SUV crested a hill, and Jack spotted Show Me Army Depot in the distance. Numerous checkered water towers and the tops of large industrial buildings jutted above the forests that covered the depot. He estimated the distance between the water towers at several miles.

"It's a big place," Jack said under his breath. Despite not wanting this assignment, his new depot impressed him. As one of the largest military depots in the free world, it covered 90 square miles and employed over 2,000 people. It had its own roads, security, fire department, cafeteria, hotel, and even a small clinic with a doctor. One major difference was the depot had no other military personnel; he was the only one.

Jack looked in the rearview mirror. "Wake up, girls. We'll arrive at our new home in a few minutes."

Soon all three girls strained in their seats to see through the front window.

"Where is it, Dad?" Mary said. "All I see are a bunch of trees."

"We're still a few miles away. But if you look above the trees, you'll spot the water towers. See them? That's Show Me Army Depot."

"Do animals live on your base, Daddy?" Janet asked.

"Yes, Janet. It has deer, rabbits, squirrels, and many other wild animals. And there's a big lake right behind our new house. It's full of fish, frogs, and maybe even beavers."

Janet clapped her hands. "Dad, can I keep a beaver at our new home?"

"No honey. Beavers are wild animals. It's wrong to make them pets."

Janet frowned. "Darn."

Jack followed two large semi-trucks onto the exit for Show Me Army Depot. He noticed the northbound exit looped up and over a large overpass-type bridge that spanned the busy highway and a set of railroad tracks. As he looked down from the exit, he saw the highway and tracks sat within terrain that some would call a small canyon. The trucks came to the end of the off-ramp and turned right towards a gate marked **Truck Entrance**.

Jack drove straight ahead to a series of booths and gates like those seen on a toll highway. Above the gate stood a large World War II-era sign that read **Show Me Army Depot**. Behind the gates, a blacktop road led to the interior of the depot. Thick forests bordered the gate area and the road.

Their vehicle slowed, and two middle-aged security guards, one male and one female and wearing blue uniforms and ball caps, stepped from the first booth. Jack stopped and rolled down his window.

"Good evening," Jack said. "I'm Colonel Jack Black Eagle."

"Welcome to Show Me Army Depot, Colonel," the male guard said. "They told us to expect you."

"Thank you." Jack smiled at the two guards. After ten seconds his smile disappeared. "Aren't you going to ask for my identification?"

The two guards exchanged glances. "Sir, the current commander changed our security procedures. We're forbidden from checking identification and searching vehicles. If we have a good idea of who is in a vehicle, we're required to let them through."

"I see. When did this happen?"

"About a year ago," the male guard said. "Joe Harper, the union vice president, said checking identification was an unfair labor practice. He said it made employees late for work and it had to stop. It's plumb stupid if you ask me, Colonel."

Jack felt his blood pressure rise. He got out of the SUV and faced the two guards. "Effective immediately you'll check my identification and search my vehicle according to current Department of Defense security protocol every time I come through this gate. That's regardless of your current orders. Please pass that on to all the security personnel. Is that clear?"

Both guards attempted to stand at attention. "Yes, Sir," they said.

They checked Jack's ID and did a careful inspection of his vehicle. They even opened the car's doors and hood. Finally, they used a small mirror to examine the vehicle underneath. The girls loved it and peppered the guards with questions about their new home.

When they finished Jack called them over. "Let's start over. I'm Jack Black Eagle. It's nice to meet you both. What are your names?"

"Sir, I'm Benny Miksic," the tall guard said. He motioned to his partner. "This here lady is June Miksic."

Jack shook both their hands and introduced the girls.

"Are you two married?" Jack asked.

"No, we get that a lot," June said. "We're cousins."

"Isn't the union president here also named Miksic?"

June nodded. "Yessir, Don Miksic is our union president. He's another cousin of ours. You'll find a lot of Miksic, Klinder, and McEntire names around here."

"Good. I'm looking forward to meeting everyone and especially Don Miksic."

"Oh, you'll meet him soon enough Colonel, and he's going to love meeting you," June said.

Jack ignored her last comment. He nodded towards the truck gate. "I followed those trucks in. Do you get many here after work hours?"

"Most nights a few trucks arrive early for their deliveries," June said. "We let them park here for security purposes."

Jack nodded at the response. "Well, I've got some tired kids in the car. Can you direct us to the guest house?"

"No need for the guest house, Colonel." June darted into the booth and returned with a set of keys. "These are the keys for Quarters #1, your permanent residence. It's ready for you to stay there tonight. The morale office stocked it with pots, pans, dishes, and all the towels and linens you'll need. You're all set. At least until your household goods arrive. I wouldn't be surprised if the kitchen has fresh milk and bread."

Jack accepted the keys and smiled. "That's great. How do I find our quarters?"

She pointed down the road. "Go through the gate and drive down the main access road. A mile past the headquarters building you take a left. That road leads to your quarters. If you miss the turn, you'll stop at the security gate for the depot's industrial facilities."

Jack got back in his car. He waved at the two guards and pulled through the gate. For many miles thick forest surrounded their vehicle.

"Wow. Fort Bragg didn't have this many trees," Jack said.

Soon the trees thinned, and they drove into a group of buildings arranged like the center of a small town. A large red brick building with a tall flagpole dominated the cluster. A large sign read **Headquarters, Show Me Army Depot**.

Jack pointed. "There's my new office, girls."

The headquarters had a well-manicured lawn with numerous large trees. Jack guessed the buildings dated from World War II. He liked being part of this historic and still vital facility.

Five minutes later Jack turned left onto 'Maple' street. Before long, their quarters came into view. His girls gasped.

"Wow! What a beautiful old house," Mary said.

Jack turned into a long driveway leading to a rustic, two-story home built with hand-hewn logs cut from the depot's own forests. A huge front door and shuttered windows framed the front of the home. The home had a lush lawn and sat inside a small forest of towering maple trees. Behind the house, a path stretched from the home's back door to a dock on a large lake. The dock held two small rowboats.

He said a silent thank you to whoever threw away the 1940's rulebook and built such a beautiful set of quarters.

Jack stopped the car. The three girls bolted from their seats and ran to the back yard.

"Stay out of the water!" Jack yelled at his screaming girls.

With no one around, he opened the tailgate and uncaged the dogs and cats. The animals leaped from the vehicle and streaked after the girls. Jack entered the new home and paused to take in the interior. He sighed and brushed a tear from his eye. "Dammit honey, I wish you were here to see this," he said to himself.

For a seventy-year-old home, its interior delighted him. The living room had a wood burning fireplace and hardwood floors. The upstairs held bright and airy bedrooms with many windows in each. The bedrooms contained standard issue Army cots identical to what Jack used in Afghanistan. Jack laughed when he saw the cots. He knew the girls would love them.

He judged the kitchen and bathrooms adequate but better than many of their previous Army quarters. He found every room spotless, and this pleased him to no end. In the family room, a large picture window gave him a stunning view of the back yard and lake. He saw no other homes on the lake.

Jack spotted the girls in the backyard looking into the forest circling the house. He stepped out and joined them. The family's two cats and two dogs sat in a row next to Janet. His girls and their animals stared into the trees.

"What do you see girls?"

Carol pointed. "It's a herd of deer, Dad."

Jack followed her point and saw a dozen deer standing in the forest a hundred feet away. The animals stood like statues and stared at the family.

"Wow," Jack said. "There's a lot of them. I guess the depot has a large deer population."

They're so pretty," Carol said.

For a minute they all stared at the deer. Soon a doe and two fawns approached and headed straight for Janet. They stopped and all three nuzzled her outstretched hand with their wet, black noses.

Janet giggled and wiped her hand on her dress. "It's yucky."

"Janet, please say thank you to the deer and ask them to go away," Jack said.

Janet looked at her father. "Awwwww, do I have to? I want to keep them."

"No, Janet. What did I say about making wild animals pets? Make them go away."

"Okay." She dropped her hand. The doe and fawns backed away but still stared at her.

Jack stepped forward. He clapped his hands and yelled. "Yaaahhh!"

The three deer bolted away to the rest of their herd. They stopped, turned, and stared at the family.

"You scared them, Daddy," Janet said.

"Janet, deer and people don't mix. They're welcome to eat the acorns and grass around our house, but you cannot play with them or make them your pets. Is that clear?"

Janet put on a little girl frown. "Okay Daddy."

Jack headed towards the house. "Girls let's go inside and see the house. It's big enough that each of you can have your own bedroom."

The girls squealed and sprinted for the back door with their cats and dogs close behind. For the next half hour, the three girls and four animals bounded through the empty house. They tried every light switch and validated that every toilet and faucet worked. Soon everyone met in the kitchen.

Mary said, "Dad I'm hungry; what's for supper?"

Jack looked in the refrigerator. It held the basics of milk, cheese, butter, and bread. He would hit the local grocery store tomorrow. "There's not much here, but I can make us something. Do you want to go to a restaurant or eat here?"

"What do we have to eat here?" Mary said.

Jack pulled a familiar blue can from his backpack and held it up to the girls. "Do you want spam sandwiches?"

All three girls smiled and yelled. "Eat here!"

Before long Jack had a pan going on the stove. The meat sizzled and filled the kitchen with its familiar aroma. The girls sat on the kitchen's ancient linoleum floor and played a word game as their father cooked. Jack moved to the sink. He glanced out the kitchen window and saw three deer standing in the middle of the back yard. They stared at him through the window. Jack made sure Janet could not see him. He moved his hand up until he pointed his index finger at the deer. He dropped his thumb. *Bang!* The deer jumped but did not run away. Jack smiled.

Chapter 5

July 10, 2015, Show Me Army Depot, Missouri

Jack entered the small auditorium located at the rear of his headquarters. Patriotic bunting adorned the walls, and cake and punch covered several long tables in the back. Thirty minutes earlier Jack completed the traditional ceremony where he received the Show Me Army Depot flag from his predecessor. This simple hand off, witnessed by depot employees and invited guests, confirmed his responsibility for the massive depot.

Jack looked dapper in his blue Class A uniform. A new Silver Star medal, awarded for his actions at COP Armstrong, topped off his five rows of ribbons. His girls, each wearing an Easter dress, burst through the door behind him. They paused for a second to examine the room, but soon ran to the refreshments.

It took Jack a long time to purchase the dresses for his daughters. At the department store, he didn't have a clue what he needed to do. He wandered around the dress aisle in a daze; his girls following behind him. A helpful clerk suggested he contact a female relative. Jack face-timed his grandmother. Once she popped up on his smartphone, the selection and fitting of each girl's dress went like clockwork.

At Jack's request his deputy, Ross Kelly, joined him in the reception line to introduce the dozens of important guests. The line started, and the mayor of Cedar City; a rural city located twenty miles up highway 61, stepped up to Jack.

The well-dressed man, older and shorter than Jack, shook his hand. "Ethan Edwards, Colonel; welcome to Missouri. We have a lot to talk about as your depot is the largest employer in this part of the state. I want to make sure you and I are on the same sheet of music in terms of creating good paying government jobs."

"I'll do my best Mr. Mayor and I look forward to supporting your wonderful city. I'm excited about living a small-town life again."

The mayor turned to a younger woman. "My companion, Sarah Simpson."

Jack took the woman's hand. "Nice to meet you, Ms. Simpson."

Sarah looked in her mid-forties with blond hair and blue eyes. She wore a low-cut white dress that highlighted a perfect figure and shapely legs. When he focused on her face, Jack's breath caught in his throat. He wondered if the stunning woman standing before him appeared on the covers of beauty magazines.

"Nice to meet you, Colonel Black Eagle," she said. "Please call me Sarah. Are you Native American?"

"Yes, I am. My father was Lakota Sioux, and I spent a lot of time on the reservation with my grandparents. In fact, I would say I spent most of my childhood there."

"How nice. I have several Cherokee ancestors on my mother's side."

Jack felt no attraction to the mayor's girlfriend but for some reason he couldn't help the words that came from his mouth. "Sarah, I'll bet people tell you all the time how beautiful you are. I'm certain you never sit at home on a Saturday night."

Sarah giggled but said nothing.

The mayor gave Jack a withering look and took Sarah's arm. "Come along now, Sarah. Colonel, I'll send an invitation to dinner soon so I can update you on the community." Before Jack could respond, the mayor guided Sarah past him and away from the receiving line.

His deputy leaned into him. "Careful, Colonel…she's the mayor's girlfriend; you might get a lot of parking tickets."

Jack shrugged and said, "She's attractive, but I'm not sure why I said that." He put the exchange out of his mind and continued to shake hands.

Soon he spotted a large man approaching. The man was in his mid-sixties, and he had short, gray hair, a chiseled face, and three days of beard stubble. The man towered over Jack and outweighed him by at least fifty pounds. Despite his age, he displayed a trim waist and large biceps. He wore a clean white t-shirt under denim overalls. A ball cap that stated 'CAT Diesel Power' sat on his head.

"Sir, this is Don Miksic; our union president for the past twenty years," Ross said.

A huge hand gripped Jack's and squeezed it. "Don Miksic, Colonel. I'm president of National Government Workers Local 1801." The pressure on Jack's hand increased. "I'm looking forward to seeing what caliber of leader you are. The depot needs a good leader; especially after three years of Colonel dickhead."

Jack attempted to put some force behind his own grip, but he could not compete with the muscles that bulged in the union leader's arm.

Don continued. "We have several outstanding grievances that need your review. I hope as a new member of management you can be fair and impartial and see the union's point of view."

"Does the union's point of view include eliminating security procedures at the depot's entrance?" Jack said.

Don's brow furrowed. "I don't know what you're talking about, Colonel."

Jack felt real pain from the crushing grip. When he could take no more, he pointed his index finger straight out relieving the pressure on his hand. He rotated his own thumb up and over and placed it on top of the first joint of Don's thumb. He placed his left palm on top of his own thumb and pushed it down. Don's hand moved down several inches. The big man's eyes opened wide, and he let out a mild grunt of pain. Jack released Don's hand and stepped back.

A small smile creased the union president's mouth. "Good move, Colonel."

Jack doubted anyone else saw the exchange, but he braced himself in case Don decided to swing at him.

Jack's new secretary, a middle-aged woman named Kristi, appeared from behind Jack. She glared at the big man. "Do you kiss your mother with that mouth, Don? Why don't you move along and do something you're good at; like stuffing your mouth with cake."

Don turned to her. "I'm looking out for the depot and its employees. I'm a veteran and a bronze star winner, and I think the depot commanders should fight for their employees."

Ross chimed in. "Don, don't start your crap now. This is the Colonel's reception. We'll discuss the union's grievances later. "

Jack shook his protesting hand. He glared at the big man. "It's nice to meet you too, Don. Maybe next time we get together we won't have to assault each other. Now that I'm in command, I'm going to make this the best depot in the world, and I look forward to teaming with the union on it."

"We'll see how that goes," Don said. He raised a great paw to his right. "I want you to meet my family."

Kristi faded back into the crowd, and Don moved off in search of the refreshments. Jack looked at Ross, but his deputy acted as if this was an everyday occurrence. The interaction showed that union and management relations on Show Me Army Depot were in a terrible state. Could he fix it? If he couldn't, he had an impossible task ahead of him.

A woman and three men stepped up to Jack. He thought the woman might be close to six feet in height. Jack put her age in her late thirties. She had stylish brunette hair cut above her shoulders. She wore no makeup but displayed a classic 'girl next door' beauty. She also wore bib overalls, but no cap.

"I'm Natalie Miksic, Colonel. Don't take my father too seriously. Once you get to know him, you'll see he's a big softie."

Jack chuckled. "A big softie? That's what I was thinking, Natalie. I'm glad that big softie didn't pound me into the floor like a nail." Jack gave his hand one final shake. "Do you work here at the depot Ms. Miksic?"

A frown crossed her face. "I do work here Colonel, and my brothers do too. It's practically a family tradition. I'm on nights down at the bomb line."

"That's wonderful. I know it's the experienced employees that keep this place running." Jack turned to Ross. "How soon can I get down to the bomb line for a tour?"

"We can make it happen within a few days, Sir," said Ross. "I'll have Kristi get it on the schedule right away."

Jack turned back to Natalie. "I'll get there as soon as I can. When I visit, will you show me around? I'd like to hear first-hand from an hourly employee about the good and bad things in the line."

A huge smile appeared on her face. "Wow. We never see the commander on night shift; that'll be a real treat. It's a date." Jack smiled but Natalie's smile cracked.

"Sorry, it's not a date date," she said. "We'll see you at the line, and I'll show you everything." Her eyes grew wide, and her cheeks blushed. "I mean I'll show you the bomb line. I'll show you everything at the bomb line. I'll give you a tour of the bomb line."

Jack said nothing. Natalie looked down and said, "I'm going to stop talking now." She kept her head down and gestured to the man next to her. "Colonel, this is my brother Will."

Will shook Jack's hand. "Welcome to Show Me Depot, Sir." Will stood a few inches shorter than Jack but had a trim build like Jack's. He also had on bib overalls, but his red ball cap stated 'International Harvester'. Will's body started to tremble, like he experienced a small seizure, and words blurted from his mouth. "Shit, cock, fuck, colonel."

Jack cocked his head but said nothing.

Kristi again appeared from behind him. "Will, did you forget to take your meds today?" she said.

"You mind your own business, Kristi. I've got everything covered." Will nodded to Jack. "It was nice to meet you, Colonel." He turned and headed towards the cake and punch.

"Sir, you'll have to excuse Will," Natalie said. "He has Tourette's syndrome, and sometimes things slip out. Despite his affliction, he's smart as a whip. He's the only one in our family to earn a college degree. He runs a forklift down at X-Ray."

Jack nodded. "It's fine Natalie. I've known many people with worse disabilities. I'm certain it doesn't affect his work. In fact, I'm sure he's a great conversationalist."

Natalie gave Jack a sly smile and continued with her introductions. "This is my other brother, Cecil."

Cecil also wore bib overalls and had the same build as his brother. His ball cap said 'Cedar City Lumber'. "I'm a supervisor down at X-Ray with Will, Colonel," Cecil said. "Please come down and see us sometime."

"I will," Jack said.

"And this is my baby brother Howard," Natalie said. "Everyone calls him Howie."

A young man in his late twenties and tall like his father, but with the build of an Olympic athlete, stepped up and shook Jack's hand. He also wore bib overalls along with a green 'John Deere' ball cap. The young man kept his head down and barely acknowledged Jack.

"It's nice to meet you, Howie," Jack said.

The young man said nothing for several seconds. Finally, words spurted from his mouth. "It's nice to meet you Sir. I think you and your family will like it here. Missouri is a great place to live, and there are lots of things to do. I drive one of the depot's ammunition trucks so I'm always around. Maybe you can come and ride around with me someday. Well, I'll see you later."

Before Jack could say anything, Howie gave an awkward wave and walked off. At no time did he meet Jack's eyes.

Natalie again apologized. "I'm sorry Colonel. Howie is very shy. Mom died when he was five, and he never came out of his shell. He rarely speaks with anyone no matter how hard they try; even pretty girls. In fact, his words to you are the most he's spoken in several years."

"It's fine Natalie. I enjoyed meeting your family, and I'm looking forward to working with you. Believe it or not I'm even looking forward to working with your dad. I'm certain I can get on his good side." Jack gestured. "I hope you can stay and enjoy the refreshments." Natalie smiled and moved off into the crowd.

Soon a uniformed police officer approached. The man appeared much older than Jack but wore his uniform well.

Ross greeted the man warmly and introduced him to Jack. "Sir, I want you to meet a great friend to the depot; Cedar County Sheriff Uwell Yates."

Jack shook his hand. "It's nice to meet you, Uwell. I'm glad local law enforcement could make it here today."

"My pleasure, Colonel. I earned my bones working here as a depot security guard. A person learns a lot operating under the strict requirements of government security. When I left and ran for Sheriff, I promised I would always look out for the depot commanders and their families." He handed Jack his business card. "Please call me if you ever need anything from local law enforcement."

"I'll do that," Jack said. "If I can help you in any way please ask."

"That's great, Colonel. I'm sure I'll be in touch." With that, the sheriff again shook Jack's hand and departed.

A loud crash echoed from the back of the room. Jack turned to see Janet with several plates of cake on the floor around her.

"I'll take care of it Colonel," Kristi said. "You stay put." She hurried off.

Jack turned back to see a short, very overweight Asian man standing in front of him. He placed the man's age in his mid-thirties. He wore a spotless white chef's outfit to include a starched toque hat.

The man gave a short bow and shook Jack's hand. "Colonel, I'm Victor Chow. It's so nice to meet you."

"I'm pleased to meet you, Victor. Thank you for coming."

"It was an honor to witness your ceremony. Also, congratulations on your silver star award. It is obvious you are a brave man."

"Well thank you. I give credit to the great soldiers I served with. Victor, it appears you're dressed for work in a kitchen."

"Yes, I own the China King Buffet downtown. I serve authentic mandarin Chinese cuisine at reasonable prices. I apologize for my attire, but I had an engagement and had no time to change."

"Please don't apologize. Your work apparel is fine. Is your heritage Chinese?"

"Correct. I come from eastern China."

"The reason I asked is I thought you might be from my late wife's original home of Korea."

Victor's smile twisted and his right eye twitched. "No…China." He smiled at Jack. "Colonel, I appreciate the sacrifices made by the members of the armed forces. I hope you and your family can visit my restaurant soon. I always give the depot commander a fifty percent discount."

"That's very generous. My family loves Chinese food, so I'm certain we'll visit soon. I hope you can stay and enjoy the refreshments."

"I'm sorry, but I cannot stay. Please; my restaurant's door is always open." Victor gave Jack a quick bow and headed for the door.

Jack turned to Ross. "Is he our caterer?"

"No, Sir. We gave a blanket invitation to the local chamber of commerce. I guess he decided to attend."

"Is his food any good?"

Ross nodded. "It's delicious. I eat there all the time."

Many additional guests passed through the line, eager to meet the new commander. Jack's hand throbbed from so many greetings. Soon the last guest approached.

"Colonel, this is Joe Harper, the local's vice president," Ross said.

Jack put the man's age at around fifty, and it appeared he purchased his out-of-style three-piece suit from a thrift shop. Sweat stains soiled his collar, and his palms were slick with perspiration when he shook Jack's hand. A comb over, glued to his scalp with an entire can of fragrant hair mousse, failed to hide his long term balding. His selection of eyewear proved the oddest part of the man's appearance. He wore a pair of bright yellow, designer eyeglasses; ones suitable for a much younger and hipper man. His appearance and eyewear screamed that Mr. Joe Harper was an odd duck.

Joe smiled revealing nicotine-stained teeth. "Colonel, welcome to Show Me Depot. I know you met Don Miksic today. I can assure you that despite what Don says, the union is ready to work with you."

Jack released Joe's hand and covertly wiped his palm against his trousers. "I'm glad to hear it, Joe. I told Don I look forward to working with the union."

"That's good. I must warn you about Don though." Joe lowered his voice and stepped close to Jack. "He's a dedicated union official and all. But he often says one thing even though he means something different. You can always come to me if you need something that Don won't agree to."

Jack bristled at Joe's attempt to undercut Don Miksic's authority. His smile vanished, and he said, "Joe, I appreciate your offer, but one of the most important tenets within the US Army is the chain of command. I intend to do everything possible to work well with Don and the union and I will not seek you out if I have a conflict with him. Ignoring Don means a nonfunctional organization, and I won't do that. I will make it work." Jack motioned towards the serving area. "Please keep that in mind as you enjoy the refreshments."

Joe took a quick breath, and he looked like he wanted to say more. After a few seconds, he nodded to Jack and scurried off.

Jack and Ross left the receiving line and mingled at the reception until the last guest departed.

"Well, I'm glad that's over," Jack said. He turned to his deputy. "Ross, good work by everyone on the change of command. It was a great welcome to Show Me Army Depot. Please thank everyone for their help. Also, get my schedule set up with tours of all key depot areas. Let's start tomorrow.

Ross nodded. "Already on it, Sir. And I'm going to handle a lot of the tours myself."

"Great. For now, I'm taking my girls to lunch and for ice cream. I'll see you in the morning."

Jack found his girls in a corner at the back of the auditorium sitting on the floor. A stack of plates holding half eaten slices of cake surrounded them. Janet dozed as she leaned against the wall. Jack thought he might have to skip the ice cream after lunch. He lifted Janet into his arms and looked at Mary and Carol. "Thanks for being good during my reception. I know you girls don't like these events, but they're important for me, and I appreciate you attending."

Mary smiled at Jack. "No problem, Dad. But now you owe us lunch, and we're going to make you pay."

Carol chimed in. "Yeah, Dad, and I want some new Pokémon cards like you promised."

Jack laughed. "I did promise, so let's get going. We'll do lunch and some shopping, but we still need to unpack some boxes at the house." They headed for the door and Jack smiled. Show Me Army Depot had some interesting people. But the best thing was it was far from Afghanistan. No one would shoot at him here.

Chapter 6

July 11, 2015, Cedar City, Missouri

Victor Chow stood and counted the money in his cash register. He served many customers last night, and many bills filled his hands. He failed to deposit last night's proceeds at his bank's night drop, but fortunately his business attracted no prowlers. He would make his deposit tonight. He wanted no loss of the money that he put towards his 'retirement' account. An account that North Korean intelligence agencies had no knowledge of.

He looked up as a small Asian man in an expensive suit knocked on his restaurant's locked door. Victor recognized the man, a minor North Korean official assigned to the United Nations in New York. The man served as his handler for his current mission, and he had not coordinated this visit with Victor. A vein in his forehead started to throb as he unlocked the door and let the man in. He looked past him and spotted a black sedan with diplomatic plates sitting in his parking lot.

Victor later wondered if the difficulties of his important mission caused him undue stress, for upon seeing the sedan, he recalled the events that led to him working with this idiotic handler.

Big Guard swung his fist and connected with Kwan Il Sung's nose. The boy's head whipped around flinging blood and snot on the wall of the interrogation cell. Baling twine secured the emaciated youth to a large wooden chair. While three other guards cheered, Big Guard positioned himself for another blow to Kwan's frail body. The look on Big Guard's face told Kwan he suffered no ordinary beating.

Kwan arrived at Big Guard's concentration camp two years earlier. Kwan's parents died soon after arriving. He did not kill them, but his actions led to their deaths.

The year Kwan turned eleven; a famine devastated the rural population of North Korea. Three million people died from a failed rice harvest and gross mismanagement of North Korean agriculture. His alcoholic parents, never ones to overcome hardship, retreated to the comfort provided by bottles of Soju; a cheap alcoholic beverage distilled from rice. Despite the massive food shortages, North Korean leaders provided plenty of Soju for national consumption.

Kwan did what he could to find food for himself and his little brother Ji Hun; the only person that returned Kwan's love. For over a year he kept his family alive. But the famine persisted. Soon others harvested the tree bark and insects that Kwan needed to survive. His neighbors even guarded the night soil found behind party headquarters. They, not Kwan, screened the privileged people's shit for undigested grains of rice and millet. Despite his best efforts, Kwan and Ji Hun grew even weaker. One morning, Ji Hun failed to rise from his sleeping mat.

Kwan, furious at his parent's failure to provide even the smallest amount of sustenance, denounced them to the village commissar as South Korean sympathizers. North Korean justice pounced on the hapless family. Kwan and his parents entered the Yodok Reeducation Camp within a day of Ji Hun's death. Kwan's sole possessions upon arrival were the clothes he wore, and a small photograph concealed in his shoe.

Three months later his parents succumbed to the inhuman hardships of the camp. Kwan, however, thrived. With his fists he obtained food from the other orphans; more than he ever had in his former life. Later a sharp knife, stolen from a camp kitchen, allowed him to eliminate rivals and rise within the child gang's leadership. Two years after arriving, Kwan led the twelve hundred feral, orphan children that resided in the city-like camp.

"Thought you could fool us forever, didn't you, you little prick," Big Guard said. "But tomorrow we're going to stand you up to a post and sight in our rifles using your heart for a target." Big Guard jabbed his fist into Kwan's stomach.

"Ooofff!" Kwan said. Spit mixed with blood ran down his chin.

"So boy, where is my lighter? Did you trade it for rice with that ass wipe down in the village? If he has it, tell me, and I'll get it from him. Tell me where it is, and I'll go easy on you until your execution."

Big Guard drew his fist back for another strike. Suddenly, the door to the interrogation cell flew open, and a well-dressed man, followed by the guard lieutenant, stepped into the room. The man wore polished black leather shoes, dress pants, a starched white shirt with a tie, and a tailored sport coat.

The man yelled. "Do not strike that boy!"

Startled, Big Guard turned towards the newcomer. "Who the fuck are you to give me orders?"

The man held up several papers in his left hand. "That boy is my prisoner. I signed for him, and I am taking him with me."

Big Guard took a long swig from a bottle of Soju. He wiped his mouth with his sleeve. "This little bastard stole something from me, and I'm getting it back. You can have him when I'm done, Fancy Pants."

He turned his back on the man and pulled his arm back for another strike. The well-dressed man produced a pistol from beneath his jacket. A loud boom battered the ears of everyone in the concrete-walled room and a round pierced Big Guard's head. Blood and brain matter pelted Kwan, and the dead guard fell to the floor. Kwan's ears rang, and he spit gore from his mouth.

A guard sitting by the door reached for his AK-47. The well-dressed man placed the pistol's hot muzzle against the guard's forehead.

"Don't move," he said. The guard froze, and a stain formed in his trousers.

The man turned to the lieutenant. "Clean this boy up and have him in my sedan in ten minutes. For every minute past my deadline, I will shoot one of these guards. When I run out of guards I'll shoot you, Lieutenant. Do you understand my instructions and time constraints?"

The lieutenant's face paled, and he nodded. The man holstered his weapon and stepped from the room. The lieutenant screamed at the guards.

Seven minutes later two guards bundled a still bleeding but cleaned Kwan into the back seat of the man's black sedan. The guards turned and ran. The man signaled to his driver to move out.

Bureau 39, North Korea's government operated, criminal organization tasked with bringing foreign currency into the North Korean regime, had its newest member.

They changed his name to Victor Chow and enrolled him in the schools reserved for the most important persons within North Korea. Within seven years Victor completed his education. He spoke several languages, held numerous spy craft skills, including weapons and hand-to-hand combat, and lived abroad as he conducted missions for Bureau 39.

He executed all his missions alongside the man who saved him from Yodok. Thirteen years after becoming a spy, North Korean agencies considered him the second-best agent in their arsenal. Who was Bureau 39's best agent? The man who saved him. An odd fact of Victor's service was, even after many years of working together, he still didn't know the man's name.

In 2013 Bureau 39 severed his working relationship with his savior. They offered no explanation for the change, and the well-dressed man dropped off the Bureau 39 communication network. Months later Victor learned Russian gangsters murdered the agent during the sale of counterfeit US one-hundred-dollar bills.

Without the calming influence of the nameless man, Victor's stress grew. He gained weight, he displayed erratic behavior, and his technical skills suffered. At least once his actions risked exposure of the North Korean government. His superiors tolerated his poor performance because they had no one skilled enough to replace him.

In 2014 Bureau 39 cancelled his ongoing mission, negotiating a steady supply of counterfeit Viagra for the Italian mafia, and sent him to Cedar City. His task there; conduct reconnaissance on the nearby Show Me Army Depot. His current handler termed it an important mission vital to the future of North Korea. Victor did not question the assignment, but he rolled his eyes at his handler's embellishment. Upon arrival he used Bureau 39 funds to open a Chinese restaurant that explained his presence in the small town.

His intelligence gathering went well. The internet provided tremendous amounts of information on the depot's operations along with maps and satellite photos that displayed key facilities. Victor could not believe the amount of sensitive information found on America's internet. Even the stupid Europeans never placed this much critical military information into the public domain. For months he sent large reports to his handler.

Victor also placed microphones under each table in his restaurant. Later he advertised a twenty-five percent discount for depot employees. While the stupid Americans crammed their mouths with his food, they talked nonstop and provided him even more intelligence. Best of all, his microphones identified a potential inside man. Victor knew some funds in a Mexican bank would turn the man if needed.

The handler's loud cough brought Victor back to the present. That his handler noticed his daydreaming ignited Victor's rage. Without a word, he punched the handler in the forehead knocking him unconscious. He dragged him to the kitchen and fished keys from the man's pocket. He threw the keys to Jose, his much older, illegal immigrant cook.

"Move that vehicle to the back of the restaurant and cover it with the tarp in the utility closet," Victor said. "Make it quick."

Jose took the keys and ignored the unconscious man.

When the handler regained consciousness, he found himself seated in the restaurant's small office. Victor handed him a glass of water and two aspirins.

"You made a poor choice coming here in such a noticeable vehicle. Your actions threatened my operation, and I don't like that. I trust it won't happen again?" The handler stared at Victor but swallowed the painkillers.

"Excellent. Now, why are you here?"

For the next hour, the agent told Victor about the planned invasion of South Korea, and the need to eliminate the logistics capability of Show Me Army Depot. Victor grasped his country's occupation of South Korea, a nation flush with food due to its powerful economy, would eliminate overnight the hunger and starvation still found in his homeland. Something he yearned for since the first day he joined Bureau 39.

"Victor, you are the expert on this American depot," the handler said. "You must formulate a plan to seize Show Me Army Depot and destroy its critical infrastructure nodes. In addition, you will lead our forces in the attack. You must inflict complete and irreparable destruction. Destruction that leaves the Americans unable to deploy their munitions against our nation's forces." The handler pointed to a calendar on the wall. "Your attack begins two days before this year's Chuseok holiday, and there can be no trace of North Korea's involvement." He handed Victor a piece of paper. "This is a list of key depot personnel. You will eliminate these individuals when you attack the depot."

Victor saw the incoming Commander's name on the list. He kept silent about his depot traitor. He wanted the handler to have minimal information on his plans.

"What forces do I lead?" Victor said.

"You have two groups of fighters. The first is a team of Korean People's Army Special Forces led by a seasoned officer."

Victor nodded. His training by the unnamed man resulted in him spending one month with his nation's Special Forces. He learned a lot during that month.

"I can use them," Victor said.

"Your second force is another small team of soldiers. However, this team consists of ISIS regulars from Syria."

Victor's face turned crimson, and he screamed at the handler. "What idiot decided that? I have studied these fools." He laughed once. "The celebrated ISIS members have no tactical skills, and they lose battles as often as they win them. If they do happen to win, they broadcast their so-called victories, beheadings, and rapes on whatever media they can find. The Americans then track them down and kill them." He crossed his arms and glared at the handler. "Any ISIS force is not suitable for this operation."

The handler cowered before Victor but forced a reply. "They are an adequate fighting force, Victor. A former British soldier with combat experience leads your ISIS team."

"This is still unacceptable. I remind you that my life is at great risk if anything goes wrong."

The handler composed himself and glared at Victor. "And I remind you that all North Koreans should leap at the opportunity to risk their lives for the Dear Leader." He dropped the glare and leaned closer to Victor. "Look at the benefits to your operation. Religious fanatics who thrive on suicide tactics make up the ISIS organization. Leaving behind many dead ISIS commandos would divert any blame away from North Korea. Don't you agree?"

Victor considered the handler's scheme.

The handler continued. "In addition to two teams of fighters, you'll have new North Korean technology in support of your operation." He handed over several point papers. "I'll send additional information on the operation in coded message traffic. And remember Victor, if this mission fails it will anger Bureau 39."

Victor rose and stood over the sitting handler. "Now listen carefully my dear handler. If this operation fails, and I trace it to a leak or mistake on your part, I'll come to New York and find you. You won't like it if I come all the way to New York to see you." Victor glared at the man for several seconds and stepped away.

The handler stood and straightened his tailored suit. "Our business is complete. I'll send the coded messages soon."

Victor took the man's arm and led him to his vehicle. He removed the tarp, and the handler got in his sedan.

The handler made a U-turn in the parking lot and stopped next to Victor. He lowered his window. "One more thing; I'm sending you an assistant."

Victor made a dismissive wave. "I don't need or want an assistant."

"We are not concerned with your needs or wants. Our superiors are troubled by your recent erratic behavior." The man touched the knot in the center of his forehead. "I share their concern. Your assistant will see that you follow the mission through to completion. He arrives today. Get him spun up on your operation immediately."

Victor stepped towards the vehicle, but the handler sped away throwing loose gravel onto Victor's shoes. He stood for a full minute; his fists clenched the entire time.

Victor sat drinking tea and waited for his new assistant. They finished the lunch rush an hour ago, and his restaurant held only himself and Jose. He thought of his arrogant handler and his jaw tightened. Did this assistant intend to kill him after the operation? Then that stupid handler could take credit for all his hard work.

A loud clang came from the kitchen, and Victor yelled. "Keep it down back there!"

Jose, his left eye bruised and swollen, appeared at the door. "I'm sorry sir. I will try not to make so much noise."

Victor glared and waved him away. Jose darted back into the kitchen. He was undecided on if he would kill Jose when the operation was complete, or just turn him into immigration. That he even considered letting him live meant he was getting soft, as the Americans said.

Victor considered his actions reckless after he entered the depot yesterday. But he so desired to see his target from the inside before he started his operation. He even met the new colonel. He wrung his strong hands together and took several deep breaths. It concerned him when the man stated he looked Korean. Was he suspected?

The front door to his restaurant opened, and a tall, but young, Korean man, a boy almost, stepped inside. He had long hair and wore blue jeans, cowboy boots, and a polo shirt. A fake gold Rolex adorned his wrist.

The young man walked up to Victor's table. "I'm Johnny Park. I was told to meet you here."

The man spoke perfect English with no trace of an accent. Victor's practiced eye saw Johnny carried neither a knife nor a gun. *This boy is not a trained agent. His handler sent him an amateur!*

"Welcome, Johnny," Victor said. "I was told to expect you." Victor pointed to the back. "Please go through the kitchen and out the back. There is a warehouse on the other side of the alley. Go inside and take a seat. I need to lock up, and then I'll join you and update you on our mission."

The young man cocked his head. "A warehouse? Well, ok." He took a step away from Victor but paused. "This is a restaurant, right? A real restaurant? Can I get something to eat? I just had a long drive and I'm starving."

Victor's cheeks grew hot. "The warehouse first Johnny, and then you'll eat. I promise."

Johnny shoved his hands into his pockets and nodded. "Okay, yeah, the warehouse."

The young man turned and walked to the kitchen. When he was gone, Victor sighed and went to the front door and locked it. A garish late model sports car with California plates and a dented front fender sat in front of the restaurant. Victor rolled his eyes. His assistant didn't even have enough brains to park around back.

Victor hung the closed sign on his restaurant's front door and headed to the kitchen. He walked past Jose, who chopped vegetables for tonight's meal, and continued out the back door. He crossed the alley and entered an unused warehouse leased by Victor. The large building stood empty except for a few chairs. Johnny Park stood in the center of the building thumbing his smartphone.

Victor put out his hand in greeting and walked towards the youth. "Welcome, Johnny. I am pleased to have you participate in our operation." When he reached him, he sent a lightning punch into the boy's solar plexus.

The air rushed from Johnny's lungs. "Oooofffff!" he said. The boy's hands flew to his midsection, and he dropped onto his side. He looked up at Victor and gasped. "What did…you do that for? You are…Victor Chow, aren't you?"

"Yes, I'm Victor Chow. A better question is who are you, and what are you doing here?"

Still holding his stomach Johnny spoke. "I'm Johnny Park from Los Angeles. They sent me here to assist you during some operation.

Still gasping for air, Johnny sat up. He kicked at the chef's leg. Victor dodged it and, despite his weight, executed a roundhouse kick to the boy's head. Johnny collapsed and struggled to move.

"So, you attack me, Johnny. I guessed correctly. You are here to kill me and take over my operation. You want it all for yourself."

Johnny tried to stand, but still suffered from the kick. "I would never kill anyone!" He slumped back to the floor. "I don't even know what the operation's about. They told me to come here. That's all!"

"You cannot fool me. You are a born killer. Did they tell you how and when to kill me?"

"No! I would not have come if they wanted me to kill you. Honest." Johnny winced and looked up at Victor; his right eye started to swell.

"Did they tell you to spy on me? Answer me. Quickly." Victor raised his arm to strike the young man.

Johnny squirmed on the floor and placed his hands on top of his head. "Yes! Yes! They told me to spy on you. I'm…I'm supposed to keep my eye on you and send a report every week."

Victor lowered his arm. "Ah, the truth comes out. But you are an amateur. A trained spy could have killed me ten times over." Victor leaned over the boy and grabbed a fistful of his hair. He pulled Johnny's head back and looked into the terrified face.

"Why are you here? Speak up." Victor released him, and Johnny's head dropped.

"They have my nonnie and pawpaw."

Victor's brow furrowed. "That makes no sense."

"My grandparents. They snuck over the Chinese border; they wanted to see their relatives in North Korea. But they never came back." Johnny paused, still trying to catch his breath. "Somehow, they got caught. A few months later this guy showed up at my apartment. He said North Korean police arrested my grandparents and put them in prison. He said that I worked for him. He told me if I went to CNN or the government, they would kill my grandparents."

"I don't believe you." Victor raised his fist.

Johnny waived his arms over his head. "No! No, it's true. They have my grandparents. I'll show you." He pulled out his wallet and spilled its contents on the floor. He snatched a photo from the floor and held it out to Victor. "Here's their picture."

Victor took the photo. He recognized a teenage Johnny Park sitting on a park bench. A younger version of Johnny sat next to him. A husband and wife, Johnny's parents, stood on both sides of the bench, and an elderly couple stood behind the two boys.

"That's my grandparents. I haven't seen them in three years."

Victor continued to study the photo. "Do you have a younger brother?"

"That's my little brother Tim in the photo."

"Where is he now?"

"Tim and my parents died in a fire when I was sixteen. My grandparents raised me after that."

Victor looked at Johnny. "Do you have a job?"

"Why do you need to know-"

Victor yelled. "Answer me!"

The boy's shoulders slumped. "No. I live off the money my handler pays me."

"What tasks do you do for him?"

"I follow people and photograph them. Koreans most of the time. Sometimes Chinese people. A bunch of times I drove trucks full of electronic gear and other stuff down to a port in Mexico. That's it. Before this, I never left the west coast."

"Did you ever kill anyone?"

"No!" Johnny shouted. "I told you I won't do that."

Victor looked at the youth that cowered before him. This stupid boy's presence confirmed his handler's foolishness. He viewed the photo once more.

"Stand up," Victor said.

Johnny looked up at Victor. "Are you going to kill me?"

"No, I am letting you live. Now stand up."

Johnny moved watching Victor the entire time. He stood before the spy with his head down.

Victor frowned. "Tomorrow I will verify your story. If you lied to me, you won't like what I will do to you."

"I'm not lying. I'm-"

"Silence!" Victor scowled at Johnny and returned his photograph. "You are now my assistant. Your cover story is that you are a new waiter at my restaurant."

"A waiter? I've never done that before."

Victor's jaw clenched. "I will teach you and you will learn quick. If not, we will return to this warehouse. Do you understand?"

Johnny nodded. "Yes, Sir."

"After that, you will assist me in an operation vital to my government. This operation benefits North Korean children much like your brother Tim. When we are successful, your grandparents might live to see another day. But if you lie to me or fail me in any way, you and your grandparents will surely regret it."

Johnny stood straighter. "I want my grandparents back. I won't fail you."

Victor pointed at the door. "Go into the kitchen and see Jose. He will give you something to eat. After work tonight we will discuss my plan for Show Me Army Depot."

Johnny turned and walked towards the door. Victor shook his head and followed behind him.

Chapter 7

July 13, 2015, Show Me Army Depot, Missouri

Jack opened the large metal fire door and stepped into the bomb production facility known as 'X-Ray.' He decided not to ask about the name's origin. The noise from monstrous machines, escaping steam, and bursts of compressed air battered Jack's eardrums. The smell of paint and overheated hydraulic oil wafted through the air. At the room's center, a dozen employees in work coveralls loaded heavy, steel bomb casings onto a moving assembly line. He looked past the employees but could not see the other end of the building.

Jack turned to his deputy. "How large is this building?"

"It's about a mile long, and we're in the southernmost portion," Ross said.

Jack paused for a moment to consider the building's size, then resumed walking. "What happens in this portion of the building?"

"This is bomb prep." Ross said. "We receive the bomb casings here. Then we clean and service the casings and paint them. Once that's finished, we send the casings to the next building for explosive loading. When we load the explosive into the casing it's considered a live bomb."

Jack noticed the employees worked quickly and with great efficiency.

Jack approached a group huddled around several bombs. "Hi, I'm Jack Black Eagle. What type of bombs are these?"

A big woman holding a clipboard slapped a bomb. "Colonel, these are Mark 82, five-hundred-pound high explosive bombs going to the US Air Force."

Jack smiled. "That's outstanding. I'm a huge fan of Mark 82s. You guys must do a good job because every Mark 82 I saw dropped in Afghanistan worked like a charm. They blew the crap out of the Taliban. In fact, these bombs saved my life many times."

The employees smiled and crowded around Jack. "We don't get to hear much about our bombs dropping in the real world," the woman said. "Maybe you can come by during one of our lunch breaks and tell us about it."

"Only if you buy me a Coke."

"Deal." the woman said.

Jack watched the employees as they prepared the bombs for additional work. He shook each employee's hand and resumed his tour through the building.

Soon he entered a long, enclosed tunnel. "Ross, why is this building so large? Wouldn't moving the operations closer together be more efficient?"

"It's much more efficient, Colonel," Ross said. "But the distance between the different sections of the production building is a safety feature. If a bomb ever exploded during production, it'll damage a portion of the building instead of the entire line. Limiting the damage to one area makes it easier for us to repair and restart the line."

Jack looked down the long tunnel. "That makes sense. Let's make sure we never have an explosion like that."

"Will do, Colonel." They walked for several minutes and arrived at another large building. Thick, concrete walls with no windows, and a few doors, enclosed the building.

"This is our explosive loading operation," Ross said. "Each employee that works here is trained for six months before they're allowed around the large quantities of high explosives." Ross pointed. "There is another tunnel behind this building that connects to the bomb assembly building and then the loading dock."

Jack opened a large metal door and stepped inside. The pungent odor of raw explosive punched Jack in the gut and took him back to Afghanistan. This same sharp smell covered the battlefield after the air strikes that defeated the Taliban force and saved COP Armstrong.

He spotted Don Miksic and three others standing atop two large platforms. A sturdy wheeled cart holding eight upright bomb casings sat between the platforms. Fans blew hot air around the interior. Soon Jack's perspiration dampened his uniform.

Jack climbed a set of stairs to the platform and stood next to the big union president. Don grabbed a flexible hose extending from the ceiling and placed it into the open end of a bomb. He opened a valve and liquid explosive poured into the bomb.

Don turned to Jack. "Welcome to X-Ray, Colonel."

"Thank you, Don. I'm getting my introductory tour, and so far, this line is amazing. I had no idea what went on here."

He shook Don's hand, and this time the union president played no games. However, the man's grip still impressed him. He wondered if Don picked up the bombs himself instead of using a forklift.

"Colonel, where did you learn that thumb hold you used on me?"

Jack chuckled. "A Korean punk I knew almost broke my hand with it once. My First Sergeant knocked him out before he could do any permanent damage. Later I had a guy teach it to me just in case."

"It's a good one. I'd hang on to it if I was you."

Jack nodded. He wiped the sweat from his forehead. "Why is it so hot in here?" He noticed the employees handled the heat much better than he did.

Don pointed to the ceiling. "The TNT is over three hundred degrees Fahrenheit when it comes out of the pots upstairs. There're six pots above us and each holds six hundred gallons of molten TNT. The pots and molten explosive heat up the entire building."

Don filled his second bomb. Jack looked into it and watched the explosive harden. He thought it looked like candle wax. After a few moments his brain yelled at him that he stood a few inches from two hundred pounds of cooling high explosive.

He took a step back from the bomb. "How is this one doing?"

The union president examined the cooling bomb. "It's doing fine, and it'll pass all the quality checks." He glanced at Jack. "Don't worry, Colonel; it's safe. It won't go off until the Air Force drops it."

Jack let out a breath he didn't realize he held. "Glad to hear it."

Don turned to Jack. "Colonel, I acted like a jackass at your reception the other day and I want to make amends. If you're willing, I'd like to take you out for a beer."

"I'd like that, Don. Give Kristi a call with the time and place." Jack waved to the other employees and rejoined Ross at the bottom of the platform. His deputy also perspired freely.

The two men returned to their sedan and drove off towards the ammunition storage area.

When they could no longer see X-Ray Jack spoke. "Ross, so far, I've only visited bits and pieces of the depot. How big is Show Me Army Depot?"

"Colonel, the depot is sixty thousand acres in size," Ross said. "We need that much space for the quantity of ammunition stored here. For safety purposes we separate the munitions by set distances."

"That makes sense. What does a storage magazine look like?"

Ross pointed off to Jack's right. "There are some now."

Jack saw a neat row of large concrete igloo-like structures. Each had a large metal door for access and a concrete loading dock. Numerous rows of magazines stretched for several miles. One magazine had its door open, and employees on small, yellow forklifts shuttled pallets of ammunition to a large truck. Small metal cylinders, sitting behind the operator, stored the propane fuel for the forklift's engine. While they watched, a forklift operator hit his brakes too hard, and a pallet fell at least ten feet to the ground. Wood boxes shattered, and cased mortar rounds spilled onto the pavement. Jack tensed but nothing happened. Ross's face flushed and he accelerated away from the area.

Jack took a deep breath. "How many magazines do we have?"

"Three thousand."

Jack stared at Ross for a full five seconds. "Did you say three thousand? Why so many? How can we maintain so many structures?"

Ross chuckled. "Most new people have the same reaction, Colonel. We have that many because that's the square feet needed to store our ammunition. Don't worry about the cost; the magazines are simple, but well-built structures so they require little funding to maintain them. We also have two hundred outside storage pads storing unserviceable ammunition; things that don't need protection from the weather."

Ross pointed ahead. "Here's a pad now."

Jack saw a small gravel parking lot sitting fifty feet off the road. Neat stacks of rusty bombs sat throughout the pad.

"So how much ammunition do we store in the depot today?"

Ross again chuckled. "We have over five hundred thousand tons."

Jack stared at his deputy for several seconds. "You're kidding," he said.

"I'm not kidding, Colonel."

"That's unbelievable, Ross. I never knew the Army had that much ammunition. When I served in the 82d Airborne Division, we thought a few tons was a lot. Now you're telling me I'm responsible for half a million tons of it?" He pinched the bridge of his nose. "You're making my head hurt."

They rounded a corner and passed over several railroad crossings. Jack spotted a locomotive pushing loaded rail cars onto a siding.

Jack looked at Ross. "So, we have our own railroad?"

"We do," Ross said. "Show Me depot operates the largest railroad in the Department of Defense. We do have a few small rail shipments out to some of the larger bases every year. If another Desert Storm comes along, we'd send out entire trains loaded with ammunition."

"Have we ever rehearsed loading and shipping out complete trains?"

Ross shook his head. "We don't need to, Colonel. We did several during Desert Storm so we can do it again if needed."

Jack thought for a few seconds. "Ross, we need a power projection rehearsal on our training calendar as soon as possible. The world is a dangerous place, and I want this depot ready."

"Sir, a rehearsal requires a lot of effort. I don't think it's necessary."

Jack waved at the road ahead. "Pull over please so we can talk."

Ross pulled over and parked. Jack turned to him. "Ross, they sent me to Show Me Army Depot for a reason. I don't plan to highlight this to our employees, but this depot has the highest number of accidents and injuries, the largest amount of inventory losses, and the greatest number of late shipments of any depot out there. That's not how we support warfighters overseas; it's how we get them killed. With all due respect to the depot's skills, I'm here to eliminate its shortcomings and prepare it for war. We will do a rehearsal for a rail out load first thing next quarter."

Ross frowned. "A rehearsal means trouble with the union, Colonel. They'll consider it a slap in the face of each employee, and Don Miksic will scream to our local congresswoman. You don't want her staffers around here getting into our business."

"I'll coordinate with the union, and I'll get their support. You make the rehearsal happen."

Ross sighed. "I'll get with the staff and get one scheduled."

"Thanks, Ross. Now let's see the rest of the depot."

Chapter 8

July 15, 2015, Show Me Army Depot, Missouri

Jack drove his government sedan through miles of scrub prairie. He wondered if he would ever get used to the sight of so many storage magazines. He passed a large magazine, and the distinctive lines of a Vietnam-era UH-1 'Huey' helicopter came into view. Jack perked up. He liked the idea of seeing the depot from the air.

Jack studied the old helicopter. It still sported a classic olive drab paint job along with faded cavalry sabers on its bulbous nose. A washed-out United States Army decorated its tail boom. Large loudspeakers hung on each side of the aircraft below the open cargo doors.

He pulled up behind a pickup parked near the helicopter. A man got out and waited for him. Jack put his age at sixty-five or so. He stood maybe five foot eight and had a wiry build. He had on well-worn hunting boots, blue jeans, and a checked shirt. Tufts of Nordic blond hair, speckled with a gray, peeked from under his white cowboy hat.

The man stuck out his hand. "Good morning, Colonel. I'm Liam Torgerson. The depot's agriculture and wildlife specialist."

Jack shook his hand. "Jack Black Eagle. It's nice to meet you, Liam."

"I appreciate you meeting me out here." Liam waved his arm taking in the land surrounding the two men. "This is my office, and I do my best work out here."

"Liam, any day I can get grass under my boots is a good day. How long have you worked at Show Me Depot?"

Liam chuckled. "A long time, Colonel. After Vietnam, I did odd jobs but soon I hired on with the depot. My hunting and farming skills got me into the land management department." He paused and looked at the land around them. "I enjoy my work and don't plan to retire anytime soon." He pointed at the helicopter. "If you don't mind, I've arranged a flight. We can cover a lot of ground that way."

"Sounds good," Jack said. "Lead on."

Jack and Liam approached the helicopter. A man and a woman left its shadow and walked towards them. He pegged the woman's age at about thirty years old and looked an awful lot like Liam.

"Colonel, this is my daughter, Rita," Liam said. "She works in production but today she's helping me with hogs. She'll be our shooter."

Jack shook Rita's hand. "Nice to meet you, Rita. You must be a good shot if you can hit an animal from a moving helicopter."

She blushed and said, "Well, I don't like to brag but I hit more than I miss. Dad taught me how to shoot when I was young, and I took to it."

"I'm looking forward to it and I'm sure I'll pick up a few pointers."

Jack turned to the pilot. The man had a build like a human fireplug. He needed a shave, had buzz cut salt and pepper hair, and wore a stained Army-issue flight suit. He wore a loud Hawaiian shirt over his coveralls. Jack put his age at close to fifty, and the 101st Airborne Division patch sewn on the shirt's right shoulder identified him as a combat vet.

"Sir, this is Tony Simpson, our pilot," Liam said.

Jack shook his hand. "Hi, Tony. You have an impressive helicopter. Are you the owner?"

Tony cracked a huge smile. "She's mine. I picked her up cheap when the Army sold her as surplus. I make a living doing odd jobs that require a vertical lift helicopter."

"That sounds great, Tony," Jack said. "I haven't flown in a Huey since I was a lieutenant in Korea. I'm looking forward to a ride."

Tony continued to smile but launched into a completely different subject. "Say, Colonel, did you know in 1963 'Surf City' was the first surf tune to top the national charts? Did you also know the song is sung by Jan and Dean and not the Beach Boys as a lot of people assume?"

Liam rolled his eyes, but Jack responded as if he got questions like that every day. "I'm familiar with the song, Tony. My mother had their album when I was a young boy. I think Jan and Dean are great, but I was not aware of their 1963 chart ranking."

Tony's eyes sparkled. "That's all-right Sir. I'm glad you know the difference between Jan and Dean and the Beach Boys. Most people don't and it's a real shame. They did all the work, and the Beach Boys got all the fame. In my opinion Jan and Dean were the real pioneers of surf music." Tony looked at Liam and back at Jack. "It's pretty obvious that I enjoy surf music."

"Not a problem," Jack said. "Everyone needs a hobby." Jack paused. "Tony, I met Sarah Simpson at my change of command. She said she works for the mayor. Is she a relative of yours?"

A dark shadow swept across the pilot's face. For a second Jack thought Tony would not answer his question. Finally, he spoke. "Sarah's my wife. We got married twenty-five years ago. We don't get along too well, so she lives with the mayor now."

"I'm sorry Tony. I didn't mean to pry into family business."

Tony took a deep breath. "It's ok, Colonel. Sarah and I changed during Desert Storm, and coming home made no difference. We've lived apart ever since."

Jack did not reply.

Liam broke the awkward silence. "Tony, Rita are you two ready to go?"

"We're ready, Dad," Rita said.

Tony turned and walked back to his helicopter. Jack and Liam got into the helicopter and buckled in. Liam handed Jack a headset.

Rita sat on the right side of the aircraft with a rifle case between her feet. In his pilot's seat, Tony now wore a green Army-issue aviator helmet with a boom microphone. Soon the engine screamed, and the spinning blades made their familiar thumping noise.

Tony spoke over the intercom. "Where to, Liam?"

"Tony, take a quick spin at two thousand feet. I want the colonel to see the depot from the air. After that, we're moving turkeys, and we'll shoot feral hogs near reservoirs four and five."

"You got it," Tony said.

For ten minutes they flew while Liam pointed out important depot facilities and his agriculture and forestry activities. Even at two thousand feet the depot stretched for miles, and its forests were larger than Jack realized. Soon a glint of sunlight from a large open area caught his eye. He pointed.

Liam nodded and keyed his microphone. "Tony, take us over to the rail yard."

The helicopter turned, and soon Jack saw the yard. He estimated its dimensions as one-half mile long by one quarter mile wide. Twenty separate rail spurs ran through its center. A dozen empty rail cars sat in the yard, and Jack guessed it could hold several hundred more. It showed how the depot could move entire trains in one day.

Jack keyed the intercom. "I've seen enough. Thank you."

"Tony, head to the old five-inch line," Liam said.

A few minutes later Tony called. "The line's coming up. I'll make sure you and the colonel see the action."

With that, the helicopter made a slow banking turn. Jack looked down onto a large clearing surrounded by forest.

"Sir, I also manage the depot's wildlife," Liam said. "Today we're relocating wild turkeys. I need to move this large flock to a less populated area, so they don't starve this winter." Liam pointed at the clearing. "If you look closely, you can see the net we use."

Jack spotted a dark line running across one side of the clearing. The rolled-up net stretched one hundred feet, and a dozen turkey decoys sat in front of it. He caught movement near a decoy. Jack looked closer and recognized at least twenty live turkeys strutting around the decoys. The turkeys focused on the colorful, inanimate objects; even ignoring the noisy helicopter above them.

A large cloud of smoke appeared, and a dozen small rockets thundered across the clearing dragging the net over the turkeys. Most collapsed to the ground in shock, and the net fell on top of them. However, a few reacted and streaked from under the falling net. Jack admired how well the net and rockets worked in capturing the quick birds. A man in camouflage ran into the clearing and waved at the helicopter. He sprinted into the forest chasing the few escaping turkeys.

"That's my son, Conner," Liam said. "He'll run those turkeys down and get them back in the net."

Jack wondered if Liam exaggerated his son's running abilities. He knew turkeys ran awful fast. He decided to humor him. "Run them down? Remind me to never go jogging with Conner."

Liam laughed. "Tony, head for the reservoirs." The helicopter turned away from the clearing.

"Liam, what is a feral hog?" Jack said.

"They're domestic pigs that are now wild animals, and they're very destructive. I've seen forests where they killed and ate everything. They now number in the millions and they're damaging ecosystems throughout the South. If I can't keep their numbers down, they'll destroy the forests that cover Show Me depot. If the forests die, they become huge fire hazards sitting in the middle of all this ammunition."

Jack spotted a large pond in the distance. "How do you reduce their numbers?"

"Most of the time we trap them. But some of the hogs are too smart for a trap, so we shoot them from the helicopter."

Tony came on the intercom. "Gunner, we're three minutes out."

Rita removed a sporting rifle with open sights from its case. She held the rifle with the barrel pointed down.

"One minute out," Tony said. "Gunner, lock and load."

Rita stretched her safety belt until she leaned out the large door. The wind rushing by buffeted her hair and clothing. She inserted a thirty round magazine and charged the weapon. Tony stroked a small MP3 player attached to the Huey's dash. The speakers under the aircraft burped and broadcast a maniacal laugh. The rapid drumming and twanging guitars of "Wipe Out" by the Surfaris blasted from the speakers.

Jack laughed and clicked the intercom. "You use surfing tunes for psychological operations?

Tony turned and smiled at Jack. "It's the only thing that works, Colonel. Rock, jazz, classical, even punk doesn't scare 'em. I figure it's the great beat that drives 'em nuts." Tony turned back to his controls but continued his conversation. "Did you know the Surfaris released this song in 1963? It made them famous. Also, it's in ten different Hollywood movies to include Dirty Dancing and Toy Story 2."

"I didn't know that, Tony." Liam rolled his eyes again, but Jack smiled and looked out at the ground.

"Starting our first run. Gunner, you're weapons free," Tony said. Rita brought the weapon to her shoulder and waited. "Three targets at two o'clock."

Jack stretched up in his seat and saw three hogs running in front of the helicopter. The animals looked nothing like farm-bred pigs. In fact, they looked like an actual wild boar. Dark coarse fur covered their bodies including their legs and tails. Curved tusks jutted from the long snout of the largest hog. Jack shuddered. He vowed to never meet that hog in a dark forest.

They caught them in the open, and now the hogs ran for their lives. Tony throttled back, keeping the animals in perfect position for his shooter. Rita fired and a hog stumbled and fell.

Jack nodded in approval at Rita's marksmanship. Suddenly Tony yelled into the intercom. "Kill those fuckers, Gunner! Hurry up, they're getting away! Do you want them coming to your home and raping and killing your family? Kill 'em! They're dirty murdering hogs!"

Rita said nothing and tracked the two remaining hogs. She fired and a second hog fell and rolled. The last hog jerked to the right. Rita shot and dirt spurted up next to it. The terrified animal darted into the forest, and the helicopter pulled away.

"Goddammit! You missed him, Rita!" Tony said. "You left that hog alive, and now he's out to get you! We're moving on to reservoir four. Weapons hold."

"Weapons hold," Rita said.

The helicopter turned, and Jack saw another body of water several miles ahead. Jack gave Liam a questioning look.

Liam shrugged and covered his boom mike. "It's nothing. He does it all the time."

Jack covered his own mike. "What's the story with his wife? I stepped in it when I mentioned her."

"I don't know all the details," Liam said. "They married before they left for Desert Storm. They served in the same reserve unit along with Sarah's younger brother. The brother went on a mission with Tony and never made it back. Sarah blamed Tony. They separated after they came home."

"They're still married after all this time?"

"Tony says they never finished the paperwork." He chuckled a few times. "You should see him around the mayor. They get into a shouting match or fist fight two or three times each year. Neither one ever presses charges though." Liam leaned back into his seat; his story finished.

"Walk, Don't Run" by The Ventures poured from the speakers. Soon they closed on the next reservoir.

"Starting our run," Tony said. "Gunner, you're weapons free. Six targets at one o'clock."

This time six hogs ran in front of the helicopter. A large hog led the pack. Jack spotted the long tusks protruding from the omnivore's mouth.

Tony spoke. "Looks like we caught one of your big boys, Liam."

Liam glanced out the door. "Yeah, he's about three hundred pounds; not too big. Save him for last, Rita."

Jack's brow furrowed. He wondered what Liam's cut off was for a big feral hog.

The hogs squealed and shook their heads but stayed together while running in terror. Tony again yelled abuse at Rita but kept the running hogs in perfect firing position. Jack had never seen anything like it. He prayed the high-strung pilot would not stroke out and crash the helicopter. Rita shot the five smaller hogs and concentrated on the large boar.

"What the fuck are you waiting for? Waste him!" Tony said.

Rita fired twice at the running hog. Each time the animal dodged, and Rita missed. It darted into the forest, and the helicopter turned away.

"God damn it!" Tony said. "You missed him! What do I have to do? Fly and pull the trigger for you? Weapons hold. Weapons secure."

Rita looked at her father and rolled her eyes. Liam smiled but said nothing. She put the weapon on safe, unloaded the magazine, and cleared the live round from the chamber. She put the rifle back into the case and closed it.

Liam came on the intercom. "Tony, let's drop the colonel off at his vehicle."

Several minutes later Tony brought the aircraft in for a gentle landing fifty yards from Jack's sedan.

Jack keyed his mike. "Thanks a lot, Tony. I enjoyed the ride."

Tony turned in his seat. "My pleasure, Colonel. I rent a small hangar out at the airport. Come by anytime, and we'll have some beers, spin some tunes, and talk about the old days."

Jack smiled. "You can count on it."

"Sir, I'm staying on the aircraft," Liam said. "Do you have any questions for me?"

"No, I'm good. I appreciate the tour and I'll visit again soon."

Jack jumped down to the ground and walked to his car. He turned, and the helicopter rose with a rush of wind and debris. Liam and Rita both waved at Jack. As he watched the helicopter fly away, he wondered if Tony should see a therapist. He got into his car and drove back to his headquarters.

Chapter 9

August 3, 2015, Show Me Army Depot, Missouri

Janet swiped at the water and grabbed for a small frog. She missed and splashed lake water onto one of the cats. The animal let out a miserable meow and shook itself like a dog. It used its tongue in a feeble attempt to dry its fur.

"I'm sorry Ajax," Janet said.

"Girls let's explore the forest," Jack said.

His girls turned and smiled at him. "Yaaaay!" Janet said. They forgot the frogs and looked at the dense trees.

Jack turned the small rowboat towards the far bank and rowed hard. Soon he beached the boat across the lake from their quarters. The dogs and cats leaped from the boat and tore into the forest. The girls dumped their life jackets in the bottom of the dinghy and ran up the bank into the trees. "Don't go too far," Jack said.

Jack tied the boat off and stepped into the woods. The trees were large and thick in this part of the forest, but the undergrowth was thin and would not hinder their exploration. He took a deep breath of the clean, forest air. Jack never tired of walking in a forest, and he took every opportunity to teach his girls about the plants and animals they encountered. Soon he spotted the girls, led by Mary, walking towards him.

They joined him, and Jack took Carol's hand. "Let's stay together and see what we can find." The small band walked deeper into the trees.

Before long Jack pointed to a patch of ground. "Girls, what do you see in that mud?"

All three knelt down around the spot and examined several indentations.

"Those are deer tracks," Jack said. "A large deer, called a buck, walked through here this morning."

Carol looked at her father. "Dad, how do you know it's a deer?"

"When I was your age, my grandfather taught me how to identify and stalk animals from the tracks they left in the ground.

"When you were on the reservation?" Carol said.

Jack nodded. "Yes, Carol. I know it's a deer because that's the shape of their hooves." He stuck his finger into a track and traced its outline. "This was a buck because the tracks are large, and the heavy deer pushed his hooves deep into the mud. Bucks are bigger and heavier than a girl deer called a doe. I know he came through this morning because last night's rain made this mud. The points on the tracks show the direction he walked." Jack pointed to his right and his left. "He came from over there and walked through this mud and continued up that direction."

All three girls looked at the tracks. "Woooooowwwwww," they said together.

"Girls, did you know bucks have antlers?"

"Like Rudolph?" Janet said.

Jack chuckled. "Yes Janet, like Rudolph, but here the antlers have a different shape."

"I wish we could see some deer antlers," Carol said.

Jack looked at his middle daughter. "Stand up, Carol." She gave him a funny look but stood.

"Turn around and take ten steps forward."

Mary and Janet watched their sister. Carol turned and counted off ten steps and stopped. She looked over her shoulder at her father.

"Now look down," Jack said.

Carol looked down and gasped. She snatched an object off the forest floor and ran back to her sisters. "It's a deer antler!" she said.

Her sisters jumped up to meet her. "That's so cool," Mary said.

For several minutes they passed the shed antler around and examined its shape and size. Carol could not take her eyes off her new prize.

Not far away, He Who Watches lounged on the tall grass growing under a sweet-smelling acacia tree. He stood and scratched his back against the rough bark of a pine tree. After a minute he reached under his arm and scratched his side where an unseen stick had poked him during the night.

He looked at the thick forest that surrounded him, then cocked his head. Miles away he heard several large machines moving down a road. Normally he avoided a place that contained so many humans and their large, noisy machines. But this land held something important to the spirits. He did not like this place, but he would do as the spirits wished.

He sniffed the air and felt his stomach rumble. Much prey roamed this forest. Once he caught something, he would satisfy his hunger. He sent out his senses. However, instead of prey, he felt the special human as she approached his forest. His curiosity piqued, he left his nesting area and moved towards her.

Jack and the girls entered a small glade. The surrounding trees stilled the air but allowed rays of sunlight to filter through the forest. Jack found it very calming. He promised himself to spend more time in the depot's forests.

As the girls moved ahead of him, the hair on the back of his neck stiffened. He stopped and looked behind him. He saw nothing but noticed a faint, musky scent. He studied the forest for a few more moments then resumed his walk with his girls. He suspected a big buck hid from them among the trees.

Soon they arrived back at the lake. The cats jumped in the boat. Jack called the dogs several times but received no response.

He looked at his youngest daughter. "Janet, where are the dogs?"

She concentrated for a few moments. "They're close but they don't want to come."

"Tell them to come back to the boat. It's time to go home."

"Oh wow!" Janet said. She looked at her father. "Daddy, they're looking at a bear."

Jack cocked his head. "A bear? That can't be right. Are you sure? What kind of bear is it?"

"It's black and it's big."

Jack frowned. "I think you're mistaken, honey. I'm certain no bears live around here; people drove them away from this part of the country a long time ago. Are you sure it's not a big dog?" He peered into the woods but saw nothing.

He turned to the girls. "Just in case, I want you girls to get into the boat. Janet, tell the dogs to get back here now or I'm leaving them."

Her bottom lip quivered. "I'll get them Daddy. Please don't leave them. They don't' like sleeping outside all alone."

Mary and Carol got into the boat with the cats, but Janet remained on the bank and gazed into the forest. She turned to Jack. "They're coming now."

"Okay thank you, honey. Now you get into the boat too."

Janet scrambled into the boat. Soon Jack heard the rustle of leaves and a few low yips. Both dogs stopped at Jack's feet, and he looked them over. They showed no ill effects after their run through the woods. Mud coated their paws and legs, and large burrs dangled from their fur. Jack groaned. He knew an unpleasant task awaited his girls upon returning home. After he lifted each dog into the boat, he looked at Janet. "Where's the bear now?"

Janet stared into the forest. "He went away."

"Okay, that's good. I'll speak to Mr. Torgerson about it but I'm sure it was a dog."

"Okay, Daddy."

She sat and held one of the cats while Jack rowed back across the lake. Ten minutes later they docked, and the animals and girls bailed out of the boat in a rush.

They were halfway to the house when Jack yelled at them. "Girls, get those dogs cleaned up!"

Carol frowned and whined, "Dad, do we have to? It was Janet's idea to take them."

Jack pointed at the garage. "I don't care. I want all three of you to clean up the dogs together."

The girls stomped to the garage and dragged out the hose and a large wash tub. Mary filled the tub, while the dogs waited next to Janet.

From his hiding spot across the lake, He Who Watches observed the human cubs placing their dogs into a tub of water. He found it strange and had no idea why they did it. He wondered if their cats would go into the water next.

He gave a human-like shrug and turned and walked deeper into the forest. The large feral hog, tucked under his right arm, ceased struggling a while ago. His left hand clamped the hog's mouth shut; stopping any possible terrified squeals. The hog's hooves floated five feet above the forest floor, and it shuddered against him as he walked.

Thirty sunrises ago he arrived at this lake and watched the human family. He learned the youngest cub had senses like his own; something he found in no other human he encountered.

When the humans entered his forest today, he followed them. Their actions puzzled him. Many times, they passed by edible roots and berries without stopping. Weren't they hungry? Didn't they need to eat the food when and where they found it? He stayed close to them throughout their visit.

He Who Watches sensed the human male, a warrior, was descended from the original humans of this land. The male moved easily through his forest and appeared to enjoy the experience. Most humans avoided his forests at all costs. At one point during their visit the male almost detected him. He strengthened his hide sensitivities and deflected the male's curiosity.

He was curious about the animals that accompanied the humans. Silently he called the dogs over and examined them. They sat at his feet, and he squatted and stroked their fur. He knew these dogs could not hunt or herd animals and they were too small to protect their masters. So why were they here?

He ignored the cats; they were good for nothing. He detested cats. They're so stupid and so smug. He always made it a point to never communicate with them.

As he examined the dogs, he sensed a threat. He rose to his full height and scanned the forest. He discovered a large hog following the humans. Thick hide covered the massive animal, and huge tusks curled from its mouth. Recently, an even larger rival bested the animal. Open wounds covered its shoulder and it limped from the fight that drove it from its territory. Anger coursed through its veins; it wanted revenge on anything it could find. Hunger also drove it toward the humans. It would kill and eat the cubs' animals or even the smallest cub if it could catch them.

He hated the greedy hogs, released into the forest generations ago by the foolish humans. Even this forest surrounded by many humans and machines was not immune. In many parts of the forest, large swaths of soil were uprooted by the hogs as they dug for insects and edible roots.

He stole behind the feral hog. Soon the humans crested a small hill and were out of sight. He moved in and seized the hog in his arms. He underestimated the strength of the wounded animal. It struggled against him, and his shield slipped. The special cub sensed him. He restored his defenses and sent her a change to his appearance. Fortunately, it fooled her.

He sent the dogs back to the humans, and they got back in their boat and moved across the lake.

He rubbed his chin with his free hand. The spirits sent him here because of this cub. He had no doubt. Her mind wielded powerful but undeveloped senses. Still, in the future he needed to shield his mind from her. Although he followed the spirits' bidding, he had no desire to reveal himself to this human family.

Now he walked away from the lake. The hog's musk and the smell of droppings matted into its fur filled his nostrils. He Who Watches wrinkled his nose in disgust. When he was safely away from the young cub, he pelted the hog's mind with his senses. He dropped it to the ground. The confused animal staggered around him in a daze. He Who Watches moved to its front. With one swing of his massive fist, he severed its spine and it flopped to the forest floor.

He tore the animal open and ripped out its liver and heart. He tore off a back leg and headed for his sleeping spot in the forest. He left the remainder to the coyotes and other forest scavengers. There were more hogs available for his next meal.

Chapter 10

August 12, 2015, Cedar City, Missouri.

Jack stepped into the tavern located a few miles from his depot. The building that housed the tavern was old. Jack guessed someone built it just after World War II. With its proximity to the highway, he wondered if it was an old auto parts or tire store. The large sign perched on top of the building stated **THE OUTHOUSE** in blaring red neon letters. The tavern's dirty windows held colorful neon signs that advertised popular beer brands from the last fifty years. About half of the signs worked.

The gravel parking lot behind him held at least thirty cars and pickup trucks along with an equal number of motorcycles. A boisterous crowd packed the bar; everyone talked and laughed over blaring honky tonk music. The smell of stale beer wafted from the rough wooden floor, and the aroma of burgers and fries poured from the kitchen.

The patrons were men in blue jeans, t-shirts, and beat up ball caps; the owners of the pickups. A few female faces dotted the redneck crowd. In addition, thirty men and women wearing biker leathers swarmed three pool tables located on one side of the tavern.

Jack spotted Don waving from a table in the back. Before he could move, someone yelled. "Hey, Colonel!"

Jack spotted June Miksic sitting with a friend. He stopped long enough to say hello and headed towards Don's table.

Don, Will, and Cecil rose and shook Jack's hand. Natalie also sat at the table. Jack sat. He noticed they all drank their beer in cans, even Natalie.

"Where's Howie?" Jack said.

"He's around here somewhere," Don said. "Can I buy you a beer?"

"I'm not a drinker," Jack said. "I'll have a soda,"

Don frowned at Jack. "Their soda machine is broken. All they got is beer."

Natalie shoved her father's shoulder. "Dad, don't be so difficult." She turned to Jack. "It's no problem, Colonel, they have soda here. I'll get it." She gave her father a dirty look. "I was about to get myself a glass of wine." She stood.

"Thank you, Natalie," Jack said. "I've got the next round." She smiled at Jack and moved towards the bar. Joe Harper appeared and joined their table.

Don glared at his vice president. "Nice you could join us, Joe."

Jack turned to Don. "I'm glad we could get together. I think it's good for us to get to know each other. "

"I want to get to know you also, Colonel. I think it's wise to know a man's motivation before making agreements with him. Wouldn't you agree?"

"I do. I found it difficult working with the Iraqis and Afghans. You never knew what type of man you dealt with. Many times, we got burned by the people who said they were our allies."

Don nodded. "It was the same in Vietnam. It made it real difficult to get results."

Jack looked at Don. "When were you there?"

"Sixty-seven to sixty-eight and again from sixty-nine to seventy."

Jack nodded. "So, you went through Tet?"

"I did. My unit got caught in Saigon. We fought house to house for days…never thought it would end. But it was a hell of a good time." A far-off look and a hint of a smile passed across Don's face. After a few moments, he returned to the conversation. "Tell me about your Silver Star, Colonel. How many men did you kill to earn it?" Will and Cecil leaned forward and watched Jack.

Jack took a deep breath. "Most of the time I avoid talking about it. It makes me uneasy."

Don frowned. "That's bullshit. You should be honored to talk about it. I talk about my bronze star and purple heart all the time."

Jack threw Don's question back at him. "Okay Don, how many men did you kill to earn your bronze star?"

"I think around twenty." Don closed his eyes for a moment. "They dropped us in Bien Hoa province a week before Tet. We sent out a patrol and stumbled on a large Viet Cong column. Their commie generals were moving it for their big offensive, so the unit didn't run away like they usually did. They formed up and came straight at us. I killed seventeen with my M-16 and one with my forty-five."

Jack kept his face passive as he realized what a natural born killer Don was. The big man continued with his story. "Later that night it got quiet, and I tried to get some sleep. A gook got too close to me and woke me up. I didn't want to highlight my position in the dark, so I caved his head in with some rebar I found. I don't know how many died from the mortars and artillery I called in, but when it was over my unit walked out, and Charlie didn't."

Don took a drink of his beer and again looked at Jack. "Come on, Colonel. Tell us about Afghanistan." When

Jack said nothing, Don lowered his voice. "It's ok, Colonel; I'm sure the bastards deserved it."

Jack nodded his head. "They did." He took a deep breath and let it out. "I was on a routine inspection in Kandahar province. I was in the area when the Taliban hit one of our outposts." Jack twisted his wedding band around his finger as he recalled COP Armstrong. "That place was a dump positioned in a God forsaken location. It wasn't worth a shit to anyone. But it had a platoon of US Army soldiers that the Taliban wanted to kill or even capture. The Taliban concentrated a lot of fighters there, so I think they wanted to capture our guys."

Jack paused and looked at Don. "You know, capture them and put them on the news so they could get the USA to back down." Don frowned but offered no comment. "The reinforcements couldn't get there in time, so I went in instead. I'm pretty sure I killed nine, maybe ten with my M4. I got one with my sidearm; an Afghan traitor who murdered one of our guys inside the outpost." Don frowned upon hearing about the murder. "Like your situation Don, I don't know how many died from the F-15s I called in, but my unit made it through. The Taliban won't recover in that sector for a long time." A dark look fell over Jack's face. "I wanted to kill a lot more of the bastards."

Don slapped the table, and the empty beer cans jumped. "That's outstanding, Colonel! I'm glad to see a real fighting man take over at Show Me Army Depot."

"Way to go, Colonel," Cecil said.

Will's body shook, and he stammered, "Cocksucker. Fucking. Taliban. Bastards."

All three Miksic men grabbed their beers and toasted Jack. Joe Harper said nothing. Jack's eyebrows rose. Don and his sons clearly enjoyed a good fight story. He hoped that's all it took to get Don and the union on his side.

Natalie returned and handed a glass of cola to Jack. Before he could drink, the tavern's front door opened, and a tall, naked man walked in. The music continued, but the discussion and laughter died down at the site of the nude man. Jack recognized Don's youngest son Howie. The young man had toned muscles; like he lived in a gym. He carried an open beer can but set it down as he passed a table.

Jack turned to Don. "Isn't that Howie? Why isn't he wearing any clothes?"

The woman who tended bar threw her dishrag to the floor and yelled at their table. "Goddammit, Don! I told you I'd call the cops if this happened again!"

Natalie put her hands on her hips and frowned at her father. "Oh, Dad, you didn't? This is no way to treat Colonel Black Eagle. I'm sure he doesn't want any part of this."

"Part of what?" Jack said.

Don, Will, and Cecil said nothing. Howie walked into the center of the tavern.

"Well, I need to get behind the bar," Natalie said. She stood and left the table.

"Why?" Jack said. "What's going on?"

Natalie stepped behind the bar. She yelled at her brother. "Don't do it Howie!"

Jack knew Howie heard his sister, but he ignored her. The young man walked up to the largest biker in the bar. Both men were the same height, but the biker looked bigger in his leathers.

Standing less than two feet from the man Howie looked him in the eye. "I need your clothes, your boots, and your motorcycle."

Jack recognized the phrase from a famous science fiction movie. "Oh shit," Jack said.

Several of the bikers laughed but most scowled at Howie.

"You forgot to say please," the big biker said.

A biker who stood behind Howie slammed a pool cue across his shoulder blades. The cue broke and flew across the room. The broken cue dropped a redneck sitting at a table. Howie, unfazed but with a huge red welt across his back, planted a right cross on the big biker's jaw. The man went down in a heap.

Three bikers rushed Howie. Don, Will, and Cecil launched themselves from the table at the nearest group of bikers. The other bikers and the blue jean-wearing rednecks rushed together with fists flying. The tavern degenerated into clumps of screaming, fighting patrons. Jack stood, stunned, watching the spectacle. Joe Harper screamed and ran for the front door; his arms high in the air.

Natalie stood behind the bar with the bartender. June Miksic, still in her security uniform, stood with them. The three women yelled at four biker women pointing and yelling at them.

Jack needed to escape this looney bin before he got punched. If the police arrested him during a bar brawl it could end his career. Before he could move, two bikers headed his way.

Jack held up his hands. "I don't want any trouble guys," he said.

"I hear you're the colonel from the depot," said one biker. "They fired me five years ago. I hate that place."

Jack realized reasoning with the bikers wouldn't work. He moved into a combat stance. "Then you must be a fucking idiot," Jack said.

The biker's eyes opened wide, and he swung at Jack's head and missed. The man followed through, and Jack sidestepped and jabbed him in the ribs with a strong left. As the man rotated, he punched him in the side of the head. The man cried out and stumbled away.

The second man moved in and threw a quick punch. Jack ducked, but the biker's left grazed the top of his skull. The pain corkscrewed into his head, but he kept his bearings. The biker overextended leaving him bent over. Jack straightened up and brought his knee up into the man's stomach. The breath rushed from the man's lungs, and he grabbed his midsection. Jack sent a downward strike to his cheek, and the biker collapsed.

The first biker returned, landing a blow that clipped Jack's chin. Jack raked his shoe down the biker's shin and stomped hard on the top of his foot. The biker bent forward, as if to massage his injured foot. Jack laid a powerful right against the man's jaw. He collapsed on top of the other biker.

Jack danced around the floor, trying to keep at arm's length from any aggressor. Two times bikers came after him. Both times he stopped each biker's attack by landing blows that sent them sprawling. He risked another quick look as he tried to find Don. He spotted Natalie still behind the bar. June Miksic had a large biker woman in a choke hold, while another woman rushed her. The bartender stood behind June and threw punches at the attacking woman. Another woman tried to protect her face as Natalie hit her with a flurry of punches. Three other women tried to get at them, but the narrow space kept them out. Through it all 'Bad to the Bone' by George Thorogood and the Destroyers blared from the jukebox.

Seconds later Jack saw stars and fell to the floor. A heavyset biker caught him unaware and tagged him with a haymaker. The biker failed to press his attack. Jack cleared his head and stood.

"You made a big mistake letting me up, fatty."

He hit the biker with a hard jab to the forehead. The man's plump hands flew to his face, and Jack punched him in the stomach. Now his hands flew to his middle, and he bent over. Jack brought his knee up into the man's face. Blood poured from the biker's broken nose, and he fell to the floor.

Jack looked across the room. He saw at least two bikers throwing punches at every male Miksic. Don Miksic turned and threw a biker over a pool table like he was a bale of hay. Three bikers rushed towards Don. The big union president wrapped a biker up in each arm and used his outstretched leg to hold off the third. Jack came up behind the man going after Don. He jabbed him in the kidney, and the man arched his back in pain. He tapped the other kidney and shoved the man hard to the side. The man fell and crawled away across the beer-soaked floor.

Still holding the bikers, Don smiled at Jack. "Thanks, Colonel. He was a pesky one. You having fun yet?"

Don twisted his body to the right and threw the biker under his left arm underneath a pool table. He pulled the other biker up like a rag doll and punched him in the stomach. The biker collapsed at Don's feet.

Don appeared calm and collected after his exertions. The big man's breathing seemed normal and unhurried. Jack panted like he was on a twelve-mile road march while carrying a heavy rucksack.

Jack yelled at Don. "Let's get Natalie and get out of here!"

"Now? I'm having fun!"

Jack used his strongest command voice. "Now, Sergeant!"

Don came to the position of attention. "Yes, Sir!"

Jack pointed to the women behind the bar. "You lead."

Don punched and threw bikers to get them out of the way. He spared any rednecks he came across but shoved them away. The fight still raged behind the bar. Natalie had two women cornered against the wall, and she kicked and punched both. June punched a fat biker woman who charged Natalie. The woman flew backward taking two other women with her. Jack couldn't see the bartender.

Don reached the bar and pushed the biker women out of the way. Don grabbed Natalie, and Jack grabbed June Miksic. "We're getting out of here, June. You're welcome to follow us." He pointed at the front door. "Get moving, Don."

The big man moved through the room like a bulldozer cutting a road through a forest. The others followed close behind while the jukebox played 'Honky Tonk Man' by Dwight Yoakam. They burst through the front door and staggered into the parking lot. Jack heard sirens approaching and tires screeched on the asphalt highway. The smarter patrons spilled out the door, ran to their vehicles, and gunned them from the parking lot.

Jack glared at Don. "Don, you are the craziest mother I have ever met." Jack paused to catch his breath. His voice rose as his anger caught up with him. "Where do you get off starting a bar fight for my benefit? Wasn't my silver star good enough for you?"

Don rubbed the sweat off his forehead. A dumb ass grin split his face. "Whoooeee that was fun," he said. "I think we should do it again next week."

When Jack said nothing, he continued. "You said it yourself, Colonel. You need to get to know someone before you start making deals with them. Now, I think I know you better. You're going to do good things at this depot, and I'll do what I can to support you."

Jack stared at Don. Before he could say anything, three county patrol cars pulled up no more than twenty feet away. Five deputy sheriffs jumped from the cars and ran into the bar. Sheriff Uwell Yates walked up to Jack's group. Don's nose bled, Jack's scalp bled from the punch he took, and Natalie covered her black eye. Only June was untouched.

"Hi, Uwell," June said. "Nice night."

Uwell nodded to June. He studied the group for several long seconds. Finally, he walked towards the tavern and called over his shoulder. "I didn't see a thing."

Jack turned and walked to his car. He yelled over his shoulder. "Good night, June! Nice seeing you!"

June laughed. "Good night, Colonel! You take care of yourself!"

Chapter 11

September 2, 2015, Nogales, Mexico

Abdul Barry scanned the empty desert terrain ahead of him. "I thought it was quite difficult to sneak across the US border," he said.

The teenage coyote shrugged his shoulders. "It was at one time, but now the Gringos practically beg people to cross. Sometimes the border patrol even looks the other way when they see us." The boy let out a quiet chuckle. "Telemundo states the border patrol is in trouble with the American politicians for sending too many of us back to our homes."

Abdul considered the young man's claims unlikely but said nothing. He looked over his shoulder at his fighters following him through the scrub bushes and cacti of the Mexican desert. A small smile formed. His casually dressed, and well-groomed men looked very much like Americans to his trained eye. They were all young; Saudis, Iraqis, Syrians, and Egyptians drawn to ISIS and its promise of an Islamic caliphate. In addition to their religious fervor, they also enjoyed the murder and rape of any nonbelievers after ISIS captured a new village.

Playing such an important role in forming a true Islamic government pleased Abdul. His mission would bring great rewards to ISIS. With a North Korean nuclear device, the caliphate would become a powerful force in the Middle East.

Abdul had a tall and muscular build but displayed a baby face and wavy, dark hair. His soft features and English background made his first days within ISIS difficult.

However, his military skills, developed during six years in the British Army, soon eliminated his colleagues' insults. He fought hard and led his forces well. Within six months of arriving, he defeated several Syrian and Kurdish units and captured much important territory. His success on the battlefield brought him to the attention of senior ISIS leaders. He would never forget the meeting where Abu Bakr al-Baghdadi selected him to lead this historic mission.

The fighters he selected for the mission were proven in battle but also the most devout in their Islamic faith. Abdul knew that many had little initiative, but he could live with that. They followed orders, and this meant they would do well. He also looked for men who could get by in America. He found three young Saudis who spoke flawless English and appointed them team leaders.

He returned his gaze to his front. Ahead of them the hidden lights of a small American city filled the night sky with a soft glow. After twenty minutes of walking, they came to a tall, chain link fence. Multilingual signs attached to the fence declared the area an unauthorized port of entry. It even identified the United States code that Abdul and his men violated, and the penalty for crossing illegally; five thousand dollars.

The coyote found a specific fence post and turned to Abdul. "Watch this."

He reached up and pulled a section of the fence away from the post.

"Impressive," Abdul said.

He turned and signaled to his men with a quiet bird call. One at a time his fighters ran to the fence and stepped through to American soil. He went through the open fence and saw a neat row of hooks affixed to the fence post. When the last fighter went through, the coyote hooked the fence back on the pole. Abdul stopped and stared at it. He stood no more than five feet from the fence but could not see the young smuggler's alterations.

"The simplest solutions are the best," the Coyote said. He pointed. "It is two miles to your vehicles. Walk quickly and there's still no talking. When we get there, I want the rest of my money."

Abdul nodded at the young man. "As agreed, when we get there."

They soon reached their goal; a rundown campground on the outskirts of Nogales, Arizona. Two large, late-model motorhomes sat at the farthest end of the parking lot. His men held back while Abdul knocked on the door of the closest vehicle. The door opened to a middle-aged Iraqi couple. Earlier, his ISIS superiors informed him the married couple immigrated to America after the first gulf war. Shocked at the degenerate lifestyles of the Americans, the couple provided support to Islamic terrorists fighting to eradicate the western way of life; first to Al-Qaeda and now to ISIS.

The man spoke in Arabic. "Welcome. Everything is ready. Bring your men in now. We leave soon."

Abdul nodded and went to his Saudi team leaders. "Split your men between these vehicles. Instruct them to lie on the floor and cover themselves with the blankets inside. While we travel, they must always remain concealed. I know they are curious about America, but under no circumstances are they to look from a vehicle's window. The risk of discovery is too great." The Saudi's nodded and moved off. Soon the fighters filed into the vehicles.

Abdul found the coyote standing at the edge of the parking lot. He produced a tight roll of hundred-dollar bills and handed it to the young man. The coyote smiled and shoved the roll into his blue jeans. Abdul placed his hand on the young man's shoulder. "You did your job well my friend. Will you have any trouble getting back?"

The coyote straightened and puffed out his chest. "No trouble; I have crossed the border many times."

"Be careful. Brave men such as you are rare, and I may need your services again." The coyote smiled at the praise and turned to go.

Abdul pulled a stiletto from his boot and spoke to the coyote's back. "One more thing..."

The young man turned. Abdul stood inches from him. The coyote brought his arms up, but the long, thin knife went under his ribs and up into his heart. The teenager let out a quiet gasp. Abdul removed the knife. The boy's eyes rolled back into his head, and he crumpled to the ground. Abdul wiped his knife clean on the boy's shirt. He removed everything from the boy's pockets including two rolls of cash totaling forty thousand dollars.

The old couple approached and handed him a piece of heavy plastic and a shovel. They ignored the dead boy. He wrapped the body in plastic and hefted it over his shoulder.

"I'll return in thirty minutes," Abdul said. Carrying the boy and the shovel, he walked into the desert. Soon he found a good spot behind several large boulders. When he had a hole three feet deep, he rolled the wrapped body into it. He refilled the hole and placed two large rocks atop the grave to deter scavengers. He walked back to the RV Park and kicked fresh sand over the pooled blood. Abdul entered the nearest motorhome and went to sleep.

At sunrise, the motorhome driven by the man's wife drove from the parking lot. Thirty minutes later the second motorhome departed. Both vehicles drove up Interstate 19 towards Tucson. Abdul sat in the passenger seat, while the old man drove.

"Remember to stay one or two miles above the posted speed limit," Abdul said. "If the police pull us over, make no attempt to evade them. Follow their instructions. I will pose as your son and answer all their questions. I'm certain I can get us through any traffic stop.

"What if a policeman wants to come inside?" the man said.

Abdul pondered this. "Let him come. I can handle one policeman."

He kicked his feet up on the vehicle's dash and took in the scenery. He found this desert rugged but beautiful. Not like the deserts of Iraq and Syria. Was that because this desert had no war to mess it up? He shrugged at his own question.

Two hours later they entered Tucson. Ten minutes after that they parked inside a small warehouse located in a poorly maintained industrial park. Abdul stretched and followed his men out of the motorhome onto a concrete floor. Paint peeled from the walls, and large spots of oil and grease dotted the floor. Stale paint fumes came from an old paint booth in the building's rear.

The man and his wife came to Abdul. "Everything is as you requested. We also have warehouses in Amarillo and Wichita. The one in Wichita holds the vehicle you require." He handed him the key fob for the vehicle.

Abdul nodded. He knew another warehouse waited near their target in Missouri. He looked around the spacious and well-lit building. Guessing it could hold fifty motorhomes if required, he conducted an inspection of the warehouse as the couple followed, then checked the building's doors and windows and ensured they locked correctly. Heavy black paint covered the insides of the windows. Air conditioners cooled the space, and tables held food, soft drinks, microwaves, flat screen TVs, video game systems, and DVDs. Many comfortable chairs and cots for sleeping filled the space.

The warehouse had a restroom and two small offices. Maps and photographs of their target rested on a desk in the first office. Prayer rugs, along with an arrow pointing towards Mecca, covered the floor of the second office. Abdul nodded to the couple upon seeing the second office.

Seven wooden crates sat near the offices. Each had a shipping label that showed they came from Shenyang, China. A customs declaration attached to each box stated they contained industrial sewing machines.

Abdul used a crowbar to open them. Six crates held the AK-47 assault rifles and two PKM light machine guns they needed for the operation. He selected a rifle and cycled its action. The weapon had Chinese markings and a light sheen of oil. The seventh crate contained their ammunition. Solvent, gun oil, and cleaning kits in two large shopping bags sat next to the crates.

"What about my weapon?" Abdul said.

The woman handed him a small box. He opened it and removed a small .380 caliber pistol and leather hip holster. He loaded the weapon and holstered it underneath his shirt. He rotated his body, testing the holster's fit.

"This will do," Abdul said.

The couple smiled at each other, and Abdul walked them to the door.

"You have done well. Carry out your normal routine until our departure date. If anyone asks, inform them you are on a well-deserved vacation to see America." The couple smiled at Abdul. "Once you deliver my team to

Missouri, return to your home and wait for further instructions."

The couple gave a slight bow and left.

Abdul found a comfortable recliner and sat. He called his team leaders to him.

"Assign the weapons to your men and have them conduct a thorough cleaning. When they finish, have them eat and rest. Tonight, we will discuss the plan to assault the American ammunition depot. I plan to conduct many rehearsals, so inform your teams. I want no mistakes once we enter the American depot."

The Saudis nodded and moved off. Abdul tilted the recliner back and closed his eyes for a short nap.

Chapter 12

September 4, 2015, The Pentagon, Arlington, Virginia

The Chairman of the Joint Chiefs of Staff, General Anthony Yellin, walked from the elevator and stepped into the Joint Operations Center. Due to his previous instructions, the busy service members present didn't call the room to attention as he entered. He glanced at the three huge projection screens dominating one wall of the important room. Three tiered rows of desks, arranged in a semi-circle, sat in front of the screens. A handful of officers and senior enlisted personnel sat among the desks. Yellin knew the start of any real-world crisis would fill the empty desks.

A briefing chart on the center screen displayed facts on the nation's small military operation going on in Northern Iraq. Information on Afghanistan filled the screen on the right. A blue field filled the remaining screen.

Yellin felt the nation erred badly with its decades-long focus on the Middle East and its oil reserves. The United States had plenty of fossil fuels, and numerous threats to our national security operated in other parts of the world. Threats his nation disregarded at our own peril.

The center, also known as 'The Tank', sat three stories below the Pentagon and maintained around-the-clock contact with United States armed forces located around the world. Yellin knew many of the younger officers referred to the center as 'The Washing Machine'. Years ago, he asked one of the officers why they used that name. The young officer laughed and told him. "When there is a crisis, we go to full staffing. Soon the generals and admirals arrive and start giving orders. When that happens, the staff officers start spinning, and spinning, and spinning."

Yellin smiled as he headed for the far side of the room and the video teleconference connected to Seoul, South Korea. He sat in front of the camera and spotted the US Forces Korea operations officer, Major General Franklin Smith, on the screen. Smith wore his exercise shorts and t-shirt, and a female Army captain in her army combat uniform sat next to him. PowerPoint charts sat on the table in front of him. He glanced at the clock; it showed 6:00 AM in Korea. He knew someone in Korea, probably the captain, put this briefing together in the middle of the night.

"Good morning, Franklin," Yellin said. "Intelligence told me you've got some significant changes to North Korean ground forces. I had some free time, so I thought I'd run down and hear it first-hand."

"Sir, glad you could join us. The information is a few hours old and very shocking. If you're ready, we'll get started."

Yellin nodded, and Franklin signaled to the captain to start her briefing. The young woman ran through a series of charts that displayed a dramatic increase in message traffic from important North Korean military headquarters. They also showed these same headquarters on the move to locations closer to South Korea. Soon the conclusion slide appeared. It read: **Once the identified headquarters reach their final locations, North Korean military forces in significant numbers could attack South Korea within ten days.**

Yellin placed his copy of the briefing slides on the table. "Franklin, does General Dunson agree with this conclusion?"

"Sir, in the absence of any other intelligence, he thinks it's valid."

Yellin shuffled through the slides. "Say again the moving ground forces."

"Sir, they are relocating their four infantry corps headquarters in their first operational echelon." the captain said. "Also, two mechanized infantry corps and one armored corps in their second operational echelon and their two artillery corps and their two army group headquarters."

Yellin nodded. "What about their strategic rocket forces?"

"Sir, there is no movement by any rocket or missile batteries. However, their meteorological support unit relocated to its wartime location. They sent out updated weather reports this morning. In addition, messages from the strategic rocket forces headquarters to subordinate units increased by fifty percent."

"Any change to their air force and air defense?" Yellin said.

"Their tactical air forces show no movement. However, this is inconclusive, as these forces operate from their existing locations in the event of war. They are repositioning air defense radars to cover the moving headquarters."

Yellin wrote notes on his charts for a full minute. He looked up at the screen. "Thank you, Captain; that was a good update. Franklin, if these movements mean the North Koreans are preparing for war, it's bad news. What does your boss need from me?"

"Sir, he wants the Reagan strike group moved to the Sea of Japan and B-52 bombers moved to Guam. He knows the administration won't like it, but he wants the prepositioned brigade set moved to Busan with the personnel to follow. He wants them visible to the North so they can see the consequences. In addition, he wants the deployment list for Korea operations plan 8121 activated. That's it for now. However, if the north continues to ramp up its preparations our needs will increase."

"Okay, I've got it," Yellin said. "I'll speak with the Secretary of Defense today and get these forces moving. Tell your boss to make face-to-face contact with the Koreans. We need to know if they'll support our show of force. I don't know where this is going but I'm ordering Pacific Command to dust off their contingency plans. We'll set up twice daily video teleconferences until this blows over."

"Understood, Sir," Franklin said.

Yellin stared into the camera. "Let's pray it does blow over Franklin. The Tank is out."

He placed the charts into a folder marked TOP SECRET and headed for the elevator.

General Yellin and the Army Chief of Staff, General Marion "John Wayne" Sturm, closed the door to the Oval Office behind them. The Secretary of Defense, the Secretary of State, the National Security Advisor, and the White House Chief of Staff remained behind with the

President. The two generals walked a few paces and faced each other in the tight confines of the hallway.

Yellin knew most Americans were unaware the grand and imposing White House was a very small building when you considered the large number of personnel it held, and the important work done there. A few feet away, five young, female administration staffers manned a half dozen desks that sat in the small space between the oval office and the chief of staff's office. As the generals stood there others came and went. No private places existed within the building's office areas.

"Well, that sucked," Sturm said. "They gave us nothing. No Reagan strike group, no B-52s, and no prepositioned stocks." He ran his hand over his bald head and looked back at the oval office. "Did you see their faces when you recommended we move those forces? You would have thought we asked them to wipe our butts."

Yellin allowed a small smile in response to his friend's earthy comment.

"After all this time they still don't trust us," Yellin said. "At least we have approval to activate the deployment process for the Korea operations plan. We can get some units and materiel loaded and even moved to port. Honestly, I expected them to shut us down completely."

Sturm looked around the small space. "Do you think they have any coffee around here?" Seeing nothing he turned back to Yellin. "Anthony, you and I both know activating the deployment list means squat to the North Koreans. It'll take loaded ships leaving port and heading for Korea for them to know we're serious." He studied the young women that stared into laptops just a few feet away. "I'm astonished the administration rates their nuclear negotiations with the Iranians more important than our defense of South Korea. The only reason they approved anything is the threat to the world economy if war breaks out in Asia. Hell, they must know a war there pulls Japan in too."

Yellin nodded. "A fifteen-thousand-point drop in the stock market would piss off their big money donors." He considered his dilemma for several seconds. "We need to get more hard intelligence on the North's actions. Something the national security staff cannot wish away and confirms the danger to the South."

The Secretary of Defense walked out of the oval office. He spoke with the two generals. "Tony you'd better be right on this. We don't need speculation; we need solid information so the President can make an informed decision. He's got much more important matters on his mind."

"More important than our ally's survival?" Yellin said. After an awkward pause, he spoke again. "Mr. Secretary, I hope to God I'm wrong for the sake of South Korea and for our military people stationed there, but we need to move those forces. Just activating the deployment list is not enough, and our weak response emboldens the north. It's stupid and it's reckless."

The Secretary stiffened. "The President and I believe the exact opposite. Movement of our forces will provoke the North Koreans into a more dangerous response, and we cannot take that chance. You have your orders so carry them out. The state department will contact North Korea through the Swiss and sort this out." He looked down his nose at Yellin. "Keep me informed."

The two generals watched him disappear down the hall.

Sturm frowned. "I didn't know you went by Tony?"

"I don't. But addressing a subordinate with the wrong name is his leadership style."

Sturm barked out a booming laugh. Several staffers sitting at nearby desks glared at the large general officer.

"Let's get out of here," Yellin said. "We're running out of time."

Chapter 13

September 13, 2015, 1900 (KST) Pyongyang, North Korea

Twenty-four-year-old Park Mi Sook, a senior manager within Bureau 121, North Korea's preeminent cyber warfare agency, entered the team area housing her subordinates. Expensive cosmetics, along with Rodeo Drive clothing, accentuated her natural beauty. Pink highlights, the current trend in South Korea, streaked her hair, and a small Louis Vuitton bag hung from her shoulder. All emphasized that Mi Sook had a value to the North Korean regime well above the average citizen.

Upon entering the large suite, she observed the young, well-dressed men and women sitting in work cubicles arranged around the room. Their hands flew over state-of-the-art laptops connected to thirty-inch flat screens. Network cables ran between the desks and snaked into the floor. Colorful posters decorated the walls, and K-Pop music played from hidden speakers. Bean bag chairs, an adult-sized tricycle, and a few beach balls covered a large open floor. A refrigerator with glass doors held cans of soft drinks, iced lattes, energy drinks, and bottled water. It looked like any technology development office that operated within Google, Microsoft, or Facebook.

The thirty people before her were a few of the over six thousand North Koreans who conducted cyber warfare actions against her country's enemies. All were well trained and, despite their nation's international isolation, well versed in the most recent information technology programming skills. North Korea used their expertise to steal valuable information, or when they wanted a message sent. In fact, their most recent cyber-attack damaged thousands of computers at South Korea's major television networks. The networks were unable to broadcast for hours and took weeks to recover. This bold attack troubled the intelligence services of South Korea's many allies.

She clapped her hands for attention. When she had it, she addressed her group. "I hope you're all prepared. Tonight, we begin an important battle in support of our nation. We all worked hard to achieve this goal, and tomorrow you'll be legends in the world of computer hackers." Many of the young men and women smiled and exchanged glances across their computer workstations. "You will also receive significant rewards upon completion of our task." She glanced at her smartphone. "Make your final preparations; our start time approaches. The Dear Leader and I need your best."

Mi Sook's targets were two small American cities: Cedar City, Missouri and Richmond, Kentucky. She had no idea why her nation found these locations important. Her task was to shut down all communication within those cities. She selected the large neighboring metropolitan areas of Kansas City, Missouri and Louisville, Kentucky for her malware insertion points. Local network operators would fight back and eventually contain the malware. Despite this, the malware would create large swaths of territory with no communication capability; no internet, no cell phones, no land lines, and no television. Cedar City and Richmond would sit well within each silent territory. Two days later each copy of the malware would erase itself and leave the networks undamaged and with no evidence of North Korean involvement.

One hour later Mi Sook returned to her team. She again checked the time and announced, "One minute to go, people. Get ready. You must defend your work or add additional malware as their network security people fight to save their systems."

The start time arrived, and the programmers concentrated on their screens. After five minutes several reported the malware active and spreading. Soon all reported successful malware activation. A large flat screen on the wall displayed a map of the United States. Red shading on the map showed the real-time movement of the virus as it spread from town to town.

The malware's spread looked like a living thing that pulsed across the screen and consumed additional uninfected terrain. It reminded Mi Sook of a film she had once seen of an Ebola virus, as it attacked and devoured red blood cells in an African victim. She shuddered and turned her back on the map. She hoped their malware would stop where their models predicted.

Three hours later the virus ceased its movement. Mi Sook studied the map. The shading around Kansas City formed a rough circle four hundred kilometers in diameter. A smaller circle surrounded Louisville but still encompassed the target city. Within the two areas every household, business, and government agency, encompassing over twelve million people, had no functioning phone or internet.

As her team recovered from their efforts, Mi Sook retreated into her office. She slapped her smart phone into its holder on her desk. Her favorite song, 'Toxic' by Britney Spears, burst from the Bluetooth speakers. Mi Sook turned it up to a piercing volume. Soon she danced like a partying student in a Boston nightclub. The young woman gyrated and swayed in the middle of her office as her hackers crowded around her open door. Soon they laughed and applauded and a few even danced themselves. When the song ended, she stood next to her desk gasping for breath. She spotted her subordinates at her door. Her hand flew to her mouth in surprise, and she laughed. Her laughter grew and she turned her back on them. The group drifted back to their desks to continue their work.

Chapter 14

September 13, 2015, 1900 (CST) Gulf of Mexico

Captain Chae Min Soo stood on the bridge of the freighter, MV Chong Chan Gong. He looked out the window and scowled. He hated the superstructure changes and paint job that disguised his beautiful ship. He also detested the Myanmar flag they flew. He felt his ship, North Korea's largest and fastest, should not sneak around in the darkness like a common criminal. His ship's history proved she was an exceptional criminal; therefore, she should sail the seas with her head held high. Chae sighed as he knew his desires did not reflect the reality of his business.

Chong Chan Gong left the Nampo shipyard that built her in 1979. Since then, she sailed the world's oceans nonstop. When she reached a port, she tied up just long enough to receive or unload the illegal cargo purchased or sold by his nation. Despite this difficult schedule, Bureau 39 kept her well maintained and even gave her a complete overhaul every ten years. Luck also blessed the ship. In over thirty years of smuggling, only once were they ever stopped and boarded. After an international outcry, the offending authorities released the vessel's cargo of ballistic missiles to its original destination; Yemen.

Chae smiled at the memory and looked at his first mate. "What is our location?"

The mate consulted his flat screen. "Two hundred kilometers south of Houston. We'll reach our launch point in thirty minutes." He looked at the captain. "Should we start?"

Chae looked at the darkening sky and the radar scope. It showed no other vessels in the vicinity.

"Very well; begin our preparations."

The first mate grabbed a phone and barked out orders. Chae walked to the man standing in the shadows at the back of the bridge. The man wore a flight suit and carried a black helmet. Gold flight wings adorned the top of the helmet. The leather name tag on his flight suit read Captain Hwong Chong Um with Korean People's Army Air Force below his name.

"You can launch in thirty minutes," Chae said. "I expect no problems, but this is our first time doing this while under way. Please be thorough as you inspect your craft."

Outside flood lights turned on and lit up the ship's forward deck. The pilot turned away from the light. "I intend to Captain," Hwong said. "Thank you for your assistance; I look forward to our return journey. Now I must see to my aircraft."

The pilot turned and left the bridge without bowing. Chae frowned at the man's back. He added another slight to the long list of constant, minor insults from the much younger man. He wished for a world with fewer fighter pilots strutting around. Chae moved to the window and peered down at the freighter's deck.

Hydraulics whined, and two cargo cranes, sitting side by side in the center of the deck, tilted forward towards the ship's bow. The whine stopped when the cranes reached a twenty-degree angle. Crewmen pounded large steel pins into holes locking the cranes in place. The false cranes now formed a sturdy ramp twenty-five meters long.

A wide roll-up door in the ship's superstructure opened. Half a dozen technicians pushed a dolly holding a small, swept-wing jet onto the deck. The aircraft sat on a small sled that fit into rails welded to the ramp. Hydraulics again whined, and a portable lift raised the sled onto the ramp. A technician locked the sled into place. Others rolled empty drop tanks along the deck towards the jet.

Captain Hwong walked around the jet and observed the activities. Fifteen minutes later the jet sat on the ramp with its wing tanks attached. The technicians dragged hoses to the jet and filled it with fuel.

The pilot stepped onto the wing and entered the jet's small cockpit. An aide held his helmet and assisted him buckling into the seat. Chae noticed Hwong had no parachute. He suspected the top-secret jet had no ejection seat either.

The wings and small fuselage helped Chae identify the aircraft; a 1950s-era MIG-15 fighter. Developed by the Soviets after World War II, it served as his nation's primary fighter aircraft during the Korean War. Although long obsolete, his nation still flew several squadrons of the tough little jet. But this jet had a strange appearance. Instead of a gaping maw to suck in air for the jet engine buried within, the nose of this aircraft resembled a three-sided pyramid covered with small vents. It also had a redesigned tail consisting of two vertical stabilizers that jutted up in a V configuration. In addition, the engine's exhaust now exited the aircraft through a rectangular nozzle lined with angular edges.

At dinner, one evening Captain Hwong told Chae the unusual jet's black skin consisted of a high-tech radar absorbing material or RAM. This material made the jet undetectable to modern military radars. Hwong stated North Korean scientists reverse engineered the complex material using samples from a United States Air Force F-117 stealth aircraft shot down over Serbia in 1999.

Chae laughed and stated he knew all about the Americans' RAM material. When the arrogant pilot disputed his claim, Chae told him how he, a humble ship's captain, purchased the RAM materials from Serbian leaders for five hundred kilograms of uncut heroin. After his tough negotiations, another five hundred kilograms remained within his ship's hold. Hwong showed a small amount of respect after that conversation.

Chae looked upon North Korea's own stealth fighter. That his small nation could build such a wonder of technology impressed him. In addition to its stealth, it retained its armaments: a twenty-three millimeter cannon in each wing and two AA-2 Atoll air-to-air missiles inside an internal bay.

With fueling complete, the technicians sealed the tanks. Teams carrying four large rockets approached the back of the aircraft. They mounted the rockets to the rear of the aircraft, two on each side, under the vertical stabilizers.

Chae gave commands that turned his ship into the wind. The pilot waved from the cockpit and closed the canopy. The stealth fighter's single jet engine spooled up. After a few moments the engine screamed. The noise pounded Chae's ears even in the enclosed bridge.

Soon the pilot throttled the engine up to full afterburner, and the technicians ran from the deck. A few seconds later, the rocket engines ignited with a loud bang. Tongues of flame three meters long scorched the deck and accelerated the jet up the ramp. Clouds of dense gray smoke obscured Chae's vision, and he lost sight of the fighter. He spotted the spent rockets and the jet's sled as they dropped into the sea ahead of the ship. The smoke cleared, and he scanned the sky around them for the jet.

An ear-splitting shriek slammed them when the jet flew by a few feet above the bridge. Everyone ducked. The helmsman even let out an involuntary cry. The man blushed and he gave several polite bows to his colleagues.

Chae frowned at the pilot's hot-dogging. He hoped the Americans shot the pretty little jet from the sky with the pilot in it. And if they didn't maybe he would sail past the snob when he ditched his fancy jet after the mission.

Chae struggled to keep sight of the small fighter against the darkening sky. He suspected Hwong would have no trouble flying through American airspace.

Hwong flew in the night sky at twenty thousand feet. He checked his gauges as his engine roared behind him. His jet performed well so he scanned the dark sky around him for any approaching aircraft. Soon he spotted the lights of Houston. He considered taking a detour over the big city. His previous flights over Japan and South Korea proved no radar systems could detect him. However, he opted for caution and studied the city from a safe distance. He hoped one day he could meet one of the gun-toting cowboys that lived in the large American state.

His destination was an isolated mansion located thirty miles from the target American base. Before he departed from North Korea, his superiors told him North Korean agents searched the Missouri countryside for an airfield to house his jet. During one of their trips, they spotted a concrete runway leading to a large mansion. They learned the founder of a large avionics company owned the mansion. The wealthy American used it as his primary residence. To commute to his various factories, he built a private landing strip for his Cessna business jet. The mansion even had a small hangar large enough to house the stealth fighter, additional ammunition, and a rented fuel truck. The agents declared it an ideal location to base the jet.

The North Korean government directed a sympathetic South Korean entrepreneur to invite the wealthy American and his family to South Korea for an all-expenses paid business trip. He scheduled the trip during the Chuseok holiday. When they departed for South Korea, the agents entered the mansion and waited for his arrival. Hwong assumed the agents would kill the numerous maids and butlers that remained in the mansion.

This was certainly an important mission, and he expected a promotion and more flying time upon his return to North Korea. But the thing he desired most was the title of first North Korean astronaut. He imagined blasting into space with the Russians and visiting the International Space Station. After that, he would need an aide to keep track of all his appointments with beautiful women.

Several hours later Hwong initiated his descent towards the mansion and its airstrip. He would have no trouble landing in the dark. He had over one thousand hours flying his stealth jet at night.

He took a long look at the terrain below. He looked forward to his stay in the mansion. He hoped it had a television so he could view American shows featuring cowboys and gangsters. He made a decision; once he landed, he would send one of the agents out to get him a cheeseburger. He wondered what they tasted like.

Chapter 15

September 13, 2015, 2100 (CST) Show Me Army Depot, Missouri

Abdul Barry took the exit and headed towards Show Me Army Depot. He glanced at the bridge that led to the entrance of the depot. He saw clearly that the destruction of this bridge would cut off vehicle access to the important facility. He studied it for potential placement of the explosives. He didn't think it would be too difficult to bring down the concrete and steel structure.

He forgot the bridge as he approached the depot's main entrance. He spotted a security guard waiting for him in the far-left lane of a very large entrance. He saw the guard turn and speak to his partner. The other guard appeared to shoo away a small animal. That guard then turned and watched as Abdul approached.

Abdul knew two guards manned the gate at this time of night. He shut off his headlights and slowed. His British-made SUV displayed diplomatic plates stolen four months ago from an embassy-owned sedan parked in a shady Washington D.C. neighborhood.

He pulled up to the big security guard and stopped. He rolled down his window, and the guard peered inside. Abdul had an expensive shave and haircut and wore a neat polo shirt over khakis and penny loafers. He looked like he belonged in the stylish SUV. He smiled at the guard.

"Good evening, Sir," the guard said. "How can I help you?"

"Good evening, officer. I'm Captain Winters with the British Army. I have an appointment with Colonel Black Eagle."

Upon hearing his British accent, the security guard relaxed. Abdul noticed the man's partner turn and look off towards the forest that surrounded the gate area.

"Welcome to Show Me Army Depot Sir. Office hours are from eight to four. Colonel Black Eagle isn't in now."

"Dear me, let me clarify. My appointment with the Colonel is tomorrow. We're meeting on the issue in Korea. But we spoke earlier, and he invited me to his home for a short visit."

"I understand, Sir. Could I see some identification, please? I have nothing in my notes, so I'll need to call the Colonel."

"Of course." Abdul handed over a perfect copy of a British Army identification card.

By this time the other security guard stood at the corner of the guard hut. The man focused on the line of trees about a quarter mile distant.

The guard studied the ID and compared the photo against Abdul. "Sir, if you give me a minute, I'll call Colonel Black Eagle and let him know you're here."

"Thank you. Do you mind if I stretch my legs? It was a long drive from the consulate in Dallas."

"Not a problem. Stay by your vehicle, please."

Abdul opened his door and stood. He made a show of swinging his arms, while the guard entered the booth. The other guard ignored him and whistled towards the forest. The second guard's behavior baffled Abdul. He approached the booth's door. Inside, the guard had his back to the door and didn't see his approach. Abdul drew his pistol and shot the guard in the back of the head. The big man dropped like he suddenly had no bones. He pivoted and shot the second guard in the back, and the man fell. Keeping his weapon up, Abdul stepped past the second guard. He spotted a small animal with dark fur around its eyes and a bushy, ringed tail as it ran toward him. When it saw him, it turned and ran back to the forest. At his feet a small bag of dog kibble leaned against the booth's back wall.

He returned to the guard booth and waited a full minute. When no one responded to the gunshots, he retrieved a small handheld radio from his vehicle and keyed it.

"Hamza, bring the truck up now. Make it quick. Mr. Harper, please come to the security gate."

One minute later a large yellow rental truck pulled up behind the SUV and parked. The driver jumped out and rolled up the rear door. Abdul's team, wearing camouflage pattern military fatigues purchased at a Mexican flea market, stood in the back of the truck. All carried their weapons, and loaded magazines filled the ammunition pouches strapped to their chests.

Abdul yelled at the Saudis. "Get those signs on the road and on the other side of the bridge! Hurry! Get them in place before a vehicle shows up."

The fighters pulled signs and traffic barriers from the truck and carried them towards the bridge. The signs ordered vehicles away from the closed depot. A car came from the highway and headed for the group. The terrorists dropped their signs and readied their weapons.

Abdul yelled. "Don't shoot! He's with us!"

The men relaxed and resumed their tasks. The vehicle pulled up next to the truck and parked.

A man got out and approached Abdul. "Are you in charge? I'm Joe Harper." He stuck out his hand to Abdul.

Abdul ignored the hand. He looked at Joe's glasses and laughed. When he finished, he spoke. "I lead these fighters. Do you have what I need, Mr. Harper?"

Joe dropped his hand. "I have the stuff." Joe smiled. "Hey, is that an English accent? I thought you guys were from Saudi Arabia or something, and the others were from Korea."

Abdul looked down his nose at Joe. "I was raised in Great Britain. You can call me Abdul."

Joe looked at the activity around him. "What do I call these other guys?"

Abdul raised one eyebrow at Joe. "Mr. Harper, listen to my instructions. You will communicate only with me. You will not speak with my men. In fact, throughout this operation I want you to always avoid my fighters."

Joe's brow furrowed. "Why should I do that?"

"First, most do not speak English. Second, they all grew up hating the Americans who suppressed their religion and bombed their countries. Each one would sell their own mother to an Israeli brothel if it meant they could cut your throat." Abdul paused to let this fact sink in. "You do want to live long enough to spend the money we're paying you don't you Mr. Harper?"

Joe swallowed hard. "Yes, I do." His face paled as he looked at the gunmen around him.

"Our things, please," Abdul said.

Joe opened his trunk and removed two large, folded banners.

Abdul turned to the Saudis. "Get these up on the buildings."

"One for the entrance and one for the truck gate," Joe said. "There's a ladder behind the building." Joe spoke the last two sentences to the Saudis.

Abdul grabbed Joe's lower jaw with his right hand and turned his face toward his own. "Speak only to me Mr. Harper."

Joe nodded and Abdul dropped his hand.

The Saudis laughed at Joe, grabbed the banners, and ran off.

Joe pointed to three semi-trucks sitting in front of the truck gate. "There are drivers sleeping in the cabs of those trucks."

Abdul gave instructions to a fighter. Four men ran to the trucks and pounded on the doors. Soon the ISIS soldiers had three men and a woman out of their cabs and down on their knees.

They heard the woman's loud sobs from a quarter mile away. "What are you going to do with them?" Joe said.

The AK-47s popped, and the four drivers fell forward. The fighters laughed and dragged the limp bodies to the nearby forest. Joe shook and he looked at Abdul.

"Relax, Mr. Harper," Abdul said. "They felt little pain. Do we need to move those trucks?"

Joe stared at the truck gate. Even at this distance, the gate's lights illuminated the blood smeared on the pavement. "No, they're fine where they are. They won't attract any attention."

"Excellent. Now the uniforms please."

Joe produced two Show Me Army Depot security guard uniforms and handed them to Abdul. He gave them to two fighters.

"Put these on." Abdul pointed at the guard booth. "Get the dead guards' caps, belts, badges, and name tags and put them on." He turned to two other fighters. "Drag the bodies out to the forest behind the gate."

Abdul turned to Joe. "Give me the maps."

Joe handed four hand-drawn maps of Show Me Army Depot to Abdul, and pointed to locations on the map. "First, go to the security office located here." He looked at his watch. "The security team takes its lunch break in thirty minutes. You should catch all of them in the office at that time. The front entrance has a camera on it." He handed a key to Abdul. "Use this and go in the back door. They won't know you're there until it's too late. The fire department sits next door to security, but they don't have any weapons." Abdul referred to the map as he listened to Joe. "Once you capture the first responders, you can round up all the employees working tonight and get them into the cafeteria."

"Are any of the employees armed?" Abdul said.

"No, they don't have any guns; this isn't the Wild West. There should be no more than a hundred people between the fire station, X-Ray, and the ammunition storage area. All the night shift employees eat their lunch in the cafeteria at ten P.M. If you hurry, you can catch them all at the same time."

"Are there any other security cameras between here and the security office?"

"No other cameras," Joe said.

Abdul pointed out a location on the map. "What about the headquarters area? Is there anyone there?"

Joe shook his head. "No one. The only other person around is the depot commander." He pointed at a spot on the map." That's his home. It's just him and his kids. I recommend you pick him up last."

Abdul studied the map. "I see the bridge, the railyard, and the security office. How far is it to the cafeteria?"

"Seven or eight miles."

"Excellent work, Mr. Harper." Abdul folded the map and examined the vice president. "How much did we pay you for your assistance tonight?"

Joe Harper stood taller and puffed his chest out. "Two million dollars, but I don't care about the money."

"Why is that Mr. Harper?"

Joe frowned. "They all hate me." He wrung his hands together. "I do my best to improve this place, and all they do is push me around. It's because I'm not from around here." He paused. "But I'll show them. Tonight, I'll use Victor Chow's satellite phone to send an email to Washington D.C. stating Show Me Army Depot is on strike. Everyone will know how important I am after tonight." Joe's face twisted into a sick grin.

Abdul stared at Joe. He would look for any opportunity to kill this idiotic traitor once the operation ended. "Mr. Harper, in a few minutes we will move into the depot. I require your assistance until our mission is complete. After that, you are free to go." He pointed at the forest. "Conceal your car in the tree line and ride with my associate." Joe nodded and walked off.

"Please hurry, Mr. Harper," Abdul said. Joe broke into a jog.

Abdul inspected the banners hung by his men. Across the top of each, large red letters stated, '**Show Me Army Depot Management BROKE OUR CONTRACT!**'

Underneath that, it read '**NGW Local 1801 ON STRIKE!**' Smaller letters at the bottom of the banner stated '**Management locked us out! All union members report to the union hall for picket duty!**'

He walked to the guard booth and retrieved his ID. He faced his disguised guards. "I want you to turn people away for as long as possible without firing your weapons. The longer we keep the American police unaware of our actions here the better. We'll return soon to mine the bridge with explosives. Do you have any questions?" The two men shook their heads. He gave them a PKM machine gun and a radio.

By this time the Saudis had their small convoy ready to move. A security vehicle they found parked behind one of the buildings sat first in line. The SUV with a Saudi driving, and Joe Harper in the passenger seat, sat behind it. The rental truck, with the remainder of the ISIS soldiers, was last.

Abdul sat in the passenger seat of the security vehicle and placed his small pistol on his lap. He looked at the driver. "Let's go and keep your speed below forty kilometers per hour."

The man smiled and drove away from the gate. The two other vehicles followed.

Chapter 16

September 13, 2015, 2145 (CST) Show Me Army Depot, Missouri

Jack sat in the family room of his quarters reading. He still wore his army combat uniform. He was too tired to change when he got home from work. His girls were in bed, and the television and internet were off due to the blackout.

Preparations for the movement of ammunition to Korea continued at a moderate pace. Most of their work occurred during the day shift while a small crew, led by his deputy, worked at night. The rail cars for the first train were almost complete, and the first Union Pacific locomotives arrived tomorrow night. After that, they would send a steady stream of two trains each day to the designated ports. His people would load and ship trains until the Army planners stated they had enough. Other depots, none as big as Show Me Army Depot, also prepared their ammunition for deployment. Although no planes or ships had departed the United States, military members at dozens of bases prepared their equipment for expected movement to Japan and South Korea.

Jack checked his cell phone for the hundredth time that day; still no bars. He wondered what high tech screw up caused the immense outage. So far, there was minimal impact on his depot's work. His people established procedures for operating without the internet, and the depot's radios still worked.

Jack looked up and saw both dogs sitting by the front door. He put his book away and placed a leash on each dog and slipped out the door. Soon they walked down the dark road that led to the depot's main road. Jack took his time and stopped at every other tree for the mandatory smells and leg lifting. He took deep breaths of cool night air while he walked.

When Jack neared the main road the security gate came into view. This gate served as the final stop for any vehicle entering the portion of the depot holding live ammunition. Two hundred meters from the gate, he spotted the security guard standing outside his hut smoking a cigarette. Jack decided to walk over and speak with the man once the dogs finished their business.

One of the dogs whined. Jack followed the dog's gaze and spotted the headlights of three vehicles as they moved down the main road towards the gate. Soon he made out a depot security vehicle, a very nice luxury SUV, and a large rental truck. The small caravan of vehicles looked out of place to Jack. He reached for his radio but found it missing. Jack frowned. He looked back towards his quarters, a mile distant, where his radio sat.

Jack watched the vehicles pull up to the gate and stop. The guard put out his cigarette and said a few words to the driver of the security vehicle. Jack heard two sharp pops, and the guard fell to the ground. Jack's heart started to thump, and his thoughts went to his sleeping girls. He trembled as he crouched down behind a tree. He pulled the dogs close to keep them quiet.

Two men stepped from the security vehicle. One wore civilian clothes, and the other wore a camouflage uniform. They grabbed the fallen guard by the legs and pulled him into the guard hut. The two men came out of the hut and raised the gate.

At that moment a security pickup truck approached the gate from the opposite direction. Jack's muscles tensed.

No! It's a trap. Go back!

The security vehicle stopped at the gate, and June Miksic stepped out. She spoke with the men that stood by the raised gate. The man in civilian clothes raised his arm and pointed it at June. Jack heard another pop. June managed to run about twenty feet before she collapsed. The two men retreated to their vehicle and signaled their comrades.

The drivers of the SUV and the rental truck jumped from their vehicles and ran forward. Both wore military camouflage uniforms and carried AK-47s. Jack recognized their military training in their movements. The two men advanced on June's prone body. One placed the muzzle of his weapon against her head and fired.

Jack's blood boiled, and he clenched his fists. A terrorist group of some kind just killed June and the other guard. But why were they here? Why did they pick his depot? He needed to notify security and the county sheriff. His small security department couldn't handle even a small number of terrorists.

The two men dragged June's body into the guard hut. One came out and tucked her pistol into his pants.

Jack scowled at the terrorist. *I hope you shoot your dick off you cocksucker.*

The well-dressed terrorist walked to the back of the rental truck and rolled up the door. Three men in camouflage, and armed with AK-47s, jumped down and went to June's pickup. They made a U-turn with the pickup, and all four vehicles drove off.

When the vehicles drove out of sight Jack left the dogs and sprinted to the guard hut. He entered and checked the fallen guards; both were dead. Jack looked for their radios, but the terrorists took them. He had to get to his radio.

Jack ran towards his quarters and pulled the dogs along behind him.

The terrorist vehicles pulled into a large gravel parking lot and parked behind several pieces of construction equipment. One of the Saudis and three fighters jumped from the rental truck. The Saudi spotted the security office a block down the street; beyond that sat the fire station.

They left the rental truck and moved to the rear of the security building. Their earlier rehearsals for attacking the building, aided by a detailed drawing of the building's interior, had gone well. From the American traitor's update, they knew the guards sat in their break room and ate dinner. One guard manned a desk and monitored the depot's alarm systems and radios.

The terrorists wore the same black bandanas they used in Syria. They stood around the door and pulled the bandanas up over their noses. The Saudi slipped the key into the lock and flung the door open. His three subordinates charged into the building with their rifles at their shoulders. The Saudi followed.

The ISIS soldiers moved down the hall to the break room. Quiet talk and the smell of warmed leftovers came from the room. The soldiers burst into the large room. Five men and one woman gaped at the soldiers, their forks and spoons frozen in midair. Before any could move, the soldiers sprayed the room with automatic fire. Several of the guards screamed, and one terrorist laughed, but no one heard them over the roar of the guns. In less than six seconds they killed or mortally wounded every guard.

The Saudi moved farther down the hall and entered the office housing the radios. A single guard stood near a large desk. The man clenched his eyes shut and his hands covered his ears. The Saudi chuckled at the man's pose and shot him in the stomach. The guard's eyes opened wide, and his hands tried to hold his blood within the wound. The guard fell to the floor, and the Saudi fired once more into his head. He took the dead guard's sidearm and fired five rounds into the radio base station.

The Saudi yelled at his subordinates. "Check the other rooms!"

He stepped into the break room. It looked like a slaughterhouse and smelled of blood and fecal matter. He shot each guard in the head and stripped them of their weapons and radios.

His subordinates returned and reported no one else in the building. The men took all the trash cans, paper, and wood chairs they could find and dumped them into the break room. Before long they had a pile four feet high. The Saudi lit the paper on fire. Soon dark smoke filled the room, and flames reached for the ceiling. A fighter pulled the building's fire alarm, and they ran out the door.

The alarm screeched, and they ran next door to the depot's fire station. They found a window and watched five firemen gather around their trucks. All wore either gym shorts or pajamas and pulled on their turnout gear. The Saudi and his team again gathered near a side door. They burst into the station and pointed their rifles at the firemen. The five firemen froze upon seeing the terrorists.

"Stay where you are," the Saudi said. "Get your hands in the air. Do as I say, or we will shoot you."

A fireman with a white helmet stepped forward and yelled. "What the hell's going on? We don't have time for some stupid anti-terrorism drill. We have a fire alarm, and we need to respond."

The Saudi shot him in the chest. The man dropped to the floor, and his white helmet rolled under the nearest fire truck. The other firemen gawked at their dead captain. The Saudi knew it took a few seconds for the reality to sink in. He waited. The four firemen raised their hands. One man looked ready to run.

The Saudi pointed his rifle at the man. "Running does no good. Do what we say, and you will live."

The Saudi waited a few more seconds, and the man made no move. He nodded to his men. The three terrorists shoved the firemen out the door to the waiting vehicles.

The Saudi keyed his handheld radio. "We finished the security office and fire station. We have no casualties, thank Allah."

Abdul responded. "Good. Return at once. We need to capture the remaining employees at the cafeteria."

He took one final look around the large vehicle bay. He turned off the lights and went out the door.

Chapter 17

September 13, 2015, 2150 (CST) Show Me Army Depot, Missouri

Jack ran through the front door of his quarters. The exhausted dogs followed and collapsed on the floor panting.

He caught his breath and grabbed his radio from the coffee table. "Security, this is the Commander. Come in security, this is the Commander." No one answered. "To any security officer, this is Colonel Black Eagle. This is an emergency. Please respond."

The radio squawked. "Colonel, this is Shorty Cramer. I heard your call."

Jack said a silent thank you. "Shorty, are you a security officer?"

"No, Sir, I'm not part of security. I'm a truck driver but sometimes I listen in on the security channel."

"Shorty, this is important. We have terrorists on the depot. They shot June Miksic and another security guard. I can't get hold of security so the terrorists may have killed them too."

The radio remained silent for several seconds. "Colonel, did you say someone killed June Miksic?

"Yes. They killed June and another guard. Maybe others. I don't know what's happening, but our people are in serious danger. Where are you?"

"Sir, I'm in my truck near the cafeteria. I'm late getting to my lunch break."

"Are you driving?"

"No, Sir. I pulled over when I got your call."

Jack began to pace. "That's good, Shorty. Shut your engine off and kill your headlights. The terrorists have at least four vehicles. If your lights are on, they'll see you." Jack waited.

"Okay, Colonel. My lights are off."

"Shorty, have you seen a yellow rental truck or a civilian SUV? The terrorists are in those vehicles."

"Gosh, Colonel. I saw a dozen people get out of those vehicles and go inside the cafeteria a few minutes ago. I was wondering who they was."

Jack's brow furrowed. "What's in the cafeteria?"

"That's where the night shift eats their lunch. There must be a hundred people in there now. Hell, I'd be in there if I hadn't got behind in my work."

Jack thought for a moment. "Shorty have you heard any gunfire?"

"No, Sir."

Jack let out his breath. "That's good. It means they'll use our people as hostages. I'm just relieved they're not killing them outright." Jack still had no idea why terrorists selected his depot for some type of incident.

"Colonel, I'm a veteran," Shorty said. "What can I do to help?"

Jack heard Shorty's voice trembling. He thought for a moment. "Shorty, you're the only person who can see the terrorists. Get out of your truck and get to a safe place where you can observe the cafeteria. I need you to keep tabs on them."

"Well shoot, Colonel. I can do that. It's like pulling guard duty back on the old John F. Kennedy."

Jack smiled. "That's great Shorty. Keep your eyes on that cafeteria but stay out of sight. I'll call you back as soon as I can. Jack out."

Jack herded his sleepy girls, still wearing their pajamas, onto the dock. Each carried a backpack with their clothes and a sleeping bag. Jack carried a plastic shopping bag filled with bottled water, crackers, cookies, and a jar of peanut butter.

"Get into the first boat girls, the one we used before," Jack whispered.

"But, Dad, we don't have our life jackets," Carol said.

"We don't have time Carol; so we're going to risk it," Jack said.

Mary gave her father an odd look but said nothing. They each stepped into the boat, and Janet lost her balance. To keep from falling into the water, she jumped to the bottom of the boat with a loud thump. Her sisters laughed.

Jack gave them a soft shush. "Remember our game, girls," he said. "No talking."

The still-groggy girls sat in the boat and grew quiet. Jack rowed across the dark lake. The two cats stood in the front of the boat and looked ahead of them. He wanted the cats to stay home but gave in to Janet's whines. He knew their presence would calm her during their night of camping. Their dogs, who would bark and possibly draw attention to the girls, remained in their home.

Ten minutes later he beached the boat on the familiar mud bank. The cats darted into the dark forest, and he helped the girls out of the boat. Jack looked back across the lake. So far, no vehicle had approached their home. He grabbed the small tent he'd thrown into the boat and led the girls into the forest.

"Girls, there's still no talking." Jack and his girls walked away from the lake. Silence surrounded them, and not even a light breeze stirred the trees. Soon they came to a small clearing. "Okay, we're here," Jack said.

Jack set up the tent and helped each girl lay out her sleeping bag. Soon all three lay in their bags ready to resume their night's sleep.

"Janet, call the cats so they can sleep with you," he said. "I don't want them in the forest."

"Okay Daddy," Janet said.

A few seconds later both cats ran between his legs and into the tent. Jack sat on the ground outside the tent's door.

Carol looked at her father. "Dad, where's your sleeping bag?"

"I don't have one. I'm a soldier. I sleep in my uniform. Now let's all go to sleep. I brought water and snacks for your breakfast in the morning. Good night girls."

Janet and Carol said, "Good night, Dad."

Mary gave her father a withering stare. She lay down and closed her eyes. Soon Janet and Carol fell asleep.

Jack reached in the tent and shook Mary's shoulder. "Mary, come with me. Don't wake your sisters." Mary slipped from the tent and followed her father for a short distance.

Jack got down on one knee in front of his daughter. "I think you know we're not camping, don't you?"

She crossed her arms in front of her chest. "What's going on Dad?"

Jack stared at her. She looked like her mother in that pose. He pushed the thought away.

"Mary, you're almost a teenager, so I need to tell you what's going on." Mary stood taller but she kept her arms crossed. "Do you know about terrorists? Do you know what they do?"

She nodded. "Sure. We studied them in school. They killed all those people on 911 in New York."

"That's correct honey. Well, some terrorists came to Show Me Army Depot tonight and they killed some of our friends. Someone you know." Mary gasped and covered her mouth. "I brought you girls here to hide you. They may come to our house to try to hurt me or you girls."

She let out a small gasp, and a tear rolled down her cheek. "Are they really here, Dad?"

"Yes, they're here, and I need you to take care of your sisters and keep them safe."

Her eyes grew wide. "But Dad, you'll be here with us."

"No honey I won't." Mary drew in a sharp breath. "The terrorists took many of our friends hostage. I need to go to the police for help."

"No, Dad. Let someone else go." She flung herself at her father.

He held his daughter tight. "Mary I can't. You girls are safe as long as you stay here. The terrorists won't know to look for you here in the forest. You go to sleep and in the morning, you keep your sisters here and away from the lake and any roads. If any forest animals come around, you get your sisters into a tree. They won't stay long. It may be tomorrow night, but I will come and get you."

"Dad, this is wrong. You almost died in Afghanistan, and now it's happening again." Mary sobbed and looked at the ground.

Jack looked at his daughter. "Who told you about Afghanistan?"

Mary took a breath. "A television reporter stopped Grandpa and Grandma at the mall. Grandpa said he didn't want to talk to him, but he turned on his camera anyway. He talked about you running through the enemy in Afghanistan; he said they tried to kill you."

Jack knew the man from his broadcasts. He hoped he would meet him someday so he could punch him in the mouth for scaring his girls. "Mary, I was never in that much danger. But here, tonight there are moms and dads with kids like you in terrible danger, and I'm the only one who can help them."

She wiped the tears from her eyes with the back of her hand. She didn't speak for several moments. Finally, she nodded. "Okay, Dad. I can do it. I'll take care of Janet and Carol." She clenched her fists and frowned at her father. "But be careful. We need you."

"I promise I'll be careful. Thank you, Mary. I knew I could count on my big girl."

Jack gave his daughter a long hug and held her hand on the walk to the tent.

She got into her sleeping bag and tucked her arm under her head. He zipped the front flap shut, then stood and jogged back towards the lake.

Ten minutes later the boat bumped up against the dock. Jack tied it off and froze. He spotted headlights moving up the road towards their quarters. He slipped off the dock and angled into the trees. He hid on the forest floor and watched the approaching vehicle. Soon he recognized June

Miksic's security truck. Its headlights went out a hundred yards from the house. The truck turned towards his house and pulled up to the front door.

Three men carrying AK-47s exited the truck and went to the front door. Soon the door opened, and the men entered. Jack frowned. He wondered how the terrorists obtained a key to his front door.

Jack heard the dogs barking, and the lights went on in all the rooms in the house. The dogs continued to bark. A few minutes later two shots rang out, and the barking stopped. The men came out the back door and swept the surrounding yard. Finding nothing, they even went into the garage. Jack heard them opening and closing the doors of his SUV.

The three men left the garage and returned to their truck. They ignored the dock and its boats. The men spoke together for a short time and got in the truck. Jack stood behind a large tree and watched them drive away.

He needed to get law enforcement on his depot now. The blackout left him with one option; make his way to Highway 61 and flag down a ride. But first, he needed a weapon. Jack's own firearms sat miles away in the Security arms room. He knew Liam Torgerson kept a few rifles and shotguns in his land management office. The office, more of an equipment storage building used as an office, sat on the other side of his headquarters. The terrorists using security's trucks ruled out him driving his car or riding a bike; too visible. Jack took off running through the forest.

When he came to the depot's main road he slowed and crept to the edge of the trees. Staying concealed, he scanned the area where his guards died. Soon he spotted the outline of a security pickup sitting within the trees across the road. Cigarettes glowed in the truck's cab. The terrorists waited for any unsuspecting employees to pass through the gate.

Jack kept to the shadows and moved away from the truck. Soon he again ran through the thick trees.

He Who Watches listened to the soft breathing of the human cubs. He scanned the area around them. Except for a few mice that gnawed on fragments of bleached animal bone, nothing moved in the forest.

He knew many humans died tonight in this place; killed by human intruders. He sensed many others in grave danger. When he scanned the intruders, he found they came from a distant land and traveled long to get here. Dark thoughts and deeds, along with hatred and ignorance, filled their minds. He Who Watches shuddered at the things he glimpsed. They were demons here to harm the cubs, the human male, and many others.

The spirits brought him here to find and protect the youngest cub. The spirits told him the young cub would affect the world someday. Fortunately, the human male followed He Who Watch's subtle hints telling him of this hidden spot in the forest.

He Who Watches decided he also needed to protect the human male. The loss of their mother years ago traumatized the cubs. It impacted the smallest cub the most; even affecting her health. If anything happened to the human male, it could cost the youngest cub her life.

He looked at his sleeping charges through a small screen on top of the tent. He liked the noisy, high-spirited cubs.

Their laughter and carefree thoughts, so common to the young of all forest animals, made him feel content and upbeat. In his solitary life, he never felt that way.

He saw the two cats looking back at him through the screen. *Stupid cats. You cats stay with the cubs and go to sleep.*

One of the cats responded. *What if we don't want to?*

He stomped the ground with his huge foot, and the tent shuddered. *If you leave the cubs, I will find you and step on you.*

We will stay! Both cats sent.

He Who Watches stood and moved deeper into the forest. The cubs were safe here. He would check on them while the human intruders remained nearby. But for now, he needed to catch up to the cub's father.

Chapter 18

September 13, 2015, 2155 (CST) Show Me Army Depot, Missouri

Abdul opened the cafeteria door, and his fighters shoved the firemen inside. The large room echoed with boisterous laughter and conversation. Several employees stood near the microwaves and coffee pots located along one wall, but most sat at large tables located in the center of the room. Open doors to male and female locker rooms stood on the other side of the room. The air smelled of hot coffee and reheated leftovers along with pine-scented cleaner.

No one noticed the fighters' entrance. Abdul fired his pistol into the ceiling. Several women screamed once and stared at the terrorists. Fighters ran to the employees by the microwaves and used their AK-47s to push them towards the tables.

One man protested his rough treatment. "Hey, don't touch me." They pushed him harder, and he took a seat.

Abdul motioned to two fighters to check the locker rooms. They returned, shaking their heads. The four firemen shuffled to the tables and sat. A few employees whispered questions to them. The firemen kept their heads down and said nothing.

Over a dozen fighters, their weapons leveled, surrounded the ninety employees. A few male employees stood up from their meals. Someone yelled. "These exercises suck!"

Abdul raised his voice. "SIT DOWN!"

The men looked at the rifles held by the fighters and sat. All the ISIS fighters, except for Abdul, covered their faces with black bandanas.

"Ladies and gentlemen please remain quiet, and I will tell you what is happening," Abdul said.

Many of the employees smiled at Abdul's men. In the center of the room an employee tried to stand, but a large man pulled him back down. Abdul noticed the large man watching his fighters. The large man had a dangerous aura about him. He told himself to keep an eye on the big man.

An employee, the same one who protested earlier, stood. "Why should we listen to you? We've gone through these exercises before and they're always a waste of time." He crossed his arms across his chest and smirked at Abdul.

Abdul turned to him. "I was about to ask for a volunteer. You have excellent timing."

He shot the man in the forehead. Blood spurted on several nearby employees, and he dropped to the floor. Now many of the women screamed, and a dozen men stood. Abdul's fighters prepared to fire.

Abdul's pulse quickened as he watched the blood pool around the dead man. He wanted to shoot someone else but decided one was enough for his demonstration.

He yelled into the room. "DO NOT MOVE!" This froze the employees again, and they stared at him. "If you move, my men will kill you, and I want you alive." He holstered his pistol and moved his hands in a downward motion. "Please sit down. No one will harm you." The men looked at each other, and one by one they sat. "That's it. Good. Sit down and we will hurt no one."

Once everyone returned to their seats, Abdul spoke. "Ladies and gentlemen, I can assure you this is no exercise." He stood tall and faced the employees. "I come from Syria, and I am known as Abdul al-Britani."

"What do you want?" an employee said.

Abdul turned but missed who spoke. He did not appreciate being interrupted. "What I want is to stop your facility from providing ammunition to the Zionist military forces that fight us in Syria and Iraq. These Zionists oppose our peaceful operations and commit many war crimes with your munitions. We will dismantle, so to speak, important parts of your depot so it cannot send ammunition to the Middle East or anywhere else."

Abdul paced in front of the staring workers. "We know that you are simple employees of the criminal Zionist-backed American government. You are trying to earn a living and feed your families." He stopped and smiled at the employees. "None of you care about Iraq, Syria, or Afghanistan and you made no decision to send the ammunition used in war crimes."

Abdul enjoyed the terrified looks on the employees' faces. Lecturing these Americans felt much like when he taught Sharia law to the conquered people of Iraq and Syria.

"Because you are innocent of the crimes of your government, we hold no malice towards you. You will remain here, while we work to shut down your facility." He gestured towards his men. "Three of my fighters will remain here with you. If you try to escape or contact anyone, we will kill you."

Three fighters carried video cameras mounted on tripods. They positioned the cameras about ten feet apart and faced them towards the employees.

Abdul motioned to the cameras. "In the morning we will return and interview many of you. We want to record your opinions on the illegal wars your government inflicts on peace-loving Islamic peoples. Once we complete the interviews, we will leave you unharmed."

Abdul's smile grew. The videos would earn significant funds for ISIS when brokers sold them. Many news networks would pay well for footage of his fighters beheading US citizens on American soil.

He took a piece of paper from his pocket and read it. "Where is Will Miksic?" No one moved.

"Will Miksic, please stand up. You won't be harmed."

A man stood and faced Abdul. "I'm Will Miksic." The man's body shook. "Shit, Iraq, fuck, cock."

Abdul's smile vanished. "Very funny, Will Miksic." He pointed his pistol at him.

"No!" A tall woman yelled and leaped from her seat and stood in front of the employee.

"Please don't hurt him," she said. "He has an illness called Tourette syndrome. He can't help what he says. He doesn't mean any harm."

Abdul dropped his arm and laughed. A few of his fighters joined in. "I have heard of this disease." He looked at Will. "Don't worry; I won't shoot you because of your affliction. Will Miksic, do you have the keys to the magazines?"

Will nodded. He reached under the table and raised his right arm. He held a large key ring holding hundreds of keys.

"Excellent," Abdul said. "Will Miksic, you will come with us and unlock the magazine where you store the C4 explosive." Abdul looked at the woman. "Please return to your seat miss. We won't hurt your friend. Once he completes his important task, he will return here to wait with the rest of you."

The woman sat. Abdul signaled, and Will walked towards him. Three feet from him Will again shook. His keys jingled like a large baby rattle. Abdul focused on him.

"Fuck, shit, dick, Iraq," Will said.

Abdul again laughed. This time all his fighters laughed. Even a few of the employees laughed. Abdul put his arm around Will and walked him to the door.

"You make me laugh, Will. Few people can do that."

He yelled at his men in Arabic, and they ran outside. Three fighters remained; their rifles pointed at the employees.

The SUV and the rental truck drove down the dark road. Since entering the ammunition storage area, their headlights illuminated a continuous stream of ammunition storage magazines. After several miles, Abdul's brow rose as he grasped the true size of the American depot. He wished he had enough time and men to blow this Zionist facility off the face of the earth.

"Turn here," Joe said. "It's in the fourth magazine."

Will stirred in the back seat. "Joe, why are you helping these guys?"

"Because they're paying me a lot of money, you dumb hick." Joe turned in his seat and looked at Will. "Why do you care? No one in this damn depot ever gave a rat's ass about anything I did before."

"You're a Goddamn traitor," Will said. "I'm going to make sure everyone in the union knows it." He began to shake. "Fuck, cock, traitor, shit."

Joe laughed. "You can tell the union whatever you want. I'll be in South America counting my money. I'll toast you with a margarita while you flap your gums to your idiot union friends."

"Shut up both of you," Abdul said. "I will shoot the next person who speaks." Both men ceased talking.

The vehicles pulled up in front of a magazine, and the large truck backed up to the loading dock. The truck's door rolled up, and the ISIS fighters stepped out.

Abdul pointed at the massive metal door. "Open it my funny friend."

Will unlocked the large door and tugged it open. He used a large brick to hold the door against the magazine wall.

Abdul entered the structure and his jaw dropped. The magazine had tall concrete walls that stretched thirty meters to the back wall. Before him hundreds of wood boxes sat six high on pallets arranged in neat rows. He walked to the nearest pallet. The stenciling on the box stated 'CHARGE, DEMOLITION M112 COMP C4.' He stopped at another pallet. These boxes read 'CHARGE, DEMOLITION ASSEMBLY M183 COMP C4.' On the adjacent pallet the boxes read 'CORD, DETONATING, M978'. He recognized the items from his time in the Army.

Abdul turned to one of the Saudis standing in the door. "This is what we need."

The Saudi smiled.

Abdul stared at the explosives and rubbed his chin. He wondered if he should use explosives to execute the employees in the cafeteria. It would work but it would make a terrible mess. Also, he did not want his cameras damaged. He decided they would use their knives. They worked well in Syria and made dramatic video.

He stepped outside the magazine and saw the Koreans pull up in their vehicles. Their rented box truck backed up to the dock and parked next to his. The truck's door rolled up, and fifteen armed commandos, wearing North Korean-issue camouflage uniforms, stepped onto the dock. Victor and the North Korean Special Forces leader he met yesterday, Major Lee Chae Jul, approached him.

A camouflage uniform stretched across Victor's ample frame. The uniform's buttons were ready to pop, and a white undershirt showed through gaps in his blouse. A small pistol rested in a holster on his belt.

"Is it here?" Victor said.

"Yes, it's here," Abdul said. "More than we need."

Victor and Major Lee walked into the magazine. When they returned, they both smiled at Abdul.

"I like that the Americans provide the explosives for the destruction of their depot," Abdul said.

"I agree, it is quite ironic," Victor said. He turned to Major Lee. "How much do we need?"

The officer referred to a small notepad. "To ensure complete destruction, we need five hundred kilograms on each end of the bridge and fifty kilograms for each rail spur."

Victor nodded. "That is one thousand kilograms for the bridge. That is your task, Abdul." He faced Major Lee. "The rail yard has twenty spurs, so that is also one thousand kilograms for you Major Lee." He waved his hand. "Get the trucks loaded."

Major Lee shouted orders to his men. Soon both groups carried boxes of explosives to the trucks. The Koreans stacked their boxes into a neat cube in the back of their truck. Abdul's fighters threw the heavy crates into a loose pile in the back of their truck. When they finished two of his fighters sat on the crates and smoked cigarettes.

Major Lee turned to Victor. "Where are the detonators?"

"How should I know?" Victor said. "Check inside the magazine."

Major Lee barked a command. Two soldiers saluted and ran into the large magazine. The ISIS fighters pointed and laughed at the two Koreans. After five minutes the soldiers returned and reported to Major Lee.

He nodded at his soldiers and turned to Victor. "There are no blasting caps or detonators in the magazine. My soldiers searched it three times and found nothing. We have no way to set off the explosives."

Victor's face flushed. "What? That cannot be correct." He ran into the magazine. A minute later he ran back out and grabbed Joe Harper.

"You said the explosives would be in this magazine!"

"They're here," Joe said. "You loaded your trucks with everything you need."

"No! We need detonators to set off the explosives."

Joe shrugged. "Can't you set it off by shooting it or setting it on fire?"

Victor clenched his fists. "No!" Spit flew from his mouth. "You stupid Americans designed C4 so it will not explode when you shoot it or set it on fire! We must have the detonators."

"Someone must've moved them," Joe said.

Victor got into Joe's face. "I'm starting to regret paying you a lot of money, Mr. Harper."

Major Lee yelled at him in Korean.

Abdul pulled out his stiletto and displayed it to Joe. "Mr. Harper, where are the blasting caps?"

Joe's eyes grew big, and he backed away from the three men.

Will laughed. "Joe, you're a dumbass; they're in another magazine."

Victor turned to Will "What did you say?"

"I said the blasting caps are somewhere else. They were never here."

Victor's eyes narrowed. "Why is that?"

"Keeping blasting caps in the same magazine with bulk explosives is way too dangerous. Only a fool would do that. They're stored somewhere else for safety reasons." Will's body began to twitch. "Cock, fat ass, fuck, shit."

Victor stared at Will. He walked up to the taller employee and punched him in the face. Will swung at Victor, but the spy dodged it and sent a kick to his head. Will fell to all fours and blood dripped from his lip.

"If the detonators were never here, where are they?" Victor said.

"I don't know!" Will said. "They're in some other magazine." He gestured at the open door. "I didn't even know this magazine had C4 in it. There are too many for me to keep track of. We use the storage planning system to locate the ammunition. Cock, fuck, gook, dick."

"Then use the storage planning system to find the detonators," Victor said. "Hurry, before I kick you again."

"The system is down," Joe said.

Victor waved his arms in the air. "Make it functional. Immediately."

Joe shoved his hands in his pockets. "It runs off the internet, and we have no internet with the communication blackout. But we can search different magazines until we find the detonators."

"How long will that take?" Victor said.

"I don't know," Joe said. He would not look at Victor. "A long time."

"How many magazines do you have?" Abdul said.

Will shook his key ring. "Just over three thousand, and I have three hundred keys with me."

Victor did not move for a moment. Then he grabbed Joe and slammed him against the magazine door. He drew his pistol and placed the muzzle underneath Joe's chin.

"We will take the explosives and begin our work," Victor said. "You find those detonators and bring them to me by the time the sun comes up, or I will shoot you. Is that clear Mr. Harper?"

Spittle ran down Joe's chin and he stared at Victor. He nodded. "I'll find them."

Victor pushed the man away. "Johnny, you stay with this idiot while he searches. Contact us by radio when you find the detonators."

"But I wanted to stay with the group and help plant the explosives," Johnny said.

"Do as I say!" Victor said.

Johnny grabbed the heavy key ring from Will and handed it to Joe. He pulled the trembling man away from Victor and to the pickup. They drove off and stopped at the next magazine.

Victor pointed at Will. "Abdul, return this babbling fool to the cafeteria and begin your work at the gate." The fat spy faced the Korean leader. "Major Lee prepare your target for destruction. The detonators will arrive as soon as they can."

Abdul nodded and yelled instructions to his men. A fighter grabbed Will and pushed him into the back of the rental truck.

Victor turned to Abdul. "I'm coming with you. Use the explosives you have and prepare the bridge for destruction. When you finish, set up defenses so no one can remove the explosives. We may have to hold off the police until we find the detonators."

"My men and I look forward to a fight with the Americans," Abdul said.

Victor's jaw clenched. "Don't be too happy. We must stop this depot from sending its ammunition to South Korea. If we fail, my government will deny your caliphate the nuclear weapon it desires."

Abdul smiled. "Victor, you are correct to worry. But Allah placed me in much worse situations, and I always achieved victory. Your Johnny will produce the detonators, and we will complete our mission."

Victor scowled. "I will stop worrying when the bridge and the rail yard are rubble. Now get moving before I lose my patience."

Chapter 19

September 13, 2015, 2300 (CST) Show Me Army Depot, Missouri

Abdul drove towards the depot's entrance. The rental truck carrying the explosives and his fighters followed close behind. His men that surveilled the ammunition gate reported they could not find the depot's military commander or his children. They were not in the home when they arrived; it appeared he and his family had fled the house in a rush.

Victor's jaw clenched. "A senior member of the United States Army is now unaccounted for in the middle of our operation."

"He is one man looking after his children," Abdul said. "What can he do against our greater numbers?"

"Do not underestimate this man. He killed many Taliban and rescued an isolated American unit while in Afghanistan."

Abdul shrugged. "My fighters are better than the Taliban. I'll assign another three men to search for the missing American once we reach the entrance."

"No. Send three men after you place the explosives on the bridge."

They arrived at the entrance and exited their vehicles. Victor pointed at the bridge. "I want explosives on both ends of the bridge, so it collapses and blocks the highway and the rail lines. With the bridge down, no one can get in or out of this depot. In addition, we can stop highway and rail traffic supporting this facility."

Abdul nodded. "I concur."

He gave the instructions to his Saudi subordinates. His men jumped in the large truck and drove towards the bridge. A vehicle left the highway and headed across the bridge towards the entrance. The vehicle approached, and Abdul identified it as an American police cruiser. The Saudi driving the truck pulled over and stopped.

Victor turned to Abdul. "You handle this." He stepped behind the guard booth.

Abdul turned to the two ISIS fighters dressed as security guards and spoke in Arabic. "Get ready to kill that policeman."

One guard fed a belt of ammunition into the PKM machine gun that sat on the booth's floor. Earlier, the two bogus guards removed the booth's window glass to accommodate the large gun.

The cruiser had a typical police paint job; white with green trim. Cedar County Sheriff in large gold letters adorned its sides. The car held one occupant. The cruiser drove up next to the rental truck and stopped.

Abdul watched as the Saudi got out of the truck and spoke with the police officer. The young man pointed towards the security booth, and the police officer followed his point. Abdul waved at the officer.

The Saudi returned to his truck and drove it away from the police cruiser. The truck veered to the right; well away from the path of the expected gunfire.

Abdul saw the officer bring his microphone up to his mouth. He turned to his men in the booth. "Shoot him," Abdul said.

A fighter picked up the machine gun and dropped it on the desk. He centered the police cruiser in the gun's sights. The weapon fired, and two dozen rounds shredded the cruiser's hood, windshield, and dash. Abdul watched the man die with the radio still in his hand.

The gunner ceased fire, and the other guard sprinted up to the cruiser and opened the driver's door. He put a bullet into the officer's head. The radio called for the deceased deputy, and the ISIS fighter shot the radio.

Abdul yelled at the fighter. "Drive the car into the forest behind the gate!" The false guard pushed the dead policeman across the seat. Soon the cruiser moved off the road and towards the trees.

When the guard returned, he carried an M4 carbine taken from the cruiser. He gave the weapon to Abdul and resumed his position in the booth.

The men smiled. "Allah favored us," one said.

"Yes, he did," Abdul said.

Victor walked up to Abdul. "The policeman used his radio before you killed him. At least two other police cars will respond to this location within the next ten minutes. You need to stop them on the highway before they reach the bridge, so we can continue our work. Be prepared for them to approach from both directions."

Abdul turned to his guards. "Get up on the bridge and stop the Americans from approaching. Use both machine guns."

The two men grabbed the machine gun and ran towards the bridge. Abdul followed close behind. One detoured to the rental truck and grabbed the other light machine gun and several cans of ammunition. A fighter went to where the road met the bridge and faced north. The other fighter did the same but faced south. Both men positioned their weapons to fire down onto the highway.

Abdul went to each man and checked their setup. Both could spot approaching traffic for several miles.

He called the two men to him. "Two American police vehicles are on their way. Stop them at least one thousand meters away. After that I want no vehicles to pass. Also, the police may try to gain access to the depot on foot." He pointed at the rail lines lying between the highway and the depot's perimeter. "If the police try to cross the railroad tracks, fire on them and stop them." Abdul placed his hands on the two men's shoulders. "Tonight, you became the first ISIS fighters to ever fire on American law enforcement. Grateful Muslims everywhere will know your names." Both men stood taller.

"Take your positions," Abdul said. "When we finish mining the bridge, I will reinforce you in holding off the police."

Abdul watched as the men returned to their positions and lay down behind their guns. Soon two vehicles with flashing lights and wailing sirens approached from the North. When the vehicles came in range the fighter fired several quick bursts. When the tracers connected with the vehicle, he fired much longer bursts.

One half mile from the depot exit, deputy sheriff Ben Crockett spotted many small, bright flashes on the highway overpass that funneled traffic into Show Me Army Depot. At the same time, small streaks of green light connected with the state police cruiser two hundred meters in front of him.

The damaged cruiser turned into the median and rolled. The heavy vehicle's velocity threw it into the air and sent it through five complete rotations. Mud and debris flew from the cruiser until it stopped upright on four flat tires. The lifeless body of the female state trooper, still belted into the seat, hung half out the shattered driver side window.

Now the green tracer rounds zoomed past his vehicle. Ben pumped his brakes and dodged the debris that littered the road. He slid into the median and stopped next to the destroyed cruiser. He could hardly recognize the twisted and shattered vehicle.

Ducking the fire from the bridge, Ben ran through the grass and dove behind the wrecked cruiser. Rounds continued to hit the smashed vehicle. Glass, bits of metal, and flakes of automobile paint pelted him. He knew no simple assault rifle spat rounds at him. The weapon fired fast, and it sounded like the light machine guns the Al Qaeda terrorists used during his time in Fallujah. He crawled over to Leslie and checked for a pulse.

He took a deep breath and grabbed the radio handset at the top of his shirt. "Officer down! Officer down! This is one lima forty. I have ten thirty-two shots fired in the vicinity of the Show Mc Army Depot entrance. Whoever's shooting has the entire highway under direct fire. They killed Leslie and took out my cruiser with heavy fire."

"Roger one lima forty we're rolling backup and an ambulance to your location," dispatch said.

Ben spotted a semi-truck coming down the highway towards him. He tried to flag down the truck, but machine gun fire drove him back behind the car. With the truck two hundred meters away, the unknown gunner shifted his fire. Dozens of rounds hit the engine compartment of the big rig. Oil, diesel fuel, and hot coolant spilled onto the highway, and steam billowed up over the hood. The driver slammed on his brakes. The gunfire appeared to cut a brake line because the rear end of the long box trailer swung forward and tried to pass the braking tractor. Additional rounds hit the truck's windshield leaving a neat grouping centered on the driver. The jackknifed truck slid down the highway directly towards him.

Ben used the distraction of the truck to sprint away from the destroyed cruiser. He dodged the swinging trailer that went on to smash into both police vehicles. He heard a tremendous crash followed by a loud 'whoosh' from a gas tank bursting into flames.

Ben dashed up the highway. Once out of range, he slowed and stopped. He put his hands on his knees and sucked in great gasps of air. He watched the flames consume the crashed vehicles, then turned and heard the faint sirens of the approaching backup. By force of habit, he reached for his smartphone to call his wife. Ben found no phone in its holder. He looked at his burning SUV and sighed.

Major Lee pointed. "Stop the truck there," he said.

The truck carrying him, and his soldiers stopped near a loading dock located on the west side of the rail yard. Behind him his soldiers rolled up the truck's door and jumped out.

Major Lee left the cab and looked at the large rail yard. Tall poles that held mounted flood lights surrounded the yard and lit up the entire area. Ten soccer fields could easily fit into the large area. A dozen empty rail cars sat waiting for movement into the depot.

He heard one of his soldiers groan and then speak. "This is going to take all night."

Major Lee walked up to the soldier and slapped him hard across the face. All the soldiers stiffened to attention.

"Anyone else have a comment?" he said. No one moved.

He faced his gathered team. "Private Yun is correct; we have a difficult task tonight. However, it is an important one." He looked into each man's eyes. "What I say to you now is top secret. Our enemies in the south would torture me without mercy to learn of it, but it is important for you to know why we conduct this dangerous mission."

The soldiers glanced at each other. "Two days from now our nation's armed forces will attack into South Korea to reunify our great nation." He paused as the eyes of his soldiers grew wide. "I expect many difficult battles, but our nation will prevail." He gestured at the rail yard before them. "To support the invasion, we must prevent this depot from sending its munitions to the American and South Korean militaries. Failure here would endanger our nation and the Dear Leader."

Lee pointed into the yard. "We will mine these tracks and we will defend this location until the detonators arrive. When our mission is complete, we will return to our homeland and help our comrades defeat the corrupt South." He paused to let his words sink in. "I expect all of you to accompany me when I march into Seoul and arrest the puppet South Korean president. After that we can adjourn to a quiet bar for a fine meal of kimchi, rice, and Soju." His men smiled. "Are there any questions?" No one spoke.

"Senior Sergeant Kim," Lee said.

The senior sergeant ran up to Major Lee and saluted. "Sir."

Lee gave his orders. "Sergeant, I want charges laid at the north and south end of each rail line. When you finish placing the explosives, start digging defensive positions at the southern end of the rail yard. We will defend against anyone who tries to stop us. Once we have the detonators you will initiate the explosives in sequence with enough delay for us to reach a safe location."

"Yes Sir," Kim said.

Lee continued. "I want sensors placed around each side of the rail yard. I also want our surveillance drones up in the next fifteen minutes. I want to spot any approaching enemy force long before they get here."

A pained look crossed the Senior Sergeant's face. "What is it?" Lee said.

"The batteries for the sensors and drones did not survive the trip from Wonsan."

"None of them?"

Sergeant Kim looked at the ground. "None. Salt water leaked into the container. I checked them myself."

Major Lee frowned. "We now occupy this installation. Speak to the fat spy and get American batteries for our systems."

"The batteries are not compatible, Sir. We must have batteries manufactured in our homeland."

Major Lee took a deep breath and held it. He let it out. "Fine. Forget about the surveillance tools. Just complete your work."

The senior sergeant saluted. He turned and rattled off orders to his junior sergeants. In a few moments, the men ran into the yard carrying boxes of explosives to the points designated by their leader.

Major Lee placed his hands on his hips and watched his team move to their task. He trained them hard, and one of his soldiers died as a result. But that training meant he would put his men up against any other Special Forces team in the world.

However, as he observed his men a small butterfly quivered within his stomach. The missing detonators and now the damaged batteries were bad omens for this mission. He reached into his trouser pocket and stroked the lucky coin given to him many years ago by his wife.

Suddenly Major Lee whipped his body around and brought his rifle to his shoulder. He swung the rifle from right to left and scanned the nearby tree line for a target. He paused and stared hard at a large shadow. After a full twenty seconds, he lowered his weapon and examined the dark forest. He had exceptional hearing, and something in the trees had made a noise. But he saw nothing. He slung his rifle on his shoulder. He took one more look at the forest and headed towards the southern end of the rail yard. He rubbed his lucky coin while he walked.

He Who Watches stood motionless and watched the human intruder walk away. His carelessness allowed the human to detect him, but he blocked its mind before it could use its terrible thunder stick. Dismissing his close call, he observed the other humans among the iron roads. He knew the large metal beasts came through this area. Their round feet traveled on the iron roads in front of him.

The smell of the massive metal beasts and the loud screeching of their metal feet always distressed him. He hated it when they called to the others of their kind. He often heard nearby dogs and coyotes howling in reaction to the call of a metal beast. Throughout his life, he avoided areas like this one. But he knew this new group of human intruders would kill the cub's father if they could. So, he watched them and puzzled over their actions among the iron roads.

He scanned the leader's mind; the one that detected him. He determined the intruders wanted to destroy the iron roads to prevent the passage of the metal beasts. Destroying the iron roads pleased him. If they caused no harm to the human male, he would let them destroy the iron roads. With no iron roads, he would not have to see or hear the dreaded metal beasts.

Despite this, he would keep a close watch on this group. But for now, he needed to check on the other human intruders and the human male.

Chapter 20

September 14, 2015, 2345 (CST) Show Me Army Depot, Missouri

Jack jogged up to Liam Torgerson's office. It sat inside a large clearing half a mile from the main road. Windows, two garage doors, metal siding and peeling paint marked it as a typical depot building. He spotted several pickup trucks parked in front of the garage doors. He opened the front door, and a pitch-black interior greeted him. Jack entered and fumbled for the light switch. He kicked a trash can across the floor and made a terrible racket.

Someone let out a high-pitched scream. "Eeeeeyaaaaahhhh!" Two figures charged out of the darkness and attacked him.

Jack wondered why the terrorists were inside this obscure and hard to find building. Were they everywhere inside his depot? He did his best to defend himself; he swung at shadows as they moved around him.

Jack connected two good punches, but his attackers struck back. One kicked him in the stomach. The air rushed from his lungs, and he gasped.

One attacker yelled at the other. "Hold him, Conner!"

Jack recognized the voice. "Liam it's me!" Jack yelled. "Colonel Black Eagle!" He felt his assailants pause but both continued to hold his arms. Jack ceased struggling. "Liam. It's me, Jack. I need your help."

Someone scrambled over to a wall, and the office filled with light. Liam stood by the light switch wearing red gym shorts and a white undershirt. He carried a sawed-off baseball bat. A man recognizable as Rita's brother, and wearing underwear, stood next to Jack.

"Colonel, what are you doing here?" Liam said. "It's the middle of the night!" He slapped the short bat into his palm. "You just about met my persuader. We've had some things go missing, so we thought you was the thief coming back for more." He walked towards Jack. "I'm awful sorry. I hope Conner and I didn't rough you up too bad."

"I'm fine Liam, but we have a big problem. Turn out the lights; we don't want them to see us."

Liam's brow furrowed. "Why do I need to turn out the lights? What are you talking about, Colonel?"

"I know this sounds crazy, but terrorists have attacked our depot."

Liam frowned and looked at the clock. "Colonel, it's very late for a training drill. Security usually runs them before lunch so we can get back to work in the afternoon."

"I'm telling the truth, guys. I saw them murder June Miksic and the night shift guard at the ammunition gate. Look at this." Jack pointed to the blood stains on his uniform's sleeves.

Both men gasped. "God damn," Liam said. He walked over and hit the light switch. He went to a cabinet and took out a small kerosene lamp. Soon they crowded around the small circle of lamplight.

"My God, June Miksic," Liam said. "I can't believe she's dead."

"They're the only ones I know of," Jack said. "If the terrorists came through the main gate, I suspect they killed those guards as well. And I can't get anyone from security to answer my calls."

"There are nine or ten people on security duty tonight," Conner said.

"I believe the terrorists got to our security people. I just hope they're captured and not dead.

Liam's eyes opened wide. "God damn."

"Why did the terrorists pick Show Me Army Depot?" Conner said. "What do they want?"

Jack rubbed his chin. "I don't know. Most terrorists target unarmed locations like a hospital or a mall. It makes no sense for them to attack a secure base like our depot. I have no idea who they are or how many are here."

"Where are they now?" Liam said.

Jack shrugged. "No idea. I spotted three terrorists hiding in a truck at the ammunition gate. That's why I'm on foot. Some others may be at the cafeteria holding our night shift people hostage."

"God damn," Liam said.

"Shorty Cramer's watching the terrorists at the cafeteria. He saw them go into the cafeteria from his truck. He thinks a lot of our people are inside."

"Did he say how many terrorists were in the cafeteria?" Liam said.

"No. He mentioned a couple of vehicles to include a large rental truck. The truck I saw could carry a lot of terrorists."

"What are the police doing about this?" Conner said.

"I don't think the police know with the communication outage."

Liam's brow creased. "The police have to know."

"Think about it, Liam," Jack said. "We have no phones or internet, and our gigantic depot is twenty miles from Cedar City. We could have hundreds of terrorists running around here, and the police would never know."

They heard a rapid popping noise outside. The three men rushed out the door. More pops in several short spurts followed by a long unbroken string came through the air above the trees.

"Well, the police will know soon enough," Jack said. "That's gunfire; and it's near the depot's entrance. Shooting that close to the highway; the police will respond soon."

"I think that's a light machine gun," Conner said.

Jack nodded. "I think you're right. I saw others armed with AK-47s." He turned to his friend. "Liam, what firearms do you have here? It's obvious these terrorists are trigger happy. I need to get to the cafeteria and free our people before they start executing hostages."

"Sure, Colonel, I have a few guns. But now that the police know, shouldn't we let them handle the terrorists?" The men paused and listened to another long burst of gunfire.

"I wish I could, but I don't think they can get past a machine gun. Do they have an armored car or a surplus MRAP?"

"No," Conner said. "They have Crown Vics and SUVs."

Jack nodded. "The only option the police have is to block the highway and wait for help. And waiting is the worst thing possible in a hostage situation. The terrorists can kill our people according to their plan. It's happened many times around the world. I need to get to the cafeteria before they get organized."

Jack's radio squawked. "Colonel, this is Shorty. Are you there?"

Jack grabbed his radio. "Shorty, I'm here. What can you tell me about the cafeteria?"

"Those vehicles I saw took off, so I went to the cafeteria and looked in the windows. I hope you're not mad. I'm sure no one saw me."

"It's ok," Jack said. "What's happening at the cafeteria?"

"I saw the terrorists, and it looks like they have all the night shift people inside. They put our people in the center of the cafeteria, and the terrorists are guarding them."

"Did they have any of our security people?" Jack said.

"No security, but I'm pretty sure I saw our firemen there."

Jack exchanged looks with Liam. "How did our people look? Did you get a count of the terrorists?"

"Everyone looks ok, and I spotted three terrorists inside. They're carrying those cheap ass AKs like they sell at the sporting goods store downtown. One thing looked odd, Colonel. The terrorists have several fancy video cameras set up in the cafeteria like they're going to film something."

A sick feeling settling into Jack's stomach, but he kept his concerns to himself. "Shorty, that's a good update. Get back to your truck and wait for me. I'll be there soon. Jack out."

Jack turned to Liam. "I'm going to the cafeteria to free our people."

"Why do they have cameras?" Liam said.

"Dad, they're going to film themselves murdering our employees and get in on the news," Conner said. "It's what they do."

Liam's hands clenched and he walked in a small circle returning to Jack and Conner. "That is God damn unbelievable," he said. "Colonel, we're going with you." Conner nodded at Jack.

Jack looked at the men standing before him. "I appreciate the offer, but you're civilians. I can't ask you to risk your lives going up against terrorists."

Liam snorted. "Colonel, do you think this is the first time we've ever heard gunfire? I fought in 'Nam, and Conner has tours in Iraq and Afghanistan."

"I'm still in the Guard," Conner said.

"Why hell, I had a poacher take a shot at me three seasons ago," Liam said. "And you've seen how Rita shoots. You want her on your side." Jack said nothing. Liam spoke in a low voice. "Colonel, you would have to tie us to these bunk beds to keep us from getting the bastards who shot June Miksic."

Jack's shoulders slumped. "Thank you, Liam. To be honest I didn't want to go alone."

Liam gave Jack a huge grin and slapped him on the back. "God damn, Colonel. It'll be like hunting feral hogs."

Jack hoped it could be that easy. As they filed inside the building, he noticed the two men's clothing. "Liam, why are you sleeping in your office?"

"We planned to hunt hogs at dawn, and it's easier to sleep here." Liam pointed to Rita who snored in a bunk bed tucked against a wall.

Conner stuck out his hand to Jack. "Colonel, I'm Conner Torgerson. Sorry I kicked you."

Jack examined the younger man. He pegged Conner's age at around thirty-five, and he had the same wiry build, light skin and blond hair as his father.

Jack shook his hand. "Nice to meet you, Conner. Don't worry about it. When this is over, I'll kick you and we'll be even."

Conner grinned. "I heard about COP Armstrong during my tour in Jalalabad."

"Are you Army?" Jack said.

"Missouri Army National Guard; I'm a warrant officer in military intelligence. I saw the analysis of that stuff you collected off that dead Taliban. We took out some real bad guys with that info. I wanted to say thanks."

Jack drank water from a bottle offered by Liam. "Glad I could help; although, I had a lot of luck getting it. Are you a linguist?"

"Yes, Sir. I speak Pashto, Dari, and Arabic. I also know some German and French."

Jack nodded. "I'm glad you're going with me, Conner."

Liam walked over and shook Rita awake. While they dressed, Liam filled Rita in on the situation. Soon all three stood wearing boots, blue jeans, and camouflage shirts and hats.

"Liam let's see your weapons," Jack said.

Liam opened a closet. "We've got Rita's rifle, a bolt action thirty ought six, a pump shotgun, a .22 revolver, and about two hundred rounds of ammo."

"Less than ideal against AK-47s but they'll have to do," Jack said. "Rita, you take your rifle. Liam, you get the deer rifle. Conner, you carry the shotgun. I'll make do with the pistol." He headed to the door. "Are you all up for a run tonight? We can't take your truck; the terrorists at the ammunition gate are waiting for that."

"I've got an idea, Colonel," Liam said.

He led Jack to three quad bikes parked behind the building. "We use these when we hunt feral hogs. We can keep our lights off when we're on the roads." Liam snapped his fingers. "Better yet, we can avoid the roads and follow the fire breaks through the forest. There's no way the terrorists know about our firebreaks."

"Don't they make a lot of noise? What if the terrorists hear us?" Jack said.

"We modified them so we can sneak up on the hogs." Liam used a flashlight to illuminate an oversized muffler attached to the quad vehicle. "Listen to this."

He started the engine and twisted the throttle. The small vehicle made almost no sound. The metal parts rotating inside the engine made more noise than the exhaust coming from the muffler.

"All three have a muffler like this," Liam said. "Once I drove into a hog before he knew I was there." He laughed. "You should've seen that sucker take off."

"Dad, I'm taking my bike," Conner said.

He walked over to a shed and pulled out a well-used dirt bike. The motorcycle's exhaust also vented to an oversized muffler. Conner kicked the motor to life on the first try. The cycle made no more noise than the quad vehicle.

"Our objective is the cafeteria, but we need to take out the group at the ammunition gate first," Jack said. "They're in a pickup truck on the north side of the road beyond the gate. All three have AK-47s."

Liam took charge. "Conner, you lead. I'll follow you, and the Colonel will follow me. Rita, you trail. I want to stop at least one hundred yards behind those guys and approach them on foot. Keep your lights off." He looked at the sky. "We have a half-moon tonight so we should be able to see ok. Let's move at a good clip."

They mounted their vehicles, and the small convoy sped away from the building. Jack found it surreal that three men and one woman, in rural Missouri and armed with hunting firearms, rode recreational vehicles to do battle with international terrorists. He would have one hell of an after-action review for the Army; if he survived the next few hours.

Ten minutes later they sped down an unmarked fire trail. Soon they turned onto a much smaller trail. Jack had little experience with the small, but powerful, vehicle. It took all his concentration to stay on the trail while keeping up with Liam. At one point he hit a depression, and his boots left the vehicle's foot pegs. The front tires hit another bump and threw him back into the seat. Jack's pulse raced and he reduced the throttle.

Soon, Conner slowed and stopped. The rest pulled up and shut off their vehicles. All four riders dismounted.

Liam grabbed Jack's arm and whispered. "You did good, Colonel. You must ride all the time."

Jack said nothing; his heart still thumped from his close call.

Liam looked at Rita and Conner. "Check it out."

Without a word Conner and Rita put their weapons at port arms and slipped into the forest.

Jack moved to follow, but Liam grabbed his arm. Liam shook his head and pointed at the ground. Jack nodded and crouched at the base of a large tree.

Ten minutes later they both returned. The group huddled. Conner pointed into the forest and spoke in low tones. "The ammunition gate is two hundred yards in that direction." He swung his point thirty degrees. "The terrorists are in a security pickup one hundred yards that way. It appears two are asleep with one on guard. He's smoking cigarettes and watching the road. I didn't see any weapons but I'm certain they're armed like the Colonel said."

"What's the plan?" Liam said.

Jack looked at Conner. "Can you interrogate these guys if we capture them?"

"I can, Colonel, but that's risky. It's four against three, and we can't afford to get into a wrestling match."

"That's a valid concern Conner, but we need intelligence on these guys," Jack said. "Lead us to the truck. If you can take one of them alive with little risk, do it. If it goes to shit; take them out."

Conner and Rita nodded and headed towards the terrorists. Jack and Liam followed. He cocked his head as he saw how easily the brother and sister moved through the forest. They looked like ghosts as they flowed over and around the logs and leaves that littered the forest floor. Jack worked hard just to keep from tripping. Soon they halted and huddled again.

"The truck is one hundred feet in front of us," Conner said.

Jack looked but saw only trees.

"Rita and I are heading in. Colonel, you and Dad wait here."

Liam and Jack nodded. Conner and Rita melted into the forest. Jack stood for several minutes but moved to a large tree and waited for Conner's signal. A few moments after he reached the tree, a scream came from the truck's location, and Conner's shotgun fired once. Liam moved towards the unseen truck and left Jack behind.

Before he could take a step, Jack caught movement from the corner of his eye. A dim shape lurched through the dark forest twenty feet to his left. Jack made a slow turn and recognized a man carrying an AK-47 in one hand and what looked like a roll of toilet paper in the other. The same hand holding the toilet paper clutched his pants hanging halfway to his knees. The man had no idea Jack watched him.

Slow is smooth, smooth is fast.

Jack drew his pistol and fired into the man's center of mass. The man sagged, and Jack shot him again. The figure fell to the ground. Jack approached the still form. Keeping his gun pointed at the figure, he checked for a pulse and found none.

Someone grabbed his shoulder, and he almost screamed. He turned to confront his attacker. Liam directed Jack's pistol up in the air, and at the last second, Jack recognized his friend.

His heart pounded, and he whispered. "Don't sneak up on me like that!"

Liam smiled. "Sorry, Colonel."

Jack gestured towards the body. "This guy's dead. I think he was taking a crap. What happened at the truck?"

"They got one guy."

Liam led Jack to the security truck. A dead terrorist sat slumped in the cab. Conner and Rita crouched at the front of the truck scanning for threats.

Conner looked at Jack and whispered. "Did you get one, Colonel?"

"I did. What happened here?"

"We caught one guy in the truck. He lit a cigarette right when I grabbed the door handle. I had to shoot him. Sorry, Colonel."

"That's all right. I'm just glad you're ok. Where's the other one?"

Conner pointed. "I think he's in the guard shack at the gate."

They heard a bird calling from the direction of the gate. "That's no bird from around here," Liam said. "That's got to be a signal to his buddies."

"Get ready," Conner said. He yelled in Arabic. "My gun went off by accident! But praise Allah, I am not hurt! You can come back to the truck now!"

Jack smiled upon hearing Conner's excellent Arabic. A man carrying an AK-47 stepped from the guard hut and looked at the truck.

The terrorist yelled at them. "What's going on? I heard more than one shot! Is Nabil hurt?"

"Nabil is fine! But he got scared like he is a woman!" Conner laughed. "Come look; he shit his pants!"

The terrorist took a few tentative steps toward the truck. "Nabil, are you injured?"

"Nabil went to clean the shit from his dirty ass," Conner said.

The terrorist laughed, but raised his rifle and fired half his magazine at the truck. The four ducked, and the rounds stitched the truck's cab and the surrounding trees. The man turned and ran up the main road.

"Stop him," Jack said.

Liam stepped clear of the trees. His rifle barked, and the running man dropped his rifle and fell forward. Rita and Liam ran to the prone terrorist and drug him into the woods.

While Jack kept guard, Conner used the flashlight app on his phone to study the terrorist in the truck. He placed the dead man's assault rifle on the hood of the truck and ran off to find the terrorist Jack shot.

Liam and Rita returned to the pickup carrying the dropped AK-47. They pulled the dead terrorist from the cab and drug him into the forest. Conner returned with the other man's rifle and spread the contents of the dead men's pockets on the hood of the truck.

A small radio on the truck's hood squawked. "Unit Two, I heard gunfire from your area."

Conner looked at Jack. "Do you want me to respond?"

"Yes. Say they stopped and killed a lone employee in a truck. They remain on guard at the gate."

Conner responded to the speaker saying, "Yes Sir" and "praise Allah" many times. Jack thought Conner spoke better Arabic than most Iraqis he'd known. Soon Conner ended the transmission.

"Did he believe you?" Jack said.

"I think so. The guy had a British accent, so I had trouble understanding him. He said when they completed their work at the entrance; he would call this group back."

"What would the terrorists be doing at the entrance?" Liam said.

"He didn't say, and I didn't want to ask. I didn't want to press my luck."

"You did fine, Conner." Jack turned to the items on the hood of the truck. "What have you got?"

"Sir, the terrorists are Arabs," Conner said. "Most likely from Egypt, Saudi Arabia, or Iraq. They had Mexican pesos in their pockets, and the uniforms are knock-offs of the old woodland battle dress uniform purchased in Mexico."

"So, we know how they got here," Jack said.

"All three shaved off their beards so they could blend in better over here. But now they're growing them back, and that tells me they're Jihadists."

"Are they Al Qaeda?" Jack said.

Conner displayed a small black flag featuring white Arabic letters. "They're ISIS. Their plan to film themselves executing their prisoners confirms it. They've killed innocents like that dozens of times in Syria and Iraq."

Jack thought for several seconds. "So, ISIS finally made it to the US." He rubbed the stubble on his chin. "But it still puzzles me that they came here; a military base in the middle of nowhere. It doesn't make any sense."

Jack looked at the three men. "Good rundown, Conner." He turned to Liam. "We need to get to the cafeteria." Jack grabbed one of the AK-47s and examined it. "We need more firepower to handle the next group of terrorists. Rita, you keep your rifle, but Conner, Liam, and I will switch to the AK-47s. Gather up all their ammunition before we leave."

Liam turned to his son. "Conner, same drill. Stop about a quarter mile behind the cafeteria."

They turned and headed back into the woods.

Chapter 21

September 14, 2015, 0030 (CST) Show Me Army Depot, Missouri

Jack left his quad as Conner stepped from the forest. Liam and Rita followed him as all four came together to get Conner's update.

Conner pointed. "The cafeteria is two hundred meters that way, Colonel."

Jack sniffed the air. "What's burning?"

"The security building is on fire," Conner said. "It's pretty far away, but from what I could see it's pretty much gone."

Jack looked in the direction of the cafeteria. "There's nothing we can do about that now. Our focus is the hostages." He faced the Torgersons. "This time we'll all go together. I need to know how many terrorists are inside, their location, and what they're doing. Let's go."

In a few minutes, they came to the cafeteria. They faced a large brick wall with industrial windows set high above their heads; the cafeteria's rear wall.

"Conner, Rita, you two find the best windows to see what's going on inside," Jack said. "Liam and I will stay here. Keep out of sight but spot those terrorists. Get back here ASAP." The siblings moved off towards the back of the building.

Liam pointed above them and whispered. "Those windows lead into the locker room showers." Jack nodded.

When they returned, the group huddled and exchanged information with whispers.

"Shorty's correct," Rita said. "Our people are inside along with three terrorists." She pointed to orient Jack and Liam to the locations within the building. "One terrorist is on a chair in front of the hostages, one's walking back and forth in front of the hostages, and one's over by the counter. The one by the counter looks like he's sleeping. All three have AK-47s."

"How do our people look?" Jack said.

"Everyone looks ok," Conner said. "About half of them are asleep. The others are watching the terrorists. I did see blood on the floor, so I think someone's hurt."

Jack's jaw clenched and Liam put his hand on his shoulder. "Don't worry, Colonel. We'll get them out."

"Can we go in the front door?" Jack said.

Rita shook her head. "It's too far from the sitting terrorist. He'll hear us and react before we can. He'll shoot us, or the hostages, and the others will join in. It's the same for the back door."

Jack looked at the window above his head. "Can anyone see me if I go through this window?"

Liam shook his head. "No, there's a wall that shields the room from the door. Even if a terrorist is in there taking a piss, he can't see into the showers."

Jack thought for a moment. "Here's the plan," Jack said. "Liam and I will enter through this window. We'll lure the terrorists in one at a time and take them out. Conner and Rita, you two go to the front entrance and wait. If you hear a commotion, it means we screwed up. You come in shooting. They'll be focused on us, so you can get in fast and take them out before they can harm the hostages."

"Sounds like a plan, Colonel," Rita said.

Jack slung his weapon over his back and allowed the others to boost him to the window. He pushed it open and heard a small squeak. He froze. When nothing happened, he scrambled through and dropped to the floor. The concrete room smelled of chlorine and water dripped from a shower head making loud metallic plops. Liam soon appeared in the window, and Jack helped him down. Both men crouched on the floor of the shower.

They crept from the shower, and Liam checked under the stalls. They inched towards the door to the cafeteria. Jack peeked out and spotted a terrorist on a chair to his left and the sleeping terrorist by the coffee pots. He pulled back when the roving terrorist passed the door.

Jack guessed he had about thirty seconds until the terrorist returned. He scanned the large room. Half the employees had their heads down on the tables trying to sleep. Don Miksic sat in the center of the group and Natalie and Will sat across from him. Will had his head down, and Natalie rested her chin on her hand. Don stared directly at Jack. The roving guard returned, and Jack ducked again.

Jack signaled to Don that he wanted Natalie to come into the restroom. Don pointed at himself and tilted his head. Jack shook his head no. He tried communicating several more times even pointing to the sign in the restroom entrance that said 'WOMEN.' Finally, Don whispered to Natalie. She stiffened but kept her eyes on the table. Natalie stood, and the roving guard paused.

"I have to use the restroom," Natalie said.

The roving guard spoke with the guard on the chair.

He turned to her. "Okay. You hurry or I shoot you." The two terrorists laughed.

Natalie walked into the restroom. She wore her normal blue jean overalls and a white T-shirt. She approached Jack, and tears welled up in her eyes.

He put his hand on her arm and whispered. "Hang on, Natalie. Conner and Rita are outside. We're going to get everyone out."

Natalie brushed the tears from her eyes and nodded. She took a deep breath. "What do you need me to do, Colonel?"

"Get the walking guard in here so we can knock him out. Once he's down, we'll get the others in here."

Natalie looked at Jack. "How can I do that?"

"I don't know," Jack said. "Wave at him or something but get him in here."

Natalie nodded. Jack and Liam crouched on both sides of the entrance and waited. Natalie walked over to a toilet and flushed it. When she heard the walking guard approach, she stepped into the door and flashed the terrorist a big smile. The man walked past the entrance.

Jack looked at Natalie. "What's wrong? Did he see you? Why didn't he come in?"

Natalie frowned. "I don't know. I've never lured a man into a restroom before."

"Try again," Jack said.

The guard approached again, and Natalie moved to the door. This time she put her hand on her hip. The guard appeared, and she smiled and formed her lips into a silent kiss. The guard again continued past the door.

Jack tiptoed up to Natalie. "What's the problem? We need him in here."

Her hands formed clenched fists and she turned to Jack. "Would you like to try it, Colonel? I think he might be gay!"

Jack smiled. "I'm sorry, Natalie. You're doing great. Try again. Please."

Again, the guard approached. Natalie's chin jutted up in the air, and her slim jaw hardened. She undid the snaps on her overalls and let the bib fall to her waist. She undid the snap on her bra. After a few seconds of wiggling, she pulled her bra down out of her t-shirt and threw it into the corner. Natalie lifted her t-shirt exposing her pert breasts. Jack stared and hoped she didn't consider him a leering pervert. Liam looked at the floor; his face red.

Natalie glanced at Jack and stepped into the entrance. This time the man stopped. Natalie darted back into the restroom and stood against the far wall. She dropped her t-shirt, but her nipples showed through the thin material. In a few seconds, the terrorist came to the door and stared at Natalie. She stared back at him. Jack and Liam froze. The man walked towards Natalie, and they slipped behind him.

Before they could hit him, the radio on Jack's belt blared. "Colonel, this is Shorty. Come back."

The terrorist swung his weapon towards Jack. Jack dropped his own weapon and moved inside his opponent's swing. He tackled him above the waist, and both men fell. Liam swung his rifle butt at the terrorist's head. His swing missed, and he fell on top of the terrorist and Jack.

All three men threw punches as they battled for the rifle that lay underneath them. The terrorist yelled in Arabic and his elbow connected with Jack's shoulder. Jack grimaced when the man's breath, reeking of Chinese food and cigarettes, hit him full in the face. He tried to move, but Liam was on top of him. A shadow fell over them. Jack looked up to see the terrorist from the chair aiming at his head. Natalie screamed, and Jack heard the blast of a rifle.

Chapter 22

September 14, 2015, 0100 (CST) Show Me Army Depot, Missouri

Jack cringed. When he felt no pain, he opened his eyes. He continued to scuffle with the terrorist and he and Liam appeared uninjured. A huge hand reached down and grabbed the terrorist by the back of the neck. The man grimaced and ceased struggling. Don Miksic pushed Jack aside and hauled the terrorist off the floor and slammed him into the block wall. The terrorist's eyes rolled up into his head, and Don released him to fall to the floor. Jack sat up and saw the terrorist who tried to shoot him lying in the door with his head twisted at an awkward angle.

Don had the dead man's rifle slung over his shoulder. "About time you got here, Colonel."

"I heard a shot," Jack said. "Who fired?"

Don gestured to the room outside the door. "Rita killed the terrorist sleeping by the coffee pots."

Natalie kept her back to the men and buttoned up her overalls. Don spotted his daughter's cast-off bra and scowled at Jack.

Jack ignored his look. "Are there any more terrorists here?"

"No, just the three. The others left a while ago."

"Did they hurt anyone?"

"They killed Klinder when they came in, but everyone else is ok."

Jack nodded. "Don't let anyone leave. We don't know where the terrorists are, but they're watching the roads. Our people could drive into them." Don turned and walked out of the room. Jack and Liam picked themselves up off the floor. Jack examined himself and found several new bruises on his chest. Liam grabbed his rifle and left the room.

Natalie walked over to Jack and paused. She grabbed his arm and reached up and gave him a quick kiss on the cheek. She gave him a big smile. "Thank you for saving us, Colonel. When the terrorists showed up, I remembered you lived on the depot. I knew you wouldn't run and hide." She grabbed her bra from the floor and stuffed it into her pocket. "Please don't tell anyone I showed you my breasts. A lot of terrible gossips work here, and some are in that room. If they knew, I'd spend half my time defending my reputation."

"I…I would never tell anyone, Natalie."

Her smile got even wider, and she gave him another quick kiss; this time on the lips. "And you really don't want Dad to know." She winked at Jack and stepped over the dead terrorist in the entrance.

Jack rubbed his cheek and touched his lips. "What the hell?"

He grabbed his rifle and walked out the door.

Jack sat at a table with Liam, Ross Kelly, Shorty Cramer, Don, Will, and Natalie. He nursed a much-needed cup of coffee. Rita and Conner, along with a few men from the cafeteria, stood guard outside. The unconscious terrorist, trussed up with duct tape, lay in a locked janitor's closet. The rest of the employees sat around them.

"Colonel, when can we go home?" an employee said.

Jack stood and addressed the group. "You're all safe now, but we don't have a count on the terrorists or their location. You've all seen that they won't hesitate to kill one of us. For now, I need you to stay here while I come up with a plan."

"Can we call our families and let them know we're safe?" another employee said.

"You can. However, you're forgetting about the communication blackout." Everyone pulled out their cell phones, but no one had any bars. "I'm sure your families are fine. I don't' know for sure but I suspect the terrorists are not in Cedar City. I think they want something here at the depot. Please be patient, and I'll get you all home soon." The people turned away and Jack sat down.

Jack looked at Shorty. "Your radio call almost got me killed Shorty."

"Sorry, Colonel," Shorty said. "I spotted two people skulking around the entrance and I thought they were terrorists. I didn't know it was you guys here to rescue everyone."

"Thats ok, Shorty." Jack said. "You did what I told you to do. It's my fault I didn't warn you we were here." Jack took another drink from his coffee.

"Colonel, the terrorists took Will when they went to get some ammunition," Don said. "He can tell you something about them."

Will looked at Jack and nodded. He had a black eye and a lump on the side of his head.

"Tell me what you know, Will," Jack said.

"Joe Harper took the terrorists straight to a storage magazine. He had a map and knew the exact one to go to.

They made me open it. I didn't want to, but they said they'd kill me if I didn't."

Jack and Liam both gasped. "Joe Harper's working with the terrorists?"

Will nodded. "Yes, Sir. He said the union could go jump in a lake for all he cared. He said they paid him a lot of money, and he's going to Mexico or South America when the terrorists are done." Will's arms began to wave. "Shit, fuck, traitor, cock."

Jack frowned. "It's ok, Will. You did what you had to do to stay alive, but Joe Harper's actions are shocking." Jack's jaw clenched. "What ammunition did they take?"

"They took over two tons of C4."

Jack sat up straight. "Two tons!"

"They're on a demolition mission," Don said.

"Yes, but what are they blowing up?" Jack said. "Did they get anything else?"

"Just the C4," Will said. "But they screwed up big time. They didn't get any detonators. That dumbass Joe didn't know we don't store blasting caps with explosives." He chuckled. "They about killed him; they were so mad at him. He's out there now going through magazines one by one looking for blasting caps or detonators."

"Where is he?" Jack said. "What magazines?"

"I don't know. Hell, he could be anywhere by now Colonel."

"Well, that's good news. That gives us time to stop whatever they're planning." Jack crossed his arms. "Will, tell me about the terrorists. Describe them; where they come from, what they wore, and how they acted."

"Well, I saw two groups with about fifteen men in each, and they're carrying the C4 in two rented trucks." He started to shake again. "Ccccock, cock, cocksucker, shit, prick." Natalie rubbed her brother's shoulder until he calmed down. "One group is all Arabs led by some British guy. He wore real nice duds, and he did a lot of the talking." Will paused. "Colonel, the other group is Asians."

"Asians?" Jack said.

"Do you think it's China?" Ross said.

Jack shrugged. "I have no idea. Keep going, Will. Did you hear any of them speak?"

Will nodded. "Yes Sir, they spoke a lot. That fat fucker that runs that Chinese restaurant downtown was with them. He talked a lot, and he did this to me." Will pointed to his injuries, and his body trembled. "Fat prick, fuck, cock, cook."

"Victor Chow from China King Buffet?" Jack said.

"That's him," Will said. "I think he's their leader." He looked at his sister. "He makes some damn fine sweet and sour pork though."

"This story keeps getting stranger and stranger," Jack said. "What did their language sound like?"

"It's hard to describe," Will said. "I never heard anything like it. That fat Chinaman spoke with another man a lot. He kept calling him 'so rung' or 'so young'. It was something like that."

"You mean *so ryong*?" Jack said.

Will's eyes opened wide, and he pointed at Jack. "Yes Sir, that's it."

Jack leaned forward. "Tell me about their clothing."

"They wore cheap-looking camouflage uniforms with their rank on their collars. Like the Germans in those old war movies."

Jack's brow furrowed and he looked at Ross. "We're in real trouble. They're Koreans."

"Why would South Korea send terrorists to Show Me Army Depot?" Don said.

Jack kept his face neutral. He didn't want to piss off Don. "They're North Koreans."

"Oh," Don said.

Jack rubbed his chin. "Victor Chow must be a North Korean agent sent to spy on Show Me Army Depot. I don't have a clue why ISIS is working with them. That's not in any intelligence summary I've ever read. But North Korean soldiers operating within the United States, means they're dead serious about invading South Korea.

Jack looked at his employees. "I need to contact the Pentagon and let them know what's going on. I also need to warn the local police to stay off the depot. They could never stand up to North Korean soldiers and well-armed ISIS terrorists."

Jack looked at his phone again. "I'll bet this damn communication outage is part of this North Korean attack." He looked at his deputy. "Ross, the news reported two outages, correct?"

"Yes Sir," Ross said. "One around Kansas City that we're in and one in eastern Kentucky. I'm guessing Bourbon Army Depot is in that blackout zone. It's a big ammunition depot like us."

Jack slapped the table. "I'll bet terrorists are in Bourbon Army Depot like here.

"But why would the terrorists attack depots?" Ross said. "We don't have any soldiers or families here and we don't have any military equipment. You think they would want to attack a big base like Fort Hood or Fort Bragg."

"No listen," Jack said. "It makes a lot of sense. If the North Koreans could shut down Show Me Army Depot and Bourbon Army Depot, our combat units in Korea would not have enough ammunition for extended combat operations. They carry enough ammunition for three days of combat. They must have resupply on the fourth day, or they're toast. Even the Air Force's fighters and bombers would run out of ammunition."

Jack's insides turned cold as he thought of his in-laws living so close to the North Korean border. "With us taken out, the North would have a good chance of winning a war against the South." He looked at his deputy. "Ross, is there any way I can reach the Pentagon through this communication blackout? I must warn them right away."

Ross shook his head. "Everything we have runs on an AT&T backbone. When AT&T went down, we went down. No email, no internet, and no phones of any kind. It's the same for Bourbon Army Depot."

"What about that big radio tower by the old security office?" Natalie said. "Maybe you could use that to call someone."

Jack looked at Ross. "What old security office?"

"We moved to the current security building in the '90s," Ross said. "We never tore down the old office and antenna."

"What did they use such a big antenna for?" Jack said.

"I can tell you about that," Don said. "When I hired on after Vietnam, they told me Show Me depot was a communication hub for civil defense. They used that antenna for shortwave radio communication with other civil defense sites."

Jack looked at Ross. "Do you think the radio gear is still there?"

"We leave our unused buildings in good shape," Ross said. "The radio might still be there."

"We need to find out." Jack turned to Liam. "I need to speak to Conner and Rita."

Liam ran to get his kids, and they returned in a few minutes.

Jack turned to Don. "If I told you to put this depot out of commission; to stop it from sending ammunition to Korea, how would you do it using two tons of C4?"

Don thought for a moment. "The first thing I'd do is take out the railyard to stop the movement of any trains. Turn that place into a plowed field. When that's done, I'd blow up the bridge leading into the depot. With the bridge gone you have no truck shipments in or out of the depot."

Ross nodded. "I agree. If we lose the rail yard and the bridge, it'll take at least a month to get us moving again. And that's working on repairs twenty-four seven."

Jack turned to Conner and Rita. "I need to send you two out into the depot. Can you handle it?"

"Tell us what you need, Colonel," Conner said.

"I need info on the terrorists," Jack said. "Conner you go to the entrance, and Rita you go to the rail yard. Take radios, your motorcycle, and a quad bike. Stay hidden but find them. I must know their locations, numbers, weapons, and activities so I can target them and destroy them. Let me know as soon as you find them."

"Too easy, Sir," Conner said. Rita gripped her rifle and nodded. They turned and ran from the building.

Jack looked at the employees around him. "We need to get these people to safety. Is there a defendable location close by?"

"X-Ray," Don said. "It's about a mile away. They can go to the bomb fill building. The walls are three feet thick, and we can block the doors with empty bomb casings. No one could get in."

"Good," Jack said. "You're in charge, Don. Stay off the roads but get this entire group into X-Ray and hole up. We cannot have anyone else become a hostage."

Don clenched his fists and scowled at Jack. He barked at him. "Defend? Dammit, Colonel, we need to attack!"

"What's your problem Don?" Jack said.

Don stood. He grabbed an AK-47 and chambered a round. "I'm not going to X-Ray. I'm taking the AK-47s we have and I'm going after the terrorists. I'll take Will, Natalie, and some of the guys. We'll surprise them and we'll cut them to pieces."

"Don!" Jack said. "I got it. You want to kill these bastards. But we don't know anything about them. We don't even know where they are."

Don clenched his fists, and his knuckles turned white. "I thought you liked to fight, Colonel. You're not afraid, are you?"

Jack glared at him. "I saved your ass, didn't I? I say what happens on this depot, and you're not going."

"But we can take 'em," Don said. Will and Natalie nodded in agreement.

Jack stood and faced the big man. "Don, go back to your infantry training. We need to see the enemy, see the battlefield, and see ourselves. Right now, the only thing I know is I have six AK-47s, a deer rifle, a shotgun, a pistol, one soldier, and one hundred civilians. I cannot attack the enemy without more information." Jack ran his hand over his short hair. "We may end up taking these guys on, so that means I need you. I can't have you chasing terrorists around the depot without a plan and getting yourself killed. For now, I want you to take these people to a safe location. Please do that for me, while I try to get hold of the Pentagon."

Don's shoulders slumped. "Okay, Colonel. I'll do it." He squinted at Jack. "But I want in on any stand-up fight when it goes down. I want to kill these bastards *real* bad."

Jack nodded. "I promise, Don. Hide the dead in the forest and take the prisoner with you when you go. Don't leave any clues for the terrorists."

Don, Will, and Natalie moved off to notify the employees. Five minutes later Don led them single file into the trees. Will and Natalie, both carrying AK-47s, brought up the rear.

Jack turned to Liam and Ross. Shorty Cramer stood next to the two men. "Shorty, why are you here? Why didn't you go to X-Ray with the others?"

Shorty grimaced. "Colonel, do you still want to talk to the police?" He looked at Ross as he spoke.

"Shorty, if you know a way, spill it. You won't get in trouble."

"Okay, Colonel. Follow me." Shorty led the three men to his ammunition truck. "I installed a police band radio in my truck last year so I could talk to my nephew in the state police. I know it's against regulations, but I like to keep in touch with him since his momma passed away."

"Shorty, that's outstanding," Jack said. Ross and Liam nodded.

Shorty keyed the radio. "Ricky, this is Uncle Shorty. Come back."

After a few seconds, the radio squawked. "Uncle Shorty, I can't talk right now. There's a big emergency at the Show Me Army Depot entrance. Wait…Uncle Shorty, are you calling from the depot? Are you inside the depot now?"

Shorty nodded. "Yes, Ricky, I'm on the depot, and I have Colonel Black Eagle here. He needs to speak with whoever is in charge out there. Right now."

"Wait one," Ricky said

Two minutes later a different voice came on the radio. "This is Uwell Yates, Cedar County sheriff. Who is this?"

Jack pumped his fist and grabbed the microphone. "This is Jack Black Eagle calling from Show Me Army Depot."

"Colonel, what the hell's going on? A state trooper is dead, and there's some nut with a machine gun shooting at us from your bridge."

"Uwell, I don't know all the details, but I have many dead employees and thirty armed terrorists on the depot."

"Jesus Christ," Uwell said. "How'd they get in?"

"I don't know. Keep your men away from the gate. You can't go against their heavy fire. But you must prevent the terrorists from getting to a school or hospital. Can you handle that?"

"We'll keep them inside the depot, Colonel," Uwell said.

"Can you contact anyone outside of the blackout zone? I need to alert the Pentagon."

"No, nothing works," Uwell said. "I sent a patrol car to the state capital just to update the governor. I can have a car carry your message to the capital. They can contact Washington for you."

"I'm going to try something here first," Jack said. "If it doesn't work, I'll get back with you.

"I'll stand by for your call," Uwell said. "Colonel, have you seen my missing deputy anywhere? His last transmission put him at the depot's gate."

Jack paused. "I'm sorry Uwell. We haven't seen him."

"Damn. Well please keep an eye out for him."

"I'll do that Uwell. Show Me depot out." Jack turned to Ross and Liam. "Let's go. If I can't get hold of the Pentagon we're screwed."

Chapter 23

September 14, 2015, 0130 (CST) Show Me Army Depot, Missouri

Jack and Liam burst into the last office in the old security building and almost tripped each other in the process. Jack hit the light switch, and the one remaining bulb in the ceiling went on. A floor-to-ceiling cabinet sat in the back of the room. Jack opened it and saw shelves filled with 1970s era radio equipment. The official heading on a faded memo tacked inside stated: Federal Civil Defense Administration.

"This is it," Jack said.

Cables ran from the backs of the radios, and several plugs lay on the floor. Jack connected them all to a handy outlet.

Ross walked in the door. "It's still here. I can't believe it. Do you think it works after all these years?"

"I don't know," Jack said. "Cross your fingers." He held his breath and flipped the power switch, and three of the four radio sets lit up. "It works!" He looked at his partners. "Do you guys know how to work this thing?"

"Colonel, why don't you run through the frequencies until you hear someone speaking English," Ross said. "When you do, break into their conversation."

Jack rotated a large knob, and static burst from a small speaker. A voice speaking Spanish came on the line. He continued scanning and heard many more languages. Soon he heard two men speaking English. Their topic; tips for growing heirloom tomatoes.

Jack grabbed the microphone. "Mayday, mayday, mayday. This is Show Me Army Depot calling from Missouri." He looked at his friends and shrugged his shoulders. "Mayday, mayday, mayday. Show Me Army Depot calling please come in."

The voices on the radio paused. One said, "Give me a second Victor Kilo Seven Zulu Zulu. Unknown caller this is Kilo Hotel Niner One Two. I'm on a private call with a friend. We don't appreciate jokes on short wave radio in this part of the world."

Jack keyed the radio. "This is no joke, Sir. I have a real emergency and I need your help."

"Who is this and what are you trying to pull?"

Jack took a deep breath. "I'm Colonel Jack Black Eagle, United States Army. I'm in command of Show Me Army Depot in Missouri. In the United States. We're in a communication blackout, and I need your help to contact the Pentagon."

The radio stayed silent for a long time. "If you're Colonel Black Eagle, which unit did you serve with in Afghanistan?"

Jack looked at Ross and Liam. "How does this guy know I served in Afghanistan?" Both men shrugged, and Jack keyed the radio. "I served with the 82d Airborne Division."

"Where did you fight? Where did you earn your silver star? What outpost?"

"Combat Outpost Armstrong," Jack said.

The voice on the radio said, "Victor Kilo Seven Zulu Zulu, I'll call you later. I need to deal with this right now."

Another voice with an Australian accent came on. "Sounds like fun. Always good talking to you Kilo Hotel Niner One Two. Victor Kilo Seven Zulu Zulu out."

"Sorry, Colonel Black Eagle," the voice said. "I had to make sure it was you. Tell me about your emergency."

"There's an incident going on inside my depot, and I need help contacting the Pentagon." Jack paused. "How do you know so much about me?"

"They had an article on your silver star award in the Army Times. I read it a couple of months ago."

"I guess I missed that article," Jack said. "Can I have your name?"

"I'm Danny Mitchell and I'm a contractor working for the Missile Defense Agency in Kwajalein Atoll."

Jack cocked his head at Liam and turned back to the radio. "You're in the Pacific? What time is it there?"

"Yes, Sir I'm speaking to you from beautiful downtown Kwajalein where it's a balmy seventy-four degrees and sunny. The time is six thirty pm and it's September fourteenth. What time is it in Missouri?"

"It's one thirty in the morning," Jack said. "You sound like you talk on the radio a lot, Danny."

"Sorry. I was a disc jockey in Milwaukee before I took a job here. How can I help you, Colonel?"

Jack grabbed a cast-off chair and sat in front of the radio. "Danny, I need you to call the Pentagon. This is hard to believe, but my depot is under attack by terrorists. I'm unable to contact anyone because of this damn blackout."

"No kidding? Real terrorists? I heard about the communication blackout, but nothing about any terrorists."

"No one knows they're here except us," Jack said. "That's why I need to speak with the Pentagon."

"I have a military telephone line right here in my quarters, Colonel. Who would you like me to call?"

Jack pulled out his wallet and went through his business cards. "Danny, I want you to call my old boss from the 82d Airborne Division, Lieutenant General Cord McNally. He's the joint staff operations officer at the Pentagon." Jack gave the number to his new friend half a world away.

"Not a problem. I'll dial the number and connect my telephone to the radio. I'm letting you do the talking on this one."

"I can handle that, Danny," Jack said. After a few moments, he heard the phone ringing over the radio. After the fifth ring, a sleepy voice answered.

"Whoever this is, it better be God damned good."

Jack smiled and he yelled into the radio. "General McNally! It's Jack Black Eagle! I'm calling from Missouri! Sir, there's an urgent situation here, and I need some help!"

Liam and Ross jumped up and down, and Liam pounded Jack on the back.

"Jack? My phone says you're calling from Kwajalein. Why are you in the Pacific? Your command is in Missouri."

Jack heard the general's familiar temper and took several deep breaths. "General, I'm calling from Show Me Army Depot. I'm still in Missouri. We're in the communication blackout zone. The only way I could get through to you is with an old ham radio set. I have a friend in Kwajalein hooking us up through his phone."

"Ok, so why are you calling me in the middle of the night and pissing me off?"

"Sir, North Korean Special Forces and ISIS terrorists attacked my depot this evening. They killed a lot of my people and they're getting ready to destroy my infrastructure to stop me from deploying ammunition to Korea. Bourbon Army Depot in Kentucky may be in the same situation. I think the North Koreans do intend to invade the South if they're conducting military operations inside the US."

The line went silent for a few moments. "How do I know this is the real Jack Black Eagle? You're telling me a big tale on an unsecured line. You could be someone playing a prank, so they can record it and put it on the internet."

Jack thought for a moment. "Sir, you gave me a set of your old eagles in your office in Afghanistan when I made the colonels list."

McNally responded. "Okay, it's you. Give me a second." Jack heard the general groan as he got out of bed. "I'm heading downstairs to get some coffee. Run me through what's going on at Show Me Army Depot. It sounds like I need to wake up the Chairman and Homeland Security."

For the next ten minutes, Jack updated his old boss on the North Koreans and ISIS terrorists on Show Me Army Depot.

The general's temper again made an appearance. "This is unbelievable!"

Jack frowned. "Sir, if I could, I'd text you photos of the dead bodies. The terrorists are real."

"Relax Jack; I believe you. I'm pissed they got to you without anyone knowing. All our billions spent on intelligence and border security, and they walk right into your depot." The general cursed; Jack suspected he dropped his coffee cup. "Ok colonel, you're the guy on scene. What do you need from me?"

Jack thought for a moment. "I need Delta Force or Navy SEALs. Maybe even Infantry to clear these bastards out of my depot. They've got too much firepower for the local police. And Sir, I need it quick. They had a traitor inside my depot, and he gave them two tons of C4 from my magazines to destroy my rail lines and bridge." Jack looked at his watch. "My first trainload of ammunition for Korea leaves in eighteen hours. If they wreck my infrastructure, it'll take me a month to get any ammunition moving to the Korean theater."

"Okay, Jack. I'll get the ball rolling and let you know what we can send your way. You be prepared to receive them and get them into the fight."

"Will do Sir," Jack said. "What does it look like in Korea? My in-laws still live north of Seoul and last time I spoke with them they refused to relocate."

"It's lousy. The North is still on their side of the border, but they have most of their key units no more than two hours from the demilitarized zone. They've fooled our national leadership with their announcement about an exercise. With their big holiday starting, even the South Koreans are on the fence. If they're not careful, they'll peace talk themselves right into Kim Ha Jun's back pocket. Jack, how do I get back to you?"

"Danny, are you still on the line?" Jack said.

"Yes, Colonel, I'm here," Danny said. "General, I'll keep this radio connection open with Colonel Black Eagle. You can call me back and I'll connect you."

"Acknowledged," McNally said. "Jack, keep your head down. McNally out."

The line went dead, and Jack thanked Danny for his help. He turned to his friends. "Now we wait."

The Chairman of the Joint Chiefs of Staff stormed into his office with Sturm and McNally following close behind.

Thirty minutes ago, the three men briefed the President, the Secretary of Defense, and the Director of Homeland Security on the terrorist attacks in Missouri and Kentucky. Yellin threw his briefing folder on his desk and walked over to the shelves lining the wall. He grabbed a silver chalice presented to him by King Abdullah of Saudi Arabia. Without a word he turned and threw the heavy object against the bulletproof windows of his office. The chalice made a huge bang and left a small chip in the thick glass. Sturm and McNally tensed but said nothing.

"I cannot believe they refused to send Seal Team Six," Yellin said. "And that idiot labor secretary. Where does he get off telling me a strike by union employees shut down that depot? Does he think we're complete morons?"

"To be fair he did have emails and photos from a union official in Missouri showing they're on strike," Sturm said.

"But I have Colonel Jack Black Eagle telling me that's bullshit, and that terrorists are inside his depot killing his people." Yellin wrung his hands together as he looked up at the ceiling. "My God. A senior Army officer has already killed several terrorists. What the hell does the administration think is going on there? What do I have to do to get them to believe us; FEDEX the bloody head of a terrorist to the White House?"

Yellin stood in the middle of his office and took several deep breaths. He pointed at his friend Sturm. "You'd better get ready because once this is over, I'm resigning. I'll go to the Washington Post and tell the entire world about this incompetent administration, and how they failed to act."

"Calm down Anthony," Sturm said. "What are we going to do now?"

The chairman started to pace in front of his desk. After a few moments, he looked at Sturm. "You think I'm kidding about resigning?"

Sturm nodded. "I know you don't kid. What's our plan?"

The Chairman yelled to his executive officer in the outer office. "Toby, get in here!"

An Army brigadier general stepped in the office. "Yes, Sir?"

"Get me Deangello Fogle at Fort Bragg. Wake him up. I need to speak to him right away."

The executive officer raced from the room. Yellin paced as he waited for the call to connect. The phone on his desk buzzed, and he pushed its button.

"Major General Fogle on the line Sir," Toby said.

Yellin heard a click. "Major General Fogle here, Sir."

"Dea, it's Anthony Yellin. You're on speaker phone with Sturm and McNally. Listen up. Do you have anyone in lockdown for a training jump?"

"Yes, Sir. I have the third battalion of the five oh four jumping later today."

"Dea, this may result in you and me losing our stars, but I have a serious crisis going on."

"What do you need, general?" Fogle said. "I'm ok with retiring as a one star."

Yellin chuckled. "It's colonels if we're lucky, Dea." He took a deep breath. "We have North Korean and ISIS terrorists in at least platoon strength on Show Me Army Depot in Missouri and Bourbon Army Depot in Kentucky. We think they're trying to take out our capability to deploy ammunition to South Korea. If they knock out those two depots, the North has a green light to invade South Korea."

"You're kidding," Fogle said.

Yellin rubbed his forehead as he spoke. "By God, I wish I was kidding, but it's true. They've killed some people on Show Me Army Depot but so far, their deployment capability is still intact. I have zero information on Bourbon Army Depot. The local police are outgunned and cannot engage. I need you to launch one C-130 full of light infantry to each depot ASAP. Make sure they have live ammunition. Pull it from your ready stocks if you need to. I want your forces to parachute in and conduct a movement to contact and destroy those terrorist forces."

"Has the National Command Authority blessed this movement?"

Yellin stared at a small US flag on his office wall. "That's the rub, Dea. There is no NCA approval for this movement of forces. In fact, a few minutes ago the administration denied my request to send Navy SEALs." He threw his hands in the air. "Hell, the administration thinks the entire thing is a fairy tale. I'm out of options and that's why I'm calling you."

Yellin's phone remained silent for several moments. "Hooah, Sir. We can do it. I'll get two rifle companies moving but I need someone to speed up the four fortieth air wing."

"We'll make that happen, Dea." Yellin gestured, and McNally left to make the call. "We'll call the wing right after this. We'll tell them it's an exercise. Make sure you give your leaders a good mission statement and commander's intent because you'll lose contact once they drop into the blackout zones. And Dea when I say I need these forces deployed right away, I require wheels up no more than two hours from this phone call. I need ninety minutes or one hour if you can make it."

The line went silent again for several seconds. "We'll make two hours General."

"Good man. One other thing; the situation in Korea is going to shit. I know you're not included in the Korea operation plan, but I need you to pull in your entire division and prepare it to deploy. I'm adding your division and several Air Force fighter squadrons to the front of the line for a rapid show of force. I'll need you to parachute into South Korea in a very visible manner. It'll send a strong signal to North Korea."

Yellin heard the younger general take a deep breath. "Sir, I'll have my division ready to go. We can deploy for South Korea once the Air Force provides the aircraft."

Yellin smiled at Fogle's can-do attitude. "Dea, I appreciate this."

"It's my pleasure, General. Unless you have other instructions, I must get my units off the ground."

Yellin looked at Sturm and the big man shook his head. "That's it. Good luck to your soldiers and God speed. Dea, if you cannot stop these terrorists, it means the start of a second Korean war."

"I understand Sir."

"Yellin out." He disconnected the call and looked at Sturm. "I hope they make it in time."

Chapter 24

September 14, 2015, 0600 (CST) /0700 (EST) Fort Bragg, North Carolina

Major General Deangello "Dea" Fogle watched the two C-130 Hercules aircraft turn and fly off in different directions. He failed to meet the time he promised the Chairman, but two aircraft full of paratroopers launched in two and one-half hours would go into the record books.

Earlier, he tried to stay out of the way while sixty-four soldiers marched into each four-engine transport. The soldiers carried all their small arms to include their M240 machine guns. They had more than enough firepower and warfighting skills to handle any terrorist force. He shook his head. North Korea and ISIS initiated military operations in the middle of the United States, and no one in Washington knew anything about it. He still found it hard to believe. To top it off the Chairman of the Joint Chiefs of Staff deployed military forces while he kept the White House in the dark. He hoped he never experienced another morning like this one.

He lost sight of the aircraft and walked back to his vehicle. His aide opened his door. "Let's skip breakfast, Rick," Fogle said. "I've got a division to deploy."

A South Korean expat with a green card sat in a deer stand high in the top of a large tree off Manchester Road in Spring Lake, North Carolina. His perch gave him an unobstructed view of Pope Field.

Seven years ago, the man's large gambling debt at the nearby Moratok Indian casino, and his far-left social media postings, brought him to the attention of North Korean intelligence. Threats to reveal his addiction to his wife, along with a monthly stipend, convinced him to conduct a few intelligence gathering tasks each year for his new friends.

Yesterday his handler sent him south from his apartment in Raleigh to the huge Fort Bragg military installation. The handler ordered him to report by phone the departure of any military aircraft carrying soldiers from the large base. His handler provided him camouflage clothing, the collapsible deer stand, a pair of binoculars, and a disposable cell phone with two preset numbers.

Now, when both cargo aircraft flew over his hiding place, he dialed the first number. The phone rang five times and went to voicemail. He thought it odd that no one answered but he left a detailed message and hung up.

He dialed the second number. After two rings a man picked up. "Yes?"

"Two C-130 aircraft carrying armed soldiers departed Pope Field, in North Carolina at 7:00 A.M. eastern standard time. One aircraft headed due west and the other flew northwest."

"Message received," the unknown man said.

The man in the tree spoke again. "I had two numbers to call, but the first one went to voicemail. Is that standard procedure? Because I think I need to speak to a live person."

"What are you talking about?" the unknown man said.

The observer repeated his question.

The unknown man screamed into the phone. "How should I know? Do your damn job!"

The unknown man's screams startled the observer, and he dropped the phone. When he recovered, he climbed down and retrieved it. It still worked so he tried the first number six more times with no answer. He shrugged, climbed back up to his spot, and resumed his observation of the air base.

Soon the unanswered call dominated his thoughts. He felt his handler would blame him for the missed communication. He wanted to call his handler and explain the situation, but he had no permanent phone number for the man. His handler always contacted him. He sighed and resumed his observation of the base. He wanted to continue getting paid by North Korean intelligence and he did not want his wife to find out about his gambling.

Second Lieutenant Paul Craig sat on the C-130's uncomfortable nylon webbing bench. The rough seat gave him a terrible itch on his butt. However, with the soldiers jammed next to him and with his gear and reserve parachute sitting on top of him, he could not reach his ass. He clenched and unclenched his butt muscles for over a minute, but it didn't work. He sighed. He would take care of it when his parachute opened.

Craig scanned the aircraft's dark interior. Most of the soldiers dozed but a few thumbed through their smartphones. He doubted any had a signal, so he suspected they watched downloaded movies or read books. Craig occupied the last seat in the back of the aircraft on the left side. This meant he would be the first person out the door on this side of the aircraft. Standing in the door made some of the newer guys nervous, but Craig had over eighty parachute jumps. He had no problem with the procedure. His company commander sat across from him on the far side of the aircraft. The man's head rocked back and forth atop his reserve chute as he slept. He would be the first person out on that side.

He rode in the most recent version, a "J" model, of an aircraft that began service in 1956. Designated a 'Super Hercules,' it had four turbofan engines spinning huge six-bladed propellers. This morning it carried two platoons from his unit; Alpha Company, 3rd Battalion of the 504th Infantry Regiment.

Dim lights tried to illuminate the inside of the cavernous aircraft. The aircraft's crew chief, a junior Air Force noncommissioned officer, sat on the ramp next to the unit's two jumpmasters. A small tablet lit up the crew chief's face as he read. Small drops of hydraulic fluid dripped from the ceiling leaving a two-foot-wide puddle in front of the door. Craig tried to swallow but his dry throat resisted. He forced his eyes from the leaking fluid and prayed the aircraft would hold together long enough for him to jump out of it.

The aircraft interior smelled of belches and farts produced by the captive infantrymen. Each half hour the aircraft's massive air conditioning system sent a burst of cooled air into the top of the cargo bay. It looked like someone shooting several enormous CO2 fire extinguishers down at the soldiers. Afterward the offensive smells went away but soon returned.

He wore his earplugs as the engines and spinning propellers filled the cargo area with a dull roar. When the aircraft changed direction, servos whined, and hydraulics moaned. He felt thumps throughout the aircraft's deck. Every few minutes even bigger thumps shook the fast-moving aircraft. Craig once told a blind date that a ride in a C-130 was the same as being eaten by some great dinosaur. Once inside its cramped, dark stomach, you're carried along and jostled among the other unfortunates it swallowed. You're accosted by foul smells and gases shoot in at you while you're digested. Your ears are injured by loud noises, and you're thrown about when the dinosaur jumps up and down and roars at other dinosaurs. A budding fine arts major, the young woman appreciated Craig's poetic license, but he still failed to score that night.

Craig had a parachute strapped to his back and a reserve chute sat on his stomach. He carried his full 'combat load' to include rucksack, radio, and ammunition. His M4 carbine, the standard issue weapon for most of his soldiers, sat in its weapons case tucked under his left arm. With his equipment and parachutes, he carried one hundred and sixty pounds of gear.

Sleep eluded Craig. His first jump as a brand-new commissioned officer riled his nerves. He looked at the soldiers around him. He barely knew the men in his new platoon. Fortunately, his platoon sergeant, an experienced sergeant first class, led the platoon through Afghanistan and knew his stuff. He knew his platoon sergeant would help him get through this first real-world test of his leadership. Craig spotted him dozing as he sat next to the aircraft's crew chief; he served as one of the jumpmasters for today's mission.

And what a mission. Their operation order stated a large terrorist force operated in Missouri, and his unit would find them and eliminate them. Intel stated the force included armed North Korean soldiers, and they had already killed many government employees.

At first, Craig didn't believe it. It sounded like an elaborate but routine training exercise. After the briefing they issued everyone live ammunition. That was not standard procedure for an exercise. Later, while they donned their parachutes, he spotted the division commander speaking with his company commander; something he had never seen before. Soon a female photographer took photos of the soldiers as they shuffled into the aircraft. She started to cry and looked at the soldiers as if they were dead men. A cold knot grew within his stomach, and the certainty he participated in a training mission vanished.

Now he felt the aircraft descend to their final jump altitude of one thousand feet. Both jumpmasters rose and waddled in their heavy gear through the cramped cargo bay. They shouted and slapped the tops of helmets waking people up.

Craig looked down at the line of soldiers next to him. His radio man, Private First Class Washington, yawned and rubbed the sleep from his eyes. His first squad leader, Sergeant Juan Cadena, sat next to him. Beyond him Private First Class Jessie Newton sat crushed between two much larger infantrymen. He knew nothing about the young female medic. Females were not part of an airborne infantry platoon, but their usual medic suffered a broken leg two days ago. The brigade's medical company gave them Newton as a temporary replacement. Craig hoped the young PFC could keep up with whatever happened today. He also hoped she got zero chance to prove her medical skills.

The aircraft reduced its speed to the jump velocity of one hundred and twenty miles per hour. It felt like someone stepped on the brakes of a speeding car. All the paratroopers slammed forward and crushed the ones sitting in the front. Many soldiers let out an involuntary "whoa!" followed by shouts of "move it!" or "get off me, fat ass!"

The jumpmasters now stood by the rear doors facing the front of the aircraft. Both men extended their arms forward towards the jumpers with their palms out. Together they yelled. "Get ready!"

The two platoons of soldiers straightened up and returned the yell. "Get ready!"

Both jumpmasters pointed to the outside row of seated soldiers and raised their arms over their heads. They yelled. "Outboard personnel stand up!"

Again, all the soldiers yelled. "Outboard personnel stand up!"

The outside row of soldiers stood and faced the rear of the aircraft. Craig attempted to stand but failed. He tried again but could not rise from his seat. Finally, his platoon sergeant reached down and unbuckled the safety belt that held him in place. Craig's face turned red, and he stood. Private Washington lifted the flimsy seat and used the attached Velcro strap to tie it out of the way.

The jumpmasters pointed at the two rows of soldiers sitting in the interior of the cargo area. They raised their hands over their heads. "Inboard personnel stand up!"

The entire plane shouted the command, and the inboard rows stood. At this point, the commands started to come faster.

"Hook up!" the jumpmasters said.

"Hook up!" the soldiers said. Each jumper took their static line snap hook from their parachute and snapped it on a heavy steel cable running above their heads.

"Check static line!" the jumpmasters said.

"Check static line!" the soldiers said. Each jumper tested his static line's connection to the cable and felt for any obstructions.

"Check equipment!"

"Check equipment!" The jumpers tugged on their helmet straps and ran their free hand down their body checking their equipment.

"Sound off for equipment check!"

"Sound off for equipment check!" Starting at the back of each line, the last man slapped the leg of the man in front of him and yelled. "Okay!"

Each jumper completed this, in turn, all the way up to the first jumper.

Craig felt the slap to his leg and pointed his knife hand at the jumpmaster.

"All ok, jumpmaster!"

The loadmaster opened the personnel doors located at the rear of the aircraft on both sides. Cold air rushed into the aircraft. It chilled the ranks of soldiers and amplified the ear-splitting noise. The wind buffeted Craig, and he lowered his body and spread his feet to maintain his balance. The cold air caused his eyes to water and his nose to run. The high velocity air soon carried away his tears.

The loadmaster folded down a small metal step at the base of each door. With the steps in place, each jumpmaster planted his feet against the base of the door and grasped its sides. Still wearing their parachutes and equipment, they pushed their bodies out of the door into the wind. Keeping a firm grip, they looked for any dangerous obstructions on the cruising C-130. Craig knew a parachute snagged on the aircraft's exterior could disrupt the entire jump. They also looked ahead of the aircraft. Satisfied, the men pulled themselves inside.

The jumpmaster looked at Craig and pointed. "Stand in the door!"

All the soldiers yelled. "Stand in the door!"

Craig shuffled forward and rotated to the right. He stepped into the door and placed both hands down on each side. Craig looked down at the countryside rushing by below. A huge forest dotted with open pastures stretched to the horizon. He spotted several houses with pickups in their driveways and tractors parked near small barns. A herd of cattle scattered when the great aircraft buzzed them. Up ahead he spotted some large factory-like buildings; their target military base. A small dark object in the sky forward of the C-130 caught his attention.

Before he could get a closer look, the jumpmaster slapped Craig's butt hard and yelled. "Go!"

Craig leaped into the aircraft's slipstream and counted out loud. "One-one thousand! Two-one thousand! Three…"

His static line, still connected to the cable inside the aircraft, pulled the parachute from the pack on his back. The parachute filled with air, and his body jerked hard. He went from 120 miles per hour to a few miles per hour in a few seconds. A loud groan escaped his lips.

Without warning, a huge explosion rocked the aircraft. Craig thought a contraband grenade, hidden in some hardcore soldier's equipment, got loose and exploded inside the aircraft. He felt the heat of the explosion on his face. He realized the explosion was too large for a simple hand grenade. The soldiers around him, swinging below their parachutes, screamed. He jerked against the parachute's risers to catch a glimpse of the stricken aircraft, but the expanding shock wave pummeled him. A huge black bat screamed at him, and he passed out.

Chapter 25

September 14, 2015, 0900 (CST) Show Me Army Depot, Missouri

Jack stood in the center of one of Liam's large agricultural fields. Six-inch-tall hay waiting for its next cutting covered the mile long rectangle of ground located close to the X-Ray production buildings. A few round bales from last year's cut and an older tractor sat at the far edge of the field. Liam, Conner, and Rita stood next to him.

Watching the approaching C-130 through binoculars provided by Liam, he lowered them and turned to his companions. "A few more minutes and we'll see their parachutes."

Three large stake bed trucks sat behind them. Once the infantry company hit the ground, he would load them into the trucks and move them closer to the invading terrorists. After that he'd turn the job over to the company commander. He would not tell the infantryman how to do his job, but he would keep an eye on him.

Earlier Jack called Conner and Rita back from their scouting duties. He wanted them to brief the arriving company commander. They confirmed that two groups of terrorists operated on the depot; the North Koreans at the rail yard, and the ISIS terrorists at the depot's entrance. All carried AK-47 rifles, and Conner spotted two PKM machine guns with the ISIS group. Thankfully, neither group appeared to have any mortars or RPGs.

Both groups worked hard placing explosives on the rail spurs and on the depot's bridge. The groups also dug numerous fighting positions close to the mined explosives. The invaders' actions to defend their work confirmed they lacked the crucial detonators.

Jack spotted a jumpmaster pop out of the aircraft's open door and pull back in. "They'll start in a few moments," Jack said. "Once they're on the ground, it takes them about ten minutes to assemble. They're going to love that we have trucks ready for them."

His team smiled and nodded. Jack knew seeing soldiers from the famous division parachute into Show Me Army Depot excited his friends. Jack felt great relief at placing the dangerous task of eliminating the enemy terrorists into the hands of professionals.

A few seconds later the first soldiers leaped from the aircraft. Jack heard a smattering of applause from the employees watching from X-Ray. He let out a held breath once he saw the leaping soldiers.

A noise above him caused Jack to look up. A small object streaked through the sky and headed straight towards the lumbering cargo plane. The object connected with the aircraft's left side at the point where the wing met the fuselage. A large explosion erupted against the aircraft. A few seconds later the sharp report reached them. A chorused moan came from the employees at X-ray.

"Holy shit!" Jack said. "A God damn missile hit that C-130!"

He knew the explosion doomed the large aircraft. Seconds after the explosion, a jet screamed over them. Jack ducked but caught sight of a black, swept-wing jet fighter tearing through the sky. The fighter zoomed past the aircraft and climbed away.

Jack tore his gaze away from the jet and watched the C-130. Ten parachutes floated behind the stricken plane. The five parachutes on the right looked fine, but burning fuel covered the other five. The burning canopies left smoky smudges in the sky, and their precious cargo plummeted to the ground. Jack choked back vomit and watched the five men die.

Jack again focused on the C-130. Flame poured from both jump doors, and thick smoke trailed the aircraft. The damaged wing fluttered and attempted to tear itself from the fuselage. Despite the pilot's best efforts, the plane dove to the left; straight towards them. Jack turned to his team. All three stood frozen; their eyes wide.

Jack yelled. "Move!"

He pushed his friends away from the aircraft's path and towards the edge of the field. They stumbled and broke out into a run and Jack followed.

He yelled again. "Don't look at it! Run!"

He glanced towards the aircraft that now filled the sky. They were so close to the engines and screaming propellers, he knew no one heard him.

The aircraft flared and hit the ground. The bottom of the C-130 crumpled from the impact but it rebounded into the air. Jack saw the pilots' faces grimace as they struggled with their controls. For a second, he thought they might save it, but, at the top of its bounce, the damaged wing tore free and hit the ground. The lone wing, its propellers still spinning, flipped into the air and cartwheeled. It sailed over Jack and his team; missing them by a few feet and landed a hundred yards away.

The wing still attached to the aircraft retained its lift and rolled the aircraft. The upside-down C-130 slammed into the three parked trucks carrying them past the still running group. Jack felt the ground shake as the sixty-ton aircraft skidded across the field. His ears protested the horrid sound of metal tearing, and his heart mimicked the rapid thumps of the propellers beating against the hard soil. The wreckage slid for a quarter mile and sagged to the ground. A huge trail of burning fuel and debris littered the ground behind it. Fire burst through great ruptures in the broken aircraft and consumed it in earnest. Clouds of thick, black smoke gushed into the sky. No one got out of the inferno.

Jack spotted the black jet complete its turn. It appeared the aircraft planned to strafe them or the downed plane. "Take cover!"

They dove into a shallow ditch at the edge of the field. The black jet shot over them with an ear-splitting scream but held its fire. Jack raised his head and watched it recede in the distance. When he could no longer see it, he stood.

He looked at the wrecked and burning aircraft. The crash and flames made it unrecognizable. Only the large vertical stabilizer, upside down and half buried in the ground, looked familiar. Their trucks lay on their sides smashed beyond repair. The smell of burning kerosene, mixed with melted plastic and scorched flesh, assailed his nostrils. Ammunition within the wreck popped, and the hay around the shattered plane started to burn.

He knew the Pentagon would have no knowledge of this crash. They might figure it out when the Air Force tagged the aircraft as overdue, but that would take at least four to five hours. A knot formed in Jack's stomach. Show Me Army Depot was once again on its own.

Jack looked at the Torgersons. Conner sat with his head in his hands, and Rita sobbed as she watched the aircraft burn. He needed to get them moving. "Conner, Rita, check on the surviving paratroopers. Go easy with them; I'm certain they're in shock. Help them through it."

The two pulled themselves together and jogged towards the parachutes still billowing in the light wind. Jack and Liam walked towards the dead paratroopers. Small wisps of black smoke marked their landing spots.

When they arrived, they checked the soldiers' vitals, but the fall killed all five. They covered the bodies with what remained of their parachutes. Jack said a silent prayer and asked the Great Spirit to watch over the dead men's families. They collected their weapons, ammunition, equipment, and radios.

He looked over at the surviving paratroopers. All had their helmets off and sat on the ground. Jack walked towards them. A soldier stood and walked towards him. The young man had a gold bar on the front of his uniform. He came closer, and Jack stopped when he recognized a dust-streaked, but familiar, face from Afghanistan.

Chapter 26

September 14, 2015, 0930 (CST) Show Me Army Depot, Missouri

Jack sat with Don, Ross, Liam, and Lieutenant Craig within the X-ray production building. Craig's hands still shook as he drank a cup of X-Ray coffee. Will and Natalie stood behind their father listening to the discussion. Conner and Rita departed a few minutes ago to again monitor the two groups of terrorists. Outside, the aircraft continued to burn, but the depot's firemen, armed with an AK-47, headed for their station and its fire trucks. The black jet had yet to reappear, but Jack kept everyone away from the windows and doors.

Jack ran his hand over his short hair and sighed. "With this blackout, and the White House thinking we're on strike, there are no more reinforcements coming to Show Me depot." Don frowned and crossed his arms at the strike comment.

Jack continued. "We're the only ones that have any intelligence on the two enemy groups. We also have four trained infantrymen and a dozen assault rifles."

"Five trained infantry," Liam said. "I served in Vietnam."

"Six infantry," Don said.

Jack smiled at his two friends. He looked at everyone around him. "I'm afraid it's up to us to save our depot. Can I count on you all to follow Lieutenant Craig and myself when we go after the terrorists? We need to take out both groups before they find those detonators."

"You can count on the Torgerson family," Liam said.

"I've never served but I'm a good shot," Ross said. "I have three trophy bucks in my living room to prove it. I'm in."

"Colonel, I say we attack the group at the rail yard right now," Don said. "We have enough rifles and the soldiers from Fort Bragg. When we're done with the Koreans, we'll use their weapons to arm more of our people so we can attack the Arabs at the entrance."

"I agree we can put together a halfway decent fighting force," Jack said. "But how would we get there? We can't do it with three ATVs."

Don slammed his fist down on the table sending their coffee cups flying. "Goddammit, Colonel! You're not chickening out again, are you?" He scowled at Jack. "It's easy. We load everyone on the fire trucks and take them to the rail yard. It's like when we used to ride a deuce and a half to the combat zone in Vietnam. It'll be a piece of cake." Natalie and Will nodded.

Jack frowned at the big man. "Don't give me any of your crap, Don. You're forgetting the terrorist's jet. We might get close to the rail yard, but the terrorists at the entrance can see us coming miles away. They'll call in that jet, and it'll blow those bright red trucks right off the road before we get there."

Don clenched his jaw and looked up at the ceiling. "Well, we need our own Goddamn air support!"

Jack and Liam looked at each other and smiled. Liam nodded at Jack.

"You're right, Don," Jack said. "We need Tony Simpson and his helicopter."

"Tony?" Don said.

"It's not perfect, but his helicopter can move us to an attack position much quicker than any truck," Jack said.

"Tony can use the terrain and trees to stay hidden from a jet. We can be on top of the bad guys before they know it. The surprise helps us big time. It could work."

"Don, didn't you serve with Tony during Desert Storm?" Liam said.

"I did," Don said. "I was one of his crew chiefs." He scratched the back of his arm and furrowed his brow. "He's a sneaky little shit but he can fly the hell out of that helicopter."

Jack looked at Liam. "Do you think you could get him to fly with us?"

"I can get him," Don said. "Give me two of the ATVs. Natalie and I'll go and convince him." Don slammed his fist into his palm.

"Done," Jack said.

The group stood and walked outside. Don and Natalie mounted the ATVs. Don's vehicle sagged with his weight.

Jack gave some final instructions to Don. "We need that helicopter back here as soon as possible. Stay away from the police. Uwell Yates might try to arrest you for your own safety, and I can't afford to lose you. If you can't get that helicopter, we don't stand a chance, so make it happen."

"Don't worry, Colonel," Don said. "I know where he is; we'll get him."

Don nodded at Natalie, and they gunned the throttles on the ATVs. In a few moments, they entered the forest heading for the depot's perimeter and the nearest county road.

Twenty minutes later Don and Natalie reached the fence that marked the depot's perimeter. The current level of security in the United States required a perimeter fence of five strands of agricultural barbed wire mounted on five-foot high metal posts. Signs identifying Show Me Army Depot as a US military facility, and a restricted area, hung on the wire every quarter mile.

Don and Natalie pulled up to the fence. Don found a sturdy tree branch and battered down a section of barbed wire. The ATVs shot across the fence line and accelerated across a local rancher's pasture spooking several dozen cows. Natalie let out several whoops to get the cattle out of their way. Soon they went through a cattle gate and stopped on a paved road.

"Which way, Dad?" Natalie said.

Don pointed to the left. "The McEntire ranch is that way. We'll borrow a pickup to get into town."

They turned and sped down the asphalt road. The wind tugged at their clothes and hair as they topped out the machines at forty miles per hour. Soon they spotted a large Mack truck with a stock trailer headed towards them. They pulled their ATVs off the road and flagged down the approaching truck.

Don turned to his daughter. "Tell him it's an emergency, and we need a ride to the airfield. Don't say anything about terrorists, or he'll think we're nuts. Make sure you smile big at the man."

She frowned at her father. "Dad, I'm not going to whore myself out just to get a ride in a truck."

Despite her protest, Natalie wiped her face with her handkerchief and spruced up her hair. The truck stopped next to them. Natalie jumped up on the running board.

A few moments later she called. "Dad, I need you to speak to the driver."

Don frowned. *Now What?* He walked to the driver's side of the truck.

Natalie had a big smile on her face. "Dad, I'd like you to meet Kitty Evans from Springfield."

Don looked up at the driver. The ugliest woman he'd ever seen, in her late fifties, sat in the rig's cab. Kitty smiled revealing a missing front tooth and a plug of snuff under her bottom lip. Her hair needed washing and brushing.

"Nice to meet you, Don," Kitty said.

Natalie smirked at her father. "I thought you would like to inform Kitty of our emergency."

Don clenched his fists. He looked up at Kitty and pulled his lips back in a forced smile. "Well, Miss Kitty it's like this…"

Before he could continue, Kitty put her hand over her mouth and giggled like a schoolgirl.

Don and Natalie jumped from the cab of the truck and ran towards Tony's hangar.

Kitty leaned out her window and yelled. "I hope you find that lost little girl!"

She blasted a deep note from her horn and pulled away. Natalie stopped and waved. Don ignored the truck and headed towards a man-door on the hangar's side. He tried the door and found it locked. He stepped back a few feet and rushed forward, putting his shoulder into the door. The jamb popped with a loud ping, and the door burst open. They stepped into the dim hangar and spotted the outline of the large Huey.

"He's here." Don pointed. "Natalie, get that big door open. I'm going to find Tony."

"Okay, Dad." Natalie headed towards the door.

Don headed to the back of the hangar. He spotted two doors to his left. He opened the first door and found a small restroom. A toothbrush and washcloth sat on the lip of the small sink. He opened the second door and stepped into a large office. Blinds on all the windows shielded the room from the morning sun. Don saw a desk covered with maintenance manuals. A flimsy card table next to it held a hot plate and an ancient Mr. Coffee. Dirty paper plates filled a small trash can sitting under the table. Metal shelving holding cardboard boxes, aircraft parts, and containers of lubricant lined one wall. The aroma of old grease, new plastic, boiled eggs, and stale beer tickled Don's nose. He spotted a form on a small cot located beyond the shelves.

He flipped the light switch and bathed the dirty room in bright fluorescent light. Don crossed the room, kicking several empty beer cans underneath the cot. He shook the sleeping form.

"Tony, get up. It's an emergency." The form failed to stir, and he tried again. "Tony, get up. We need your helicopter."

The pilot pulled his blanket tighter and mumbled. "Go away whoever you are."

Don ripped the covers off Tony and grabbed him by his neck. "God dammit Tony get your ass up."

He forced Tony up until the pilot stood on top of his cot wearing nothing but his dirty white briefs. Don's hand remained at his neck holding him in place. Tony groaned from the pain, and he grabbed Don's wrist. He took in the huge man standing no more than a foot away from him. His eyes grew wide, and his hands covered his groin.

"Don, why are you in my office?" Tony said.

Don released him and stepped back. "There's an emergency at the depot. I came to get you and your helicopter."

Natalie ran into the office. "I got the hangar door open, but I don't know how to get the helicopter outside."

Tony grabbed his blanket and covered himself.

Don stuck his finger in Tony's face. "Get dressed. I'm moving your helicopter out of the hangar. I'll make sure it has fuel and I'll preflight it for you. When you come out, I'll fill you in on everything. And if you're drunk, I'm going to beat it out of you." Tony pulled the blanket tighter to his chest and said nothing.

Don grabbed Natalie and walked out. Tony, still standing on his cot, watched them go. After a few moments, he stepped down to the floor. He sighed and grabbed his flight suit and boots.

Five minutes later Tony hovered ten feet off the ground in front of the hangar. He watched his rpms and listened to his engine. He appreciated the way Don prepared the helicopter for takeoff like he did during the war. Regardless, the big man still scared the shit out of him. He snuck a look at Don sitting in the back of his helicopter. Don scowled at him, and he turned back to his controls.

Tony keyed his mike. "She's ready to go. We'll be at the depot in ten minutes."

"The depot can wait," Don said. "Take us to my ranch. I need to get Cecil and Howie."

Tony said nothing. Don's instructions confirmed something he'd known since Desert Storm; raging nutcase thy name is Don. Most parents hid their children from ruthless terrorists. Not Don. He gets his kids together and leads them into battle against the terrorists.

Tony applied power, and the helicopter rose into the air. He nudged the cyclic forward, and the helicopter gained airspeed. When he reached three hundred feet, he turned the aircraft east towards the Miksic ranch. Cloudy but clear skies made it a beautiful day for flying. Tony also knew the great weather gave any terrorists plenty of opportunities to see and shoot at his helicopter. He sighed.

Five minutes later they approached the ranch that consisted of two neat homes and half a dozen small barns surrounded by acres of pasture. He knew Cecil Miksic and his family lived in the second home.

"Coming up on your place Don," Tony said.

Don's voice came over the intercom. "Set her down in the front yard and don't scare my cattle."

Tony brought his chopper in and landed close to Cecil's house. Don and Natalie jumped out and ran through the front door. Tony had plenty of fuel, so he kept the engine idling.

Three minutes later Don, Cecil, Howie, and Natalie ran out of the house. Don had an AK-47 in his hands. Howie and Cecil each carried a duffle bag stuffed with shotguns and rifles. Natalie followed with a large ammunition can in each hand. They jumped in the helicopter and belted themselves in. Tony turned and saw that Don had the muzzle of his rifle pointed towards the floor.

"Make sure you secure those cans," Tony said.

"I was a crew chief for ten years," Don said. "I haven't forgotten. Now take off and head east. We need to get some more guns."

"More guns!" Tony said. "You have two duffle bags full of guns."

Don glared at Tony. "Head over to Rory Klinder's place. He has something we need."

Tony turned and looked at Don. "Rory Klinder! That guy's even nuttier than you, Don. One time I flew over his house, and he shot at me with a deer rifle. I'm keeping plenty of distance between me and that lunatic."

Don's jaw clenched. "Shut up and do what I tell you. Your precious helicopter won't get a scratch on it. He lives alone so here's how we're gonna do it."

Don proceeded to explain the plan for their arrival at Rory Klinder's ranch. When he knew Don could no longer see him Tony rolled his eyes but lifted the helicopter into the air. Five minutes later they approached an isolated ranch. Tony saw at least one hundred head of cattle grazing in pastures that surrounded a house and barn. The house hadn't seen paint in fifty years, and overgrown bushes and trees clung to its sides. Several broken tractors and piles of ruined implements sat in the home's front yard.

Tony hovered in front of the house. He popped his MP3 player into its holder and blasted the Beach Boys' "I Get Around" at the shabby house. He could swear he saw the glass in the home's windows shaking. He handed a microphone to Don.

Don spoke over the music. "Rory, this is the government. The United Nations sent us to confiscate your guns, your cattle, and your land. Come out now so we can take you to prison."

The front door flew open, and a skinny man in his seventies ran out towards the helicopter. The man wore stained bib overalls over a filthy t-shirt. A crumpled ball cap covered his long, white hair. He attempted to aim a double-barreled shotgun at the helicopter while he ran.

"Go!" Don said.

Tony flew up and over the house. The crazed rancher backpedaled but Tony was soon out of range.

Don continued with his plan. "Rory, that's no way to treat your government. Now surrender so we can impound your guns and take you to prison. We have lots of foreigners waiting to move onto your ranch."

Cecil, Howie, and Natalie howled with laughter. Tony watched it all from his pilot's position. He saw little difference between crazy Rory and the crazy Miksic family. He landed on a small hill about a mile away from the ranch. Tony and his passengers stared hard at Rory's house.

"Wait for it," Don said.

A minute later they spotted a small dust cloud coming from the ranch. The dust cloud pierced the surrounding pastures and headed straight towards the idling helicopter. The cloud came closer, and Tony made out Rory Klinder riding a beat-up quad ATV. His shotgun rested on a rack that sat above the vehicle's front wheels.

With the ATV seconds away, Tony applied power, and the helicopter leaped from the ground. The little vehicle tore underneath the climbing chopper and skidded to a stop. The furious rancher grabbed his shotgun and jumped off his machine. Tony circled out of range of the shotgun, and Don used his AK-47 to place a round into each of the ATV's four tires. They flew back to the ranch and landed in front of the house. The skids hit the ground, and Don, Cecil, and Howie jumped from the chopper and ran inside.

Tony looked back towards the hill, but the house blocked his view. Ten minutes later Don ran out of the house carrying an M60 machine gun in his right hand and two full ammo cans in his left. The machine gun looked like a toy in Don's massive hand. Cecil and Howie followed close behind carrying two full ammunition cans in each hand. Tony wondered who was stupid enough to sell a machine gun and two thousand rounds of ammunition to a maniac like Rory Klinder. All three leaped into the back of the helicopter.

"Go!" Natalie said.

Tony pulled pitch, and they shot into the air as Rory staggered around the side of his house. With sweat pouring down his face, the old man ran after the helicopter. When a fence barred his way, he stopped and fired both barrels. Tony heard the pings of bird shot hitting the bottom of his helicopter.

Tony keyed the intercom. "Can we please go to the depot now?"

"We still have a couple of stops to make," Don said. "Head to the hospital. When we're finished there, we're going to stop at Channel 27's building over on industrial avenue. We've got some assets to pick up."

Tony's shoulders slumped and he turned towards Cedar City.

Chapter 27

September 14, 2015, 1045 (CST) Show Me Army Depot, Missouri

Victor Chow paced near the completed fighting positions at the south end of the rail yard. Major Lee stood behind the spy; smoking a cigarette and watching him pace. The remainder of the Special Forces team lounged in their holes smoking or talking among themselves.

Hours ago, Abdul Barry lost contact with his men at the security gate. After that, the fighters guarding the captured employees at the cafeteria failed to answer their radio calls. When Abdul went to investigate, he found the commandeered security truck still at the gate. Blood covered the cab, and he found no trace of his men. At the cafeteria, he found more blood, and again no sign of his fighters or their hostages.

The missing terrorists, and the arrival of the aircraft from Fort Bragg, caused Victor to wring his hands with worry. Despite the blackout, the American authorities somehow discovered his activity on Show Me Army Depot. His call to his stealth aircraft handled their response. The pilot reported no one from the large cargo plane survived.

So, what happened to the six missing terrorists? Did the Americans send another military force, this one undiscovered, to the depot? Had the aircraft from North Carolina masked the arrival of American Special Forces? Was a sniper rifle, held by a US Navy SEAL, even now trained on him? Victor shuddered and peered into the dense forests around him.

He grabbed the radio off his belt. "Johnny, this is Victor. What are you doing? Do you have the detonators yet? We need them here at once."

The radio squawked. "Johnny here. Joe thinks this magazine is the one. We should be at your location soon."

Victor enunciated each word. "Johnny. Listen. To. Me. You and that idiot vice president have one more hour. If you are not here by then I'm going to find you and beat you both. Do you understand me?"

The radio remained silent for a few moments. "One hour; we got it."

Victor put the radio back on his belt and resumed his pacing. He lit another cigarette and watched the forest.

Joe walked up to the magazine door. His eyes itched and his nose ran from the fine dust present in every magazine. They lost count a long time ago, but Joe guessed their search covered over fifty magazines at least.

Fatigue dogged both men. However, the money waiting for him in Bolivia and his fear of Victor Chow kept him going. He wondered how he failed to spot the Chinese cook's insanity. He wished the crazy spy would drop dead from a massive stroke.

Johnny grabbed the key ring and unlocked the magazine. Both men pulled open the large metal door.

"I got this one," Joe said.

He stepped into the magazine and flipped the light switch. Like half the magazines they visited, this one had no working light bulbs. Luckily, sunlight streamed through the door. He examined the stacks and found boxes with the correct size and shape. One stack of boxes read FUZE, TIME M700. His pulse quickened. He moved to another nearby stack. The boxes read IGNITER, TIME BLASTING FUSE M60. He looked over several more stacks and saw CAP, BLASTING, NON-ELECTRIC, M7.

Joe's heart raced. "Johnny get in here!"

In a few moments, the tired young man stuck his head in the door.

Joe looked at him and smiled. "We found it."

Johnny stood straighter. "For real? You're not yankin' me, are you?"

"This is the stuff. Get the truck and back it up to the dock. Then come and help me load it."

"It's about time."

The boy turned and ran out the door. In a few moments, Joe heard the truck back up to the magazine.

Johnny ran through the door. "Where is it?"

Joe pointed to the three stacks. "Fuse igniters, time fuse, and blasting caps."

Johnny ran to the first stack, and Joe followed. In five minutes, they had the pickup loaded. Johnny dropped the large key ring on the dock and jumped down to the pickup.

"Call Victor and tell him we have it," Joe said.

Johnny grabbed his radio. "Johnny calling Victor."

Victor answered. "Do you have the detonators?"

"We have them. Where do you want them? The rail yard or the entrance?"

Victor screamed over the radio. "The rail yard you idiot! It's the most important target. Bring the detonators here to the rail yard."

"Okay, I got it. We're on our way."

Victor continued his rant. "Why are you still talking to me? Get off the radio and start driving. Get those detonators here at once. Do not stop for anything."

Johnny shut off the radio. "Jesus. Impatient much?"

The two men got into the truck and sped away from the dock.

Chapter 28

September 14, 2015, 1115 (CST) Cedar City, Missouri

Howie willed himself invisible as he walked down the bright hallway. He wore a lab coat and badge found on a coat rack in an empty waiting area. A clip board holding a cleaning schedule taken from the back of a restroom door completed his disguise. When he examined himself in the mirror, he thought he looked like a doctor. So long as no one he met looked too closely at his work boots and blue jeans.

He turned the corner and entered the hospital's flight operations office. A man wearing a blue flight suit sat at a desk with one leg draped over the top. He looked forty-five years old and had a mullet haircut. The pilot worked a toothpick while he read the latest copy of Sports Illustrated.

The man looked up at Howie. "Can I help you, sport?"

Howie closed the door. "I'm doctor Miksic from the FAA. I'm here for a check ride of your medevac helicopter." He made a show of checking the clipboard. "Are you Tom West?"

The pilot smirked. "I'm Tom West, and I fly the Medevac helicopter. But if you're from the FAA, I'm the Pope shitting in the woods."

Howie cocked his head. The pilot's arrogance irritated him; he would not let this boob stop him from rescuing his friends. His crippling shyness vanished in an instant. "Why do you say that Mr. West?" Howie gestured to his lab coat and clipboard. "I'm clearly a doctor here on official business."

Tom continued to roll his toothpick. "I've visited the FAA many times and I've never heard of you. On top of that, you're way too young for a pilot and a doctor." He dropped his leg off the desk and pointed at Howie. "I suggest you turn around and get out of my office before I call security."

Howie turned and locked the door. He stared at the pilot as he lowered the blinds on the office windows facing into the hallway. The smirk vanished from the pilot's face.

"You're correct Mr. West," Howie said. "I'm not a doctor and I'm not from the FAA; I'm an imposter. My friends are in trouble, so I need you and your helicopter. It shouldn't take long; maybe a few hours. After that, you can return here."

Tom again smirked. "What are you going to do? Force me to fly? I got into a few scrapes in college. I bet I could take you." He made no move to stand up.

Howie straightened up to his full height and pushed out his chest. "I'd prefer to fly with an uninjured pilot if I can help it."

Tom stared at Howie for a few moments. "I still think I can take you." He dropped the magazine on the desk and lunged for the phone.

Howie crossed the room in two large steps. He pulled his .45 automatic and placed it against the pilot's cheek below his right eye. Tom's eyes focused on the pistol lodged in his face, and the toothpick fell from his mouth. Howie felt the man shake through the pistol.

Now Howie smirked. "Still think you can take me?"

The pilot remained still and kept his eyes on the pistol.

Howie almost laughed at the expression on Tom's face, but he felt that would ruin his threatening display. He continued. "Now stand up." Tom stood and started to raise his hands.

"No need to raise your hands. I'm not robbing you. I want you to fly where I tell you."

Howie grabbed the pilot by the arm. "We're going to walk out to your helicopter. Act natural and speak normally to anyone we meet. If you try to run, I'll shoot you. I won't kill you; just wound you." Howie put his mouth two inches from Tom's ear and whispered. "Believe me; I'm that good of a shot." He moved his head away from Tom and spoke normally. "If I must, I'll carry you to the helicopter and make you fly with a bullet wound. Do you understand?"

Tom nodded. "I'll walk. Just don't shoot me."

Howie steered him to the door. He placed the gun in his coat and unlocked the door. "You lead the way, Mr. West."

Tom walked out the door with Howie close behind. They made one turn and saw the helicopter through the glass doors at the end of the hallway. Bright red paint along with a green cross and the hospital's name covered the helicopter. A four bladed rotor balanced on top, and the tail rotor sat inside a small shroud.

When they got to the aircraft Howie sent Tom to the pilot's seat. He walked around the aircraft and sat in the co-pilot's seat.

"Can you tell me what this is about?" Tom said. He put on his helmet and grabbed his startup checklist.

Howie donned a spare headset. "I will soon. For now, stay off the radio and get us to a thousand feet. In a few minutes we'll join up with another helicopter and follow them."

Five minutes later they orbited alone over the center of town.

"What helicopter are we looking for?" Tom said.

"It's an old military helicopter. I think they call it a Huey."

Tom looked at Howie. "An old Huey? Is it Tony Simpson's helicopter?"

"Yes, that's him."

"That man is a drunk, and he doesn't have half the piloting skills I do. I'm not flying with him." Tom turned the helicopter back towards the hospital.

Howie reached over and placed his hand on the pilot's helmet. Using a small measure of his strength, he slammed Tom's head hard against the door.

"Owww!" Tom looked at Howie. "If you do that again you could knock me out, and we'd crash."

Howie shrugged. "Terrorists attacked Show Me Army Depot last night and killed a lot of my friends. Colonel Black Eagle and my family need this helicopter to help take them out. If I can't fight with my family, I might as well be dead. It's your choice."

He again reached for him, but Tom ducked away from the outstretched arm.

"Terrorists?" Tom said. "Is that the best line you could come up with? What's really going on? Are you robbing a bank?"

Howie looked out the window for the other helicopters. "No, it's not armed robbery. Just a lot of terrorists in different locations. That's why we need helicopters."

Howie decided to use a little psychology. He crossed his arms and smirked at the pilot. "Tom, if you don't think you can hack it maybe we should go back. I'm sure your hospital has more than one pilot. Where does the other pilot live? Let's fly to his house, and I can get him instead."

Tom stuck his chin in the air. "No. No. No. You don't want Jill. She's a crash waiting to happen."

"Who's Jill?"

Tom checked his gauges. "She's the night shift pilot. You're better off with me. I can teach Tony a few things and make sure we all come home safe and sound."

Howie smiled. "That's the spirit, Tom." He pulled his hand away from the pilot. "Keep circling. He'll be here soon."

Natalie stopped outside the station's entrance. She used a window as a mirror and wiped her face and smoothed her hair. She examined the bags under her eyes and sighed. Her grandmother from the old country would roll over in her grave if she knew Natalie still had no husband. She thought back to her brief kiss with Jack Black Eagle and wondered if it would lead to something further. She pushed the thought away; she needed to focus on her family. Natalie adjusted the revolver hidden under her long sleeve work shirt. Satisfied, she walked in.

She spoke to the building's receptionist. "Good afternoon. I'm here to serve papers to your helicopter pilot. It appears he doesn't pay his bills." Natalie flashed a creased envelope containing her electric bill. The bottle blond bought her act and even supplied the pilot's name; Brock Hightower. The receptionist appeared miffed that a strange woman needed to see the pilot.

A few minutes later Natalie found the pilot's empty office. The door across the hall read 'Associates.' She opened the door to find a room with ten small office cubicles. Several reporters crowded around a police scanner and listened to radio traffic.

At the far end of the room, a trim, attractive man in his late twenties, with a dark complexion and styled dark hair, stood behind a young woman as she worked on a desk top computer. He wore a long sleeve paisley shirt, tight Levis, and cowboy boots. She had Brock Hightower in her sights. The pilot spoke softly to the woman, but she ignored him. Natalie paused. Something about the handsome pilot felt off.

She cleared her throat, and everyone in the room looked at her. "I'm looking for Brock Hightower."

The reporters all looked at the pilot, and Natalie hit him with a big smile.

The pilot stepped away from the reporter, smiled, and walked towards her. "I'm Brock Hightower."

She backed out into the hallway and stood by his office door. He followed and closed the door behind him. They had the hallway to themselves.

Brock stepped close to her. She had at least four inches on him, so he looked up into her eyes.

"I don't believe we've met miss-."

Natalie noticed he raised his heels up off the ground. She forced out a giggle. "I'm Natalie Miksic. I'm a friend of …" For a second, she could not recall the dim receptionist's name. Finally, it came to her.

"Cynthia! Yes, Cynthia. You see Brock I'm in a jam, and she said you could help me out."

Brock's voice turned silky. "Ah, Cynthia with a Y. She's a lovely girl." He paused. "But she cannot hold a candle to you, Natalie. What can I help you with?"

Brock stepped even closer and touched Natalie with his body. Natalie smelled the strong cologne he wore along with the coffee and egg sandwich he'd had for breakfast. She smiled and looked at the floor.

"Well, I feel silly asking."

Brock grinned at her. "It's not silly, Natalie. Go ahead and ask. I'm always willing to help a friend. You never know. You might get...lucky."

Natalie giggled again and struggled to keep her eyes from rolling. She'd heard better from half-drunk farm boys at The Outhouse.

She stared deep into Brock's eyes. "Well, I know it seems trivial, but I would love a ride in your helicopter. I've heard it's such a turn on and I told Cynthia that I have to try it."

She saw the smallest crack in the man's smile and knew she would need her gun. It wasn't loaded but Brock didn't know that. She strolled down the hallway towards the door that led to the helicopter.

Brock followed. "I think a flight is possible, Natalie. How about we have dinner at my place and follow that up with a moonlit flight? How does that sound?"

She reached the glass doors and spotted a light blue helicopter with white trim sitting on its concrete pad. A huge network logo and a large number twenty-seven covered its side. A camera unit and a small public address speaker hung underneath the nose of the helicopter.

Natalie leaned against the door and looked at the pilot. "That sounds wonderful Brock, but I can't wait for the next moon. I need a ride now."

Brock continued to smile but cocked his head. "Well, it would be tough to fly at this time. What is so important about going up now?"

"What's the matter, Brock?" Natalie said. "Having performance problems?"

His smile vanished and he furrowed his brow. Natalie wondered if he would start scratching his head. She looked down the hall and saw no one.

"Enough of this," she said. She pulled out her revolver and stuck it into his ribs.

Brock sucked in a huge gulp of air. His hands flew up and dangled near his shoulders. "Oh gosh; please don't hurt me."

Natalie continued to steal glances down the hall. "I won't hurt you if you do as I say."

He took another deep breath. "What do you want, Natalie?"

She looked at him. "Just what I said. I need a ride in your helicopter. I have some friends in trouble, and they need my help."

"It's nothing illegal, is it? Because I cannot go to jail."

Natalie smiled. "It's legal. But it's dangerous."

He frowned. "I don't like the sound of that, Natalie."

"Don't worry I'll be with you the entire time. If we survive, you'll be a big hero. You'll have to beat the women off with a stick, you'll be so famous."

Brock rolled his eyes. "Oh puh-lease."

Natalie stared at him.

He noticed and lowered his voice's pitch. "I mean...I can get all the women I need. I'm already a hero to the women around here."

"Good for you." She used the revolver to give his ribs a thump. "Now it's time to go. I'm going to hide this gun in my pocket, and we're going to walk out to your helicopter. You go first, and I'll be right behind you. Once we're finished, and my friends are ok, you'll be free to fly back here safe and sound."

"Do you guarantee that I can return unharmed?"

"I guarantee it. Now let's go." Natalie put the gun in her pocket and pushed Brock out the door. He walked forward but kept his hands near his shoulders.

"Put your hands down," she said.

He dropped his arms to his sides. Both his hands now pointed to the side and moved back and forth as he walked. Natalie noticed he took short steps, and his butt swished back and forth.

Natalie pushed his shoulder. "Faster."

He hopped once and sped up, but still took short, quick steps. He reached the helicopter and got in the pilot's seat. Natalie ran around the front and pulled herself up into the co-pilot's seat.

"I don't have my helmet," Brock said.

"Neither do I. Start it up and get us off the ground."

Brock sighed and grabbed a headset from a hook. He pointed to another headset, and Natalie put it on. He grabbed a takeoff checklist. The modern helicopter beeped and whirred as the electronics powered up.

Natalie spoke over the intercom. "What kind of helicopter is this? It looks nice."

"It's a Bell four zero seven utility helicopter with a Panasonic camera package." Natalie watched him go through his checklist. Soon the engine screamed, and the rotor blades spun through the air.

"Are you a good pilot?" she asked.

"Puh-lease, girl." Brock snapped his fingers and shimmied in his seat. A feminine lilt entered his voice. "I'm the best pilot in all of Missouri." He gave Natalie a big smile.

Natalie saw Brock was now much more comfortable in his helicopter. She smiled back. "Good. Where we're going, we need the best. Let's go."

Brock applied power, and they took off. From the air, Natalie spotted the receptionist watching from the front of the building. The woman turned and stomped back to the entrance. Natalie laughed.

Chapter 29

September 14, 2015, 1120 (CST) Cedar City, Missouri

Tony goosed his throttle and flew away from the building housing Channel 27, an affiliate of the network's main station in Kansas City. He keyed his intercom. "Don, why do we need three helicopters? Is it that bad at the depot?"

For several moments he received no reply. Finally, Don spoke. "It's bad, Tony. As bad as anything I saw in Vietnam. There's at least a platoon of terrorists armed with AK-47s. They killed the entire night shift security crew including my cousin June. They slaughtered 'em. If that wasn't bad enough, they snuck a jet fighter into the US." Don paused again. "I still can't believe it; those bastards got a jet fighter into Missouri without anyone finding out. We had no idea it was there until it showed up and shot down a C-130 full of paratroopers."

Tony's jaw dropped. "I didn't know. June Miksic. My God; I see her around all the time. She's a grandmother, isn't she?"

Don said nothing.

Tony's cheeks flushed and he shouted. "So why isn't the government doing anything about it? What about the police? How come a bunch of civilians in a broken-down helicopter are the only ones who can fight the terrorists?"

"God dammit shut up!" Don said. "The government did try something, but the terrorists ran a well-planned operation. They killed those paratroopers as soon as they got here. The local cops can't do anything because half of the terrorists are actual North Korean soldiers. That's why we need helicopters."

Tony turned and looked at Don. "North Koreans! What the hell are they doing here? How did they get into the country? I thought those damn airport security guys kept people like that out."

Don scowled at Tony. "I can't explain why the fucking government is so clueless. If I had a phone that worked, I'd call the White House myself and ask them."

Tony thought the conversation was over, but after a long pause Don spoke again. "I'm certain about one thing though. Once we get these helicopters, I'm going to kill every one of those fucking terrorists. Nobody murders my friends while I'm around."

Tony took a deep breath and turned his helicopter towards the neighborhood with large homes and well above average incomes.

"Hey! Where are you going? We need to wait for the other helicopters."

Tony opened his throttle and zoomed over the town. "I said I'd go but I'm getting the best crew chief I know to help me."

Don said nothing for at least ten seconds. "You must love getting kicked in the nuts. Make it fast. I don't know how long Natalie and Howie can keep those other pilots occupied."

Tony knew his wife and the mayor ate lunch at the Cedar Hills Country Club almost every day. He flew over the lavish golf course and spotted Ethan's luxury SUV in the club's parking lot.

He cleared the clubhouse and landed on the practice green sitting near the club's massive veranda. The Huey's skids sank an inch into the well-manicured grass, and patrons in golf attire moved away from the storm kicked up by the helicopter. Huge picture windows framed the club's restaurant. The diners, eating their expensive meals, rushed to the windows and stared and pointed at the intruding helicopter. Tony took the engine down to idle.

Don spoke. "You sure you want to do this? You know it won't end well."

"With what's going on, I think I have to."

"Okay, dumbass. Do you still have the mounts for this thing?"

"They're in the storage area in the back."

Tony hung his helmet on a hook and stepped out of the chopper. He looked at the stains on his Hawaiian shirt and grimaced. He knew he looked like a bum compared to the club's wealthy members, but he had no choice. He needed his wife by his side to keep him alive. She saved him several times during some hairy missions in Iraq.

He sprinted towards the wide staircase that led up to the veranda and into the club. He looked up and saw Sarah coming down the steps towards him. She wore a beautiful blue skirt with a white blouse. Her stylish high heels clacked on the marble staircase and her blond hair glowed in the sunlight. His heart leaped into his throat when he saw her. Tony waited for Sarah to come to him. He looked past her and saw Ethan standing at the top of the stairs. The mayor crossed his arms and frowned at Tony.

Sarah stopped five feet from her husband. "Tony, what the hell are you doing here? You've damaged club property, and the manager called the cops. What's got into you?"

He took a step closer to his wife. "Sarah, there's something bad going on at the depot. Terrorists killed a lot of people out there, and they need my helicopter for a fight. I'm going and I want you to go with me."

The mayor yelled. "Get that piece of shit off the club's grounds!"

Sarah looked back at him. "I'll handle this, Ethan!" She stepped in front of Tony and pushed him away from the stairs. "What are you talking about? What terrorists and why are they fighting at the depot?"

"I don't know how, but terrorists got inside Show Me Army Depot," Tony said. They killed some cops and the entire security shift." He motioned towards the helicopter with his head. "I have Don Miksic in the chopper and I'm going to help Colonel Black Eagle take on the terrorists."

Sarah glanced at the helicopter. "Is Don the one who told you this? He's a lunatic! You know I don't believe anything he says." She crossed her arms over her chest. "Why haven't we heard about this here in town? All we know is the state police shut down Highway 61. They said the bridge to the depot may collapse.

"Natalie Miksic saw it too. She told me the same story. She said Colonel Black Eagle witnessed the terrorists murdering June Miksic." Sarah's hand flew to her mouth. "Natalie said they tried to kill the Colonel and his kids. Hell, they held the entire night shift hostage for a couple of hours until Colonel Black Eagle jumped them."

Sarah again crossed her arms and started to tap the ground with her right foot. "Okay, so you're going to fight the terrorists. Why do you need me?"

Tony paused and looked at his hands. He shoved them into the pockets of his flight suit. "Because I'm scared, Sarah. Like I was before. You're the one who always gave me the courage to fly. They need my help, and I need you to get me there. Will you come with me? After this, I promise I won't bother you no more." Tony looked at his wife.

"Why can't Don be your crew chief?"

"You're better than he is, and I don't trust him," Tony said. "You said it yourself, he's a nut job. He'll probably force me to crash my helicopter into the terrorists so he can jump out and fight them hand to hand."

Sarah looked at the ground. She let out a deep breath. "No, Tony. I don't think I can go with you. I'm sorry."

Tony's shoulders sagged and he kept his gaze down. "Okay. I had to ask. I'm sorry I embarrassed you." He turned to go.

Without warning, Ethan appeared behind Sarah. He threw a large glass of beer at Tony drenching him. "Here's a beer you drunk. Go crash your helicopter somewhere else you son of a bitch!"

Tony wiped the beer from his face and charged the mayor. "Ethan, you bastard!"

Ethan swung a right and connected with Tony's chin. The blow staggered Tony and he fell. Ethan advanced with his fists raised. Tony cleared his head and leaped to his feet. Ethan swung again, and Tony ducked under his arm and stepped into him. He planted a hard left into his stomach. The mayor's breath rushed from his lungs, and he stepped back for another swing. Tony swung a right at Ethan's chin, but the mayor blocked it. Still struggling for breath, Ethan lowered his shoulder and rammed it into Tony's chest. The pilot flew back and landed on his back.

Sarah stood with her fists clenched. She screamed at the two men. "Stop it you two! Stop it this instant!" Having no effect, she focused on her husband. "Dammit, Tony! Why did you come here? You're always ruining everything! Stop fighting! Please stop fighting!"

The two men ignored Sarah. Ethan held his wounded stomach and tried to straighten up. Tony jumped up and moved towards him. He ducked another right and jabbed a left into the mayor's ribs. The mayor arched in pain. Tony used his left leg to sweep Ethan's legs out from under him, and his opponent fell back on the soft grass. Tony pulled his leg back for a kick to the mayor's midsection.

Sarah grabbed him and pushed him away. "Stop it! I'll go you bastard! Please stop fighting!"

Tony stared at his wife and panted. Ethan lay on the ground and tried to catch his breath. Water stains and grass clippings covered his expensive clothes.

"Don't go on account of me, Sarah," Ethan said.

Sarah whirled and pointed at him. "Shut up you old queen. You started this."

The mayor's mouth formed a large O. He said nothing and stayed on the ground. Sarah took Tony's arm and pulled him towards the helicopter.

After a few steps she stopped and faced Tony. "When this is over don't ever speak to me again."

Tony gave a downcast nod, and they ran to the idling helicopter. By this time Don had the machine gun attached to the helicopter's pintle mount. The rig sat in the middle of the cargo door on the helicopter's left side. An ammunition can sat in the mount, and a belt of ammunition fed into the gun. Don even found a spade grip for the machine gun.

A large group of club patrons stood on the veranda and used their smartphones to video the event. Don gave the finger to the club members as they gawked at the large helicopter.

Sarah jumped into the back of the helicopter.

When she had her headset on Don keyed his mike. "Nice to fly with you again, Sarah."

She glared at the big man. "Screw you, Don. Why'd you let Tony come here?" Don shrugged and said nothing. The helicopter's engine throttled up, and Sarah keyed her intercom. "Do you have a spare flight suit in here?"

"Check underneath the seat," Tony said.

Sarah grabbed a cardboard box and pulled out a folded flight suit. The suit had a 101st Airborne Division patch on the right sleeve. She noticed a faded name written on the inside. A pair of gloves and black combat boots lay under a folded newspaper dated six days ago. The boots gleamed in the sun; like someone spit-shined them that morning.

She clutched her old uniform and looked up at Tony. She took off her expensive shoes and threw them onto the putting green, then pulled her flight suit on over her clothes. When the suit reached her waist, she undid her skirt and threw it out the door.

She looked at Don and keyed her intercom. "I hear there are terrorists on the depot."

Don nodded his head. "Sure are. I've seen them myself. Some real murdering sons of bitches." He patted the machine gun. "But this baby will take care of them." He looked at Sarah and smiled. "It's like old times."

Sarah laced up her boots and did not look at Don. "Yeah…just like old times…yippee."

Tony applied power and pitch, and the helicopter rose from the ground. Sarah watched as bits of grass and leaves blew towards the spectators standing on the veranda.

Chapter 30

September 14, 2015, 1115 (CST) Show Me Army Depot, Missouri

Jack grabbed his radio from his belt. "Go ahead, Rita."

"Colonel, Joe Harper just arrived here with a truck full of ammunition boxes," Rita said. "And now I'm seeing some of the Koreans heading into the rail yard. Also, that British guy is here. He's talking to the fat Chinese guy."

"They must have the detonators," Jack said. "Conner, did you copy Rita's last transmission?"

"I copy Colonel," Conner said.

Jack took a deep breath. "I want both of you to move to the North side of the rail yard and wait for me. I don't know how but we're coming to you. We need to assault the North Koreans and push them out of the rail yard before they detonate the explosives."

"Copy Colonel," Rita said.

"Got it Colonel," Conner said. "I'm moving now."

Jack dropped his radio. Liam, Ross, and Will stood with him in the X-Ray supervisor's office. "Have we heard from Don yet?" Jack said.

Liam shook his head. "Nothing."

"We're out of time. We've got to attack the rail yard and quick. It won't take them long to place the detonators and set off the charges." Jack stuck his head out the door and yelled. "Lieutenant Craig!" The young officer came running. Jack grabbed him by the shoulder. "Get your people together and prepare to move. We're hitting the

North Koreans in the next fifteen minutes. They have the detonators."

Craig nodded and ran from the office. Jack looked at his companions. "We have five armed soldiers and you three, me, Conner, and Rita to take on the North Koreans." He turned to his deputy. "Ross, do you have any idea how to get us to the rail yard?"

"Our only option is Shorty's truck," Ross said. "A few of us can go in the cab, and the rest can ride on the trailer. The trailer's big enough, and we can shoot from it."

Jack grimaced. "We'll be exposed as hell, but we don't have a choice. Go get Shorty. We're leaving now."

Ross and Liam ran out of the office.

Jack wrung his hands together. "Dammit. I wish I had a tank."

Will laughed. "You do have a tank, Colonel. Hell, you have eight of them."

Jack looked at Will. "What do you mean I have eight tanks?"

Will waved his arms in the air. "We need to attack the North Koreans in the rail yard, don't we?" Jack nodded. "Well, the depot has eight locomotives that have as much steel in them as a tank, and they can take us straight to the North Koreans. They don't have a big gun like a tank, but we could ride on them and get some protection when we attack their positions."

Jack thought for a moment. "I like your idea, Will. It's better than riding into battle on the back of a semi. Where are they? Do we have anyone who can operate one?"

Will shuddered. "Ffffuck, Fuck, Train, Prick, Commander. We keep 'em at the round house. It's not too far from here. I worked on the rail team for years. I can drive a locomotive no sweat."

"You've convinced me," Jack said. "Let's go."

They grabbed their rifles and ran out of the office.

Five minutes later Shorty's semi carrying Jack and his team pulled up to the round house. Six locomotives sat on spurs located next to the large building. Jack got his first up-close look at the big locomotives. They were massive. They were as long as his house and towered twenty feet above the ground. He estimated each one weighed one hundred tons. Black and yellow paint trimmed the solid red locomotives, and United States Army in large yellow letters adorned their sides. The nearest locomotive had 4627 stenciled in yellow on each side of the cab. An identical locomotive labeled 4640 sat right behind it.

Jack took in the huge machines. "My God. They are tanks."

He heard a soft rumble coming from both locomotives, and a short blast of compressed air shot from underneath 4627. He looked at the cab expecting to see an operator but saw no one.

Will ran up to Jack and pointed. "Colonel, 4627 and 4640 are both running, and they're sitting on the main line. That's perfect. Cock, fuck, shit, train."

Jack looked at Ross. "Why are they running?"

"They used them last night," Ross said. "They leave 'em running during breaks. They hold a thousand gallons of diesel, so there's no problem if they idled all night."

Jack yelled to his people. "We're taking two! Lieutenant, you get your team on 4627! I'll lead my team from 4640!"

The soldiers and civilians swarmed onto the two locomotives. Will scrambled into the driver's seat of 4640 and throttled up the sixteen-cylinder engine. The huge diesel roared, and Jack's pulse quickened.

Will stuck his head out of the cab and looked down at Jack. "Colonel, who's going to operate 4627?"

Jack looked at Shorty sitting in the cab of his truck. He had no rifle and could not participate in the attack. He yelled. "Shorty do you still want to help?"

"Yes, Sir! What can I do?"

Jack pointed at the 4627 locomotive. "Get up in that cab. You've got one minute to learn how to drive it. Get some pointers from Will." Shorty ran to the locomotive. Two minutes later Will returned to his own driver's seat. From the ground, Jack saw each team easily fit on the rear of each locomotive.

He circled his hand in the air and keyed the radio. "Let's move out."

Both engines revved up, and a whoosh of compressed air released the brakes. The locomotives rolled forward.

Will hung half his body out the cab window and pounded on the train's metal side. "Colonel, isn't she the most beautiful hunk of steel you ever seen?"

Jack smiled. "She sure is Will."

The locomotive passed Jack, and he grabbed the handrail and swung up on its steps. He walked along the engine's catwalk and entered the cab.

He stood next to Will. "How long until we reach the rail yard?"

"Five minutes, Colonel."

Jack keyed a squad radio taken from a dead paratrooper. "Lieutenant, we're five minutes from contact. When we get there, I'm going to have Will put each locomotive on a different spur with you on the left and us on the right about fifty meters apart. I want smoke to screen the locomotives and whoever throws the switches."

"Roger that," Craig said. "Two-oh-three gunner prepare to pop smoke."

Specialist Siegel, one of Craig's survivors, responded. "Roger on smoke."

"When we're on two different tracks we'll move the locomotives in parallel towards the enemy positions," Jack said. "When we're close, we'll dismount and support each other with fire. It won't take long to roll 'em up."

"Roger, Sir," Craig said. "Infantry team, you got it?"

All four of the soldiers came up on the radio. "Roger."

"Depot team, do you copy?" Jack said.

Liam responded. "That's a good copy, Colonel. Ross and I are ready."

"Good copy," Conner said. "We're at the rail yard, and we'll throw the switches."

"We're a few minutes out," Jack said. "Everyone keep your head down."

He Who Watches stood in the forest and watched the human intruders work among the iron roads. He faced north and sniffed the air. *Two of them.*

He knew the human male traveled with the metal beasts headed to this place of the iron roads. The human male would confront the human intruders and do battle as a warrior.

He recognized now the great metal beasts were machines that served the humans. Like the green and yellow machines from his forests and fields. He chuckled to himself for his life-long misunderstanding. He vowed to throw rocks at one soon.

He sent his senses to the approaching humans. Their hearts beat rapidly, and their bodies moved in anticipation. Some had difficulty keeping their urine inside their bodies. But all would do everything in their power to expel the human intruders from the iron roads and their home. He sensed many would sacrifice their lives if required. He touched the minds of the intruders. They were unaware the metal beasts approached.

He Who Watches let out a great sigh. He abhorred the large-scale and almost instinctual bloodshed and death that awaited the two groups of humans. He opened his mind and checked on the cubs before he became occupied. He sensed their play within their hiding place. Reassured, he focused on the survival of the human male.

Both groups carried many of the thunder sticks. Even with his deception ability and his great bulk, the large number of thunder sticks could cost him his life. He scanned the forest around him. He found two herds of does and fawns about one thousand paces away and a small group of bucks two thousand paces away. He touched the animals, and they moved towards him.

Chapter 31

September 14, 2015, 1130 (CST) Show Me Army Depot, Missouri

Victor Chow again paced behind the fighting positions dug by the Special Forces team. Behind him stood Major Lee, Abdul Barry, Johnny Park, and Joe Harper. The long night drained them all, but Johnny and Joe could barely stand.

Victor went to Johnny and gave him a small pill. "Take this. I need you alert."

The young man pulled a water bottle from his back pocket and swallowed the pill. They watched six North Korean soldiers working among the yard's railroad tracks. All six connected blasting caps and igniters to the explosives in twenty separate locations. Once they ignited the detonators, the soldiers had ten minutes to get into their vehicles and depart for the entrance. They did not rush but worked steadily; their leader expected no problems.

Victor muttered curses at the six soldiers. He felt they moved too slow. He wanted to scream at them, but he knew Major Lee would protest. He lit another cigarette. As he drew in a puff of smoke, he felt several small shocks come through the ground.

"What was that?" Victor said.

The others looked at him. Major Lee took a step towards him. "I felt something. I think it was a small earth tremor. I'm sure it is nothing that could affect our explosives."

Victor felt more tremors, and he heard a low rumble punctuated by faint metal on metal shrieks. He looked up the main line track towards the sound. Half a kilometer north of the rail yard the track curved to the left. He tried to look beyond the bend, but the forest blocked his view.

Major Lee took his weapon off his shoulder and held it ready. "I hear something. What is it?"

The six soldiers out in the rail yard stood and faced north towards the rumbling sound. One waved at Major Lee and pointed. Soon all the soldiers pointed. Within moments a large red locomotive appeared from behind the trees and moved down the main line track towards them. Victor saw it would soon enter the rail yard.

He turned to Abdul Barry. "It's the employees you let escape from the cafeteria! Your incompetence is threatening my operation!"

The British terrorist ignored Victor and shot at the approaching locomotive. Major Lee barked at the soldiers in their foxholes, and they fired at the huge red target. The soldiers out in the rail yard dropped their detonators and ran towards their fighting positions.

Victor screamed at the running soldiers. "No! Don't stop! Go back! Ignite the charges! Ignite the charges!"

Several of the soldiers stopped at the nearest mines and pulled the igniters. Small puffs of smoke rose from the burning detonators.

Now both Victor and Major Lee waved their arms and yelled at the running soldiers. "Yes! Yes! Pull the igniters!"

Before the soldiers could reach any more charges two shots rang out from the forest near the approaching locomotives. A red spot burst open on one soldier's chest, and he fell to the ground in a heap. A second soldier grabbed his leg and fell to the ground. The Special Forces soldiers shifted their fire to the tree line.

Victor spotted a second locomotive following the first. "No! Shoot the trains! Shoot them. They have two of them!"

Before they could adjust their fire four small bursts appeared along the main line at the rail yard perimeter. Soon large clouds of white smoke screened the approaching locomotives. Victor heard the locomotives slow and stop, but the smoke hid their movements. The fire from the North Koreans died down to nothing.

Abdul lowered his rifle and turned to Victor. "They have an M203 grenade launcher. That means they are American soldiers. You stated this base had no military assigned to it."

"It has none. They must have survived the crash of the aircraft."

Abdul and Major Lee aimed their rifles at the unseen enemy and waited. A deafening sound blasted from the smoke cloud and battered their eardrums. Victor's breathing grew uneven, and he took several steps back. He pushed Johnny Park into a foxhole and waited. The horn stopped, but the rumble of the hidden diesel engines turned into a roar. Their horns blasted again, and the two locomotives burst from the smoke cloud. Only now they traveled, side by side, straight for the still running soldiers and the dug in fighting positions.

Victor spotted a mix of soldiers and civilians firing from both locomotives. The massive machines belched heavy black smoke and accelerated into the yard. Their horns once again blared. Victor jumped into his foxhole; his hands over his ears.

Joe Harper raced for the forest with his hands over his head. Victor took a quick shot at the union official and hit him in the shoulder. The man staggered but recovered and entered the forest. Victor yelled at him. "Run you worthless traitor! I'm keeping your money!"

He again looked at the charging locomotives. The great machines frightened him more than a beating at the Yodok Reeducation Camp. He took out his satellite phone and, with shaking hands, punched the preset number.

Jack watched as Conner and Rita climbed aboard the locomotive. The smoke screen hid his small force well, and the locomotives suffered just a few grazing rounds.

Jack keyed his radio. "Move out."

Both engines thundered, and Will and Shorty laid on the air horns.

In a few seconds, they burst through the smoke cloud into the open. Jack got a good look at the rail yard. A few empty flat cars sat on the spur the farthest to his left. Nothing stood between them and the enemy positions. Jack spotted several enemy soldiers running in front of them. They surprised the terrorists. Now he needed the locomotives to affect the fight like real tanks.

Jack keyed his radio. "Enemy in the open; use high explosive."

Specialist Siegel aimed and fired his grenade launcher. He reloaded and fired two more times. Jack counted to three and looked out the front window. The first grenade exploded ahead of the running soldiers. They dodged to the left and kept on running. Jack lost sight of the fleeing soldiers in the thick smoke but heard the second and third rounds explode. The smoke cleared and he spotted two soldiers motionless on the ground.

By now accurate rifle fire pelted the locomotives. Several rounds went through the cab, and Jack and Will both ducked.

Will let out a crazy laugh, and his body twitched. "Cocksucker, prick, fuck."

Jack keyed his radio. "Open fire!"

The roar of the rifles on the two locomotives assaulted his ears. He saw small spouts of earth around the enemy positions. The fire from the positions slowed as the Koreans ducked the incoming fire.

Jack again looked around the rail yard. He saw numerous small piles of explosives laid out along each of the rail turnouts. Several mounds of explosives had wisps of white smoke coming from them.

Jack clapped Will on the shoulder. "Stop the locomotive one hundred yards from the enemy and grab your rifle and join us."

"You got it, Colonel," Will said.

Jack opened the door and ran back along the catwalk. Several rounds followed him but went over the top of the locomotive. A round pinged off one of the engine doors above his head. Liam fired, and a North Korean soldier fifty meters to their right dropped to the ground.

Jack ran past Liam and crouched down behind him. Ross, Conner, and Rita crouched there also. Every few seconds two of them, one high and one low, would pop around the back of the locomotive and fire a burst towards the fighting positions.

Jack put his hand on Liam's shoulder. "Thanks."

Liam nodded.

Jack grabbed Ross's arm. "Ross, when we stop, I want you to get those igniters." Jack pointed behind the two locomotives at the smoking charges. "Pull the blasting cap from the C4 and throw it away. Once it's out the explosive can't go off. Try to keep the locomotive between you and the bad guys. You got it?"

"No problem," Ross said. He moved to the steps on the far side of the locomotive and prepared to jump off.

Jack peered around the engine compartment. About a dozen men fired at them from foxholes. A burst of fire hit the steel doors close to Jack's head. He ducked out of the way.

Liam fired a burst and yelled. "Careful, Colonel! There's a lot of paperwork involved if a depot commander gets killed!"

Jack winked at him. "It'll never happen, Liam." He keyed his radio. "We're about to stop. Gunner put some high explosive on those positions."

Jack once again peeked around the large engine. Seconds later two high explosive grenades exploded among the fighting positions followed by a white smoke. Jack waited for more rounds to hit, but none came. He looked at locomotive 4627 and saw Specialist Siegel splayed out on the catwalk. Blood poured from a wound in his throat. His M203 lay on the ground fifty feet behind the moving locomotive. Lieutenant Craig and Sergeant Cadena fired at the enemy while the medic pulled the wounded man behind cover.

Both locomotives stopped. Ross jumped to the ground and ran for the smoking charges. Will triggered a long blast on the air horn and ran down the catwalk. Rounds chased him as he ran around Liam and flopped down on the deck.

He rolled over on his back and laughed. "That was a close one!"

Jack looked at their objective. Half the positions still had smoke on them. The sounds he heard were no different than the battle for COP Armstrong.

He keyed his radio. "Craig, I'm sending Will over to take the place of your wounded man. We're jumping. Cover us. When we're in position take your locomotive forward another fifty meters and jump from there."

Jack shook Will's shoulder and pointed at the wounded man. "You fight with the Bragg team."

Will nodded. He ran down the steps and sprinted across the gap between the locomotives. He fired his AK-47 from the hip while he ran. Jack ran down the steps and crouched behind the rumbling locomotive. Liam, Conner, and Rita followed. All three reached the ground, and Jack yelled. "Let's go!"

He charged out from behind the locomotive. His small team followed and spread out to the left and right. All four fired while they ran. At first the infantry team on locomotive 4627 received most of the enemy fire. But when the smoke cleared, the North Koreans spotted Jack's team and shifted their fire. Dozens of rounds flew by them and pinged off the railroad tracks around them. Jack covered thirty meters before the fire became too intense. He dove behind an elevated rail bed. Rita dropped behind the same bed, and Liam and Conner crouched behind a short stack of railroad ties. All four did their best to send rifle fire towards the enemy positions.

The 4627 locomotive revved its engine and pulled forward. Jack saw Shorty in the cab and PFC Newton at the back of the locomotive still working on Siegel. Craig and his team bolted from behind the locomotive. Jack's team increased their fire, but the aimed fire at the infantry team intensified. They ran forward for twenty-five meters and hit the ground. Will Miksic continued to stand and fire at the North Koreans. The crazed employee screamed obscenities at the Koreans as rounds flew from his rifle. Finally, Craig jumped up and forced Will to the ground.

Craig's team put accurate fire onto the North Korean positions. A Korean soldier dropped his rifle and disappeared into his hole.

Jack jumped up and yelled. "Let's hit 'em!"

All four again ran towards the enemy. Murderous fire zipped through the air around them. Jack felt a round tug at his collar and heard its supersonic crack inches from his ear. It took all his courage to move forward. This time they got no more than ten meters before they had to take cover. Jack pushed his rifle over a track and returned fire. His team did the same.

Jack looked over at Craig. The Bragg team leaped up and charged. The fire from the enemy positions rose in intensity.

Jack yelled. "More!"

Even with his team a few feet away, Jack knew they barely heard him. Craig and his team moved no more than ten meters before they too had to take cover. Craig rallied his team, and they advanced again. A torrent of fire met them. They got no more than a few feet and dove to the ground.

Jack keyed his radio. "Craig, it's no use. We can't do it. My team will cover. Pull back to your locomotive."

Craig nodded at him. Jack lay on his back and looked at the blue sky above him. He knew they had a few seconds before the veteran enemy soldiers charged and destroyed his small force. Jack rolled over and fired at the North Korean positions.

He Who Watches stood with his hands covering his ears. The battle before him made an unbelievable noise. He watched as the human male jumped from the closest metal beast. The noise from the human's thunder sticks increased, and he pressed his hands even tighter.

The deer standing behind him stamped their feet and pawed at the soil; their white tails pointed up in the air. The males swung their antlers up and down and sometimes struck an animal next to them. The entire herd boiled with the need for release. He concentrated hard to keep them from bolting.

He watched the two groups of humans for several minutes. He touched the mind of the human male. At the start of the battle, the male projected confidence and saw victory for him and the others. The human male failed to advance against the human intruders, and his confidence vanished. Soon he radiated failure and doom. Now the human male thought of his dead mate and his cubs.

He Who Watches released the herd to run for their lives. He told them safety waited in the dense forest on the opposite side of the iron roads. The terrified animals surged past him, and he touched the minds of the human intruders.

He looked up at the sky. *I hope they arrive in time.*

"Gunners, target coming up," Tony said. "Lock and load."

Sarah grabbed the weapon's charging handle and pulled it hard to the rear locking it in place. A manicured nail snapped off, and she cursed out loud. "I'm ready, Tony."

Don slapped a thirty-round magazine into his AK-47 and crouched in the right door. "Ready."

"Stand by gunners." Tony thumbed his MP3 player and placed it into its holder. The steel guitar and heavy base of "Surf Medley" by Junior Brown pounded from the speakers.

Don laughed. "God, I love this!"

"Starting our first run," Tony said.

He spotted two locomotives parked at the south end of the rail yard. A furious firefight raged in front of them. It appeared the enemy fired from dug in fighting positions. He also saw figures on the ground among the yard's railroad tracks. Heavy fire reached for the figures. Movement at the forest's edge caught his attention. A large herd of deer broke from the forest and ran towards the firefight.

He ignored the deer. "Gunners, your targets are enemy troops in fighting positions at the south end of the rail yard. Note the friendlies one hundred feet in front of the fighting positions. You're weapons free."

Don brought his AK-47 to his shoulder and aimed down at the ground. Five hundred meters from the enemy positions, Tony rotated the tail of his helicopter to the left.

The UH-1 crabbed sideways while it flew across the rail yard.

"Dammit, Tony," Don said. "I want a shot."

"You'll get your turn," Tony said. "Now shut up and stay off the intercom."

"Don't you yell at me, Tony," Sarah said. She stood behind her gun and aimed at the fighting positions.

Tony spotted the deer running through the battle. He cocked his head at the sight but then shrugged. There was nothing he could do about them now.

Sarah pressed the butterfly trigger.

Chapter 32

September 14, 2015, 1135 (CST) Show Me Army Depot, Missouri

Jack slammed a fresh magazine into his rifle and sent a three-round burst into the Korean positions.

"Colonel, look!" Liam said.

Jack followed Liam's point to this right. Over thirty deer, to include at least four big bucks, burst from the forest and ran into the raging battle. He had never seen this many deer in one herd before. As one they dashed between the North Koreans and Jack's two teams, the crazed animals seemed fixated on the forest on the other side of the rail yard. The shooting from both sides dropped off.

All the participants stared dumbfounded at the suicidal deer. Jack spotted many of the North Koreans pointing open-mouthed at the large herd. From his previous tours to Korea, he knew native Korean deer were extremely rare; they lived only in the remote mountains. Most Koreans went a lifetime without ever spotting one.

A North Korean soldier jumped from his foxhole and fired at the deer. Soon five enemy soldiers stood outside their foxholes and shot at the fleeing deer. Half a dozen animals dropped but most continued on.

Jack heard the bass and guitar of surf music come from behind him. He rolled onto his back and spotted the big Huey helicopter headed towards them.

He pointed at the helicopter and yelled. "Don did it! He got Tony Simpson into the fight."

Liam looked away from the deer and into the sky.

Tracer rounds zipped over their heads and into the Korean fighting positions. He heard a machine gun firing.

"He's got a gun and he's shooting at 'em!"

He looked back at the Koreans. Many continued to take pot shots at the deer, and even turned away from their attackers. Others noticed the music and incoming gunfire. Troubled looks appeared on their faces.

Another burst of helicopter gunfire hit the center of the defensive positions. Three standing men shuddered and fell behind their foxholes. Others jumped back into their holes when the ground around them erupted with hits. Tony's helicopter passed over their heads no more than one hundred feet off the ground. In an amazing feat of flying, the big Huey crabbed sideways at over fifty miles an hour. Don Miksic leaned from the door and sent accurate rifle fire down into the foxholes.

"We'll Goddamn," Liam said. "Let's get 'em before they start shooting again."

Jack leaped to his feet.

Before he could do anything, Craig swung his arm forward and yelled. "Follow me!"

The young officer charged the enemy fighting positions, and his team let out a blood-curdling yell and flanked him. In a matter of seconds, they were halfway to the Korean positions. At least one Korean fell from the charging team's fire.

Jack turned to his team. "Give 'em cover!"

They opened fire and sent three round bursts at the enemy positions. Jack ran through a complete magazine but received little return fire from the distracted Koreans.

Jack reloaded and yelled again. "Let's go!"

He charged towards the enemy positions with his team beside him. Jack stopped and shot a soldier still looking at the deer. A red spot blossomed on the man's chest, and he fell to the ground. Jack ran forward and kept up continuous fire. Liam, Conner, and Rita did the same.

A handful of Koreans leaped from their holes and ran towards the forest. A fleeing soldier grabbed several cardboard boxes from the ground and disappeared into the trees. Jack wanted to chase them with fire, but too many Koreans still threatened Craig's team. He kept his fire focused on the center of the fighting positions.

In a few seconds Craig's team reached the first foxhole on Jack's left. They shoved the muzzles of their weapons into the hole and opened fire. Blood and bits of uniform flew from the hole. They shifted their fire and moved forward.

Jack reached the enemy line. He killed a Korean aiming at Will Miksic, and Liam shot another. The remaining Koreans dropped their weapons and put their hands in the air. All yelled in Korean. "Chong sohji ma seh oh!" (Don't shoot.). One even yelled in broken English. "Don't shoot Yankee GI!" All looked terrified with their attacker's rifles inches from their heads.

Jack tried to spot the escaping Koreans, but the trees hid them.

He turned to Liam. "Wave off that helicopter."

Liam ran back towards the locomotives and waved at the approaching Huey. The helicopter held its fire and prepared to land in front of the fighting positions. Jack ran to the open ammunition crates pilfered by the escaping Korean soldier. The labels showed they held the missing blasting caps and igniters. The escaped Koreans had sufficient detonators to arm the explosives at the depot's entrance.

Jack moved down the line of foxholes and met Lieutenant Craig. Sweat rolled off both men and mixed with the dirt and grime on their faces and hands.

Jack's hands trembled, and he took a swig of bottled water. "Good work leading that charge. They broke and ran when they saw you coming."

Craig gulped water from his camelback. He slouched from the stress. "I don't know how we did it."

"Do you have any wounded?"

"Siegel took a bad hit on the locomotive, and Will got a finger shot off. Other than that, we're ok. My insert saved me at least twice." Craig showed Jack two rough gouges in the center of his ceramic body armor. "I have two captured Koreans. One's wounded, but he'll make it."

Jack noticed Craig staring at him. "What?" he said.

Craig pointed. "You took some damage."

Jack reached up and found a long gouge on the left side of his helmet. "I didn't even feel it." He shook his head. "Jesus we were lucky."

He turned and yelled at his team. "Liam, is anyone hurt?"

Tony's helicopter came in and landed. He kept his engine running but reduced it to idle.

Liam yelled over the noise from the helicopter. "We're all ok, Colonel." The lanky employee turned and jogged towards the helicopter.

Jack turned back to Craig. "We have two Koreans also. Bring your medic forward to treat Will and the Korean. The chopper can medevac Siegel."

Lieutenant Craig stepped away and keyed his radio. Don Miksic jumped from the helicopter and ran to his son. Will made wild gestures and showed his father his still bleeding hand. Jack knew adrenaline coursed through the quirky employee. Thank God he suggested they use the locomotives. The big machines gave them the edge they needed.

Craig faced Jack. "Siegel didn't make it, and your driver Shorty bought it." Both looked at the locomotive and saw a mass of bullet holes in the cab's windshield. "That guy saved our butts when he moved the locomotive forward to cover us."

Jack recalled Shorty's earlier offer to help. "Shorty saved a lot of people today."

Ross ran up to Jack. "I got rid of all the explosives, Colonel."

"Good work," Jack said. "But some of the terrorists got away with the detonators. We need to regroup and assault the entrance right away."

Jack faced the idling helicopter. He noticed a dark object high in the sky behind the Huey. The object grew, and he recognized the black jet that shot down the C-130. Bright flashes winked at him from the jet's wings. Two lines of small explosions and spouts of dirt marched towards the idling helicopter.

Jack turned and yelled. "Take cover!" He jumped into a foxhole as the jet fighter zoomed low over the fighting positions. His ears hurt from the scream of the aircraft's afterburner. He popped his head up and watched the black jet begin a long banking turn. Other heads poked up from the surrounding foxholes. The zip tied Koreans yelled in terror at their captors.

He turned back towards the rail yard. Smoke and dust filled the air around the helicopter, but it appeared untouched. Jack had no idea why the jet's pilot missed such an obvious target. The old Army chopper leaped into the air and flew off in the direction it arrived. In a few moments he lost sight of it. The enemy jet flew high over the rail yard and followed the retreating helicopter.

Jack jumped from his foxhole and pointed at the Koreans. "Get those prisoners into foxholes."

The soldiers shoved the Koreans into the nearest holes.

"Is everyone all right?" Jack said. He heard a few yells and saw heads bobbing up and down.

Rita looked around the positions and yelled. "Where's Dad?"

Everyone scanned the area around the foxholes for the missing man. Conner pointed. "There he is!"

Jack saw a figure lying in the path taken by the jet's bursting cannon shells. Conner and Rita sprinted to the prone form.

Jack turned to his soldiers and yelled. "Medic!" PFC Newton ran towards Liam.

Jack ran after Conner and Rita. The siblings reached their father and knelt down on both sides of him. Liam lay on his back covered in dust and bits of dirt. His left leg lay under his right at an angle impossible for a leg to make. His left arm ended above the elbow. Rita squeezed the stump, while Conner prepared his belt for a tourniquet. Fresh blood saturated Liam's shirt causing it to stick to his chest. Jack gasped, and a knot formed in his stomach. The coppery smell of blood made him gag.

PFC Newton flopped down next to Liam. She cut his shirt away and slapped bandages on three jagged punctures in his chest and stomach. Liam ignored the medic and looked up at his kids.

"Please don't die, Dad," Conner said. Tears rolled down his cheeks. Rita sobbed as she took in her father's condition.

"I'll be ok Conner," Liam said. "I've had worse from an old boar hog."

Conner and Rita tried to laugh at their father's courage.

"Help me roll him; I need to see his back," PFC Newton said.

Conner and Rita rolled him onto his side. Liam's eyes closed and he groaned. She ran her hand over his spine and ribs. She finished and gestured for them to roll him back.

She looked at Jack. "The shrapnel is still inside him, and he's bleeding internally. I can't stop it here. We need to get him to a hospital."

Jack looked at the vehicles parked next to the tree line. Don Miksic and the others watched the drama from the foxholes. Jack pointed and yelled. "Don, get that SUV! We need to get Liam to the hospital!"

Don took off in a sprint.

"Colonel," Liam said.

Jack bent over his wounded friend. "Don't try to talk, Liam. We're taking you to a hospital."

Liam coughed, and blood appeared on his lips. "Colonel, we both know the terrorists have the gate blocked and there's no road through the forest. I'm staying right here."

Jack's shoulders slumped. He knelt next to his friend. "Hang on, Liam. We can still get you out of here."

Liam smiled at Jack, and blood coated his teeth. "Don't try to fool an old fooler. I know I've had it."

"Don't say that, Dad!" Rita said. She kept pressure on the severed arm and cried into her shoulder.

Liam reached up and patted her arm. "It's ok honey; it doesn't hurt." He looked at Jack. "I need some time with my kids."

Jack nodded and touched the medic on the shoulder. The young woman teared up, closed her bag, and walked towards the foxholes.

"I'm glad you're my friend, Liam." Jack stood and walked away.

Liam raised his head. "Colonel, wait." Jack stopped and turned. Liam smiled at Jack. "Don't be afraid of that jet. It's just a big turkey."

Jack had no idea what Liam meant. He nodded and smiled at him and headed for the foxholes. Once there he turned and watched Conner and Rita speak with their father. After a minute he saw their heads drop. Soon their bodies bobbed up and down over their father.

Chapter 33

September 14, 2015, 1140 (CST) Show Me Army Depot, Missouri

Tony flew low and fast over the dense forest. Every few moments a gravel road or small industrial building appeared beneath them. His gauges indicated one hundred knots; the top speed for his old helicopter.

"Why didn't he shoot us?" Sarah said. "He had us easy."

"He missed us on purpose." Stress etched Tony's voice. "But he'll come after us. He wants us flying so he can get an air-to-air kill. It's like crack cocaine to most fighter pilots." He scanned the sky above them. "Can you see him, Sarah?"

She stuck her head out of the helicopter and looked behind them. The wind that streamed past the helicopter threatened to rip her headphones off.

"He's in our six at about four thousand feet. I think he's lining up for a gun run on us. When I yell, break left."

Tony shook his head. "No, that's no good; I'm going to break right. When he flies past us you shoot him."

"Roger," she said. Thirty seconds later she keyed the intercom. "He's diving on us." A few moments later she yelled. "Break right!"

Golf ball-sized tracers flew past the helicopter hitting the trees in front of them. Tony turned right without decreasing his speed. Sara pushed hard against the machine gun to keep from flying out the door. The much faster jet could not adjust and flew by them. Sarah snapped off a quick burst, but her tracers arced through the sky far behind the jet.

"God dammit!" Tony yelled. "How could you miss him?"

Sarah whipped her head around to her husband. "Tony Simpson, if you think I'm going to tolerate your abuse, you'd better think again. If you yell at me one more time, you can land and let me out. You can take this fighter on by yourself."

Tony waved his hand in the air. "But he flew right in front of you!"

"Dammit, Tony, I mean it. Keep your mouth shut!"

Tony's shoulders sagged and he looked back at his wife. "I'm sorry, Sarah. I'll control myself." He turned and examined the sky in front of them. "Where is he?"

She again looked behind the helicopter. "He just finished a wide left turn high above us. Now he's lined up on us again." She pulled back inside the helicopter. "Tony there's no way he can turn inside us or brake with us. Also, every turn he's made is to the left."

"That's good to know," Tony said. "Let me know when he shoots again. This time I'll break right and flare. That'll give you a better shot."

"Roger." Sarah stuck her head out of the helicopter. "He's diving on us Tony. Get ready." She paused for a moment. "Break, Tony!"

Tony slammed the aircraft hard to the right and tracers shot by them. Sarah again pushed against the gun. The helicopter came out of the turn and Tony pulled the nose of the helicopter up until it stood on its tail. He brought the helicopter to a complete stop and dropped its nose.

"Get him, Sarah."

Sarah aimed at a point in the sky and fired. Tracers shot away from the helicopter, and metal links and brass casings poured onto the deck. Tony prayed the spent casings went nowhere near his engine intake. The jet screamed past the hovering helicopter no more than one hundred feet above them. Sarah shifted her fire but failed to hit the speeding jet. She released the trigger. Smoke rose off the blistering hot gun barrel and blew away in the rotor wash.

"I missed him again," Sarah said.

"Dammit!" Tony yelled. He added. "Not you, Sarah. I'm mad at myself. Keep track of him."

Tony applied power and chased the jet. Soon he had his speed back up to one hundred knots. He continued to head towards the center of the depot, and the fighter again turned left in a long turn to get behind the helicopter.

Tony came on the intercom. "Let's try something different this time."

Sarah stuck her head outside the helicopter. "What do you mean?"

"I'm going to aim this time. Put the gun as far forward as you can and hold it there."

Sarah sat on the bench at the back of the helicopter. She pulled the gun's hand grips towards her until the muzzle pointed to the left and down from the front of the aircraft.

"Okay. The gun's in place. I can even sit while I hold it."

"That's great, honey. Give me a test fire." Sarah fired off a ten-round burst, and Tony observed where the rounds hit in front of the helicopter. "Okay, I got it, Sarah. You hold the gun and fire when I tell you."

"You'd better make it quick. It's getting tough to avoid this guy."

"No shit," Tony said. "Where is he?"

Sarah looked up behind them. "He's in our six. Get ready to break; I think he's going to dive again. Wait…"

"What's he doing?"

"He's doing something different. He just dipped his nose towards us, but he pulled it back up."

Sarah screamed into the intercom. "Missile! Missile! Missile! He's fired a heat seeker at us. It's behind us and it's locked on."

Tony could not see the approaching missile. In addition, he had no decoy flares or electronic counter measures to defeat the diving missile. He scanned the industrial buildings to his front and spotted a large exhaust stack jutting from a building to his right. He recognized the depot's central boiler house. Inside it an old, but still serviceable, boiler sent superheated steam to at least a dozen production buildings. The depot employed Tony's father as a boiler operator for eighteen years. His old man told the family many stories over dinner about the cantankerous Kewanee boiler.

Tony banked into a turn and dove down to the road that ran in front of the boiler house. When the building filled his windshield, he wrenched the helicopter off the road and flew behind it. He shot down the alley with the tips of his spinning rotor blades mere inches from the boiler house and the parts warehouse behind it. Even over the straining engine, Tony heard Sarah scream in terror.

Four hundred meters behind them, the missile's infrared seeker lost sight of the helicopter and locked onto the boiler house instead. Tony pulled up at the end of the alley and watched the missile dive through the roof of the building. An explosion blew the roof off and ruptured the massive boiler. A huge cloud of steam burst from the wrecked building and covered the surrounding area.

"Sorry, Dad," Tony said.

Tony leveled off at one hundred feet and dodged several water towers. Sarah came on the intercom. "D-d-don't you ever do that again Tony Simpson."

Tony chuckled. "I won't honey. I promise. Now, where's that jet?"

Sarah took several deep breaths and leaned out the door. "He's above us flying in circles. Maybe you scared him?"

Tony craned his neck to look above the helicopter. "I doubt we scared him but I'm sure he thinks we're friggin nuts."

Captain Hwong, his mouth twisted beneath his oxygen mask, watched the antique American helicopter below. No other fighter pilot could match his skills, and he flew his nation's most advanced fighter. Yet the helicopter easily evaded him. He had no more missiles, and only sixty cannon rounds remained. The helicopter's slower speed and greater turning capability gave it the upper hand against his much faster jet. He thought for a moment. He needed to take away the helicopter's advantage.

Hwong pulled his throttle back to its lowest setting and lowered his flaps. When his aircraft stabilized, he lowered his landing gear slowing the fighter even more. His heads-up display showed his airspeed at one hundred and twenty-five knots; the slowest speed at which he could stay in the air.

Hwong slowed and followed the helicopter as it flew towards a long industrial building. The helicopter flew a meter above the ground and stayed next to the long building. He knew the enemy pilot would try another slow speed turn to throw off his aim.

Something on the ground caught Hwong's attention. Two additional helicopters sat near the long building. His pulse quickened. When he finished with this one, he would return and wait for the other two to take off. Soon he would have four air to air kills. When he found another aircraft on his return to the Gulf of Mexico, he would be the first North Korean fighter 'Ace' in over sixty years.

Hwong smiled into his oxygen mask. He dropped down behind the running helicopter. His altimeter read zero; he guessed the blacktop road that paralleled the building sat ten meters below him. The long building on his left blurred as he passed it by. His gloved finger caressed the trigger on the control column between his legs. The helicopter grew in his heads-up display gun sight, and his smile widened.

When the gun sight's pipper joined with the helicopter, he fired. The rounds went beneath the helicopter but rose to meet it. At least three rounds hit the bottom of the helicopter before it broke right. Hwong streaked past it and pulled up at the end of the long building. He looked behind his jet.

What he saw stunned him. Trailing a thin line of white smoke, the helicopter came to the end of the long building and made a quick one-eighty turn. It now flew away from him down the opposite side of the same building. Either it absorbed the damage from his high explosive shells, or they passed through the aircraft without exploding.

Hwong cursed out loud and banged his fist against his cockpit canopy. He finished his turn and dove towards the building. Still at his slow speed, he again flew above a road with the helicopter ahead. He had enough ammunition for one final burst of cannon fire. The helicopter grew in his heads-up display.

Tony felt the hits to his helicopter. He still had good control, and his gauges showed everything green.

Sarah pulled a small fire extinguisher from its mount. "Tony we're trailing smoke. I think we're on fire."

"Ignore it, Sarah. Put your gun at nine o'clock and aim it straight down. I'm gonna sucker this guy into position so you can kill him."

Sarah dropped the extinguisher. She pushed her grips into the air and pointed the gun down. She looked behind them.

She warned Tony. "He's right behind us; twenty feet above the road. He's catching up fast. Holy shit. I think he's gonna try to ram us!"

"Get ready." Tony said. "It's coming up."

This side of the building had several large steel conveyors that transported raw materials into the production line. The immense conveyors originated four hundred feet away, rose one hundred feet in height, and angled down into the top of the building. Tony flew above the maintenance road that ran under the first conveyor. He headed for the gap between the large steel support columns in their path.

Sarah screamed into the intercom. "Tony, no!"

They passed underneath the conveyor, and Tony again stood the helicopter on its tail to kill his forward speed. He dropped the nose and applied power to climb straight up.

Tony yelled into the intercom. "Fire, Sarah!"

Sarah squeezed the trigger. A lethal rain of ball and tracer rounds pounded into the maintenance road below them. She glanced at the jet and saw their pursuer had come too close to pull up. It had to follow them, or it would hit the steel columns on both sides of the road. The jet squirted through the conveyor supports and flew below them.

Time seemed to stand still for Sarah. She watched her rounds penetrate the top of the fuselage behind the cockpit. She could even see the pilot looking up at them through his canopy. He had on a flight suit like her own but wore a black helmet with gold aviator wings on top. An oxygen mask and sun visor hid his face otherwise she could have seen the man's expression. Sarah nudged her grips and walked the rounds into the cockpit. The canopy shattered and the aircraft zipped away. The jet now trailed a solid stream of black smoke. It pulled up away from the road and gained altitude.

Sarah screamed. "I got him!"

Tony said nothing. He stayed in a hover and watched the jet climb.

The wind tore at him, and Hwong wondered why so much air flowed into his cockpit. He looked around and saw little of his canopy remained. What was left had jagged holes and cracks running through it.

He looked down at his torso and legs. Blood covered his flight suit from his chest to his knees, and he noticed a huge hole in his oxygen hose. A piece of gleaming white bone, he guessed it came from his femur, sat next to his throttle. Hwong tried to check his gauges but could not raise his chin from his chest. He concentrated hard, but his head refused to move. Soon his right hand lost its grip on the control yoke and flopped next to his bloody leg. The aircraft rolled over and pitched down into a steep dive.

He knew he would never become an astronaut and he would never again hold a woman. He blinked back tears while the terrain spun below him. Hwong blacked out before his aircraft dove into a field.

Sarah did a quick jig and yelled into the intercom. "Waaaahhhoooo! We got him!"

The jet slammed into the ground and exploded into tons of scrap metal. Its fuel erupted into a huge fireball and shot thick, black smoke into the sky.

Tony watched the fire for a few seconds and turned to his controls. "Nice shooting, Sarah. We're heading back."

Five minutes later they landed at the rail yard. Ten minutes after that they dropped the prisoners off with a speechless Uwell Yates. Soon they, along with the survivors from the rail yard, approached X-Ray and the civilian employees hiding there.

Chapter 34

September 14, 2015, 1300 (EST) Bourbon Army Depot, Kentucky

Mohammed Kashani drove the Cadillac SUV south on Kentucky Highway 212. He lit another cigarette and enjoyed the aura of the expensive vehicle. Soon he took the exit leading to Bourbon Army Depot. Two large panel trucks followed him.

Kashani began life in a small Turkish village situated close to the Syrian border. When he turned two, his family left Turkey for better jobs in Germany. He received an excellent education, provided free to all immigrants admitted by the socialist state. He also worshiped at several of the two thousand mosques that operated within Germany. At age fourteen he heard his first lecture from a visiting Imam that discussed the merits of Al Qaeda, and its struggle against the West's oppression.

Kashani, now a thirty-year-old ISIS member, wore a German Army class B uniform provided by a colleague in Berlin. A small leather clutch purse, popular with European men, sat on the seat next to him. A small pistol rested inside it. He practiced with it for hours; until he could quickly draw and fire the pistol.

He yawned and cursed the operation's contact for his fatigued condition. He and his ISIS team arrived at their leased warehouse two days ago. They found it open and well stocked with food and drink. Several large shipping crates held their weapons. However, they could not find their contact; a North Korean agent. Kashani waited six hours for the agent. When no one showed up, he used a satellite phone, found in the warehouse, to dial the agent's contact number. After a dozen tries over many hours, he still had nothing.

The next morning a North Korean commando team arrived at the warehouse. The captain leading the team spoke English but had no information on the missing agent. Both team leaders worried for the success of their mission. They needed to enter the nearby American depot that night, but they had no vehicles to take them there.

The Special Forces team leader made a frantic satellite phone call to the North Korean embassy in Mexico. The embassy informed him the county morgue held their missing agent. It turned out the agent ran a small acupuncture clinic in a small town located near Bourbon Army Depot. A local housewife received treatments from the agent over many months. Three days ago, an often-absent husband discovered the agent and his lonely wife in their bed. The husband shot the agent, his wife, and himself.

Using documents they found in the warehouse, Kashani and the Captain pieced together the agent's plans for the attack. Overnight, the embassy staffers somehow pierced the blackout and rented the SUV and trucks from a local dealer.

Now Kashani smiled. Allah's will allowed him to pull the mission together. Their delay in entering the depot made little difference. Once inside his team's firepower would stop anything the depot's security force could bring against them. They would find the needed explosives and destroy the designated infrastructure. Once they completed their work, the execution of many infidel American hostages would begin. Any American response would not arrive in time.

The road he followed entered a dense forest. Kashani's brow rose. He had never seen trees so thick; not even in Bavaria. Soon the trees thinned, and he spotted the depot's main entrance ahead.

He entered the large gate area and found all the vehicle lanes but one blocked by orange traffic cones. He headed towards the open lane with his trucks close behind. Two security guards dressed in blue uniforms and ball caps stood outside a windowed booth waiting for him. He spotted no other cars or trucks anywhere. It was a perfect setup for his entrance into the American installation.

He pulled up to the gate and rolled down his window. His trucks stopped twenty meters behind him. One of the guards approached. The large black man had a clipboard in his left hand, and his right thumb tucked inside his pistol belt. Kashani spotted a 9mm handgun in the guard's holster. The strap held the handgun in place.

"How can I help you, Sir?" the guard said.

The other guard, a large white man, stood off to the side watching him. He also had his thumbs thrust into his pistol belt.

Kashani stubbed out his cigarette and put on a bored persona. He added a strong German accent to his English. "I am Captain Schmitt of the German Army. I have an appointment with Colonel Jenson."

The guard relaxed and smiled at Kashani. "Not a problem, Sir. Colonel Jenson is in today. Could I see some ID please?"

He handed over his fake German military identification card. The guard compared it to Kashani and returned it.

"Thank you." The guard pointed to the trucks behind him. "Are those vehicles with you?"

Kashani looked into his mirror. "No, I'm alone. I drove in from Chicago." He smiled at the guard. "Colonel Jenson set up our meeting a few days ago, so I drove instead of flying. Airport security is such a pain."

The guard nodded. "I believe it, Sir." He pointed to the small security booth sitting in front of the vehicle. "Please leave your car here and step into the booth. I need you to sign some paperwork so I can issue you a temporary badge. It's our security rules."

"Of course, officer," Kashani said.

He turned off the car's engine and placed his leather purse in his left hand. He stepped from his vehicle and faced the guards. His eyebrows rose. Both stood at least two meters tall, and their arm muscles stretched their sleeves tight. He noticed their uniforms had a poor fit. He also thought it odd that each wore tan combat boots instead of more comfortable leather trainers.

The two security guards watched him. Neither smiled, and their hands now hung at their sides. The nearest guard backed away from him, and his hand moved to his now unsnapped holster. Kashani shoved his hand into his purse.

I'm faster than you.

The two guards went for their guns. Kashani smiled and swung his pistol towards the closest guard. He felt a slight tug to his upper body and heard the loud report of a rifle off to his left. His arm holding the pistol dropped to his side. He looked down at his chest. A small hole above his heart allowed a red stain to flow down the front of his shirt. He looked up at the guard. The big man had his pistol aimed at him. Kashani again raised his pistol towards the guard. A small explosion burst from the muzzle of the guard's pistol. A terrible darkness enveloped Kashani.

The company commander watched the two men sprint away from the Cadillac and head towards their positions in the tree line.

He turned to the platoon sniper lying next to him. "Nice shot, Cabrera."

The soldier said nothing. He ejected the spent shell from his rifle and jacked in a fresh round.

"Target the truck's driver," the company commander said. The soldier shifted his rifle to his new target. Ten feet to his right a second sniper did the same to the driver of the second truck. Both drivers appeared stunned after witnessing their leader's death.

The two false security guards leaped into freshly dug fighting positions situated twenty feet to his left and took up their M4 carbines. The company commander looked up and down the line of well-camouflaged fighting positions. Other manned fighting positions sat behind the main entrance. His entire first platoon sat in a textbook 'L-shaped' ambush. All positions could fire upon the vehicles without hitting friendly troops.

The commander pointed a large bullhorn, borrowed from the depot's security office, at the two trucks. "Attention in the trucks! Attention in the trucks! This is the United States Army! You cannot escape! Drop your weapons and surrender and you won't be harmed!" He waited twenty seconds and repeated his message.

He watched the two terrorist drivers stare at the forest concealing his soldiers. The rear door on the first truck rolled up and banged to a stop. The soldiers around him tensed, and a man poked his head out and looked towards them. He wore a camouflage uniform with no cap and carried an AK-47 rifle. The man jumped from the truck and yelled in Arabic towards the company commander.

Keeping his head down, the captain once more used his bullhorn. "Drop your weapons!"

Before he could say another word, the man sent a burst of fire towards the hidden platoon.

The company commander yelled into the bullhorn. "Take them!"

Every weapon in the platoon fired at the trucks. Both snipers killed the drivers before they could move. Eleven different infantrymen shot the standing terrorist, and he collapsed into a bloody heap. A few shooters found the dead man an irresistible target, and the body shook with the impacts of additional rounds. Hundreds of metal jacketed bullets pierced the two trucks. Tires burst and pieces of metal flew into the air. Soon clouds of steam rose from shattered radiators, and oil, fuel, and hot coolant puddled beneath the trucks.

The noise from the gunfire pummeled the company commander's ears. Despite this, he heard dozens of men screaming inside the cargo boxes of both trucks. After ten seconds of uninterrupted fire, the door on the second truck rattled up. Armed men in camouflage uniforms spilled from the rear of both vehicles. A hail of gunfire met them, and most fell to the ground, wounded or dead. A handful of terrorists from each truck still managed to return fire. Tree bark, wood splinters, and dirt pelted the soldiers around him. More terrorists leaped from the backs of the trucks. Many fired from a kneeling position or from behind their dead comrades.

The company commander again brought the bullhorn up. "Heavy weapons!"

Eight soldiers each aimed an AT-4 anti-tank rocket at the trucks. All fired within a few seconds of each other. One rocket passed under the second truck and exploded against a tree on the far side of the gate area. The other seven exploded against the trucks, and shrapnel and jets of molten copper sliced through them. The trucks shook from the explosions, and the screams from inside got even louder.

The platoon kept up its fire. Fifty-five seconds after the firefight started, the first terrorist broke and ran towards the trees behind him. Another followed a few seconds later. Both men still carried their AK-47 rifles. One terrorist yelled at them in Korean, but an infantryman silenced him. A platoon machine gun behind the main entrance cut the runners down halfway across the parking lot.

A few seconds later a terrorist dropped his rifle and thrust his hands in the air. Soon others raised their hands, and the fire from the terrorists reduced to a trickle. His men sensed their victory, and the platoon's fire dropped. He counted seven terrorists with their hands up.

He pulled the bullhorn to his lips. "Cease fire! Cease fire! Cease fire!"

A few additional shots rang out followed by silence. He waited a full twenty seconds to make sure no more enemy fire came at them. Finally, he spoke. "Zip ties!"

The soldiers surged from their fighting positions to secure their prisoners. The medics pulled out their kit bags and went to the wounded.

The company commander stood in his hole. He gazed at the forest as his men worked. He found this unknown Army installation very beautiful, and since his arrival, he had never felt more relaxed. He wondered if the Army could make Bourbon Army Depot his next duty station.

Chapter 35

September 14, 2015, 1215 (CST) Show Me Army Depot, Missouri

Jack stared at the bodies of Liam Torgerson, Shorty Cramer, and Specialist Siegel, wrapped in ponchos as they lay on the deck of the helicopter. The loose ends of the ponchos flapped in the wind that flowed through the moving helicopter. The passengers didn't speak and avoided looking at their lifeless friends.

Tony landed between the two helicopters sitting outside X-Ray and cut his engine.

Jack jumped from the back of the Huey and grabbed Don Miksic. "God dammit, Don. When did I say I wanted three helicopters?" He pointed at Sarah. "And why is she here? I'm already on the mayor's shit list."

"We needed more helicopters for our air assault against the terrorists," Don said. "We bumped into Sarah, and she volunteered to come with us."

Jack turned to Sarah who stood behind her gun. "Sarah, is that true? Did you volunteer for this fight?"

She stuck her chin out. "I did, Colonel. I wouldn't be anywhere else." She jumped down from the helicopter and stood with the others.

Jack pinned Don with his eyes. "What about the pilots? Did they volunteer?"

A crooked smile crossed Don's face. "We'll no. We encouraged them to come, but I'm certain when this is over, they'll be really glad they helped us."

Jack crossed his arms in front of his chest. "That's fucking awesome. So, you're a union president and a kidnapper. Are there any more volunteers around here that I should know about?"

Don avoided Jack's eyes. "No, Sir. Just the pilots."

"What air assault are you talking about?"

"Colonel, you said it yourself." Don gestured at the helicopters. "We need the helicopters for mobility. Now that we have them, they can carry all of us to the terrorists' positions at the entrance. We can sneak up on them and conduct an air assault like we used to do in 'Nam."

Jack looked at the big man. "We'll talk about it later. For now, get inside and redistribute weapons and ammunition."

Don grabbed Will and walked towards X-Ray. Tony, Sarah, Private Washington, and Private Newton followed close behind. A group of smiling employees waited at the door. Jack turned back to the helicopter. Conner, Rita, Lieutenant Craig, and Sergeant Cadena waited to speak to him.

"Colonel, what should we do with Dad?" Conner said. "I don't want to leave him in the helicopter."

Jack thought for a few moments. "Is it ok if we place your dad with the others at the plane crash? He'll be safe there. When this is over, I promise we'll take care of him like he deserves."

Conner looked at Rita and both nodded together. "Dad would be ok with that."

Jack looked at Craig. "Is that ok with you, Lieutenant?"

"Yes, Sir. Placing Siegel with his friends seems right."

"Conner, Rita round up a vehicle from X-Ray to move our friends," Jack said. "I'll help."

Conner took one last look at the poncho that held his father and nodded. He and Rita turned and walked towards the building. He put his arm around his sister and pulled her close as they walked.

Jack looked at Craig and Sergeant Cadena. "What do you think of Don's idea for an air assault against the terrorists at the entrance?"

"I think he's correct," Craig said. "We know the ISIS soldiers have dug in positions like what the Koreans had. That's bad, but with three aircraft we can get a large force on top of them before they know we're there. With the sixty in the Huey firing in support, we'll be much better off than we were at the rail yard.

"Sir, it would help if we could arrange a diversion to take the enemy's attention off the helicopters," Sergeant Cadena said.

"Good point, sergeant," Jack said. "Okay. You convinced me. Let's get up to X-Ray, and I'll issue an operations order for the assault. We need to get going ASAP."

The lieutenant and sergeant came to the position of attention and rendered a salute to Jack. He returned it. The two men turned and walked away. When they neared X-Ray, a group of employees surrounded the two young men and escorted them through the door.

Five minutes later a depot fire truck arrived and parked next to the Huey. Jack watched the four firemen from the cafeteria remove the bodies from the helicopter and place them atop the hoses stored in the back of the truck. The entire operation occurred in complete silence.

The fire engine pulled away, and Jack saluted the fallen men. He turned and walked towards X-Ray. No crowd of employees waited for him.

Jack walked into the large production area that held his fighting force and the sheltered employees. Everyone sat in chairs and on empty bomb casings scattered around the large room.

Sergeant Cadena barked at the room. "Atten Hut!"

All conversation stopped, and the soldiers leaped to attention. A few of the civilians looked confused and some stood.

Jack kept moving. "At ease please."

Everyone relaxed and returned to their seats. They all looked at Jack.

A framed map of Show Me Army Depot, liberated from an office within X-ray, sat propped up on two chairs in the center of the room. Jack removed his helmet and placed it on a chair. He moved to the map and looked at the faces in the room. A wildly diverse group of people made up his makeshift fighting force. He needed a simple operations order to lay out his plan. Something his soldiers, and now his civilian fighters, could easily understand.

"Ladies and gentlemen, we have had great success against the terrorists. But they remain a dangerous force that must be removed from our depot. If they succeed it means war in South Korea and death and destruction for millions of innocent people." He pulled out a small notepad. "Prepare to receive my operations order for our attack on the entrance area."

When he had everyone's attention he began. "Situation. An enemy force of twenty terrorists and North Korean soldiers holds our entrance. Their mission is to destroy the bridge at the main gate and disrupt our ammunition resupply efforts to South Korea."

"Friendly forces are the soldiers and civilians in this room. We have our own air support and the police forces located outside the depot on highway 61 can provide minimal support." Jack paused. "Because of the communication blackout we'll receive no more reinforcements; at least none today. It's up to us to take out the remaining terrorist force."

The employees looked determined, and many nodded their heads in understanding.

"Mission." Jack looked at the clock on the wall. "At 1225 hours Show Me Army Depot forces attack and destroy the terrorists at the depot's entrance so that Show Me Army Depot can continue with its ammunition deployment mission to South Korea."

"Execution. We'll form two fire teams and conduct an air assault into the entrance area. Once we insert our teams the UH-1 helicopter uses its machine gun to suppress enemy fire. The fire teams maneuver against the enemy until they can overrun his positions."

"My commander's intent is we must prevent the destruction of our bridge at all costs. We cannot defeat our enemy and back off. Even one terrorist free to set off any demolition charges means our defeat. We must occupy the terrorist positions and disable their explosives."

Jack looked at the employees sitting around him. "Once we destroy the enemy force, and the bridge is secure, I need you to resume outload operations. We need to get our first train out tonight as planned to prevent an invasion of South Korea."

"Lieutenant Craig leads fire team Bragg and attacks on the left." Craig stood. "His team consists of Sergeant

Cadena, PFC Washington, PFC Newton, Conner Torgerson, and Ross Kelly."

When he called their names, the soldiers and civilians stood and moved to the lieutenant's side. Before Jack could continue, Don Miksic clapped for the team. Before long everyone in the room applauded and whooped for the standing fire team. The team smiled at the applause.

"Excuse me, Sir," Craig said.

Jack looked at the young man. "Yes, Lieutenant?"

"I would be honored if Will Miksic could fight as a member of my team."

Jack looked at Will. "Are you ok with that Will?"

Will looked at his family and nodded. "I'd like that." Will grabbed his AK-47 and walked over to the lieutenant. He had a huge smile on his face. The soldiers standing with him smiled and patted him on the back. Will began to shake. "Ttttits, cock, prick, happy." No one paid him any attention.

Jack continued. "Don Miksic leads fire team Missouri and attacks on the right." Don stood. "His team consists of Natalie, Cecil, Howie, and Rita. Jack looked at Ross. "Ross, I'm moving you from team Bragg to team Missouri to balance them out."

Ross nodded and moved next to Don. Lieutenant Craig led the applause for team Missouri. His soldiers barked loud "hooahs" at the standing team.

Jack continued. "Fire support and lift comes from the UH-1 helicopter manned by Tony and Sarah Simpson."

Tony and Sarah stood. The room applauded and someone yelled. "Way to go, Tony!"

Jack spotted several women in the room whispering to each other. He wondered if they traded gossip about the estranged couple.

"The two remaining helicopters provide additional lift." Jack looked at the new pilots. "I'm sorry gentlemen but I didn't get your names."

The entire room stared at the two men. Tom West stood. "Colonel, I'm Tom West and I'm flying the Euro copter medevac. You're going to see the best flying today that you've ever seen in your life." The pilot paused and spat out his toothpick. "But when this is over, I'm going to sue all of you for every cent you have."

Tom sat and crossed his arms. No one applauded, and many people booed the pilot.

"Tom, I know you're here under unusual circumstances," Jack said. "But I thank you for your support and I look forward to your flying."

Jack looked at Brock, and the pilot leaped to his feet. A few minutes ago, Natalie told Jack that her abduction of the pilot and his proximity to possible, imminent death apparently threw him out of the closet. Jack didn't care about the man's sexuality; he just needed him to fly well.

"I'm Brock Hightower and I fly the Channel 27 news chopper," Brock said. He smiled and waved to the employees sitting around him. "I'm happy to be here, and I look forward to defeating those awful terrorists. There is no lawsuit in my future. I'm having the most…liberating time."

He smiled and bowed, and everyone in the room clapped and whistled.

Brock sat and Jack continued. "We'll use aggressive flying to avoid enemy fire and apply constant psychological operations to harass our enemy. In addition, I want at least three gun runs on the enemy positions before our assault." Jack pointed to the depot entrance on the map. "Tony, I want your final approach to put us down here in front of the truck gate. Once there we can use the terrain and any parked vehicles to cover our approach to the enemy positions."

Tony glanced at the map. "I'll make it happen, Colonel."

"This completes my order. Any questions?" No one responded, and Jack looked at his watch. "We're wheels up in five minutes."

All the fighters and many of the civilians nodded at Jack. Jack barked at the room. "On your feet!"

Everyone leaped up and Jack stood on a chair. "Ladies and gentlemen last night I watched the terrorists murder June Miksic in cold blood. I had to hide my own children in the forest to keep the terrorists from finding and killing them." The employees gasped and Jack looked at their faces. "These bastards violated our depot, and they killed many of our friends. They thought we were an easy target, and we would lie down and take it." Jack again paused and looked around the room. "But they were wrong. They underestimated our love and respect for our friends and coworkers and for our depot and our nation." He held up a clenched fist. "They didn't know we would fight and fight well." Over one hundred resolute faces looked back at him. "I'm proud I'm your commander and proud to fight with you today." Jack yelled. "Now let's take back our depot and get that ammunition out the door!"

The crowd yelled and whooped. His teams, carried along by the excited employees, flowed through the exits. Jack stepped off the chair and waited for the room to empty. When the door closed, he took one final look around the room and grabbed his helmet and weapon and walked out the door.

Chapter 36

September 14, 2015, 1230 (CST) Show Me Army Depot, Missouri

Tony scanned his gauges as the big helicopter rocked under its spinning blades.

Jack looked out the helicopter's front windshield. He spoke into the intercom. "Move out."

The Huey's rotor blades spun faster until they blurred. Tony tapped his MP3 player, and his speakers blasted a cavalry charge bugle call. The employees that stood outside X-Ray jumped up and down and waved upon hearing the famous notes.

Tony keyed his radio. "Ascend to one hundred feet and assume heading zero zero zero. Maintain ground speed of eight zero knots."

He added power, and the helicopter rose and moved forward. The other pilots clicked their radios in response. Both helicopters rose and flew on each side of the Huey and behind it by one length. The heavy bass and superb guitar licks from "Apache" by Jimmy Thackery blared from the speakers. All three helicopters flew close to the treetops.

Tony swiveled his head and scanned the helicopters to his left and right. "Show Me zero three maintain your position. Show Me zero two you're drifting; pull it in closer." The news chopper inched closer to the Huey. "That's good Show Me zero two keep it there. Maintain eight zero knots." Tony keyed his intercom. "Sarah put your gun in the forward firing position again. I'll aim with the helicopter. Hit the trigger when I tell you."

"No," Sarah said. "You brought me here to shoot so let me shoot."

Tony's blood pressure spiked. "I am the pilot in command of this helicopter, and I'll tell you when to shoot." He turned in his seat to face Sarah. She glared at him. He opened his mouth to yell at her but spotted Don looking at him. The big man's face said it all...*Tony you're a dumbass and we all know why Sarah left you.*

Tony shut his mouth and closed his eyes for a second. He opened them and turned back to his controls.

He spoke. "I'm sorry Sarah. You didn't deserve that. You're a much better shot than I am, you've got more guts than me, and you're doing great. But I need to fly over the enemy positions so the Colonel, Don, and the lieutenant can see 'em. You won't have much of a shot when I fly over them. But, if you'll help me, I can shoot as we approach, and you can shoot as we pass by."

Tony again faced Sarah. Don smirked at him then looked out the helicopter.

Sarah cocked her head at her husband. "Ok, Tony. I think we can do that. I wouldn't want to disappoint the Colonel, Don, and the lieutenant. Tell me when and I'll hit the trigger."

Tony grinned at his wife and turned back to his controls. For several minutes they flew over nothing but trees scored by an occasional fire break.

Tony keyed his radio. "Show Me flight we're coming up on our first gun run. Left turn to three one five and keep it tight. Sarah, you're weapons free. Stand by for my command."

The helicopters finished their turn. "Show Me flight increase to one hundred knots airspeed. If you have to dodge enemy fire, do it but don't hit me or the trees."

Two clicks came over the radio. Now, the thrumming guitar and rapid drumbeats of "Hawaii 5-O" by the Ventures burst from the speakers. A few seconds later the trees fell away and revealed the depot's entrance.

Tony grunted and tightened his grip on the cyclic. "Fire, Sarah."

Victor Chow watched Major Lee as he worked in the center of the bridge. In a few minutes the Special Forces officer would set off the fuse igniter connected to multiple demolition charges. They corrected their mistakes at the rail yard. This time Major Lee wired all the explosive charges to one detonator.

He looked down the line of foxholes. The ISIS fighting positions faced into the depot to defend against an enemy that approached from the center of the depot. The ISIS fighters and the two remaining Korean soldiers stood in their holes smoking and talking. One fighter, his head down, read from a small book. A few rifles were propped upon the loose soil piled in front of the positions.

Abdul Barry walked towards him, and Victor turned on him. Victor waved his hand at the foxholes. "Why did you orient your fighting positions towards the center of the depot? What about the police on the highway?"

"Victor, you worry too much." Abdul took a long drag on his cigarette. "We bloodied their police, and they know we outrange anything they carry. They will not attack."

Victor scowled at Abdul. "Your light machine guns point down the main road that leads back into the depot. I see no enemy forces coming at us from the depot." He pointed up the highway. "But I can see the police forces that threaten us. Your machine guns are useless where they sit if they decide to attack."

Abdul looked over at the bridge. "Let me know when he sets off the igniters. I want to get my men deep in their holes before the charges explode."

Abdul turned his back on Victor and walked away. Victor fumed, and his hand dropped to the weapon on his hip. His pistol remained in its holster. He needed the conceited British leader, and his terrorist soldiers, for the counterattack on the rail yard.

Victor froze. Faint music came from the forest. He noticed others in their foxholes turned towards the music. Victor wondered where it came from and if it signaled a new attack by the Americans. He now heard the music clearly; he identified it as American rock and roll.

Victor turned to Abdul. "They're coming! Get your men ready!"

Abdul threw his cigarette down and yelled up and down the line of foxholes. He pulled the carbine off his shoulder and jumped into a hole.

Victor turned towards Major Lee, but he was not on the bridge. A moment later the special forces leader climbed up from beneath the bridge. He ran towards the fighting positions and waved his arms in the air. He yelled but the music drowned him out. Victor thought Major Lee tried to tell him something with the movement of his arms.

Victor yelled at him. "Ignite the charges! They're coming! The Americans are coming!"

Major Lee ran past the detonator setup that lay in the middle of the bridge.

Victor waved and shouted. "No! No! Go back! Set off the charges! The Americans are coming!" He took a step towards the bridge. He would set off the charges himself.

Three helicopters flew over the edge of the forest straight towards them.

Johnny Park stood in the large foxhole he shared with the last two Korean commandos. He had never felt so alert and alive. He peppered his companions with dozens of questions about life in North Korea.

"What television shows do you have in North Korea? Do you guys own a car, or do you ride the bus? What's your favorite food? My parents used to serve me Kimchi all the time, but I prefer pizza and hamburgers. I like Victor's Chinese food; it's delicious. Do people in North Korea really eat tree bark 'cause they're starving? I heard that some starving North Koreans even ate some people. If that's true that's gross. Even starving, I don't think I could eat a human being. Maybe I could if I had enough hot sauce. LOL! I heard when North Korean men cannot get dates they turn to their buddies for sex. Is that true? That doesn't happen in America. Well, at least it never happened to me."

The two soldiers didn't speak English, so they ignored the boy's questions and smoked their cigarettes.

All three heard faint music coming from the direction of the depot. The two soldiers grabbed their rifles and moved to the front of the foxhole.

Johnny ignored his rifle. "Hey. That's music. Where's it coming from?"

He had never seen the movie *Apocalypse Now*, so he concentrated on the depot's main road. The two North Koreans did the same.

Soon the music filled the air. Johnny stood in the center of the foxhole and played air guitar.

Jack flinched as concussions from Sarah's gun pulsed against the side of the helicopter. The rounds hit the ground well in front of the fighting positions, sending dust, dirt, and grass into the air. The impacts ran towards the center of the fighting positions and cut through a two-man foxhole. Dust hid its occupants.

Jack pointed at a lone figure standing on the bridge. Tony banked the helicopter, and the impacting rounds ran into and beyond the now running soldier. The man's arms dropped, and blood splashed the ground around him. He flopped onto his stomach and rolled over once and lay still.

"Cease fire," Tony said.

The big gun fell silent, and Sarah rotated it towards the fighting positions. However, they moved too fast, and the trees blocked her shot.

Jack keyed the intercom. "Good shooting, team. A couple more runs like that, and our assault should go fine."

Tony looked at him. "We won't catch them sleeping again. They're going to shoot back next time."

"You're right. Take me over to the police. Let's get some help."

Tony nodded and keyed his radio. "Show Me flight maintain three one five and parallel the highway. You're doing good. Stay on me."

The pilots clicked in response. Soon Jack saw the masses of police cars blocking both sides of the highway.

"Look over there, Colonel," Don said.

Jack spotted three large locomotives sitting on the tracks beyond the police barricades. 'Union Pacific' in large red letters along with a large US flag adorned the side of each locomotive.

"Those are the locomotives for our train going out tonight," Jack said.

"We'll make it in time," Don said.

Jack grabbed the radio off his belt. "Uwell, come in, this is Jack."

Uwell Yate's came on the radio. "Go ahead, Colonel."

"Start your vehicles towards the gate like we discussed. Send those locomotives forward also. Tell them to make a lot of noise."

"We can do that. Are you sure you can't wait for the National Guard?"

Jack looked out the window to see if he could spot Uwell. He could not. "We've got this handled; but we need that support."

"I had to ask. We'll be there. Uwell out."

Jack looked at Tony. "The police will hit the bridge in a few minutes. Time your next run with their arrival."

Tony nodded and keyed his radio. "Show Me flight slow left turn to one eight zero."

Jack felt the helicopter bank. The other two helicopters stayed in perfect formation. The pilots kidnapped by Don were actually pretty good.

Jack felt a commotion behind him. He looked into the back of the helicopter. Cecil and Howie, their rifles at their feet, stood in the center of the helicopter's cargo area. Both still wore their intercom headsets, but they had their arms clenched around each other like high school wrestlers. Cecil sent a quick jab into his brother's ribs. Howie responded by kicking his shin. Cecil yelped in pain, but Jack heard nothing over the screaming engine. Cecil rained blows to Howie's chin.

Don sat on the bench with his arms crossed. He ignored his sons and gazed out the door. PFC Washington's eyes grew wide, and he moved away from the two men. Sarah yelled at the two but kept her gun pointed forward.

Jack keyed his intercom. "Don, what's going on?"

Don spoke. "They're having a family discussion on who's going to kill the most terrorists. They'll be done soon."

Jack shook his head and turned back in his seat.

Sarah came on the intercom. "Tony, make them stop! If they keep this up, they'll fall out!"

Tony turned and scowled at the two men. He yelled into the intercom. "I have had enough of this! You two are ruining this trip for everyone! Now sit down this instant! If I have to come back there, I'm going to turn this helicopter around and take you both back to X-Ray! Do you hear me?"

Both men stopped and looked at Tony. After a few moments they let go of each other and sat down in their seats. Both panted hard from their exertion. They looked at each other and grabbed their rifles off the deck.

"That's better," Tony said. "Now stay in your seats and do not speak to each other until we start the assault."

Jack did his best to ignore the exchange. He hoped the attack on his depot stayed out of the official US Army history documents. He didn't want to tell anyone how he led a bunch of lunatics against international terrorists.

Jack caught glimpses of the highway through the trees. He saw dozens of police cars racing towards the large bridge. All had their emergency lights on, and he knew their sirens blared. Black clouds of exhaust poured from the three diesel locomotives, and they also moved towards the bridge.

The distinctive guitar solos of Dick Dale's "Misirlou" blasted from the speakers. Jack snapped his fingers in time to the catchy beat.

Chapter 37

September 14, 2015, 1232 (CST) Show Me Army Depot, Missouri

Victor gasped as the bullets swept towards him, and he dove into the nearest foxhole. Fresh dirt soiled his hands, face, and uniform. He recognized the lead helicopter from their disastrous battle at the rail yard. Now two others flew with it. He wondered how the Americans acquired the helicopters and why his stealth fighter no longer responded to his calls.

When the helicopters flew off, Victor jumped from the hole and ran down the line of foxholes. Ahead of him an AK-47 lay in the dirt, while a man shrieked inside his foxhole. He ran by the position and saw a blood covered terrorist curled in the bottom. He glanced at the screaming terrorist but saw no wound on the man. Abdul pulled the screaming man from the hole and slapped him until he stopped.

Victor ran to the hole containing Johnny and the two Korean soldiers. All three crouched in the bottom. "Ji Hun…I mean Johnny, did they injure you?"

Johnny got up and looked around. "I'm ok. Man, that scared the crap outta me. I never knew helicopters could fly that low."

"Get ready. They will return."

Victor faced the bridge and searched for Major Lee. He saw no one. He sprinted towards it and yelled at Abdul Barry.

"Ignite the charges! Ignite the charges!"

Abdul Barry ran towards the bridge. Soon Victor spotted Major Lee lying face up in the middle of the bridge. Victor ran towards him. He heard sirens approaching. He stopped and saw at least ten police cars of many sizes and colors coming down the highway towards him. He looked behind the racing police cars and saw three large, yellow locomotives approaching. The locomotives sounded a long blast from their horns.

An ice-cold fist punched Victor's stomach, and he screamed at Abdul. "The police are attacking, and the crazy Americans are using locomotives to attack us again. Get your men and stop them. I'll ignite the charges."

Victor again ran towards Major Lee. Abdul turned and ran back towards his men. He waved his arms and shouted in Arabic at his soldiers. Two terrorists armed with the PKM machine guns jumped from their foxholes and ran towards Abdul.

Victor reached the span's center and saw Major Lee surrounded by a pool of blood. The detonator lay on the pavement twenty meters beyond him.

Three helicopters screamed over the trees and headed towards him. American rock music with a pounding bass and screaming guitar boomed from speakers attached to the center helicopter. The unbearable music sent his hands to his ears, and he tried to run faster. The center helicopter fired, and Victor dove for the edge of the overpass.

Jack scanned the bridge ahead of him. He counted at least four terrorists in the open. "Riders in the Sky" by The Chantays boomed from the speakers.

Tony keyed the intercom. "Fire, Sarah."

The machine gun roared, and Tony walked the line of bullets and tracers toward three running men. The rounds passed the first man leaving him unharmed but joined with two terrorists carrying light machine guns. Both men's arms flew into the air, and their guns crashed to the ground. The men fell and were still.

Jack spotted Victor Chow lying on his back on the pavement below them. He also recognized the well-dressed British leader of the ISIS group. The suave terrorist brought a carbine to his shoulder and aimed at the helicopters. Before he could fire, Don Miksic sent a burst of rifle fire towards him. The terrorist dodged away from the bullets and ruined his shot. Sarah and the passengers in the other helicopters fired into the foxholes. A few rounds thumped into the bottom of the Huey.

Tony keyed the intercom. "Everyone all right back there?"

Don came on the intercom. "We're good. You have a few new holes but no hydraulic leaks."

"Roger. All my gauges are green. We're continuing with the mission."

They flew down the depot's main road, and Jack again grabbed the radio off his belt. He spotted three of the depot's fire trucks parked several miles from the gate. Employees armed with captured AK-47s lay on top of the big trucks.

Jack spoke into the handheld radio. "Show Me fire department we're starting our last run. Move forward."

A voice came from the radio. "We hear you, Colonel. We're moving now."

Tony keyed the radio. "Show Me flight stay centered on me and give me a slow right turn." The helicopter turned. "Maintain this turn and eight zero knots. I'll bring us out at two seven zero degrees."

"The helicopters came out of their long turn. "Show Me flight this is our final gun run," Tony said. Straighten it up on two seven zero. Maintain your air speed and get close to the trees. If you think you're too close, you aren't."

The other two helicopters dropped even lower to the tops of the trees. The music pounded, and Jack strained to see the gate area through the trees.

Victor picked himself up and ran towards the detonator. Major Lee lay face up in a pool of blood. He had four bloody holes running from his right eye down to his groin. Victor shuddered at what his back must look like and looked away.

He reached the detonator and scooped it up. He muttered to himself while he inspected its components. "Fuse igniter ready, time fuse connected, blasting cap crimped, detonation cord taped to the blasting cap and the other detonation cord leads."

He placed the detonator on the pavement, yanked the ring free from the igniter, and heard a small pop. Soon a wisp of smoke streamed from the burning fuse. Major Lee stated he would set a three-minute fuse. Victor ran towards the defensive positions.

He waved his arms over his head and yelled. "The fuse is burning! Take cover!"

Abdul Barry ran towards his foxhole leaving the machine guns on the bridge. Victor looked up the highway. The police cars sat three hundred meters away. The policemen stood next to their vehicles shooting at him. Victor dodged and ran faster. He also noticed the locomotives moving back up the rail line away from the bridge.

Victor yelled at the foxholes. "Forget the police; it's the helicopters! Get ready!"

He jumped into Abdul Barry's foxhole, placed his hands on his knees, and gulped air. Abdul watched him struggling to get his wind back.

Victor faced Abdul. "The police actions are a ruse. The Americans are coming in the helicopters. We must keep them away from the bridge."

"Are you sure?" Abdul said.

Victor's brow furrowed. "What do you mean?"

"Listen," Abdul said.

Victor twisted his head around and strained to hear. Soon he heard sirens; several of them. Both men looked down the road that led deep into Show Me Army Depot. At the limit of his vision, he spotted flashing lights. Soon he saw three large, red fire trucks speeding towards them.

The trucks grew closer, and personnel aboard them opened fire. Abdul turned to his men and shouted instructions. Two terrorists jumped from their fighting positions and sprinted towards the dropped machine guns.

Victor pointed. "They're slowing."

The trucks stopped next to each other five hundred meters from the defensive positions. Victor spotted people in civilian clothing on top of the trucks firing at his positions. He wondered where the depot's employees obtained so many weapons. The defending terrorists returned fire. However, the distance prevented any effective fire from either side.

Victor again heard music coming through the trees. He swiveled his head trying to find the source. The music grew louder, and screaming vocals battered him. Many of the Islamic terrorists covered their ears against the horrid music.

The three helicopters appeared above the trees far to the right of the police cars. The center helicopter streaked towards them and fired its machine gun. The rounds hit the two terrorists carrying the light machine guns. Both men reeled from the impacts and fell to the ground. A few seconds later the three aircraft buzzed low over their positions.

Victor poked his head up in time to see them disappear over the trees. "When the bridge is down, we can counterattack and take back the rail yard."

Abdul laughed. "I think you need to reassess your plan for a counterattack, Victor."

"What do you mean?"

Abdul waved his hand. "Look around you. We have a dozen men remaining. That is not enough."

Victor looked down the line of foxholes and did a quick count. He faced Abdul. "You are wrong. We can still defeat the Americans and retake the rail yard. If we fail, my nation will deny your precious caliphate its nuclear weapons."

"Calm down, Victor. We can hold long enough to destroy the bridge, but we cannot retake the rail yard." He shrugged his shoulders. "Once the Americans land in their helicopters, we are defeated. It is Allah's will." Abdul smiled at Victor. "But my dear Victor we will kill many Americans in our defeat."

Abdul yelled at his men in Arabic, and five ISIS soldiers jumped from their holes. One man carried several small cameras mounted on small aluminum tripods. He positioned the cameras facing the foxholes and the expected battlefield. The others donned heavy canvas vests. The vests had many pockets stuffed with blocks of explosives. Detonation cord ran into the pockets, and a fuse igniter hung from the front of each vest. Victor realized the terrorists wore suicide vests. Their tasks finished; the terrorists returned to their foxholes.

Victor looked around the area but spotted no explosive crates. "Where did you get the explosives for those vests?"

"My men removed them from the bridge, of course," Abdul said.

Victor's face turned crimson. He screamed at Adbul. "We need those explosives on the bridge; not inside your idiotic suicide vests!"

"Calm yourself, Victor. We left more than enough explosives to take out that bridge."

"No!" Victor pointed at the bridge. "You need to go back to that bridge immediately and inspect the charges. We cannot afford any mistakes!"

Abdul laughed at Victor. "You just set off the igniter. I am not going near that bridge while the fuse is burning. My men are prepared for suicide, but I am not."

Before either man could speak again, a terrific explosion shook the bridge. The shockwave slapped them and threw them down into the foxhole. Chunks of concrete and pieces of steel flew above them. As he lay in the bottom of the hole, Victor felt the size of the explosion did not equal the large amount of explosive placed on the bridge.

The overpressure from the explosion bounced around inside his skull and gave him a terrible headache. A loud buzzing in his ears slowly faded away. He opened his eyes and grimaced. He pushed Abdul off him and got to his feet. He looked towards the bridge. A dense cloud of black smoke covered the structure. He held his breath as he watched the smoke.

A gust of wind blew in and dispersed the smoke. Victor's hands clutched his hair, and he swayed back and forth as he saw the bridge still stood. It appeared the explosion removed the sides of the bridge as large pieces of concrete and steel lay on the highway and railroad tracks below. But most of the bridge stood undamaged. What damage he saw to the pavement looked easily repairable. He was certain the bridge could carry vehicle traffic without any trouble.

Victor turned to Abdul. "You idiot! Your stupid fighters damaged the detonation cord that linked the explosives. Only a small portion detonated. The bridge is still intact and usable by the Americans!"

Adbul stared at the bridge. "I believe you are correct." He looked at Victor "I apologize...this has never happened to me before." He brushed the dirt from his expensive clothes and stood taller. "But it makes no difference. We participated in your operation and killed many Americans. Your nation owes ISIS a nuclear weapon as agreed. Please make this point in your final report to your superiors."

Victor's breath caught in his throat. He pulled his pistol from its holster. Abdul smiled and reached for his carbine. "Please don't do anything rash, Victor. I don't want to kill you. You need to get home so you can make your report."

Again, the growing strains of rock music came over the trees. They forgot their argument and turned towards the music. Abdul yelled at his men. One fighter got out of his foxhole and crouched behind it. The man grasped the fuse igniter and waited for the arrival of the helicopters.

Chapter 38

September 14, 2015, 1238 (CST) Show Me Army Depot, Missouri

Jack looked at Tony and keyed his intercom. "Better let them know."

Tony keyed his radio. "Show Me flight one minute. When we get there, stay on the ground and wait for instructions. They'll ignore the helicopters and focus on our infantry. You'll be safe." Two clicks came over the radio.

Jack grabbed the radio off his belt. "Show Me fire department we'll be there in one minute."

"Got it, Colonel," the unseen fireman said. "Hey, we just saw a big explosion on the bridge."

"Dammit!" Jack yelled. They were just a few minutes too late. He wondered if there was a way, he could still complete his deployment mission without the bridge.

He keyed his radio. "How bad is it? Did they block the highway?"

"The bridge is still up. The explosion was pretty big, and we can see some damage, but it's still standing."

Jack looked at Tony and shrugged. "That's good news fire department. The terrorists screwed up somehow. We still need to attack. They might try to set off a second explosion. So, get ready."

"We'll be here, Colonel."

Jack turned to his team in the back of the helicopter. He keyed the intercom. "Thirty seconds to target. Get ready."

Don Miksic nodded and checked his rifle. Sarah used her feet to sweep brass and links out the door. Jack secured his helmet on his head. Again, he looked behind him. Don wore a solid black German-style motorcycle helmet complete with a chromed spike. Howie had on a Kansas City Chiefs football helmet minus the face guard, and Cecil wore a neon green construction hardhat. All three had their rifles ready.

Howie and Cecil moved to the doors and prepared to jump from the helicopter when it hit the ground. Jack saw the blood lust in both men's faces. Howie hung out of the Huey and let out a terrifying howl. Jack almost felt sorry for the terrorists. The speakers blasted The Lively Ones' classic "Surf Rider." The helicopter seemed to jump in time with the music.

They cleared the trees and headed for the truck gate. The terrorists crouched in their foxholes two hundred meters away. Most fired at the approaching depot fire trucks. A few had their hands over their ears. Jack did a double take when he spotted one man playing air guitar. A dozen shocked faces turned towards the screaming helicopters. He glanced at the bridge but did not see any obvious damage. The helicopter dropped, and Jack felt the contents of his stomach rise.

"Clear left," Sarah said over the intercom.

Don crouched in the right door. "Clear right."

A second later the big helicopter thumped hard onto its skids. The men and women of his fighting force spilled from the open doors. Lieutenant Craig led his team behind three parked semi-trucks and headed towards the tree line. His men snapped off quick shots during their run.

Don hit the ground and led his team towards an empty semi-trailer located in front of the helicopters. His team also fired as they ran. Jack stood in front of the big Huey and watched his two teams move. The enemy force responded to their arrival. Their weapons swung away from the fire trucks and towards the three helicopters and the departing teams. Rounds zipped by Jack and the helicopters.

Tony's Huey jumped three feet in the air, rotated, and set down. Sarah now had a clear shot at the terrorist positions and poured fire along the line of enemy foxholes. Several enemy fighters went down into their holes and stayed there.

A terrorist jumped from his hole and sprinted towards the helicopters. Jack held his fire as Sarah had an easy shot. He made it halfway to them when Jack spotted an odd-looking vest over his uniform. Jack banged on the Huey's windshield and pointed at the terrorist. Tony spoke into his microphone.

Five rounds from Sarah's gun stitched the runner fifty meters from the helicopter. The man fell onto his back and lay unmoving. Both his hands rested on top of the strange vest. Jack forgot about him and resumed watching his teams. Don's people crouched behind the trailer and hammered fire into the foxholes. Craig's team moved through the forest towards the nearest foxholes. At the edge of the trees, fifty meters of open ground separated them from the first enemy positions.

Jack knew that any attacking force avoided open ground when opposed by well-trained infantry. Although the terrorists excelled at murdering women and children, no tactician would ever call them infantry or well-trained. Sarah sent another long burst into the nearest foxholes. A terrorist's shoulder shattered into blood and tissue, and the man dropped.

The three fire trucks drove up and parked on line seventy-five meters from the terrorists' positions. While the drivers crouched down in their cabs, the employees on top fired at the terrorists.

Without warning, a huge explosion rocked the ground in front of the helicopters. The blast slammed Jack to the ground, and his ears rang. All three helicopters shuddered from the blast. Dirt and debris flew into the spinning rotor blades and covered Jack. He spit dust from his mouth and got to his feet. He grabbed his rifle and looked at Tony. He appeared unharmed, but a long crack ran through the Huey's windshield. The gunfire from both sides slacked but soon resumed its previous levels.

Jack looked into the back of the helicopter. Sarah sat on her butt with her head in her hands. Her gun hung from its mount with smoke coming from the hot barrel. She shook her head and got to her knees. She kept that position for a few seconds before she stood up. Tony waved at Jack and pointed. A smoking crater four feet across covered the spot where the charging terrorist lay. The dead man's legs, minus the rest of him, sprawled on the lip of the crater.

Jack keyed his squad radio. "Craig, Don, the terrorists have suicide vests. Don't let them get near your teams." He grabbed the radio on his belt and warned his firemen. "The terrorists have suicide vests. Do whatever it takes to keep them away from your trucks."

Another terrorist leaped from his foxhole. He yelled and ran toward the fire trucks. Jack fired at the man. Don also shifted his fire to the running terrorist. The man took a round to his leg and he dropped. However, he recovered and soon limped towards the big red trucks. Despite their sustained fire, neither Jack nor Don could put him down. Jack held his breath as the hobbled terrorist approached the trucks.

Heavy diesel exhaust burst from the nearest truck. The water cannon located above its cab sprayed a solid stream of high-pressure water from its internal tank. The fireman that crouched behind the cannon walked the water towards the limping terrorist. The water impacted the man's chest and knocked him onto his butt. Each time the terrorist tried to stand the water knocked him down. Soon the man gave up, and the water rolled him across the muddy ground. He exploded with a bright flash and a dirty cloud of black smoke.

The shockwave rolled over the battlefield. The Miksic family screamed in delight at the terrorist's demise. All three fire trucks inundated the terrorist fighting positions with water.

Moments after the explosion, Craig's team charged the enemy positions. They made it and occupied three foxholes containing dead or wounded terrorists. Another terrorist wearing a vest jumped from his hole. He took one step, and Cecil shot him in the chest. The man crumpled, and a stream of water blasted him back into his foxhole. Five seconds later the hole erupted in a huge explosion. Water, mud, and a shredded human form flew into the air. The Miksic family again whooped and hollered at the spectacle, and all three fire trucks honked their horns.

Jack heard the Medevac chopper behind him spool up its engine. He turned, and spotted Tom West giving him the finger. The red helicopter lifted and flew away across the top of the fire trucks.

Jack grabbed his radio. "Where's he going? We need him for our wounded personnel."

"He said he's leaving before we get him killed," Tony said.

The medevac helicopter raced over the trees away from the battlefield. Without warning, a line of heavy tracers ran across the tops of the trees and merged with the fleeing helicopter. The helicopter shuddered from the hits, and thick black smoke burst from its engine. A few moments later it nosed into the trees and became a smear of fire, torn metal, and black smoke.

A black jet, a twin of the one that attacked them this morning, screamed through the rising smoke of the downed helicopter. The enemy fighter pulled up into the sky and began a long slow turn above the depot.

Jack's jaw clenched. He faced Tony and keyed the radio. "I thought you said you shot that jet down?"

"We did," Tony said. "They must have a second one."

Jack fixed Tony with a cold stare and pointed towards the jet's path. "I need you to take him out. We can still lose if they have that fighter."

Tony shrugged his shoulders. His tinny voice came over the radio. "What can I do against a jet? We got lucky the first time."

Jack scowled at Tony. "So, are you just going to sit here and let him strafe you?"

Jack saw Tony use his intercom to speak with Sarah. He looked back at Jack. "Never mind, Colonel; we'll get him," Tony said.

Jack moved away, and Tony took off and followed the path taken by the doomed medevac. When he reached the column of smoke, he turned towards the center of the depot. The jet came out of its turn and followed the departing helicopter.

Jack watched the black jet fly off. He turned back to the battle and fired at the enemy positions.

Major Kim Kyong Ok banked his stealth fighter and looked down through his canopy. He watched the smoke rising from the downed helicopter. He'd made a good decision to leave Kentucky and head to this attack site.

He scanned the battle below him. He debated attacking the three fire trucks but worried any strafing run could hit his own nation's forces. The large helicopter took off and headed towards the center of the American depot. He identified it as a United States Army UH-1 utility helicopter. He studied another helicopter, a smaller blue and white Bell Jet Ranger, that sat on the ground idling. This helicopter did not take off.

No matter. He would shoot down the UH-1 and return to this location. Major Kim turned and flew after the utility helicopter.

Chapter 39

September 14, 2015, 1242 (CST) Show Me Army Depot, Missouri

Tony aimed his helicopter towards several water towers. "What's this one doing, Sarah?"

"He's in our six at four thousand feet and he's starting his dive. It looks like he's going to use his guns."

Tony yelled into the intercom. "I hate this shit! Let's hope he's as cocky as the last one."

Tony dodged through the water towers.

Sarah screamed into the intercom. "Missile! Missile! Missile! I think it's another heat seeker!"

Tony jinked the helicopter left and right and dove for the deck. "I need a heat source!"

Sarah stuck her head out of the helicopter and scanned in front of them. Thousands of concrete storage magazines dotted the terrain for many miles.

She sobbed into the microphone. "I don't see anything!"

Tony knew his wife had no wish to die in a dirty helicopter with the man who killed her brother. He spotted a yellow shape half a mile in front of them. "The forklift Sarah! Shoot the forklift!"

Sarah slammed the gun against the stops and hit the trigger. The gun thundered, and its rounds reached out ahead of them. Tony walked the impacts into the yellow machine. Several rounds pierced the sturdy propane tank sitting above its motor. Tony spotted a large cloud of gas enveloping the forklift.

A tracer round ignited the cloud, and it exploded with tremendous force. The shock wave pushed the helicopter sideways until the spinning rotor blades nicked the ground leaving four small parallel furrows in the earth. Tony fought the controls and pulled the helicopter away from the ground. Seconds later the missile's warhead exploded against the smashed forklift.

Tony leveled out and flew towards another row of magazines. He hopped over the nearest magazine and flew down the service road. His gauges all read green, but he knew he'd need a lot of maintenance after today.

Sarah again screamed. "Missile! Missile! Missile!"

Tony groaned. "How many missiles does this guy have?"

He looked for another forklift, but this row of magazines had none. A mile to his front he spotted the first of several outside storage pads. He could just make out its stacks of high explosive bombs.

"Fire, Sarah," Tony said.

The heavy gun thundered, and its rounds shot forward. Falling rounds churned the soil five hundred meters short of the target. Tony pulled back on the cyclic and raised the nose of the helicopter. The rounds arced upward, and the impacts walked towards the bombs.

Sarah yelled over the intercom. "You're climbing into the missile's path!"

Tony had no time to respond. He continued to pull up until the rounds walked into the storage pad. He held his position for a full second then banked the helicopter into a hard left. He dove for the nearest magazine.

A gigantic explosion erupted from the storage pad and hurled shrapnel, gravel, and unexploded bombs high into the air.

Tony saw the explosion from the corner of his eye. The shockwave hit and threw the helicopter one hundred feet to the left. He looked to his right and watched the jet's missile fly by a foot under his turning rotors. He had no idea why its proximity warhead failed to detonate when it came so close. A second later the streaking missile added its warhead to the eruption rising from the storage pad.

Tony wrestled with the controls as his helicopter flew sideways. His left skid scraped the ground fifty feet before the helicopter bounced back into the air. Tony yelped when jagged pieces of bomb casing and orange chunks of explosive whizzed past him. He got the helicopter under control and sped away from the explosion.

He leveled out at one hundred feet and turned back towards the center of the depot.

He keyed the intercom. "Sarah, you ok back there?" He got no reply. He twisted in his seat and looked back at his wife. She sat on the deck of the cargo compartment with her head in her hands. "Sarah, are you all right?"

Sarah raised her head and looked at Tony. Her tears made streak marks on her dusty face. "I'm fine! Just peachy!" She pointed at her husband. "But if we get out of this, I'm going to kill you, Tony Simpson."

Tony smiled at his wife. He turned back to his cockpit and flew on.

Major Kim's mouth fell open, and he stared at the huge explosion below him. Half a dozen unexploded bombs burst through the black smoke and tumbled high into the air. One even reached the height of his aircraft before it stalled and fell back to earth. He could not believe it; the helicopter pilot below him evaded two heat-seeking missiles in less than two minutes.

He almost disengaged and headed for his rendezvous with the ship, but his enemy's skill excited him like nothing before. He realized he would never again face an opponent like this pilot. He dropped his landing gear and applied full flaps. His jet slowed to one hundred and twenty-five knots.

Major Kim started a slow dive and approached his opponent from the right. He matched the helicopter's altitude and eased towards it. Soon he flew close alongside it. The helicopter's pilot wore a standard United States Army flight suit and helmet. Kim pushed his sun visor up on top of his helmet. From no more than one hundred feet away, the enemy pilot stared at him. He also noticed the pilot's crew chief looking at him. Major Kim executed a double take. A beautiful woman manned the helicopter's machine gun. He knew women served in the armed forces of the United States, but he had not expected to see one today. In his country, such a stunning female would never participate in combat operations. It was too bad she would soon lie with the wreckage of this old and ugly helicopter.

He ignored the woman and looked at the pilot. He placed his left hand on the control column and brought his right hand up and saluted. He held the salute until the American pilot gave him a slight wave. Major Kim dropped the salute, brought his sun visor down, and climbed away from the helicopter.

Jack stood next to Brock's helicopter and watched the firefight. Lieutenant Craig's team made steady progress against the remaining foxholes, while Don's team stood off and poured fire into the enemy positions. Another terrorist went down into his hole after he tried to charge Don's team.

Jack counted backward. "Six, five, four, three, two, one."

He waited two more seconds before a huge explosion erupted from the foxhole. The body remained in the hole, but mud and water fountained into the air.

When the last drops hit the ground, a huge explosion from the center of the depot rolled over the battlefield. Jack turned but saw nothing. For several seconds the firing died down, and everyone looked towards the sound.

Jack keyed his radio. "Tony, we heard a big explosion. Did you get the jet?" He received no response. "Tony, this is Colonel Black Eagle come back. Are you ok?"

After a few seconds, Tony responded. Jack heard the helicopter's engine and thumping rotor blades in the background.

"What do you need, Colonel? I'm kinda busy."

Jack took a step to the left as a round hit the ground near him. "We heard something. Did you get him?"

"No, Colonel. This guy's a tough nut to crack. I'm not sure we're gonna make it." The radio went silent for a moment. "Please tell my family I'm sorry."

Jack faced the center of the depot. Tony sounded nothing like the man he initially met. He sounded like a man staring into the abyss.

"Sorry for what, Tony?"

"For screwing up my marriage. Sarah and I were gonna be together for a long time, but I messed it up."

Jack used his free hand to rub the back of his neck. "Tony, fly back to the gate. We have a lot of weapons here. We'll help you with the jet. Whatever you do don't give up."

Something about the situation made Jack recall Liam Torgerson's last words. He jumped up and down and shouted into the radio.

"Holy shit! I know how we can take him out! Tony, lead that jet down the main road back towards the entrance. I have something for him. Keep him on that main road and get him low."

Jack turned towards Brock Hightower in the news chopper. He pointed at him and twirled his hand above his head. The pilot nodded and powered up his engine.

"What are you talking about, Colonel?"

"Tony, I don't have time to explain. Give me five minutes. After that, lead that jet down the road towards the gate. I'll have a surprise waiting for him at the turnoff to Liam Torgerson's building. Keep your helicopter flying."

The radio remained silent for several seconds. "I don't know if I can hold him off that long."

"You have to Tony," Jack said. "I'll be there. But keep him down low otherwise it won't work."

"I'll try, Colonel. I'm headed that way."

Jack switched to his squad radio. "Don, I need to borrow Rita." Don put a round into the chest of a terrorist wearing a polo shirt. He grabbed Rita and pointed at Jack. The Power's family increased their fire, and Rita sprinted towards him. "You take charge here. Rita and I need to help Tony and Sarah."

Don waved. "Go ahead. This thing is over in one minute."

Jack jumped into the news chopper, and Rita scrambled into the back. Brock applied power and they flew away. Jack scanned the battlefield and spotted several terrorists with their hands above their heads.

Victor ran through the pelting water towards Johnny Park's hole. Mud covered his uniform, and his boots squished with every step. Rifle fire hit the ground around him throwing water and mud into his face.

He arrived at the position. "Ji Hun, we must leave. The Americans will reach us in moments."

The two remaining Korean commandos stood with their hands up. Both had thrown their rifles away. They ducked from the rounds zipping past them but kept their hands in the air. Johnny stood in the wet hole; his hands up and his rifle at his feet.

Victor held out his hand. "Ji Hun, please come with me. We can still finish the mission. You and I together."

Johnny's brow furrowed. "Who's Ji Hun?"

"Ji Hun, come with me, please," Victor said.

He looked up, and the group of Americans to their front charged them. A huge man in bib overalls led the screaming civilians. Victor backed away from the hole. He looked at Johnny again. The young man watched him with a look of pity on his face.

Victor sobbed. "I'm sorry Ji Hun. I didn't mean to hurt you. Please forgive me."

He turned and sprinted for the tree line on the far side of the gate area. Several rounds hit the ground around him, but none touched him. He reached the trees and disappeared into the forest.

Chapter 40

September 14, 2015, 1245 (CST) Show Me Army Depot, Missouri

Jack and Rita burst into the shed behind Liam's building. "Where is it?" Jack said. "We don't have much time!"

"There it is!" Rita pointed towards a far corner.

They ran to the corner and tossed boxes, garden tools, and empty gasoline cans from their path. Jack grabbed a large bundle of netting and pulled it tight to his chest.

Rita grabbed several long cardboard boxes labeled 'Explosives.' "We got them," she said. "Let's go."

They ran from the building and threw their cargo into the back of the helicopter. They jumped in.

Jack pointed. "Brock, get us back to the main road."

Thirty seconds later they hovered over the center of the road. Jack opened the door and kicked the bundle out. Brock landed on the road. Rita jumped out carrying the boxes.

"What do I do now, Colonel?" Brock said.

Jack turned to the pilot. "Go back to the entrance. The battle's over by now, and they might need a medevac. But if we can't stop this jet, abandon your helicopter. Do not fly. You got that?" Jack reached out and shook the pilot's hand. "And thanks."

Brock shook Jack's hand. "You're welcome, Colonel."

Jack jumped out, and the helicopter leaped into the sky. He ran to the bundle and untangled and pulled it until the net spanned the road. Rita planted half a dozen metal stakes into the ground on each side of the road. She slid a small rocket over each stake. Jack helped her connect a length of wire from each rocket to metal d-rings on one side of the net. Rita connected an electric wire to each rocket and pulled the wires into the trees. She connected the wires to a battery-powered trigger.

"I'm ready," Rita said.

Jack heard cannon fire and the jet's scream coming from the center of the depot.

He keyed his radio. "Tony, we're ready. Bring that jet down the main road past the turn off to Liam's office. I need him on the deck. Force him to fly very close to the ground."

The radio squawked. "On the way, Colonel. I hope you've got something good."

Jack stood next to Rita. He looked down the road and waited for Tony's arrival.

Tony spoke into the intercom. "I didn't kill Frank, Sarah."

She turned towards Tony and frowned. "You want to talk about this now?"

Tony kept his eyes forward. "I didn't kill your brother. He committed suicide. I'm not sure we're gonna make it so I wanted you to know the truth.

"How dare you, Tony! What gives you the right to say that about my brother?"

"You never had a clue about your little brother, Sarah; never." Tony shook his head. "When you played as kids, when you grew up together, and when you both served in Iraq." He let out a long sigh. "Frank was an alcoholic, and he was too proud to ask for help. In the end, he couldn't handle it."

"I don't believe you. You just won't admit it was your fault."

Tony pulled something from his pocket. He turned and tossed it to Sarah. She caught it in midair and looked at it.

Her mouth dropped open. "This is Frank's high school ring. Where did you get this? He told me he left it with Mom. When I got home, she said she lost it somewhere in the attic."

"Your mom knew about Frank." Tony dodged around a water tower. "I tried to get him to back out of the deployment and get treatment, but he said he had to go for you. He said he would dry out." Tony sighed. "But once he got there, he couldn't take it. I don't know how he did it, but he found something to drink."

Tony dove between the familiar buildings that ran along the depot's main road and headed towards the entrance. He flew no more than ten feet off the ground.

Sarah stared at Tony. "Why didn't I know? He was my brother. I spoke to him every day."

Tony shrugged. "I suspect you couldn't see the truth because he was your baby brother. Your need to protect him clouded what you saw. Don't knock yourself for it. It happens."

The helicopter swerved around a crane parked on the side of the road. "I tried to help him; I really did. But he made me swear to keep it from you. He said he wouldn't quit if I told you. I think he tried, but it got worse. When he couldn't find alcohol, he stole cans of spray paint from the motor pool. None of us had a clue it was that bad."

Sarah's eyes filled with tears.

"Flying that last mission, we knew the war was over. I spoke with him about going home. When I looked at him, he had his pistol in his hand."

Sarah stood behind her gun and sobbed; her head down.

"I tried to reason with him. But he said it was just too hard. I begged him to stop and told him he could go home on a medical. But he said he couldn't disappoint you. He said he was sorry, and he made me swear again not to tell you. I tried to land, but he put his pistol against his chest and pulled the trigger."

Sarah let out a low moan, and tears ran down her face. "Frank, why?"

"I told everyone the Iraqis shot him. I even made sure he got his Purple Heart. I found his ring on your cot afterwards; I think it was his way of saying he wasn't coming home. I never told you the truth because I didn't want to hurt you." He paused. "I don't think it's anyone's fault he died. Frank wasn't meant to stay in this world for long."

Sarah let out a few final sobs and wiped her eyes. She put the ring in her pocket. "I have his Purple Heart at home. I look at it all the time."

Tony nodded, still looking forward. "Well, you keep it. Frank deserved it."

Sarah nodded. "I will." She looked at Tony. "Thanks for telling me about Frank." She stayed silent for a long time. "Tony, can you forgive me?"

Tony turned in his seat and looked at her. "It's ok, Sarah. It was wrong to lie to you, and I'm sorry."

Sarah smiled and looked into her husband's eyes. "No, I'm the one who needs to say I'm sorry."

Tony smiled. "Thanks Sarah. Now, tell me what that jet's doing."

Sarah returned to her gun and looked behind them. "Let me guess," she said. "Yup; he's right behind us. His flaps and landing gear are still down. He's trying to line up his guns."

Tony counted to three and steered towards a small radio tower that jutted up from the maintenance building. His move forced the jet to climb and spoiled the pilot's aim.

Tony passed the depot's headquarters and flew into the dense forests that stood on both sides of the main road. The road to Liam's office was a mile ahead.

Sarah stuck her head out the door. "He's back in our six. He went over the flagpole but he's coming back."

"How high is he?"

"Looks like about one hundred feet. He's firing Tony!"

Tony pulled on his stick and soared up to one hundred feet. The burst of cannon fire went below them.

Sarah yelled into the intercom. "Tony, stop climbing! You're giving him a perfect target!"

He shoved the stick forward and dropped back down to ten feet. "How about now, Sarah?"

She stuck her head out the door and pushed her hair away from her eyes. "He came down to fifty feet. But he's stopped. Oh, Tony, he's getting so close." She banged her gun against its rear stops, but it could not target the jet. She kicked the mount and screamed. "God dammit!"

Again, Tony popped up to fifty feet and dropped back down. He inched his speeding helicopter closer to the pavement. Soon he flew no more than three feet off the ground at one hundred knots. He kept his eyes off the road lest he become hypnotized by the yellow dashes flowing under his helicopter. "How high is he now?"

Sarah stuck her head out the door. "He's at twenty feet. Oh God, Tony. I'm looking right down his guns."

Tony flew past the turnoff and glimpsed someone standing in the trees alongside the road. They disappeared a second later. He was not a religious man, but he prayed for God to spare his wife. Sarah's scream came over the intercom. Tony closed his eyes and prepared to die.

Jack ignored the helicopter and concentrated on the approaching jet fighter. He had never seen a fighter so low to the ground; not even in Iraq or Afghanistan. Jack raised his hand.

Rita crouched in the grass; her finger poised over the firing button.

The helicopter flew by them, and Jack yelled. "Now!"

Rita hit the button. The rockets boomed and leaped into the air. They pulled the thin, but sturdy, net straight up. The jet flew into the net, and it wrapped around the fuselage, wings, and landing gear.

Rita leaped into the air. "We got it!"

Jack ran into the road and watched the jet begin a slow climb out of the trees.

Major Kim had never flown this low before, let alone within an impenetrable forest. He found it invigorating. He decided to add a similar flying course to his training regimen when he got back to North Korea.

He studied the helicopter to his front. His opponent continued to show incredible skill. He would honor the man's death with a toast of rice liquor at the officer's mess once he returned home. His gun sight pipper danced on top of the helicopter. He could have fired a long time ago, but he had no desire to end the chase. He sighed and squeezed the trigger.

Suddenly a series of bright flashes, like small explosions, appeared on the road in front of his aircraft. A thin wall of black material rose in front of him. He flew into the material, and it blanketed his fast-moving jet. Forgetting the duel with the helicopter, he pulled back on his control yoke and started a slow climb away from the road and the surrounding forest.

Soon he passed over the helicopter below him. He looked at the material flapping against his canopy and wings. A dark mesh, woven like a fishing net, shrouded his jet. He looked behind him. Several small metal tubes banged against his tail surfaces. He turned back to his controls. A movement to his right caught his attention. The enemy helicopter flew no more than fifty feet off his right wing.

Impossible! A helicopter could not match his speed. He glanced at his gauges. His airspeed read one hundred and ten knots; well below his stall speed.

Major Kim attempted to bank away from the helicopter, but his jet refused to move. He looked at his wings and spotted clumps of fishing net and wire cables jammed into his control surfaces. No matter how hard he pushed his stick, his control surfaces remained frozen. He again looked at the helicopter.

The beautiful woman in the back of the helicopter pointed her black machine gun at him. She raised her right hand and gave him a perfect salute. She snapped her hand down and crouched behind the weapon. Kim threw his arm up in front of his face.

Tony looked at the slow-moving jet. "Waste him, Sarah."

The heavy gun roared, sending hundreds of rounds into the stricken fighter. Pieces of black coating, fragments of aircraft aluminum, and dark streams of hydraulic fluid flew from the jet. When the impacts reached a spot under the cockpit canopy, the pilot's head flew up in pain. Sarah walked the rounds into the canopy shattering it. The smashed plastic fell away, and the pilot slumped forward. Blood streamed from under his helmet's visor.

The jet wobbled and Tony banked away from it. He reduced power and let the pilotless fighter climb away from him. Thick black smoke streamed from the doomed jet. It climbed to a thousand feet and nosed over into a dive. A few seconds later, the jet hit the trees and exploded.

Tony looked back at Sarah. She stood behind him in the center of the helicopter with her head down and her eyes closed.

He keyed the intercom. "Let's go see who won the battle."

Sarah opened her eyes and smiled at him. She sat on the bench and looked at the trees below them. Tony turned the big helicopter and headed for the cutoff and the colonel.

Chapter 41

September 14, 2015, 1300 (CST) Show Me Army Depot, Missouri

Jack studied the damaged bridge as Tony flew over the depot's main gate. He spotted at least two dozen police vehicles and several ambulances parked in the depot's gate area. Teams of police searched each prisoner and placed them into squad cars. Other officers, carrying shotguns and rifles, inspected the muddy fighting positions.

A long line of parked vehicles ran from the depot's entrance, over the damaged bridge, and down onto Highway 61. The line stretched for several miles.

"What the hell is that?" Jack said of the many cars.

Their helicopter touched down in its original spot next to the Channel 27 news chopper.

He keyed the intercom. "Shut down, Tony. I think we're done for today."

The engine and rotor blades wound down. Rita and Jack stepped down from the helicopter. Rita ran towards a knot of employees standing with several police officers. Jack slung his carbine over his shoulder and walked towards Ross, Don, Lieutenant Craig, and Uwell Yates standing near the truck gate. When he arrived Craig and Don came to the position of attention and saluted. Jack returned the salutes.

"Report," Jack said.

"Colonel, the firefight ended a few minutes after you left," Don said. "The remaining terrorists surrendered, but the fat Chinaman ran into the woods and got away.

Jack looked at Craig. "Any casualties?"

"No casualties, Sir. We had one person sprain an ankle when he slipped in the mud."

Jack smiled back at the four men. "Wow, that's great news."

He looked at Don. "What about your union vice president?"

Don crossed his arms in front of his chest. "He's not my vice president and no one's seen him."

Jack turned to Sheriff Yates. "Uwell, you get the prisoners. Turn them over to the FBI when you get the chance. Also, put out a bulletin on Victor Chow and Joe Harper. They worked with the bad guys on today's attack. I want them caught and charged with murder."

Uwell's eyes bugged out of his head. "You mean the guy who runs the China King Buffet is a terrorist and the union's vice president is also a terrorist?"

Jack nodded. "This is a weird one, Uwell. Yes, they're involved. But we had a lot of luck on our side, and we stopped them."

Uwell shook Jack's hand and headed for his patrol car.

Jack looked at Ross. His deputy appeared to favor one leg. "What about the bridge?" He looked at the cars lined up on the large overpass. "Is it safe to use?"

Don pointed at the bridge. "I had Will do a quick inspection on it."

Jack's eyebrows rose and Don scowled at him. "He has an engineering degree."

Jack held his hands up in mock surrender and Don continued. "The bridge took a lot of damage, but Will says placing some shoring underneath it should allow it to hold our big trucks. We'll send the trucks over one at a time just to be safe." He chuckled. "There's detonation cord and unexploded C4 scattered everywhere underneath that bridge. I think those dumbass terrorists screwed up their demolition chain. I'm betting less than half the explosives went off. Maybe even less than that."

"Then we got really lucky," Jack said. He paused for a moment. "I'll take that luck." He turned to his deputy. "Ross, we still need to get a train out tonight. What can we do to get it loaded?"

Ross waved at the long line of vehicles. "Colonel, the people in those cars are Show Me depot employees. Even with the blackout, news of the attack got around town. They started lining up behind the police barricades on Highway 61 this morning. I think we have enough people here to finish loading our first train.

Jack looked at the long line of cars. "That's outstanding." He looked back at his team. "Ross, Don get our people in place. I don't care if they're janitors, cooks, or secretaries. I need them running forklifts and loading shipping containers."

"You got it, Colonel," Don said.

Ross limped towards a parked security vehicle, and Don walked towards his family.

Jack walked towards the gate's entrance lanes. Craig walked with him. "Lieutenant, get your soldiers. We're going to welcome the Show Me depot employees back to work."

"Yes, Sir." The young lieutenant ran off.

Jack reached the first guard booth and spotted the blood covering the floor. He clenched his fists and swore to never forget the people murdered in the last twenty-four hours.

Craig ran up with Sergeant Cadena, Private Washington, and Private Newton. They stopped and saluted Jack. He returned the salutes then smiled at the young soldiers, and they beamed back at him. "Each of you take a lane. No need to check identification. Tell everyone they're on ammunition duty and to report to the cafeteria."

The soldiers ran to their lanes and waited.

Jack keyed his depot radio. "Ross, Don, I'm sending the employees to the cafeteria. You organize them from there."

Both men responded. "Will do, Colonel."

Jack pounded on the hood of the first vehicle in line and yelled. "Let 'em go!"

The lines of vehicles flowed through the gates. Soon they honked their horns. Many had US flags flying from their roof or truck bed. It looked like a massive 4th of July parade. When the cars stopped at the gates, the returning employees shook the soldiers' hands and yelled words of encouragement. Many handed bottles of water, soft drinks, and even a few cans of beer to the tired soldiers. The soldiers yelled their thanks.

Soon he heard Tony Simpson start his Huey. A few moments later the Channel 27 news chopper started its engine. Jack watched the two helicopters hover and fly off. Tony blasted one last surf tune when he passed over the gate area.

Soon a white security pickup pulled into the line of cars. Don drove with Natalie in the passenger seat. Will, Howie, and Cecil stood in the pickup's bed. The three Miksic men yelled and waved their AK-47s over their heads. The employees around them laid on their horns and hooted and hollered back at them. Jack had never seen anything like it; not even when his units returned from Afghanistan and Iraq.

The truck pulled up to Jack, and Natalie jumped out and gave him a quick kiss on the lips. Without a word, she released Jack and ran back to the truck. The Miksic family and his soldiers stared, and Jack's face turned beet red. Cecil, Howie, and Will returned to their celebrations.

Don shook Jack's hand and gave him an evil eye.

Jack ignored it. "Thank you for what you did today, Don. A lot of people are alive today because of you and your family."

"Glad we could help, Colonel. When this is over, we need to have a quiet beer someplace to celebrate."

"Sure," Jack said. "Maybe at The Outhouse. That place seems tame after today's festivities."

Natalie laughed and whooped from the passenger seat.

"You have an interesting family, Don. Take good care of them."

"I intend to, Colonel."

The truck pulled through the gate, and Craig called to Jack. "Awesome, Sir. Your girlfriend is hot, and she can fight!"

Jack blushed again. "All right, that's enough. Get the cars through the gate."

It took thirty minutes to pass all the cars through. Jack guessed over a thousand employees entered the depot. He looked at his watch. Their train might leave on time.

Chapter 42

September 14, 2015, 1700 (CST) Show Me Army Depot, Missouri

Jack pulled hard on the oars and propelled the small boat across the lake. Soon the prow ran into the soft mud of the shoreline. He jumped out and tied it to a tree. Twenty feet to his left he spotted the marks in the mud from last night's trip.

Jack took his M4 from the boat and hung it on a tree branch before he walked into the forest, soon spotting the girls' tent among the trees. Jack approached and looked inside. Mary and Carol lay sleeping on the tent floor. Both girls' heads were cradled in their rolled up sleeping bags with another bag twisted about their legs. Torn wrappers and empty water bottles surrounded their small forms.

Jack sat at the edge of the tent door and shook Mary's leg. "Mary, wake up." He shook his daughter's leg again. "Mary, it's Dad."

Mary woke and stared up at Jack. Tears came to her eyes, and she leaped up and hugged her father. "I worried about you all day."

Jack held her tight. "It's all right, sweetie. The terrorists are gone, and I'm here to take you home."

Mary wiped the tears from her eyes and sniffed her nose. She pulled back from her father and examined the grime covering his face. She released him and stepped back. Her hands formed little fists and she placed them on her hips.

She frowned. "Dad, did you put yourself in danger again?"

Jack smiled at his daughter. "Maybe a little." He grabbed Mary's arm and pulled her into another hug. He felt her stiffen, but after a few moments she relaxed and squeezed her father hard.

"I missed you," Jack said.

"I missed you too, Dad"

Jack finished his hug. "Thank you for taking care of your sisters. I didn't worry at all because I knew you could handle it." Mary smiled at the compliment.

"Now wake up Carol and let's go find Janet."

Mary's eyes went wide. She looked in the tent. "Dad, Janet's not here. She was here a few minutes ago when we laid down for a nap."

Mary turned to her sister. She put her foot on Carol's butt and shoved her hard. "Wake up, Carol. Dad's here and we have to find Janet."

Carol awoke with a start and looked at Mary. "Why did you kick me?"

"I didn't kick you," Mary said. "I pushed you. Now get up."

Carol stood and went to her father. Both hugged for a long time. Carol let go of Jack and turned to Mary. "I told you Dad would come back."

"Where's Janet?" Mary said.

Carol shook her head. "I don't know. She was next to me when we went to sleep."

Mary turned to Jack with a worried look on her face. "I'm sorry, Dad. I don't know where Janet went."

Jack put his hand on her shoulder. "Mary, it's all right. I'm sure Janet is fine. I'll bet she went for a walk with the cats. She's around here somewhere."

Jack rolled out the door of the small tent and stood. Mary and Carol followed. Both girls still wore their pajamas, but each had on sneakers.

He looked around the forest. "Which way do you think Janet went? Did you have a spot around here where you played while you waited for me?"

Carol pointed. "We used sticks and built a small fort in a clearing over there. Maybe she's there."

"Let's go check the clearing," Jack said. "I agree with Carol; I bet she's there. You girls lead the way."

Before they could take a step the sharp report of a gunshot came from the direction of the clearing. A feeling of dread washed over Jack and settled in his stomach. He sprinted towards the sound.

Jack ran through the forest and called for his daughter. He reached the clearing and stopped. Janet stood next to the half-completed fort wearing her pajamas and sneakers. Mud spots covered her pink pajama bottoms. Forty feet in front of her a cat crouched on all fours and hissed at the man standing behind Janet. The other cat lay on the ground next to its partner. The cat on the ground looked asleep.

Tears rolled down Janet's face. She looked at her father. "Daddy, the bad man killed Ajax." She sobbed and rubbed her eyes.

Jack looked at the man standing behind his daughter. Victor Chow smiled back at Jack. The spy's left hand gripped Janet's shoulder, while his right pointed his pistol at her temple. Mud spattered the fat spy's still damp uniform. Jack's rifle hung over the spy's shoulder.

"Welcome, Colonel Black Eagle," Victor said. "Please step forward. I have some instructions for you."

Mary and Carol ran up behind Jack. Mary let out a gasp, and Carol's hand went to her mouth. Jack turned his back on the spy and shielded his daughters with his body.

"Mary, take Carol to the lake and get in the boat. I want you to row back to the house and run to the gate on the main road. Someone will help you there." When neither girl moved, he pointed behind them. "Now."

Tears welled up in Mary's eyes. "But I don't want to leave you."

"I'm waiting, Colonel," Victor said.

Jack yelled over his shoulder. "In a minute, Victor!"

Jack pulled the girls close. "Mary, I cannot do this with you here. You must leave now if I'm going to have any chance of getting Janet. Please do what I tell you."

Mary looked at her father. "I love you, Dad."

"I love you too. Now go."

Mary grabbed Carol's hand, and they ran into the trees towards the lake. Jack lost sight of them and turned back towards Victor. His arms hung at his sides, and he presented his open palms. He walked towards the spy and his daughter.

"That's good, Colonel. Please come closer so we can talk." The spy smiled but his gun never wavered. When Jack came even with the cats Victor spoke. "That's close enough."

Jack stopped and looked at the spy. He had several long scratches on the right side of his face. Jack looked down at the two cats. Ajax had a bloody hole in his side. The other cat continued to hiss at the fat spy.

"Janet, tell your cat to stay away from the bad man," Jack said.

Victor's brow furrowed at Jack's statement.

"But he killed Ajax," Janet said.

"I know Janet, but I need to talk to him. Tell your cat to leave him alone; for now."

Janet frowned and looked up over her shoulder at Victor. The spy looked down at her with a perplexed look on his face.

"Janet, tell the cat," Jack said.

Janet looked at her pet, and it relaxed its crouch. It ceased its hissing but made a low growl and stared at the spy.

Victor cocked his head and stared at the cat. "How did your daughter calm that animal? It was ready to attack me a moment ago."

Jack decided to tell the truth to the spy. "My daughter has a gift; a sixth sense that allows her to communicate with animals. My wife and I wanted her to have a normal life, so we've told no one about it."

"I don't believe you" he said. "You simply trained that cat to respond to her voice."

"Believe what you want. I don't care." Jack took a deep breath. "Victor, let my daughter go. Your disagreement is with me. She had nothing to do with it."

"I cannot do that Colonel. Your daughter's presence here allows me to complete my mission to save the starving children of North Korea."

Jack frowned at Victor's comment on North Korean children. "It's useless Victor. Your colleagues are dead, and your mission failed. My depot's first train of ammunition is already on its way to South Korea. Don't make it any worse than it already is. If you surrender now, I'm sure you'll sit in a comfortable prison for a few months. When your government detains another innocent westerner, they can conduct a trade for you. It happens all the time."

"Everything you say is true, but I can still keep your depot from resupplying South Korea." A huge smile creased the spy's face. "You see Colonel, I have you."

Victor appeared unhinged to Jack. This concerned him. He doubted the spy would listen to reason or even consider the odds against him.

"What do you mean by that?" Jack said.

Victor tightened his grip on Janet. "I have your daughter, so now you're under my control." He gestured towards Jack with his pistol but quickly returned it to Janet. "You carry a radio so call your employees and order them to cease loading ammunition. They will follow your orders without question. In addition, I want the train that departed recalled and unloaded. Please do it now Colonel Black Eagle."

Jack pulled the radio off his belt. He held it for a long time and looked at Victor. He put the radio to his cheek. "Ross, this is the Colonel; come back please."

The radio squawked. "Go ahead, Colonel; did you get your girls ok?"

"Yes, I have them. Everything is optimal. I say again everything is optimal. Stand by for further instructions. We may need to cease loading operations and to recall the train."

It took a long time for Ross to reply. "Got it, Colonel; standing by."

Jack kept the radio in his hand and lowered it to his side.

Victor's smile disappeared. "You did not follow my instructions. Why didn't you order your employees to cease loading ammunition? Why didn't you recall the train?

If that ammunition gets to the Korean peninsula, my nation will have much difficulty in conquering South Korea. North Korean children will starve because of it. Give the order Colonel so you and your daughter may live."

Jack looked at the spy. "Victor, I could give the order, but my people would ignore it."

Victor's face flushed and he yelled. "Ignore it! Why is that?"

Jack held up the radio and showed it to Victor. "I used a code word in my transmission. The code word told my deputy that I'm under duress, and now he'll ignore any instructions that come from me. In fact, I'm certain he's notifying the police and my soldiers that I'm in trouble."

Victor's face held a dreadful scowl. "You made a terrible mistake. Now instead of lasting weeks, the coming war will last months, maybe even years. But my nation will take back what is rightfully ours." Victor's voice became shrill. "With the plentiful resources of South Korea, the children of my homeland will finally have enough to eat!"

Jack decided if he could not reason with the insane spy, he would push him over the edge. It might give him an opening to get Janet. "Victor, why do you keep talking about starving children?"

Victor paused and appeared to compose himself. "You know what happened to my nation. For over half a century your country tried to destroy my homeland. This naked American aggression forced us to prioritize our resources to our defense. That means our people often do not have enough to eat. And when a famine occurs it is the young who wither and die. Like my brother Ji Hun."

Jack saw the spy could soon lose control. He continued to push him. "It sounds like you're speaking from experience, Victor. Did you starve as a child? Is that why you're so fat now? Surrender, and I'll make sure your prison feeds you four times each day. You'll be even fatter when my government trades you back to North Korea."

Victor's eyes opened wide. "Shut up! You dare to speak to me like that? You have no idea what Ji Hun and I went through. Because of you, many children will die."

The spy's voice rose, and Janet again started to cry. The cat crouched and inched towards the crazed spy. Jack let out a long and booming laugh. Victor stared open-mouthed at him.

Jack looked up into the sky. "Victor, Victor, Victor." Jack dropped his gaze to his adversary. "I'm sorry you suffered when you were young and that now you're a fat bastard. However, that isn't my daughter's fault." He pointed at the spy. "Did your brother Ji Hun starve to death?" Victor's eyes blanked at Jack's mention of his brother. "If he did that's too bad. In fact, I hope more North Koreans starve like your brother. Do you know why Victor? Because the entire world despises all North Koreans. They're all so stupid the way they live as slaves to Kim Ha Jun. Do you want to know what I think about your brother Ji Hun?" Jack smirked at the terrorist. "I could give a shit about your little rat fuck brother. I'm glad he's dead and I hope some starving North Korean soldier ate him."

Janet gasped, and Jack tensed. Victor let out an anguished howl and swung his weapon towards Jack. The instant the gun's barrel moved; Jack drew the radio back for a tremendous pitch at Victor's head. The cat streaked for the spy.

Victor fired and the bullet hit Jack's shoulder. The impact shook him, and he threw the radio. It missed

Victor's head by inches. The pain from Jack's shoulder forced him to one knee.

The angry cat leaped at Victor. The twelve-pound cat slammed into Janet's chest and knocked her onto her back. With Janet clear, adrenaline surged into Jack's muscles. He charged, and Victor prepared to shoot again.

An animal's roar, so loud and deep that it rumbled inside Jack's chest, filled the clearing. The forest behind Victor exploded, and a massive shadow swept in and enveloped the fat spy.

Jack's mouth dropped open, and he fell to his knees. He stared at a great beast looming over the spy. Thick black fur covered the massive body. Jack's mind told him a large black bear stood behind the spy. It was the biggest bear ever seen in North America.

Victor turned and swung his gun up towards the black shape. A massive hand, shaped like a human's, but covered in black fur, shot out and grabbed his forearm. The bear lifted Victor until his feet swung at least four feet above the forest floor. The bear's other hand grasped the barrel of the gun and twisted it from the spy's grip. With a flick of its wrist, the bear tossed the pistol away. Victor looked into the bear's face; inches from his own.

A conflict roiled Jack's mind. Bears didn't have hands. He focused on the bear's face. He saw no long snout and no canines ready to devour the fat spy. Instead, he saw soft black fur surrounding a human-like mouth, nose, and eyes. Huge eyelashes and expressive eyebrows sat within the thick fur. Tanned, leathery skin framed a large, squashed nose. Jack's brow rose as he recognized the creature from numerous television documentaries.

Jack looked at Victor. The spy's mouth hung slack, and his vacant eyes looked at the creature holding him. The huge animal swung the motionless spy up over its shoulder. Jack's rifle fell to the ground, and the creature ignored it. Victor's legs hung down the animal's chest, while his upper body and arms hung down its back. It wrapped a huge arm around the spy holding him in place.

Janet, now holding her cat, sat in the grass at the creature's feet. She looked like a tiny doll in comparison to the massive animal. The creature looked at her, and she smiled at her new friend. Still carrying the spy, it went down to one knee. An impossibly long arm reached towards his daughter.

Jack took a sharp breath. The creature paused and looked at him.

Janet looked at her father. "It's ok, Daddy. This is the bear I told you about. He won't hurt us."

Jack stared at the animal but managed to calm himself. The creature reached out and scratched the purring cat's neck. Janet stared into the creature's eyes and stroked the black fur of its huge hand. A long index finger brushed Janet's cheek.

The creature stood. It turned and carried its burden into the forest. Jack felt the ground shake from the animal's footfalls. It took no more than a few seconds for it to disappear among the trees. Jack faced the forest but saw or heard nothing.

Jack looked at his daughter. "What did you say to it?"

"I told him thank you and I would like to see him again. I also told him to be nice to the bad man even though he did so many awful things. He said ok."

Jack smiled at his daughter. "That's good, Janet. I'm proud of you." He again examined the forest hoping to spot the animal. "Do you think we'll see him again?"

"Oh yes, Daddy. He told me to call him anytime."

Jack thanked the Great Spirit that both he and Janet still lived. He went to one knee and spoke to his daughter. "Janet, it's important that we both say that a bear scared off the bad man. The bad man wanted to hurt us, but the bear came and chased him into the forest."

"I will Daddy because that's what happened. The bear came and saved us."

Jack cocked his head at his daughter. He decided not to overthink the situation. "Wonderful, Sweetie." He held out his hand. "Let's go. We need to go home, and I need to see a doctor."

Janet stood and placed her cat on the ground. It took off towards the lake. Jack took his daughter's hand, and they walked into the forest.

Chapter 43

September 15, 2015, 1000 (KST) north of Pyongyang, North Korea

Lieutenant General Song sat across the table from the Dear Leader and his entourage of aides. Song was alone. The palace's security detail denied his aides access upon his earlier arrival. The command post surrounding them bustled with activity as it issued recall orders to the North's military. He felt small and outnumbered without General Lee at his side. Hours before, when he learned of his operation's failure, a cold, hard lump formed in his stomach. That no summary execution followed, and that they even allowed him to travel to Kim's command post, did nothing to soften it.

The Dear Leader fidgeted in his chair but said nothing as Song briefed him on the failure of Operation Ferguson, the pending arrival of the American airborne division, and the growing movement of powerful US military forces to South Korea. Song took Kim's silence as a good omen; anything less than screaming seemed good for the unpredictable leader.

When the briefing ended, one of Kim's aides, a colonel, directed questions at Song.

"General Song, Operation Ferguson failed in all respects and embarrassed the Democratic People's Republic of Korea. You proposed this operation. You even gave it your own code name. Should the Dear Leader hold you responsible for its failure?"

Song put on his best poker face and spoke to Kim. Even with a possible death sentence just minutes away, he refused to acknowledge his much more junior interrogator. "Dear Leader, it is my operation, and I would like to take the blame, but I cannot. Despite their initial success, Bureau 39 and others hold primary responsibility for its failure."

"How so?" the aide said.

Song kept his trembling hands below the conference table. "The Bureau 39 agents in Missouri and Kentucky failed in their attacks on the two depots. One agent's ill-timed role in a disgusting lovers' triangle resulted in his murder. This delayed our attack and allowed the Americans to identify and destroy our force. In Missouri, our forces entered and occupied the target depot. However, leadership failures by the Bureau 39 agent in charge resulted in depot employees attacking and defeating our force. That agent avoided capture and is now missing."

Song noticed Kim paying close attention to his explanations. "In addition, two of our stealth fighters entered American airspace in support of the operation. But a lone Vietnam-era helicopter destroyed both aircraft." Song shook his head. "I ask you, Dear Leader, how could one obsolete helicopter shoot down two of our most advanced aircraft? It makes no sense. The training for both pilots was negligent. Finally, computer modeling showed our Special Forces soldiers had a distinct advantage over the American defenders. Yet, poor leadership and inadequate training of these soldiers resulted in their defeat."

Song again paused. "Dear Leader, it wounds me to say this, but failures beyond my control in Bureau 39, the Korean People's Army Air Force, and the Korean People's Army doomed this operation."

Song sat back in his chair. He used all his self-control to keep his body from shaking in front of the most dangerous leader on the planet.

Kim stared at Song for several seconds. He turned and huddled with his aides. After several quiet, but heated exchanges, the huddle broke.

Kim returned his gaze to Song. "General Song, your excellent plan provided us with a guaranteed victory over the South. Its lack of success is a grave disappointment to the Korean people." Kim took a long draw on his cigarette. "I do not blame you for its failure." He turned to his aides. "Have the principals and deputies of Bureau 39, the Air Force, and the Army arrested."

An aide left the conference room and walked to the nearest phone. A cold shiver ran down Song's spine. He knew his finger pointing condemned at least six men and women, and their families, to immediate detention and a brutal death.

"Your plan came so close, general." The Dear Leader rubbed his chin as if he contemplated the meaning of life. "Now, what should I do with you?"

Song tensed and a sheen of sweat appeared on his forehead.

Kim opened a small jewelry box and revealed a pair of general officer stars. "Song Ho Sung, you are my new Defense Minister."

He pushed the open box across the table to Song. The Dear Leader and his aides stood and applauded. Song grasped the box and examined the four stars.

When the clapping died down, he stood and bowed to Kim. "Dear Leader, you honor me with this unexpected promotion. I will work hard to always keep your trust and confidence." Before he could stop himself, Song blurted out a dangerous question. "But what of Lee Hyun Do? Did he retire?"

The dictator showed his tobacco-stained teeth. "I would not call it retirement." Kim signaled, and a live video feed appeared on the conference room's flat screens. Song's throat tightened and he sat. He once again recognized anti-aircraft target range #57.

The camera focused on the target. General Lee Hyun Do stood tied to a new, larger wooden post. Lee wore his dress uniform, and his many medals gleamed in the sunlight. After months of chemotherapy his uniform hung on his wasted frame. Despite this, the old general stood at attention with his head held high.

The Dear Leader's hand fell. On-screen, Lee disintegrated. When the roiling black smoke covered his remains, the firing stopped, and the camera panned back from the carnage. The smoke cleared and a bloody shin and foot, still wearing a sock and black dress shoe, rested against the shattered post. The rest of the general was unrecognizable. The screens blanked and Song faced Kim.

Kim turned to his new general. "Send a message to the Americans that a rogue military officer initiated the attacks within the United States; attacks not sanctioned by the North Korean government. Inform them we handled the situation."

"At once Dear Leader," Song said.

"Once again congratulations, Defense Minister," Kim said. "I look forward to hearing many unique proposals from you on the reunification problem."

Kim stood and walked out of the room followed by his aides. Song stood and rendered a polite bow to the man's back. When Kim's elevator rose, Song started to tremble, and he collapsed into his seat. He took out his handkerchief and covered his face as he wept.

Chapter 44

November 12, 2015, 1000 (EST) Washington D.C.

Jack stood on the stage in the White House's East Room. He checked his dress blue uniform one last time and looked around the large room. A temporary wall stood on the far side of the stage. It held over eighty framed photographs of those who lost their lives in the attack on Show Me Army Depot. Jack spotted Shorty Cramer, June Miksic, Bennie Miksic, Specialist Siegel, and even Tom West. When he saw the photograph of Liam Torgerson his heart fell. He smiled and remembered his short, but satisfying, friendship with Liam.

Lieutenant Craig stood next to him in his own dress blue uniform. The young man stood with his hands crossed in front of his groin. Craig gave a short wave to an older couple in the front row of seats. Jack spotted no other family members in the audience. His girls remained in Missouri with his visiting grandparents. Jack did not want his daughters to miss school for an awards ceremony.

Don Miksic and his family stood next in line. Fresh haircuts and shaves cleaned up Don and his sons, although Will sported a new mustache. All the Power's men wore sport jackets with blue jeans. Union pins decorated their lapels.

Natalie stood next to her brothers wearing a stylish blouse and a skirt that ended above her knees. She finished it off with a chic, short-waisted leather jacket. She wore shoes with a small heel, but she still towered over every other woman in the room. Her face glowed in the room's lights. Jack's heart began to beat faster. Ever since the attack, and her brief kisses, he felt different towards her. He tore his eyes away from her.

Ross Kelly stood next to Natalie wearing a conservative, dark business suit. He looked at the room full of high-level federal and legislative leaders and he tugged at his collar.

Conner and Rita Torgerson stood next to Ross. Rita wore a colorful but tasteful pantsuit. Conner's crisp, dress blue uniform sported multiple ribbons for tours in Iraq and Afghanistan. Both stole glances at their father's photograph. Jack knew they missed their father, and this ceremony reopened fresh wounds.

Jack spotted Tony and Sarah at the edge of the crowd that circulated in front of the stage. Both wore new Army dress blue uniforms. After downing two jet fighters, Army leaders urged the couple to return to active duty. When the Army gave them an ironclad guarantee to serve at the same duty station, both agreed. Tony wore the rank of chief warrant officer four, and Sarah displayed gold second lieutenant bars.

The squat helicopter pilot held court on the finer techniques for shooting down enemy fighters to six senior Air Force officers. Despite the handsome pilots surrounding her, it appeared to Jack that Sarah had eyes only for her husband. Jack smiled. It pleased him that the tragic events at Show Me Army Depot brought the long-suffering couple back together.

Brock Hightower stood at the end of the line. He wore khaki pants, a polo shirt, and a neat Channel 27 windbreaker. Unknown to all, Brock kept his helicopter's camera recording throughout the battle with the terrorists and during the final shoot down of the enemy jet. That footage, along with video he copied from the terrorists' cameras, resulted in a news documentary entitled

'Battlefield Missouri.' The network expected Brock to receive the next Pulitzer Prize. In addition, he graced the cover of this month's 'The Advocate' magazine.

Jack spotted Sergeant Cadena, Private Washington, and Private Newton seated in the front row next to the service chiefs. All three enlisted soldiers wore new Bronze Stars with V-devices on their uniforms. All three looked uncomfortable among such high-ranking brass.

A well-dressed man stepped up to the podium and spoke. "Ladies and Gentlemen please take your seats. The ceremony begins in one minute."

Soon a man at the entrance called. "Ladies and gentlemen, the President of the United States."

Everyone in the room stood. The band played 'Hail to the Chief,' and the President entered the room and walked to the podium. The First Lady followed close behind and stood at the empty seat next to Craig's parents.

Following a short prayer by the Army's Chief of Chaplains, the President took over the podium and looked out at the audience.

"Good afternoon, everyone," he said. "Welcome to the White House. Please be seated." The President referred to his written remarks. "Two months ago, terrorism invaded our nation in an up close and personal way. A large and well-organized force of North Korean and ISIS terrorists attacked two government installations with the purpose of killing many innocent Americans. We're here today to honor the men and women you see before you for their gallant fight against the terrorists that invaded Show Me Army Depot. Terrorists that sought to diminish the flames of liberty by murdering helpless Americans in front of the nation and the world. These brave soldiers and civilians refused to let that happen."

After describing the battle that took place at Show Me Army Depot, and the impact it had on North Korean threats against South Korea, the President shifted into the awards portion of the ceremony.

"As a direct result of this terrible battle, we honor a soldier today with our nation's highest medal for valor - the Congressional Medal of Honor. That soldier is Second Lieutenant Paul R. Craig."

Everyone stood, while an Army colonel took over the podium and read the award citation. The President stepped behind Lieutenant Craig and fastened the long blue ribbon and star-shaped medal around Craig's neck. With the medal in place, the President stepped back and applauded Craig with the audience joining in. When the applause died down the President asked Lieutenant Craig if he would like to make any remarks. The young man's eyes opened wide, and he shook his head. The audience tittered at Craig's obvious discomfort.

Normally the President limited his award presentations to the Medal of Honor. But at the urging of many powerful union leaders, the President decided to present awards to all the Missouri participants. Jack received a second Silver Star and his first Purple Heart.

The Miksic clan, Ross, and Rita all received the Presidential Medal of Freedom. Will Miksic also received the Secretary of Defense Medal for the Defense of Freedom; the civilian equivalent for the Purple Heart. Don Miksic, a huge supporter of the President and his pro-union policies, could not control his glee and, upon receiving his medal, grabbed the President in a smothering bear hug. The audience laughed when two secret service agents rushed to the side of the President.

Conner also received a Silver Star and Tony and Sarah each received the Distinguished Flying Cross. The final award went to Brock Hightower. He received the Secretary of Defense Medal for Valor.

After a long round of thunderous applause, the ceremony ended. For the next hour, the crowd wound through a long line and shook hands with each awardee. Afterward, Jack's group took many photos and selfies with the famous room as their background. Jack also spent time with Craig's parents, telling them of their son's heroic deeds in Afghanistan and Missouri. Proud, but also astonished, looks crossed their faces upon hearing the details of his bravery.

Soon Jack headed for the door. Before departing he took one last look at the room. Don Miksic stood by the stage and spoke to Natalie. Both smiled at Jack and gave him a small wave. Jack smiled and waved back. His gaze lingered on Natalie...he turned and walked out the door.

Chapter 45

November 27, 2015, 0700 (CST) Show Me Army Depot, Missouri

Jack helped Janet from the boat and removed her life jacket. He removed his own life jacket and grabbed a heavy sack from the bottom of the boat. Both turned and headed towards the same clearing where they first met the creature two months before.

Silence dominated the forest, and neither said anything as they walked. With fall in full swing, a thick carpet of leaves covered the forest floor. A recent rain left the trail muddy and the leaves soft and slick under their feet. At the bottom of a small hill a small, intermittent stream of rainwater coursed through the low ground. Something caught Jack's eye. Twenty yards to his right he spotted an object in the mud.

"Wait here on the trail, Janet," Jack said.

He walked into the woods to get a better look. He found a broken pair of bright yellow glasses. Dozens of small hooves had trampled them into the mud. Several yards beyond the glasses he saw a man's shoe and a torn shirt.

Jack returned to the trail. He grasped Janet's hand and hurried her along. The FBI could search the area later. He had no worries about any agents running into Janet's friend. After seeing the animal in action and researching it online, he understood it could remain hidden from the most skilled tracker or hunter.

Soon they left the dense forest and entered the familiar clearing. Jack placed the contents of the heavy sack on the ground and looked around. He shuddered at the memory of almost dying in the remote patch of forest. A cold wind blew autumn leaves across the clearing making the scene lifeless and eerie. He reached down and zipped up Janet's jacket. Jack vowed to never return to this spot again.

They had not seen the Sasquatch since that terrifying day. According to Janet the huge animal kept to the forest, although several times she told Jack it roamed near the lake and their home. Today they planned to say thank you to the wary Sasquatch. Two twenty-pound bags of oranges, purchased during their recent trip to Florida, lay on the ground. In addition, Janet insisted on bringing an entire pumpkin pie from yesterday's holiday meal. The pie sat next to the bags of fruit.

Jack looked at his daughter. "Are you sure he's coming, Sweetie? I don't see any sign of him."

Janet paused for a few moments. "Yes, Daddy. The bear's coming. He says he wants to see me." She laughed. "Sorry, Daddy, he says he wants to see us! He's close and he'll be here in a few minutes."

Soon they spotted a black shape through the gaps in the forest. The massive form moved easily and quickly through the trees. Jack had a strong urge to turn and flee, but Janet's presence kept him in place. The creature stepped into the clearing and stopped.

Jack's mouth dropped open, and he took an involuntary step back as the creature's presence filled the clearing. He closed his mouth and tried to swallow. He looked at something that should not exist, and it disturbed him. Jack estimated the creature stood more than eight feet tall, and its weight was three to four times his own. Jack gave his head a slight shake. He suspected the creature could not conceal itself behind a full four by eight sheet of plywood; it was that big.

Dense, black fur covered it from top to bottom. In addition, fur covered the large hands and feet that otherwise looked just like a human's. It had a broad chest and its shoulders stretched four feet across. Huge muscles rippled under its fur, and its long arms hung almost to its knees.

Jack studied its face. Black fur covered the creature's head and face although it thinned around its eyes, nose, and lips. Its skull had a pointed top like a gorilla's, and fur hid its ears. But there the similarity ended. It had a wide mouth and small lips. Both appeared very humanlike. The nose had no fur and looked like a human's, but flatter and wider. It reminded Jack of a boxer's nose; pushed in after taking numerous punches.

Its eyes fascinated Jack. Large and expressive, they displayed a distinct intelligence. The creature appeared so human-like that Jack doubted it had any relation to a modern great ape.

"Dad!" Janet said. "You're being rude, and Bear is going to leave if you don't stop it." She crossed her arms and frowned at her father.

Jack looked at his daughter, and his cheeks turned red. He looked at the creature, closed his eyes, and gave it a short bow. He didn't know why or how but he sent a silent thought of apology towards the creature. When he looked again it gave him a slight nod of its massive head. Being careful not to show his teeth, Jack smiled at it and took a seat on the forest floor. He kept his eyes down.

Janet gave a little girl wave to the massive beast. "Hi, bear. Won't you join us? We wanted to see you, and we brought you some gifts." She motioned towards the center of the clearing and the bags that lay next to her.

The creature gave a slight wave to Janet and moved towards them. In three enormous steps, it crossed the clearing and stopped on the other side of the bags. The creature lowered its bulk to the ground and sat with crossed legs like Jack.

He looked at the colossal feet. Fur covered the top of the foot, and he spotted a wide, hairless sole with no arch. He saw how the tough feet produced the footprints discovered across the continent.

Janet walked to the seated creature and sat on one of its crossed legs. Its massive head towered over his daughter. For some reason, Jack felt comfortable with his little girl sitting on the giant Sasquatch's lap. He relaxed as Janet communicated with the creature.

She pointed to the bags of treats waiting for him. "These are oranges, and people eat them for breakfast. A lot of the time they make juice with them. I love them, but I let Daddy peel them for me. They grow on trees in a warm place called Florida." She looked up at the creature's face. "Do you ever go to Florida?" The Sasquatch looked down at her. It swung its head from side to side.

"Oh well, that's too bad. It's a nice place, and Disney World is there." She clasped her hands together next to her face. "Disney World is my favorite place because Mickey Mouse lives there. I got to meet him when we visited but he wouldn't speak to me." Her face scrunched into a frown. "I think he can't talk even though he talks in his cartoons. I tried talking to him the way I talk to you, but it didn't work. I kept getting some dumb guy. Oh well, maybe you'll get to visit Florida someday."

Jack smiled at Janet's comment about Mickey Mouse. She never told him she tried to communicate with her cartoon hero on their recent visit. He would have to explain it to her before their next visit.

The creature sat and listened to Janet like a doting grandparent. Its huge hand rested against her and served as living backrest. Every now and then it would nod or shake its head depending on her questions or comments. Jack wondered if the creature had a language it could vocalize. So far it had not made a sound.

Janet walked over to the bag and selected an orange for her friend. She handed it to him. "Try one. I think you'll like it."

The large orange looked like an apricot in the huge hand. Jack grimaced and silently kicked himself for not bringing more fruit. The creature brought the orange to his nose and took a huge whiff. The air flowing into the creature's lungs sounded like a large bellows found in an old timey blacksmith shop. Satisfied, the creature popped the fruit into his mouth and chewed. Jack spied rows of teeth that, despite their size, looked very familiar. After a few seconds, the creature looked at Janet, and a soft rumbling sound emanated from its throat. "Mmmmm."

Janet looked at her father. "He likes it, Daddy."

Jack smiled. "Yes, I think he does Janet."

Janet picked up the pie and carried it to her friend.

Jack warned her. "Janet, don't let him eat the pan; it might hurt his teeth."

"Okay, Daddy." She returned to her seat on his leg and held out the pie. "I brought this for you. It's called a pie, and it's made from pumpkins. I don't know where they come from, but farmers grow them. We make jack-o-lanterns from pumpkins on Halloween." Janet looked at her friend. "Do you know about Halloween?" The creature again shook his head side to side. "On Halloween, we dress up like spooks and witches and we go to people's houses, and they give us candy. I like to dress up for Halloween, but it's kind of scary." She held the pie up to him. "I hope you like this pie. Now hold out your hands."

The creature brought both his huge hands together in front of him. Janet tipped the pie from the pan into its waiting hands. He sniffed at the pie and took a small bite. He chewed, and his eyes opened wide. He looked down at Janet and made another delighted sound. The rest of the pie disappeared into its great mouth, and Janet laughed. While the creature chewed his left hand patted the ground and his head rocked from side to side. More pleased comments emanated from its throat. The animal looked at Jack and gave a slight nod.

"Janet, please tell him thank you for what he did for us," Jack said. "I don't think we would be here today had he not taken the bad man away. He saved our lives, and I'm grateful. Also, let him know we'll tell no one about him."

"Okay, Daddy." She looked up at the creature, and he looked down at her. They conversed silently for several seconds. Janet turned to her father. "He says your welcome and thank you for keeping his secret. He says he had to stop the bad men from hurting you or me because we're special. He says the forest people told him that no harm is to come to us, and he had to protect us while he is here. He also says it's important for him to stay hidden from people. He did not like us seeing him when he came to take the bad man away."

Part of the creature's response confused Jack, but he smiled and nodded. "Well, I think you're special Sweetie, but I think he made a mistake calling me special. Does he have a name?"

They again spoke silently. "Yes, but he can't tell us his name. He says it's only for his kind to know. He says to call him Bear."

Jack nodded. "Ok, Bear it is. Does he have a mate or children?"

Janet stared at Bear. "He doesn't have a wife and he doesn't have any children but he wants to go to the mating grounds soon so he can get a girlfriend. He says it's very far away, but he hopes a girlfriend will return with him to his territory here. But she must be pretty or it's no deal."

Janet covered her mouth and giggled. Several large breaths escaped from the creature's open mouth. It pounded the ground with its free hand as it laughed at its own joke. Jack let out a short laugh.

A solemn look soon replaced its laughter. Janet turned to Jack. "He says he's sorry that we lost mommy."

Jack wondered how the creature knew about Soo Jong. He nodded his head. "Tell him thank you for his sympathy."

Janet looked at the great beast. "He said it's ok we're sad but don't worry. Soon we'll have a new mommy." Janet clapped her hands. "Oh goody, goody, goody, goody."

Jack's brow furrowed and he stared at the creature. It gave him a small, knowing smile. It looked at Janet and stirred.

Janet grasped at the creature and started to cry. She buried her face in the creature's fur. "Please don't go! You just got here! I've waited so long to talk to you, and I don't want you to leave."

For a minute the creature's huge hand gently patted Janet on her back. Finally, he lifted her up towards her father. Jack leaped to his feet and took her from its outstretched arms. It placed a palm down on the ground and stood up to his full height. Jack's neck hurt when he looked up at him. The creature picked up the bags of fruit. He gave Janet a small wave and turned and walked into the forest.

"Janet, tell him to come back anytime," Jack said.

Janet thought for a moment and again started to cry. Great tears rolled down her cheeks and dropped onto her jacket.

Jack brushed away his daughter's tears. "Don't cry; it'll be ok. We can see him again while we're here in Missouri."

"No Daddy, he said we'll never see him again." She buried her face in Jack's shoulder.

Jack watched the huge shape recede in the distance. "Maybe it's for the best, Sweetie. I don't think people are meant to see him. It could put him in danger if other people knew he was our friend. Did he say anything else?"

Janet wiped her eyes. "He said goodbye cub; you're my favorite human." She rested her head on her father's shoulder and watched him go. "Dad, what's a human?"

Jack smiled. "I'll tell you when we get home." When he could no longer see the creature, he turned and carried his daughter into the forest.

Chapter 46

May 20, 2016, 1300 (CST) Federal Penitentiary, Renovo, Pennsylvania

Victor ended up in a federal prison in rural Pennsylvania. US marshals took him there after a farmer discovered him sitting in a shallow hole in a Kansas wheat field.

Dozens of government interrogators visited Victor at the prison. He could not respond to any of their questions. In fact, the prison's mental health experts stated it appeared he could not communicate at all. Even a few attempts at sleep deprivation and waterboarding produced nothing useful. Instead of speaking, Victor cried for hours and often wailed in anguish. The interrogators soon stopped coming.

When he stopped eating and soiled himself daily, the administrators moved him to a padded cell. The cell contained a padded door with a small glass window and a dark plastic bubble in the ceiling. Orderlies took away his slippers, dressed him in scrubs, and placed him in an old-fashioned straight jacket.

Victor's weight dropped. Two months after arriving Victor weighed ten pounds less than his peak weight as an agent. Months later he resembled the starving residents of the Yodok Reeducation Camp. The facility administrators directed the guards to force feed the important prisoner.

One day a young federal agent suggested they confront Victor with the one piece of physical evidence linking him to North Korea. With no other options, his superiors concurred. That night the agent taped the wrinkled photo of a young North Korean schoolboy to the window in the padded door.

Victor soon discovered the small photograph. For hours he stood and stared at it; he did not move, and he made no sound. The only time he left the photo was to sleep, for forced feedings, and for his 'baths'. This went on for weeks.

One night the slot at the bottom of his door opened, and his evening meal slid into the cell. The cardboard tray held water, fried rice, corn, and applesauce. If he consumed the food, the guard would retrieve the tray one hour later. If the food remained untouched after one hour, four large orderlies would enter his cell and force it down his throat.

That night Victor looked away from the photograph and towards the tray of food. He stared at it for several minutes. Soon, he flopped down onto his stomach and squirmed forward until his face hung over the tray. He lowered his face and ate every morsel and drank every drop of water. The guards who watched doubted this one event meant a change to the spy's mental status.

Many weeks later Victor continued to stare at the photograph, and he continued to finish his meals. One day he looked away from his brother's photograph and noticed details in his padded room. The next day he used the toilet and showered without assistance. Soon he asked for reading material. The prison psychologists took furious notes as they observed his new behavior. However, the veteran guards still questioned their prisoner's restored mental health. They kept him in an adult diaper and the straitjacket.

Now Victor sat in the center of his cell. He read from Plato's Republic while he sat on the padded floor. As he moved his foot to turn the page, the door to his cell opened. His eyebrows rose. He never had visitors after his evening meal.

Johnny Park, in blue jeans and a polo shirt, walked into the cell. The young man sneered at him. "Nice diaper, Victor."

An old Korean man wearing a department store suit followed him. The old man said nothing and stood next to Johnny staring at Victor. A third man entered the room. Victor stared at the man. The Bureau 39 agent who saved his life stood before him. The agent had a few more gray hairs but looked fit. He wore the same outfit he did on the night he shot Big Guard; expensive black leather shoes, dress pants, white shirt with tie, and a dark sport jacket.

Victor looked at Johnny Park and smiled. "Ji Hun, you're alive. They have good food here; let us eat it together."

"I'm not your dead brother you stupid psycho," Johnny said. The young man looked at the Bureau 39 agent and gestured at Victor. "I told you he's nuts. Losing at that depot sent him over the edge. Hell, he was crazy before the battle. He can't do it."

The agent spoke with ice in his voice. "Be quiet."

Johnny closed his mouth and glared at Victor. The old man continued to stare.

"Do you recognize me, Victor?" the agent said.

Victor smiled. "Of course. You saved me and you trained me to become an agent. We did many missions together." Victor paused. "I never knew your name. Later they told me you died. But you lied about that didn't you?"

The man nodded. "It was a lie. I arranged my death so I could leave Bureau 39. I'm sorry I had to deceive you. You performed well as an agent, and I liked you."

Victor looked down at the floor. "Are you here to kill me for my failure at the American ammunition depot?"

The agent shook his head. "No. I'm here for another reason. Today I work for the US government."

The agent pointed at Johnny. "Who is this?"

Victor smirked at the young man. "He's Johnny Park and he's not my brother. I know my brother Ji Hun died a long time ago."

"Victor, I know your brother's death haunts you." The agent stared at Victor. "Do you want to make sure that every child in North Korea has enough to eat? That no one starves in North Korea ever again?"

"I have always wanted that." Victor narrowed his eyes at the agent. "But how can I make that happen?"

"You can help me overthrow Kim Ha Jun and liberate the people of North Korea."

Victor did not reply. He rocked his body forward and pulled his legs underneath him. He stood, and his arms writhed within the straight jacket. A few seconds later he pulled the straight jacket over his head and dropped it in a bundle at his feet. Johnny's eyes opened wide, and he took a step back. The agent smiled.

Victor looked at Johnny. "I'm glad you made it out of Show Me Army Depot, Johnny. It was wrong to put you into that situation and I'm sorry. I hope you can see my mind is healed. I said you were my brother Ji Hun to test you. I'm pleased you're standing up for yourself."

Johnny cocked his head at Victor. A moment later he smiled.

Victor looked at his old colleague. "Please include me in your operation."

He turned to the old man and gave a polite bow. "Sir, I would like to know your name."

The old man looked at Victor. "I am General Lee Hyun Do of the Korean People's Army. However, I'm retired."

Without taking his eyes off Victor, he addressed the senior agent. "He'll do."

Chapter 47

June 16, 2018, 1000 (CST) Cedar City, Missouri

Jack crept to the door. He turned the knob doing his best to make no sound. He opened the door a few inches and peered out making sure no one saw him.

He spotted his daughters as they stood on a small, elevated platform at the far end of the room. None of the three girls dared move from their positions. Jack knew these events unnerved his girls. Hell; he had to admit the truth. Today's events flat out scared them. All three looked around for their father. Mary, now a gangly teen, stood five foot eight inches tall. Jack guessed she might add another two inches before her growth spurt ended. Carol, twelve, had her mother's hair color, figure, and height. Neither girl smiled. They wanted today's events over, and soon.

He frowned and took a deep breath. It upset him that his actions placed his daughters in that room. He hoped he could get them out soon.

Janet, now nine, appeared unconcerned with the events unfolding around her. She smiled and held one of her cats. Her other cat, the one that saved her life, sat at her feet and faced the unfamiliar faces that surrounded the girls. It hissed at them, and they laughed at its distress. Clearly the organizers of today's events wanted the cat gone from this place, but no one dared touch it. Jack had no idea how the cats got here. He hoped they would help keep Janet calm. Only losing their mother stressed his children more.

He closed the door and turned to his grandfather. Jack smiled and wrung his hands. Having his grandfather at his side filled him with the courage necessary to complete this terrifying task. Jack noticed that his hands trembled.

"Grandfather, I'm more frightened now than I was during the fight at the railyard. My knees are shaking so hard I'm afraid I'll fall before I get to the girls."

His grandfather had a grim look on his face. "Son, you can do this. Your girls need you to do this. They'll blame you for a while, but they'll recover from it like they did before." He placed his hand on Jack's shoulder. "What happens today, good or bad, becomes part of their lives and part of who they are. But that can't happen unless you get out there. Don't worry. I'll be behind you the entire way."

Jack let out another deep breath. "Thanks, Grandfather."

He looked down at his uniform once more and made sure everything was in its place.

"We need to go now son," his grandfather said.

Jack nodded. Both men moved to the door. He counted. "Three, two, one."

He opened the door wide enough for them to slip through. Both men moved across the room towards his daughters. At the halfway mark, many heads turned their way. He sped up so he could get to the girls quicker. His grandfather kept pace. Loud, ominous music blared from speakers situated around the cavernous room. He ignored the music and kept moving.

Jack hit the first step leading to his daughters and missed his footing. He fell to his hands and knees. One half of the room gasped in horror. The other half laughed at him.

His grandfather grabbed his shoulders and helped him to his feet. "Hurry, Jack."

Jack moved the final twenty feet. He stopped six feet from his girls. They instructed him to approach no closer. Mary and Carol glared at him. He wanted to apologize to his girls, but he knew he couldn't. The events that led up to this day were beyond his control. Janet giggled and smiled at her father. He thought Janet understood the ceremony that occurred around her, but with her, he never knew for sure. Everything around them frightened him, but he flashed them a quick smile. His grandfather stood to his left and guarded a precious object in his jacket pocket.

Jack noticed the other people in the room staring at him. One half of the room appeared hostile. No one smiled at him. They considered him an outsider; an intruder soon to leave their world. Jack gulped and stared back. The other half of the room appeared more supportive. Many smiled at Jack and the girls. He could tell they looked forward to the end of these events also. Jack clenched his fists and wished for it to end soon.

The large double doors at the far end of the room flew open. A huge man stood in the opening and scowled at Jack. An ice-cold feeling of dread formed in the pit of his stomach. The ominous music changed to a more familiar tune. The people within the room stood and turned towards the large man.

Natalie Miksic, looking magnificent in a beautiful white wedding gown, took her father's arm. Both walked down the aisle towards Jack and his family. Jack smiled at Natalie, and she smiled back.

Don Miksic led his daughter towards him. The big man's scowl vanished; replaced by a huge grin. The cold once again twisted Jack's stomach. He wasn't sure he would get along with his new father-in-law.

The End

ABOUT THE AUTHOR

Arnold P. Montgomery retired from the US Army with the rank of Colonel. He has numerous assignments in South Korea, Iraq, Germany, Fort Bragg, and the nation's Army depots. This is his first writing adventure. Arnold and his wife live on a small farm in Illinois.

We hope that you enjoyed this title and look forward to many more to come. Please, leave us a review! Reviews matter to all of our authors.

Take a look at some of our other award-winning series at https://threeravenspublishing.com/series-universes/

Visit us at https://www.threeravenspublishing.com and sign up for our newsletter for the latest and greatest news on upcoming titles and events.

Other series and titles you might enjoy.

AVAILABLE ON
AMAZON
JOINT TASK FORCE
13
HOLDING THE LINE
BETWEEN HEAVEN AND HELL

DECLAN FINN
DECLAN FINN
DECLAN FINN
DECLAN FINN
Demons
Forever
HONOR AT
STAKE
Live &
Let Bite
Good
Last Drop
The Dragon Award Nominated Series
FREE on Kindle Unlimited!

MYSTERY,
MAGIC &
MAYHEM
WITH A TWIST
OF ROMANCE
J.F. POSTHUMUS
ON AMAZON
FIND ME

Arnold P. Montgomery

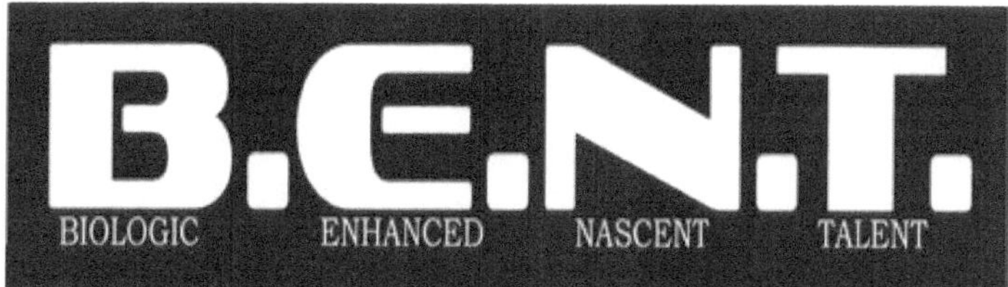

You can also keep up to date with our latest release announcements on Scifi.radio and get some of the best fandom programing on the planet.

Scifi for your Wifi

And don't forget to check out our other Sponsors and Affiliates

A southern Appalachian jewel for craft beer lovers, Buck Bald Brewing offers something for everyone. With delicious, locally brewed beverages from across the spectrum, Buck Bald Brewing offers craft brews that are consistently amazing.

From the dark and smooth Shesquatch Scottish ale, to the intense hops of Hippibilly IPA, to the puckering sour of the blackberry and cinnamon in Berry My Heart at the Trailer Park, and more than 60+ rotating brews, you'll find what you're looking for and more.

With smiling faces behind the bar ready to help you find your next favorite brew, a constantly rotating selection of delicious craft beverages, toe-tapping tunes always playing, and the biggest games on TV, you can kick your feet up in either Copperhill, Tennessee or Murphy, North Carolina and immerse yourself in the Buck Bald Brewing experience. So, come out, fill a pint, fill a growler, and fill your mind at your new favorite family-owned craft brewery.

To discover more visit us at buckbaldbrewing.com or follow us on Facebook @buckbaldbrewing and @buckbaldbrewingmurphy.

Vesper Wren's
TRAILER PARK
PIXIE
PUNCH
· A PEACH STRAWBERRY SELTZER ·
BUCK BALD BREWING

And don't forget to check out the latest edition of *Car Wars*

http://www.sjgames.com/car-wars/

Or the other amazing titles from
Steve Jackson Games

http://www.sjgames.com

…or the latest in the Car Warriors: Autoduel Chronicle fiction series.
https://threeravenspublishing.com/car-warriors-autoduel-chronicles/

Comprised of active or retired servicemen and civilian volunteers, Shepherd's Men enthusiastically raises awareness and funds for the SHARE Military Initiative (SHARE) at Shepherd Center in Atlanta, GA.

This nationally renowned program focuses on assessment and treatment for American military veterans who have sustained mild to moderate Traumatic Brain Injury (TBI) and Post-Traumatic Stress Disorder (PTSD) during post-9/11 service.

Find out more at: https://www.shepherdsmen.com/

www.ingramcontent.com/pod-product-compliance
Lightning Source LLC
Chambersburg PA
CBHW032106310726
48972CB00001B/114